Borrowed Things

Doris Schneider

Borrowed Things

A Southern story of beginnings, endings, secrets, & healing

by Doris Schneider

Borrowed Things
by Doris Schneider

Copyright © 2013 Doris Schneider

Edited by Tia Silverthorne Bach

Cover design by Jo Michaels of **INDIE** Books Gone Wild
Cover painting by Doris Schneider
Author photo on back cover by MJ Peters

Formatted for print by Jo Michaels of **INDIE** Books Gone Wild

To Jim

Acknowledgments

I have the life-experience and perhaps the DNA to feel great regard for family and friends, many of whom played a major role in enriching and refining this novel.

I want to thank Tia Silverthorne Bach, my editor and an award winning novelist, for her belief in this manuscript and her great skill at guiding without invading a writer's vision. I also want to thank Jo Michaels of **INDIE** Books Gone Wild for her artistic design of the cover and internal formatting. I am grateful to my husband, James L. Coke, without whom this story would not exist; my daughters, Elaine Woods and Jessica Rhyne, for providing support and real-life character models; and my friend Diane Bryson for her insight and challenging questions on motive and plot.

Many other friends and members of various writing groups provided feedback as well as specialized knowledge on sailing, psychology, and medicine. Of these, I particularly wish to thank Jim Keen, Don Bryson, Dr. Dennis Sinar, Angela Silverthorne, Lucy Littler, Billy Rhyne, Eloise Currie, Jan Lamoreaux, and Kaylene Wilson.

Last, I want to express my sincere gratitude to Dr. Rachel Victoria Mills, my journaling teacher, for setting me free as a writer.

Contents

Prologue

Running backwards,
in slow motion,
leaning away,
twisting to side,
lifting heavy foot,
turning,
nothing gained,
no safety found.

He follows,
wings beating,
watching as she
flails air
with weighted arms
and silent screams,
falling, pierced
by his song and sting.

Anne sits up violently, throwing the covers aside, reaching for her robe. "God! I have to get out of this house!" She stops, hugging herself and finding control.

The coffee has dripped and waits to be poured. Anne grabs a mug, fills it, and walks to the back door, shrugging into the robe and exiting the too-tight feeling of threat and hurt. On the deck, she pulls a chair against the wall, wraps the robe close against the morning chill and raises the hood. She sits, pulling her feet up into the chair, almost fetal, sipping the warm caffeine, waking head and body, separating her essence from the recurring nightmare.

Anne's deck overlooks the lake and gardens. For the thousandth time, she questions her need to sell this house and get away. It is the perfect home in the perfect location, and just ten minutes from her daughter. Above the steam of her coffee, she sees the beginning glow of light beyond the trees across the lake, and she looks away, her heart contracting at this warm reminder of her daughter and granddaughter. But Summer and Lindsay's nearness do not erase Anne's need to leave.

The real issue lingers in the rafters and beams of the house, in the siding and paint she and Steven had worked on together. Their efforts still permeate the sheetrock walls; their sweat still not dry. This perfect house is full of haunting memories of a marriage gone berserk.

In addition, it is too close to the university where Anne's generosity of spirit causes her to have difficulty saying no to requests for more of her time, although she is finally retired. And last, increasing traffic in North Carolina's Research Triangle (Chapel Hill, Raleigh, and Durham) has made cycling difficult and dangerous, too easy for a planned accident—the ultimate contradiction. She wants to stay but she needs to go, to begin a fresh segment of her life—somewhere without reminders of her past. She breathes in deeply and slowly lets it out. *Besides,* she reasons, *my children and grandchildren will want to visit me at the coast. It will be their getaway as well as mine—if I can ever get away. Six months on the market, and not a single buyer with a realistic offer.*

Everyone says I need time to adjust to single life again. Time, powerless time. It can heal physical wounds, she allows, *but not injury to the spirit and the heart. That kind of healing needs more . . . I suppose it requires forgiveness . . . but I can't pull that out of my pocket.*

Anne tries to brush the shadowy thoughts away. Like an ostrich, her head sinks beneath the sand of remembrance until she can accept the past as illusion. She has heard of people who dream fine fantasies that become the meat of novels, or others with dreams that foretell the future. Her dreams are always recycled reality, a detailed reliving of the betrayal that ended her second marriage and marked her as a relationship failure, incapable and undeserving of love. Last night and this morning, every time she closes her eyes, the moment returns—the instant his eyes looked through her and revealed his intent. But after each plunge into his darkness, she resurfaces wearing the Pollyanna mask that carries her through the day.

Anne looks up again to witness the orange glow slowly emerging, haloed by a yellow sky gradually fading to blue. The newborn light reaches the lake, shimmering, sparkling, and dancing on the water, performing for its singular audience.

Why now? I thought I had purged him even from memory, our story bottled up in some vessel to be forgotten. But it isn't forgotten. It pervades every cubic inch of air in this place, seeping into the insulation between the wall studs and rising through the floor joists. It feels like there's a cloud over this house raining negative memory. I have lived with that too long, and now there's something new, something different—a sadness, mixed with anger and disappointment. This new feeling moves inside her, circling and tightening around her heart as conflicting emotions struggle for dominance. *Shake it off, Anne.*

A prehistoric sound draws her eyes above the sunrise, and a great blue heron soars into view, gliding gently down to the dock, wings open and feathers like fingers spread. Her lips curl upward as she imitates his sound. He turns, observing the woman who greets him every morning with a voice like his own. *Click.* The shutter in her eyes, marked by the clicking of her tongue, freeze-frames the bird, saving his image for a future painting. *I should have painted you long ago, my friend. But something has suffocated the creative in me.*

She calls to him, finally releasing a bright smile. "Hello, Blue Bro." Rising and stretching, she sheds the morning's melancholy. The hood of her robe falls away, revealing tousled hair that sparks red and gold in the early dawn light. In imitation, the bird spreads his wings, and the feathers on his head rise. For a tick in time, Anne feels her own arms are wings. The moment passes, and she lowers them, weighted by gravity, accepting her limitations. The heron walks awkwardly to the edge of the dock where he too pauses, accepting his own limits, keeping his watchful distance while longing, as she longs, for more. She pulls her robe around her again and looks up at the glowing sky with renewed determination. She raises a small balled fist and shouts in a whisper. "Screw you, Time! I'll heal myself!!!"

The heron croaks. "Faaarrrkkk!"

She answers. "Faaarrrkkk!"

Chapter 1

La, God of Good Lungs

"THE SUN ALSO SETS." Anne sighs and gazes for another moment at the dawn turning to day and the heron lazily flying away, close to the water, his wing tips touching, forming concentric ripples.

A personality can be affected by events, but no matter how traumatic or disillusioning those experiences may be, it doesn't change the core of the individual. Anne Gray is the rare woman who looks delicate and sensitive, but her fair freckled skin covers a spine of steel-infused DNA, subject to periods of dark irrational self-loathing that segue into bright optimism and cheerful self-discipline. She sighs as responsibility, like a powerful magnet, draws her inside to begin the tasks of the day.

In spite of her ability to whistle and imitate bird calls, Anne cannot sing. So she tunelessly hums a love song from *Phantom of the Opera* while she roams the house and assesses the results of months of repairing, painting, cleaning, and discarding—trying to see it with fresh eyes, the eyes of a buyer. What remains of her once

5

crowded, once bustling household is a spacious quiet home. She has only her most precious belongings on display. Their presence gives her courage.

For over twenty years Anne designed scenery, creating environments to fit characters and actions in plays for the stage, making visual spaces communicate to an audience. She also tried to do that with her house. But she knows that every audience member interprets what they see according to their own life experiences and needs. So far, no one needs this house. But Noah Levinson of Chicago may already be in the air, travelling to Durham to find a new home, perhaps this one. *What strange circumstance brings him here? I wonder if he remembers me.*

The mail truck arrives while Anne waters ferns on the front porch. Crossing the lawn, she stoops and replaces the fallen "For Sale by Owner" sign, a necessary result of divorce and early retirement. *Oh, for the luxury of a realtor.*

Continuing to think like a buyer, she turns and looks at the old place, assessing it for street appeal. She knows the current real estate trend is toward a big new house with oversized bathrooms and closets and a small lot with little to no yard work. Her house is large, but otherwise, the exact opposite. She looks up at the windows to the loft above the great room, both added ten years ago by a dyslexic contractor who kept reading measurements backwards. Anne and her husband Steven became his crew. Two years later, an attached garage and shop were added with a large recording studio over them. The studio was created for but never used by her former musician husband. After their separation, she turned it into a one-bedroom apartment to help cover the increased mortgage payment due to their property settlement. The apartment that saved her financially is now a problem. It has been called to her attention that this is a single-family residence and the apartment is against the Homeowners Association Guidelines. No one wants to pay for square footage they might seldom, if ever, use. She is looking for the proverbial needle/buyer in a housing-glut haystack, someone with a child-come-home or a dependent in-law who could legally use the outlawed space.

She sighs and waves to her neighbor Ben as he drives past, on his way to teach at the university where his wife resides in the campus cemetery. She looks next door but can't tell if Barbara is home, now that she parks her car in the garage that was once filled with her ex-husband's tools. Now Barbara spends most of her time in South Carolina with her new boyfriend. *Soon-to-be-gone and long-gone friendships.*

Formerly an ideal place to raise a family, the children are all grown and gone. So it's quiet. Most people work and keep to themselves unless a large snowfall brings them together for chili and beer. Being snow-bound makes everyone lonely. Memories of chili, beer, snow, and old friendships pass through her mind, reviving the ambiguity of her need to leave.

Crossing the street to her mailbox and reaching inside, she finds an unexpected letter from Faye, her oldest friend, and instantly feels the beginning of dread. Standing in the street, Anne opens the letter. The first sentence tells of the loss of Faye's father, one week ago. Clouded with emotion, her questionable gift of too much insight and empathy blocks the moment's reality. A car rounds the corner, moving well above the residential speed limit. The driver honks and swerves, narrowly missing her and then narrowly missing the telephone pole on the opposite side. Anne stands frozen while unfocused images of Steven flash through her mind. When she can move and breathe again, she has already missed the chance to read the disappearing license plate. Anne shudders and slumps. Paranoia has long tendrils, and Steven still casts an even longer shadow. *Why is he so much on my mind today? It has been years.*

Walking back to the porch, she sits heavily with legs crossed and re-reads Faye's words. It's too early in the day to call her. *I'll try later when I can give her the support and attention she surely needs. Like me, she was a daddy's girl.*

She carries the letter and the weight of her friend's news inside, and then purposefully moves upstairs to tackle the remaining sorting problems. The usual clutter of a home office and studio, augmented by the physical remains of her campus office and many years of teaching, is in stacks on every scrap of horizontal space. Exams ended the previous week, and Anne's retirement began. She donated most of her books to the Theatre Department library and still somehow managed to bring home a roomful of stuff. She wonders now at her foolishness. The collage of theatre office remnants morphs into a still-life arrangement for a painting, symbolizing the students, the colleagues, and that all-important sense of worth and purpose.

Worth and purpose. She laughs. Even that duo began to slowly erode, along with her patience and self-image, following her divorce. One day, she threw a chair in class in an emotional explosion at the tardiness of half of her students. She realized it was time to reassess or to take an anger management class. She began planning an early retirement.

Anne feels herself being sucked in by emotional memories. *You need to walk away.*

She bumps a chair, which in turn hits the computer and jars it to life. Checking her email, she finds a lower than low-ball offer that doesn't even deserve a counter. She then opens a response to a previous message from yesterday.

EMAIL TO A. GRAY:

Arriving at 5:00 p.m. to look at the house. Thanks for the map.— N. Levinson

Yes, Mr. Levinson, I couldn't get to you; maybe you can get to me. Anne moves on to her handsome easel, a gift from Logan, the last and best man in her life, dumped due to fear of a third relationship failure. She examines the unfinished portrait of her older daughter and two grandsons. The composition, a triangle with a strong diagonal of light touching only their remarkable eyes, cheekbones, and a few wisps of auburn hair reminds Anne of her set designs— bold and clean, and always triangles. This was the first painting after Steven left, but like most creative efforts in these last years, it is far from completed. If she can make herself open paint tubes and lift a brush, she will finish it before the move. *Oh well, considering the real estate market, there may be time to paint a one-woman show—if only I could make myself begin.*

8

The phone rings. A showing to a realtor with a potential buyer is scheduled. On impulse, Anne calls Summer at work. "Hi, sweetheart. I'm selling the house today."

"Really?"

Her daughter's voice betrays a touch of panic, making Anne's heart tighten. "Stop sounding abandoned. You know I have to do this or go bonkers."

"Don't bonk, Mom. So who's the buyer?"

"I don't know. I have a three o'clock and a five o'clock. One of them."

"I see. Are we wearing our clairvoyant hat?"

"Maybe I am. The three o'clock seems very eager. If nothing else, I'll keep her here until five when the gentleman from Chicago arrives. They'll fall in love at first sight and buy it together. Of course he'll have to leave his wife first, probably an answer to her prayers." Anne chuckles. "How's that for optimism?"

"Sounds more like depraved desperation."

"Hey, I already got one offer in an email."

"How much?"

"Seventy below asking."

"Hell, I'll buy it for that."

"Really?"

"No. But I love you, Mom."

"Back at you, Summergirl."

After the phone call, Anne takes a deep breath and slowly releases it. *I'll shower and then attack the studio—no more walking away.*

At 3:30, the realtor with the 3:00 appointment calls to postpone until 4:00. At 4:00, she calls to postpone until 4:30. At 4:45 the doorbell rings.

"Come in!" Anne calls, controlling her irritation. *Almost two hours late.* She knew she wouldn't be able to hear the doorbell from the studio and abandoned that project at 3:00, filling time down-stairs while waiting for the realtor. After the second postponement, she decided to bake cookies for her granddaughter, Lindsay, and was unloading the last pan onto a cooling rack when the doorbell rang, and then rang again.

"Please come in!!" This time, she calls louder and with attitude. As the last cookie slides off the spatula onto the rack, she looks up and into the questioning eyes of a well-dressed middle-aged man stand-ing in the kitchen doorway. *Click.* She suddenly feels frumpy in her jeans, t-shirt, and oven mitt, blowing a lock of hair from her face.

"Sorry to surprise you. I'm a little early." Anne doesn't respond but tosses the cookie sheet into the sink while regaining her com-posure. "You obviously don't like surprises. Did I let myself in too far?" He smiles weakly, and her irritation disappears as her emo-tional guard goes up. When she still doesn't immediately answer, he continues, releasing boyish charm. "I could back into the living room, or just leave and drive around for fifteen minutes. But, can you keep the house smelling just like this? And may I please have a cookie to take with me?"

"Stop!" She laughs, pushing the stray lock of hair out of her vi-sion, angry with herself for the blush of pleasure rising to his com-pliment. "I was expecting someone else, an unpunctual and incon-siderate realtor. She has already postponed three times and might show-up while you're here."

"Will that be awkward?"

"No. I have actually fantasized that the two of you will fall in love and buy the house together—or start a bidding war. Is your mar-riage stable?"

"Not very."

"See, perfect solution. Here, have a cookie. Have several. If you buy the house, you can have the whole batch."

His smile takes on a wooden effort as he reaches for a cookie and dutifully tastes it. "Oh ... my ... God!" Then he takes two more.

A little too effusive, you kiss-up. Anne cools her blush, reminding herself she has a house to sell, and that she isn't interested in men, especially this one. *Once fooled, twice foolish, and there won't be a third time. Besides, I don't think foolishest is a word.*

"My childhood just flashed before me. If you don't have children, buy some. This shouldn't be wasted on old taste buds. I know this is oatmeal, but what else is in it?"

"Raisins, cranberries, pecans, and a certain spice I can't divulge without killing you. Would the old taste buds like some iced tea?"

"Yes, if it isn't southern sweet. By the way, I'm Noah Levinson."

"And I'm Anne Gray." *Ring any bells? Of course not. You would only know me by my married name.* "You've come a long way, Mr. Levinson. How was your flight?" Humor gone, her words are stiff, tinged with sarcasm.

"Please call me Noah. May I call you Anne?"

"Of course." She hesitates, knowing they're fighting for control, and he's winning. Naturally! He's a big time publisher and she's just a retired teacher, one whose work he once rejected. She looks at him more carefully. The teasing done, he seems tired and drawn. *The flight couldn't have been too rough—not a hair out of place on that upper management salon-styled head.*

One side of his mouth lifts and then abandons the beginning of a smile. "The flight was the usual. No time wasted. I used to like to read a novel between naps, meals, and cocktails. Now it's a laptop and a cell phone between a soft drink and pretzels."

Anne agrees. "There are disadvantages to modern technology. We've become our own secretaries, and carry our office with us. Why don't we go relax in the great room? A few more cookies, and then you get the tour. Is your move to Durham due to a job transfer?" They walk through the dining room and into the great room where large windows face the lake.

"Not exactly. Wow! Your pictures didn't do it justice."

"The room?"

"The view!" He opens the door and walks out on the deck as if he already owned it. "Perfect." The lake is a deep blue, reflecting the late afternoon sky. The weeping willow on the left at the edge of the water is yellow-green with new growth. The Chinese redbud, just past its peak, is still covered with intensely pink blooms, and the ornamental grasses which dominate her gardens are beginning to show their varied colors. Everything looks fresh and young and hopeful.

"Are you overwhelmed every time you step out here? You didn't send me pictures of the island. I think I understand. Some people would have come just to see it, with no intention of buying."

Anne shakes her head at the way he jumps ahead of her answers. She tells him about her first summer here when the lake's dam was being repaired and the water level was low. Many neighbors took advantage of the dry lake bed to enlarge their back yards, reclaiming land that had washed away from lack of retainer walls. Instead of adding to her yard, Anne built a small island, which fit neatly into the cove that water and wind had sculpted through years of neglect. She mortared stone retainer walls around the island and on the water's edge of her lot. A short bridge spans the six foot distance from yard to island. Beside it hangs a sign given by a latter-day-hippie friend printed with the words, "Welcome: Children, Animals, Unicorns, and Lovers". And then she met Steven.

Pure fantasy, Noah muses, *almost too precious. How would Elizabeth react?* He walks slowly down the deck steps, down the slate path, across the bridge, around the Chinese redbud in the center of the island, and onto the dock on the far side. He turns, looking back at Anne and the house, observing the brick patio surrounding the maple, the garden shed providing privacy from the neighbor on one side, and the natural fence created by trees and tall shrubs on the other. He notes the low garden walls made of stone. *A secluded fantasy world in the middle of a suburb—Elizabeth might just love it.*

From this distance he really looks at Anne for the first time. *Her hair's too short and her temper too quick. She's trying to play me, but she doesn't have the killer instinct. And I don't have the time or energy for games.*

Walking back, he notes the good condition of the siding and the roof, the freshness of the paint. "What about boats?" He stops on the steps and looks up at Anne.

"Rowboats, canoes, bass boats with electric motors, and small sailboats are allowed, but no gasoline motors. That's my canoe over there. It goes with the house."

"Good."

"We have a variety of fish and waterfowl. The gardens are mostly ornamental grasses and hardy perennials that practically take care of themselves. The only invasive grasses are in containers. I plan to mulch heavily, so weeding will be minimized."

"Is that the apartment?" He gestures to a door on the left of the deck.

"Yes. That door opens to stairs that lead to the apartment above the garage. Would you like to look at it since we're out here?"

"How do you get to it from the front?"

"There's a gate to the right of the garage as you face the house. It opens to a courtyard garden that leads back here to the patio and the apartment door. Would you like to see the garden?"

"No. Is the apartment still occupied?" Anne takes a deep breath, and he knows she is controlling her negative response to his selective interest, but he doesn't have time for her full sales pitch.

"Sue is moving to a condo in a converted tobacco warehouse in downtown Durham. It's a great place for a single person, close to restaurants, jazz clubs, theatres, Duke Hospital, the Durham Bulls stadium. Have I talked you out of this house and into a condo? Should I cut out my tongue?"

"You're funny. Is the apartment furnished?"

"It is now, but Sue's taking her furniture with her. Would you like to see it?"

"No, my schedule's tight. I'd like to see the master bedroom."

Anne hesitates, then turns and walks inside to a French glass door with lace curtains. It opens from the great room into the master bedroom. Noah follows her, understanding her reluctance. *She probably wanted to show me the smaller bedrooms first so this one would seem larger by comparison.*

Struck by the calmness he feels in this room, Noah pauses and notes each detail, surprised to see the walls are stark white. The tall queen bed, white down comforter, and several pillows in varied shades of green dominate the space. A burgundy throw is casually draped over the corner of the bed, a novel on it. Beside the bed, in place of a night table, is an antique sewing machine with a reading lamp, several more books, and a vase of dried grasses. Above the iron headboard hangs an artfully framed waterscape. Other art work and photographs of five generations of family hang in carefully planned groupings. On the faux-painted chest of drawers, a carved statue of Don Quixote holds a sword in one hand and a book in the other. Beside it is a plain wooden box, contrasting with the ornate jewelry boxes on her dresser next to pottery lamps, perfumes, and a Mardi Gras mask with plumes and sequins. He feels like a voyeur in this room that exposes the woman quietly watching him, laying bare her pedigree, her sensibilities, and her sensitivities.

Above is a slow-turning white ceiling fan. *I believe there's a fan in every room I've walked through—an excess, even in the South, but nice.* "You have a strong sense of color and design. But why are only these walls white?"

"Whenever my life begins anew, I cut my hair and paint the bedroom white." She blushes as if this information was too private and unplanned. "This isn't a large room, but you really live in the other spaces—the great room, the dining room, and the kitchen—and they actually *are* large."

"This room feels bigger than it is. I think it's because of the glass door and all the light it gives. That's a good decorator choice."

"Let me show you the other bedrooms and guest bath."

"I have to go. I can't be late for my next appointment."

Stunned, she leads him to the front door. "Did I tell you the roof and heating and air conditioning units are new? And wouldn't your wife like to see it?"

Noah stops at the door and turns. "It's all perfect. Why are you leaving?"

"That's a long personal story. Why are you coming here?"

"Equally personal!"

Anne pauses, realizing she is being rude in response to his rudeness, but she can't resist a bit of sarcasm. "Sorry. But for future reference, Mr. Levinson, what exactly turned you off? Was it a spider web I missed, the apartment and bedrooms you didn't see, the shop you didn't even ask about?"

"You're funny, Ms. Gray. I'll call you tomorrow."

Walking to his car, he hears the door close, soundly.

As she storms away from the slammed door, Anne resists the urge to scream, glad she didn't remind him of their past connection. She didn't want him to know he had rejected her a second time. The phone rings. "What!"

"Whoa, Mom. What's up? Have you sold the house?"

"Do I sound like I'm celebrating?" Anne takes a breath and softens. "Sorry, Summer. I need to calm down. I just spent a day preparing for two serious buyers. The guy from Chicago refused to answer questions about himself, and didn't even look at half of the rooms. Instead of showing him the house, I felt like I was being pulled around behind him. He was more interested in my decorating than in the property, and he ate half the cookies I made for Lindsay."

"Oh, he is no good, especially the cookie part. Why were you questioning him? Good looking?"

"No!" *Yes!* "I simply wanted to know what he's looking for . . . in a house. He says he'll be back. Right! He couldn't wait to leave and look at other houses."

"You're famous for your insight. Couldn't you get a read on him?"

"If I had to describe him, I'd use the words: angry, controlling, very smart . . . and sad."

"Sounds volatile. Also sounds like the type you tend to bring home and take care of. Be careful. What about your three o'clock realtor?"

"She postponed about four times and never showed up. I'm sure I've heard the last of her. To be honest, I thought I'd already heard the last of him."

"Excuse me?"

"He's a publisher who rejected my textbook years ago."

"Ouch! So, a book-rejecting, cookie-mooching be-back and a no-show she-rat. You *have* had a bad day."

"Put that to music, and we'll take it on the road." Anne laughs and then exhales her frustrations. "Thank you, honey. I feel better already. But don't be surprised if I give up my Pollyanna attitude and turn it over to a realty company."

"I thought that wasn't an option."

"What, giving up Pollyanna or calling a realtor?"

"Either one, my believer-in-the-human-race, financially-depressed mother."

"I'm not destitute. I just want to maximize my buying power at the coast. I thought I would be sensible for once in my life and hold out for some financial security."

"Come on, Mom, you wouldn't know what to do with a flush bank account."

"That's right. Who needs it? And you don't need an inheritance, do you?"

"Hmmm, bribery. All right, what can I do to help you? Come to the gym tomorrow. We'll exercise and strategize. And in-between, I'll tell you all the problems I'm having with my second line manager. What a creep. I think it's therapy time for both of us."

Anne winces as she listens to her daughter putting up a brave front, trying to mask the longing for her mother to stay, but also trying to reciprocate the support she has always been given.

"I'll be there. Give my angel a kiss. Tell her I'll bring the cookies tomorrow. And give the big palooka a hug for me."

"Would that be my husband or the dog?"

Anne chuckles as she sets the phone down. It rings again. "Forget something?"

"Yes, my manners."

"Noah?"

"Right! I want to apologize. My life is a little out of control right now, and I'm really tired. I like your home, and I'd like to come

16

back tomorrow morning at nine, if that's all right. I want to look at everything, but I have another appointment across town at eleven."

"You're considering another house?"

"No."

Finally, Anne listens to his voice. "And you're not going to another house *now*, are you?"

After a long pause, he responds. "I have a conference call with my wife's oncologist in Chicago and her new one at Duke."

"You don't have to explain. I've been so focused on selling the house that my antenna for other people's problems has been out of order. I'm not usually so insensitive."

"You're fine. I much prefer humor to sympathy."

"So, I'll see you at nine? I'll make coffee."

After a simple supper of stir-fried vegetables and rice, she makes the postponed call to Faye, and they talk about her father, pulling Anne into her friend's pain and loss. Then she calls her brother Earl, who listens and soothes, always her rescuer from deep moods or deep water.

For a change, sleep comes quickly only to be disturbed by a dream of Steven. In it, they are walking, talking about his betrayal. He looks like the vulnerable boy/man she first married. As they pass through an unknown whispering town, he confesses and then begs for her forgiveness. Before she can respond, strange people gather around them and drag him away. She is silently screaming as they place a rope around his neck. His eyes look directly at her, burning with condemnation. She slowly climbs out of the dream-become-nightmare.

The next morning, following coffee and a more detailed tour of the house, Anne and Noah sit in the great room, the sunlight filtering through bamboo shades, at once exotic and soothing. He seems different, no longer the CEO, man in charge. Or maybe she is just looking at him differently. On the outside, he appears to be in his mid-to-late forties, average height and build, well-proportioned, but a little soft from a sedentary job. His hair is dark and, without the salon styling gel, it curls. His eyes are brown and watchful.

Because he doesn't offer, she asks. "Is your wife's cancer treatable?"

"You go straight to the point, don't you?" He moves forward, sitting on the edge of the couch as tension follows the opening of a subject he never shares with others.

"Sorry, I do tend to say what I'm thinking, a little trait I inherited from my mother."

"I don't talk about it, but I probably should. There are lots of treatments. She has ALL—Acute Lymphoblastic Leukemia. Whether the treatments will make a difference, we don't know. When I say we, I mean the doctors and me. Liz won't discuss it."

"Why?"

"Because she doesn't want it. Treatment, I mean. She lost her mother and two sisters to cancer. She believes it will take her, too. She won't fight it, and she doesn't want to prolong her life in exchange for debilitating and degrading treatments."

Too hard. Change the subject. "Do you have children?"

"One—Joshua." Noah clears his throat before continuing. "He died of childhood leukemia several years ago."

Oh, Jesus! Great change! "I'm sorry. I guess I can understand her unwillingness to fight. If I had lost so much of my family and even one of my daughters, death would be very seductive." She sighs, trying to ward off his pain entering and filling her. "But I suppose my other daughter would keep me going, for her sake."

"Right. She needs a reason to fight. But it seems I'm not reason enough." He says it matter-of-factly, but it costs him. He sits back, the worst of the conversation over.

Shake it off, Anne. New direction, or offer him therapeutic sex now. Shut up! You don't do that . . . anymore. "Why Durham? There are surely more glamorous cities with equally good cancer centers."

"Durham has Jazz—we're both big fans."

"Well, Durham not only has the musicians; it also has the roots."

"You're a fan, too?"

She hesitates. "I'm a little bit country, but I used to know someone in the local music scene. I can make a list of musicians and places to go. So will you be moving your offices here?"

"Do you know my work?"

"Of course. I googled your name after you contacted me for a showing of the house." *Actually, I learned your name when I received your form letter rejecting my book after months of encouragement.* "Does your wife work?"

"She did. She was an editor." He hesitates and then the long penned-up words tumble out. "She loves books, and currently reads true stories about real people. You would think she'd go for fantasy or some other escapism. But she wants to know about people struggling and surviving or struggling and failing, as long as it's real. She's been like that since our son died."

"What did she like before?"

"Happily-ever-after romance adventures and children's books. She and Josh used to read together, and they would laugh and cry over the characters in their stories. They both were inconsolable over *The Little Prince* and *Charlotte's Web.*"

"I remember crying with my daughters over those same books." *Go ahead, ask.* "Did she ever edit textbooks?"

"At one time. But we no longer publish textbooks."

It's history. Let it go, Anne. "Why are you buying? Why not rent? Why am I shooting myself in the foot?"

In spite of his somber mood, he chuckles, then stands and walks to the glass door to gaze out again at the lake. "Stronger people than you have tried to redirect my thinking, Anne. So don't worry about your foot. Anyway, rentals don't provide the atmosphere she needs. I want her to feel at home, but not in our Chicago home. I think she needs a completely new environment. I want to put painful

19

memories behind her so that maybe she can imagine a future where she isn't drowning in loss. Chicago has good doctors and hospitals, but I've been referred to an outstanding oncologist at Duke Hospital whose research is targeted at her disease."

"If you want to give her the feeling of a new start, why not buy a new house? There are plenty of them around. The whole Triangle is overbuilt. This house is full of past lives, bad decisions, and ghosts of marriage past. That's why I'm leaving." *Why do I keep trying to talk him out of this house?*

He turns back to her. "She doesn't like new. And we don't have time for it. She likes, no, *loves* things that have been affected by life, things that have stories and memories. The only things she buys new are mattresses, linens, and underwear. That's an exaggeration, but not by much."

"Well, she would just get an empty but well-storied house if you buy this one."

"That's what I want to talk to you about." He sits again, tension rising as he plans how to word his proposal.

Anne shifts uneasily. "Somehow, I knew this conversation would bend."

"I don't have the time, energy, or skill to decorate, especially to look for used but interesting stuff. That's much harder than walking into a showroom and ordering a house full of new, which she would hate anyway. Liz simply *can't* do it, and she wouldn't."

"So, you want me to furnish and decorate the house for you?"

"You already have."

"Yes, but my interesting stuff will go away with me."

Noah sits forward again, all business. "This is my offer. I'll pay your asking price for the house, plus 20 percent for the furnishings. I'll have to pay the 20 percent in a separate contract so it doesn't balloon the tax value of the house. I've thought about this a lot since yesterday. I would also need you to furnish the apartment so it will be ready if we need a live-in nurse."

"Noah, please, slow down. By furnishings, do you just mean the furniture?"

"No, I mean everything—except your clothes, photos, and personal essentials."

"Your offer is generous. But how can I put a price on my history? These furnishings, these *things* remind me who I am and where I've been, both happy and scary. Actually, you're welcome to the furniture . . . except for the chaise lounge . . . but not the things." She does a quick calculation of 20 percent, and grows weak in her knees.

Noah delays, not ready to respond to her counter. "Happy and scary? Happy I understand, but explain how an object represents scary."

She sighs, unable to sidestep his determination. *Why am I doing this? Why is he asking?* But she feels sympathy for his situation and wants him to understand why she can't sell her past. She stands and walks around the room, stopping at a small piece of pottery hanging on the wall. It's a sun with a face and a lopsided smile. She removes it from the hanger and holds it a moment, letting the warmth of the memory move through her before handing it to Noah who holds it carefully and leans back, waiting for her story.

"I nearly died of a lung disease a number of years ago." She paces as she talks. "It took a month in the hospital, a botched bronchoscopy, open lung surgery, and a misdiagnosis before I was treated with prednisone and sent home with a worrisome prognosis. When the disease returned six months later, the doctors finally determined it was an allergic reaction to the pet dove in my home." She shrugs her shoulders. "I tend to rescue birds and animals—but no more birds from the pigeon family. I was terrified of dying and leaving my daughters who were only nine and eleven."

Then she smiles as the good side of the memory returns. "Anyway, a group of my students, all guys, all black, and one well over six feet tall, brought that piece to me at the hospital. They hung it on the wall in front of my bed and called it La, the God of Good Lungs. One of the courses I taught was Arts and Humanities. In it, we discussed Ra, the Egyptian sun god. They knew I would make the connection. I was touched that they came, and that they chose such a gift. They took turns lying beside me on top of the covers and acting out hilarious death scenes. They stole pillows and assorted medical supplies as they left, just mischief and an effort to keep me laughing. The nurses stopped them before they made their get-away, and they returned everything. I remember that night and those students whenever I look at it."

Anne sits in her rocker beside the couch. "Like many people in a crisis, I made a deal with God. I asked Him to let me live long enough to get my girls independent of the need of parents, and then I would happily leave this earth. After that, I never even entertained the notion that I might die. Before he had determined the true source of my illness, whenever my doctor tried to talk to me about his prognosis, I simply zoned out. I did, however, hear him say that if I lived, I would never run, play tennis, or do anything like I had done before. He said I would be an invalid. The only question was how severe my disabilities might be. I didn't believe him. By summer, I was part of a two man crew building the addition that includes this room."

Noah looks up at the high ceiling and balcony, aware of the enormous labor involved in such a project. He whistles in appreciation.

"And by the way, I can run, play tennis, ride a bicycle, whatever any healthy woman can do. And my x-rays don't even show the scar tissue that had eliminated 80% of my breathing capacity. My lungs are clear. So I guess my daughters still need me."

"That's quite a story." He smiles, and in spite of the bleak future before him, he feels energized by this woman. *You're a survivor, and I'll bet you have a bucket full of stories.* A new idea begins to form. He dangles a baited hook before her. "But that's just one example." He looks around, remembers she excluded one piece of furniture in her offer. "What about that chaise lounge? It looks like it belongs in a Hobbit novel."

"It's made of willow branches, cut and shaped while they're still green. I met a Vietnam vet at the NC State Fairgrounds who custom-made it for me. And yes, there's more to the story."

"And I suppose everything else has a story?"

"I hadn't thought about it that way, but I suppose most of the art objects do." Anne looks around, swallowing Noah's bait. "The vase on the table represents the restoration of my belief in the unending power of love and the human spirit; the statue of two children over there, on the bookshelf, is a tribute to the influence, both good and bad, that teachers have as role models for students; the dinner bell in the dining room was a gift that marked the beginning of forgiveness. Need I go on?"

"No, I'm convinced." *Now I just have to convince you.*

"Back to your wife." Anne swallows, a catch in her throat. "As I said before, if my girls were gone, I too would probably welcome death. In addition to the loss of your son, it sounds like she felt defeated by cancer before she was even diagnosed. I can't imagine what that loss or that feeling of hopeless resignation would be like."

He leans forward again. "I think you get the picture, and she has a long unpleasant treatment to go through, if I can even talk her into it. The oncologist says attitude is as important as the medication. She needs something to reawaken her interest in life. She needs *your* attitude—and maybe your stories." He pauses as he gently lays the clay sun on the coffee table, and then looks directly into Anne's eyes for the first time. "That's it! The house won't give up its history; the objects will get her attention, but she needs the stories." He pauses for emphasis. "You have to do it!"

"Whoa!" Anne laughs, pulling her knees up and circling them with her arms. "I'm not good with sickness. I empathize too much. I would be throwing up right beside her."

"You don't have to be here. Liz wouldn't be comfortable with that either. She just needs your own unselfconscious written memories—good and bad—that make you a fighter and a survivor."

"You mean write my memoirs?" she asks in disbelief.

"Not exactly." Grasping for a straw, he almost pleads. "Just do what you did a moment ago. Take one meaningful object in the house at a time, and write the story it brings to your mind, stories that emphasize positive attitude and a determination to beat the odds."

"Hold on!" Her feet hit the floor. "I'm not one of your writers. I tried to be, several years ago, but you rejected me."

"What? I'm pretty good with names, and I don't remember yours."

"I was still married. Would you remember Marshall?"

"Anne Marshall . . . you sent a manuscript for a textbook on scene design."

"You are good. Gray is my maiden name. I took it back after the divorce."

"I remember your book because Liz was the editor who recommended it. She was so excited, said it was as easy to read as a novel. We didn't reject you. We simply dropped all textbooks in order to specialize in another direction."

"You never told me that. Your letter simply suggested I try another publisher . . . and that was after what I interpreted as serious interest in my book. Is your wife's name Elizabeth Fineberg?"

"Yes. She continued using her maiden name for professional purposes."

"I liked her so much, and we seemed to click as a team. She was so warm and encouraging to me, a new writer." Anne shakes her head. "It's difficult to believe she's the depressed woman you've been describing. I was disappointed that I never heard from her after the rejection."

"Our son's illness began to escalate at that same time, and he became her focus. It's one of the reasons we ended the textbook line. She was the driving force behind it. I'm so sorry. We couldn't talk about the change in our line until we transferred the textbooks we already had to other companies. So everything that wasn't fully contracted was dropped." He pauses. "Did you get it published?"

"Yes. Harcourt-Brace accepted it."

"And has it been successful?"

"Mildly. I get a royalty check every spring and fall. It's used more as a source book than a textbook. But it will help with my retirement. Thanks for explaining. Now my perception of an injustice seems both wrong and minor. But back to your offer and conditions. You're challenging me to create a will-to-live in the mind of someone I don't really know. You are, in a sense, making me responsible for her life. No dice." She moves away, distancing herself from his needs, rehanging the clay sun.

Determined, Noah follows. "Anne, I came here looking for a house with grace and charm that would make Liz comfortable for her treatments and possibly for her remaining weeks or months. To be honest, I had almost given up. But you and this house move me. Your resilience, your humor, and your ability to communicate both are what she needs. Logical or not, you've given me a grain of hope."

Anne covers her eyes, horrified by his request.

"I know I'm expecting a lot. My amended offer is this: your asking price for the house and a separate check for 20 percent of that in exchange for your stories and the *temporary* use of your things. You can have them back."

"You want to buy the house and borrow my things?"

"Yes."

"I've written for education, adapted prose and poetry for the stage, but I've never written memoir."

"Your writing skills are more than needed for this. Just put down what you're thinking or remembering, like you did with this clay sun. If you can write a story as well as you told this one, it will be perfect. Don't try to refine or pretty it up. It might become self-conscious and contrived. Besides, there isn't time for rewrites, and I'm going to sell you to her as a would-be writer. I can even play the guilt card over not publishing your textbook."

"Assuming I'll agree to this," she says slowly, considering, "how soon would it have to be done?"

"Three weeks."

"What about closing on the house?"

"My lawyers will take care of that. Just give me a voided check and the money will be deposited in your account."

Anne shakes her head and paces again, concern lining her face. "It's too much money. I feel like I'm robbing you, using your bad luck to my advantage."

"Number one," he smiles, knowing she's caught. "The price is low. If such a house existed in Chicago, it would cost two or three times as much. Number two, I can afford it, and you are saving me the enormous time it would take to furnish a house. Number three, I got where I am because I'm good at reading people. Your stories may not change her attitude, but they will at least show her a different path than the one she's on."

Anne stops, moved by his faith and enthusiasm, and amused by the ironical twist. *So, finally she will be my editor and you'll be the publishing CEO?*

"I understand the employees call me the AIC behind my back."

"The AIC?"

"Asshole In Charge."

They both laugh, and then Anne sobers as she realizes she has accepted his offer and the conditions. "Don't use the guilt card. She liked my writing before; maybe she'll like it again."

After Noah leaves, Anne falls onto her willow chaise. Overwhelmed by his confidence in her and her own feeling of inadequacy, she tries to shut out the confusing and conflicting emotions. *Until now, I never thought in detail about the stories connected to my things, and I don't know if I want to relive any of them, even in my mind. And how can I be so arrogant as to expect my stories will help Elizabeth? But now that I know her story, I desperately want to help her!*

The day that began with measured optimism has exploded into a financial dream attached to a nightmare responsibility. She tries to make a list of objects that might have stories to give, but she can't imagine an order or an ultimate direction, much less a conclusion for the writing. *What is the real goal—to make Elizabeth fight—to simply provide a distraction while the treatment does or doesn't work—or to prepare her for death?* She remembers Noah's comments about the state of his marriage. Some of her stories would have to include her husbands. She assumes their marriage would

26

look good next to her two failed attempts. But some of her stories would naturally include her daughters and grandchildren. *Would that help or just cause more pain? Maybe I could just make up some stories. No, I hate lies. And as an editor I imagine Elizabeth would know them for false.*

Anne has known many people with cancer, and their responses and attitudes were as varied as their diseases. Some gave up and died quickly. Some fought and died anyway. But she knows one with stage four breast cancer who said, throughout all the worst treatments, "I claim my healing!" And that one is still alive and cancer-free. *Attitude, faith, determination, or whatever it was saved her. Her doctors are still stunned. According to Noah, Elizabeth has claimed death instead of life, and he expects me to swing that choice—to help her make a miracle.* Anne shudders. She was an educator, but this is not a classroom exercise or temporary scenery for a play about fictional characters. This is real.

Her mind shifts to the money and the kind of house Noah's offer could buy her and where she wants to look for property. But her moral pole draws her back to the stories and where to begin. *How can he trust me when I don't even trust myself and can't manage my own issues, much less finish a creative project?*

After hours of false starts, she breaks her healthy eating rule and makes a dinner of fried catfish and biscuits. Still later, caught between self-effacement and a growing determination to help this woman, she throws her paperwork aside, finds a CD with old beach music, and opens the back door to a lovely spring night.

Anne stands on the deck looking up at the stars and tries not to think about the loss of this place, this view, and the years behind her. She closes her eyes and lets the night clear her mind as she slowly begins to move with the sensual pleasure evoked by the music of her youth.

She doesn't hear Noah's car pull into the driveway or his knock at her front door. He finds his way through the side garden to the patio gate. "What do you call that step?"

Anne blushes, irritated that blushing seems to be her standard reaction to Noah. Regaining her composure, she laughs and wags a finger at him. "Only a bona fide Yankee would not recognize the shag, a dance born and bred on the beaches of the Carolinas."

"After I ply you with wine, and you sign these contracts, maybe you would teach me. And by the way, I'm not a Yankee. I was born in Raleigh, but moved to Chicago before puberty and dances on the beach."

"Well, Raleigh boy, you just earned some points, but I'm amazed you already have the contracts."

"My lawyers are well paid to do what I ask." He holds the wine up.

My name is Anne; I am an alcoholic. Maybe one day I'll speak the words aloud. Instead, she sighs and responds, "One glass—no plying. This filly can't hold her liquor, and I'm already a little drunk on the twists and turns of the day. I'll sign your papers, and then I'll teach you to shag." *Maybe I can toast the sale with my one glass and then put it aside. Ah, just look at him. Click. Hazy light, red wine, blue shirt, brown eyes, and all that need—woe is me, I could be so undone.* And just as quickly, she remembers her resolve and her feelings recede. She looks up to an open window in the garage apartment. "Sue!"

A flash of blonde hair fills the window. "What's up, girlfriend?"

"Come on down. A handsome stranger bought my house, and now he wants to dance." *And I don't think I should be alone with him and a bottle of wine.*

Hours later, Noah sits back and releases the seatbelt after the stewardess hands him a drink. He relives the hectic two days in Durham, North Carolina. Will this become his new home for an indeterminate period of time and medical procedures, or just another aborted attempt to save Elizabeth from herself? He wonders what she will say, wonders if he can sell the lie and open her head and heart to Anne's stories. He pulls his computer from the bag under the seat, and writes.

EMAIL TO ANNE:

I'm airborne, on the way to Chicago, putting my CEO hat back on. Thanks for the dance, but you didn't have to call Sue. You were safe. Write those stories. Make them sing.—*Noah*

EMAIL TO NOAH:

I don't know if they'll sing, but I've written the first story, and it's already deeply affecting me on many levels. As I wrote, I felt fragile. When I finished, I felt strong. In fact, it's still too fresh to talk about. I desperately want to help your wife, but I wonder if this will benefit me more than her.

Remember me to the heron when you come here to live, and teach your Elizabeth the shag. That may help her more than my poor stories. And, it wasn't *my* safety I was worried about.—*Always, Anne*

Chapter 2

Finding Pearl

YESTERDAY WAS HOT, humid, dark, depressing, and frustrating. This morning is bright and fresh, cleansed by last night's rain. Anne wore yellow yesterday to keep her spirits above the gloomy weather; today she can wear anything and feel good. She rummages through her suitcase while talking on the phone to yet another realtor.

"That's correct. I want a house in or within walking distance of a small town somewhere between Wilmington and North Myrtle Beach, preferably on the Intracoastal waterway or on a tributary. I don't want to be on the beach, but I would like the beach to be within a thirty-minute drive. I prefer three bedrooms and two baths, but I can look at something smaller that would accommodate an addition, if the location is right and the renovations aren't a money pit."

"Honey, I have several wonderful houses in developments with shopping centers nearby and a golf course, tennis courts…" It's the same response Anne has heard from every realtor she has called.

"No developments and no golf courses. Small town, not shopping center."

"Well, dear, what about a lot? We have some lovely developments on the Black River with free dock and launch access."

Why is it so difficult to get someone to listen? She decides on the blue t-shirt purchased last night. It has "Holden Beach" printed below a picture of a long-legged, long-billed bird. She bought it because it reminded her of a painting she did years ago of a solitary sandpiper running on a beach. She had named the painting "Solo"— *feeling very solo today, but also very determined.* She finds white casual pants, wrinkled but wearable. *I look like a tourist. Oh well!*

The realtor continues with forced enthusiasm. "Here's a listing that might interest you. It's a three bedroom with two baths in a mixed community outside the town of Harding."

"What do you mean by mixed community?"

"It just means that the housing varies in style and type."

"You mean there are trailers and pre-fabs and a few older houses. I'm not a snob, but I would like to invest in property that will increase in value, not decrease." She ends the conversation. *Maybe I have too specific a house and location in mind. Maybe I am a snob.*

Anne calls Greer on her cell. Her daughter answers. "Well, hello there."

Needing no further invitation, Anne complains. "It's not really the house that's so important; it's the place. I have proven I can make a house into what I want. I just don't want to settle. I want this to be the house and community I'll be happy in for the rest of my life. And if you talk to your Uncle Earl, please don't tell him I'm looking for a house near water. You know how my brother worries." Satisfied that she has finally been heard, she gives Greer a chance to speak of her day. Afterwards, her thoughts shift to Durham, and she wonders if they have arrived, wonders when Noah will begin reading her stories to Elizabeth, wonders if they will matter.

After breakfast, Anne checks out of the motel and gets back into her Honda. The waitress at the motel café mentioned a small community north of Varnumtown in response to Anne's inquiries. "It ain't much, honey. It's hardly a town, but they got a little restaurant and some nice old homes by the river, and a bar and grill my boyfriend and me go to sometimes on a Saturday night. I think there's a grocery and a drug store, but none of them big name stores. Ya have to go up to Wilmington for that, or Shallotte. Shallotte's got some nice stores."

Anne laughs out loud as she remembers June the waitress, a caricature of a stereotype, wearing more make-up than Anne owns, giving directions. "Ya go up to the red light and turn right on Route 130. Then jus' keep on till ya run into Varmittown. Take a left, cross the railroad tracks, turn right and there y'are. Do ya mind Meskins?"

"No, I'm from Texas. I grew up with Mexican Americans."

"I don't much think these is Americans. They're mostly wet-backs, men without women, makin' money to send home or to bring 'em all here. Course they're everywhere now. I don't know why they're in Pearl, though. There ain't no work there."

Why does everyone assume that a Mexican man is an illegal if he doesn't have a family, or if he's looking for work? And if this is how everyone thinks, do I really want to live here?

Now on the road, having decided to follow June's directions, Anne switches on the radio and listens to the latest stats on military deaths in the East, on children abused by priests, and the rise in the water table resulting from the greenhouse effect. *Enough with the news—I need music.* Singing along with Sarah Brightman, hitting none of the high notes and few of the others, she knows her ears deceive her when she sounds pretty good to herself. *Doesn't matter; it's a new day. Pollyanna lives!*

In what seems like a short time, Anne passes a sign with "Varnumtown, Established 1988" in peeling painted letters. An old country store is on the right, a new housing development on the left, and ahead are forked roads, both with "Dead End" signs. The first fork leads to Dixon landing, a dock where shrimp boats are tied. The next fork leads to Wildcat Landing, another dock with more shrimp boats. She likes the idea of having Wildcat Landing as her address. But the land is low, and the only houses are in disrepair or not for sale. Her childhood was spotted with hurricanes on the Texas coast, and she doesn't want to be within ten feet of sea level. She drives on. *It ain't much, honey; it's hardly a town.* Maybe she missed something. She'll look again on the return trip.

Depressed by her surroundings, Anne reflects on her search along the southeastern coast of North Carolina, a search that revealed a disturbing imbalance, a decided distance between the haves and have-nots. Seasonal residents and tourists stay in multimillion dollar homes on the beaches and in the gated golf communities while the less fortunate of the Carolina natives live in poverty. She knows many of these have been displaced from the land and the waterways once farmed or fished by their parents or grandparents and then sold for far too little. The middle class exists, but like the wealthy, in isolated developments with mostly retired couples, places where Anne would feel even more alone.

Following the Lockwood Folly River, that very name having drawn her to this location on her map, she comes to another sign: "Pearl, Population 210, Founded in 1903". She turns left, into the town. The road is called Broad Street, and for a good reason. Like many older southern towns, there are only two lanes for traffic, but there are angled parking spaces, mostly empty of cars, on each side of the road making it seem at least four lanes wide. A gas station displays a sign out front, reflecting this summer's high cost of gasoline: "Regular, One Arm; Unleaded, One Leg; Premium, First Born". *Encouraging! Someone has a sense of humor.*

On the left is a small grocery store. Opposite it is the Juarez Bar and Grill. Beside the bar is the courthouse, conveniently paired. Anne laughs. Next is the First Methodist Church, opposite the First Baptist Church, and beside it a pharmacy which is also a hardware store. Based on the three cars parked in front, it's the most active place in town. On her right is an old movie theatre that might once have been a legitimate stage, then empty store fronts facing a car and lawnmower repair shop, and finally a bait shop. Broad Street ends at River Road. Across this road is a park. *You're right, June, it ain't much now; but it once was more.*

She turns right and slowly drives by some lovely not-so-very-old homes on the park side that all back up to the river. They are nicely landscaped and appear to be well cared for. On the opposite side are some older could-be-lovely fixer-uppers that she doesn't have the money or desire to overhaul. Besides that, they aren't on the river.

On an impulse, Anne stops at the end of the road, at the last of the river houses, a particularly pretty, much older low-country home. She sees a dock in the back with a red sailboat tied to a piling. She wonders if door-to-door begging for people to sell their homes is illegal. Shrugging that possibility, she goes up the walk and rings the doorbell. The house is surrounded with beautiful flowers and blooming shrubs. No one answers. She knocks.

"Just a gol-darned minute!" The door opens and a wizened face with wild gray curls frowns and then grins. "Well, how do? Can I help you?"

Click. A portrait in the making. "Hello, I'm Anne Gray. I apologize for bothering you, but…"

"You're not botherin' me. And don't stand outside. Come on in. I needed a breather, anyhow. My name is Marjorie Hester." Skinny legs protrude from navy blue Bermuda shorts. Thin but muscled arms in a T-shirt with "No Fear" printed on the front motion for Anne to enter. Anne guesses Marjorie Hester is in her seventies, and those arms and legs have served her well. She looks both fragile and strong. *Probably the bone is fragile, but the attitude is strong.*

The room is bright with window light, and has pretty but well-used furniture. Framed photographs are everywhere. Most of them are snapshots of a blonde girl, her life documented from infant to adult. There's an old photograph of a handsome couple and a portrait of an angular man with soft hazel eyes behind round glasses. Sunlight betrays dust and occasional cobwebs.

"What did I interrupt, Mrs. Hester?" *Certainly not dusting or cleaning.*

"None of your business. If you can't call me by my Christian name, you don't need to know what I'm doin'. Now, have a seat and tell me what brought you to my door."

Taken aback, Anne sits in the closest chair. "Forgive me, Marjorie. I just drove down River Road for the first time, and saw this beautiful house. For some reason, I felt such warmth in the look of your home that I thought perhaps you would be willing to take a few minutes to tell me some things about your town." *Or sell your house.*

"You call this a town? Well, it used to be. My Johnny had a clothing store, and there was a fresh food market, a dry goods store, and several restaurants. The town used to be supported by tobacco and cotton farmers and by the textile mill in the next town. That's all gone now. I guess they can grow or make everythin' cheaper somewhere else. We have bait shops and family owned fishin' businesses that barely meet their payments, and that's about all. Why? Oh, would you like some coffee? I haven't brewed the sun tea yet."

"No thanks. I just finished breakfast. In fact, a waitress at the restaurant in Shallotte recommended I come here."

"What's her name?"

"I believe it was June."

"Naw!" Marjorie laughs. "I'm surprised she sent you here. She got arrested the last time her and her skuzzy boyfriend come to Pearl. She's okay though, daughter of a friend of mine. She just don't know how to pick men. Few women do."

"I can't argue that point. My reason for asking about Pearl is that I recently retired, and I want to relocate in a small coastal town with affordable real estate and not overrun by tourists."

"Well I don't know 'bout real estate, but tourists aren't a big problem here."

Anne smiles. "Good. Do you know of any homes for sale in this neighborhood?"

"No, honey. It's all old folks on this street, and they won't sell till they die."

"Anyone about to die?"

"Hee, hee! You are a breath of fresh air. But you don't look old enough to be retired."

"I'm retiring a little early." Anne hesitates before adding, "I needed to get away and make a fresh start."

"Well, I won't be nosey. I can't help you 'bout houses here, but you could drive in the other direction on River Road. You'll come to a Catholic church on the left. The priest there is nice enough and he knows about that side of town." Without pausing, she adds, "I imagine it was a man problem. Was he abusive, dear?"

"Another church? I guess you could call it abuse." Anne plays along. "And if they ever dredge the lake behind my old house, they'll find what's left of him. I'm surprised a town of two hundred can support three churches."

Marjorie's eyes sharpen as she evaluates Anne, deciding if she's serious or joking. She decides on half-joking and smiles. *Don't think you can fool me, girl.* "Oh, you're talkin' 'bout the sign at the beginnin' of Broad Street. That was put up when the town was founded, in 1903. And that was the population then. There's a few more of us now, but we're scattered around. Some of our old farts are at the bottom of the river, too. I like to swap stories, if you know what I mean."

Anne laughs, rises, and offers her hand. "Thanks for the information and the suggestion. Do you know the priest's name?"

"Oh yes, Father Paul Santino. He's family."

"Really?"

"Well, no, not really, just sorta'. But he's a good sailor. Course I'm better. Let me know what happens. There's no work here to speak of, so we always welcome a retired person with her own income— good for the town."

Anne pauses at the door and smiles at her hostess. "I think I like you, Marjorie Hester. Here's a card with my cell phone number. If a neighbor dies, call me."

Marjorie chuckles and pats her on the back. "You'd keep 'em laughin' at the Red Hat Club."

So she sails, Anne muses as she drives away. *Maybe she's only in her sixties and the wind and sun have aged her face. And there's a Red Hat Club in Pearl?*

Anne passes another bait shop and a Mexican restaurant—closed. Following the river, the road begins a slow curve that reveals a widening of the water on her right that Anne guesses is a bay. On her left, the land slopes upward, unusual in this normally flat coastal terrain.

She sees the Catholic church above her, on a road that runs parallel to River Road. Remembering the news, she wonders if the priest is nice to everybody or just little boys? Driving farther, she finds a left turn that takes her to the white church. Built in the tradition of Mexico with a bell inside a curved stucco arch, it's similar to churches she has seen in the southwest and California, but never in North Carolina. It reminds her a little of the Alamo.

Anne parks and walks to the front. Beside the door, engraved in a metal plate, is "Saint Angelica". She turns. The view of the bay from the church is stunning. She sees a few sailboats and fishing boats, but none of the usual tourist water toys. The flora on the bank below includes live oaks and many low growing shrubs and weeds, some of them flowering. She suspects the fauna includes snakes, mice, and stray dogs. She has already seen several of the latter. What she hasn't seen is people.

Turning back to the church door, she is about to enter when a voice from behind startles her. "Can I help you?"

Anne jumps and turns. A tall man with fishing gear in one hand and a bucket in the other emerges from the side of the church and walks to her. He smiles, very white teeth and very dark eyes, squinting in the morning sun. *Click. Another portrait.* "I'm looking for Father Paul."

"Ah, good for you; you found him. I'm sorry I frightened you." He puts down the bucket, transfers the fishing rod to his left hand, wipes his right hand on his pants, and offers it to Anne.

She looks nervously at his hand and begins to extend her own. "Sorry, I'm not Catholic. Do I shake it or kiss it? And if I have to kiss it, what have you been using for bait?" He laughs and takes her hand. *Definitely not a child molester—this man could have all the grown girls he wants!*

"What took you so long? I've been waiting for someone to liven my day. I was about to clean these fish when I heard your car. Walk with me." He picks up the bucket.

Following, she mutters to herself, "Another alpha male. Well, I'm just here for information." While they walk around the church, she introduces herself and tells him that Marjorie Hester suggested she ask him about available property. He laughs.

"Ah, Marjorie! She is my friend and my nemesis, a dear rascal, but with good intentions and very good instincts. If she sent you to me, she must want you around."

"Nemesis? She said you're family, sort of."

The priest stops, but doesn't look at her. "Did she? Well now, that's interesting." He puts his fishing gear against the wall of the modest stucco house behind the church. Then he takes two folding lawn chairs and sets them under a tree. He gestures to one and she sits, after moving the chair so that its back is against the tree.

Why am I here, and how long will this take? But it's a pretty morning and she finds this fisherman/priest very interesting. She studies him while he gathers a garden hose and his cleaning and scaling equipment, toting them into the shade. His slender lanky frame makes him appear taller than he actually is. Of course, most people seem tall to Anne's own five feet, three inches. His thick black hair is graying and needs a trim; his face is clean-shaven, weathered, and deeply lined. She has no idea how old he is. She has reached a point in life where she automatically catalogues men by their age: too young; just right; older, but not too old; waiting for death. She doesn't catalogue Father Paul. He's a priest. And she's not sure why she even bothers with the others. She has no plan to start another relationship, but old behaviors as well as longings persist.

"Entertain me while I clean these fish," he says, clamping the first fish to the scaling board. "Tell me your story."

"Always a story." She tells him briefly about teaching theatre at a historically black university, retirement, selling her home, writing her stories for Noah and Elizabeth, and her dream to settle in a coastal town that reminds her a little of south Texas and life near the Gulf of Mexico. He has many fish to scale, gut, and fillet, so she goes on to tell him of her dislike for housing developments filled with idle, retired, wealthy golfers. She doesn't tell him of her divorces.

Pausing in his work, he leans back in his chair to give his spine some relief. He looks at his unexpected visitor, reading her strengths, aware of the casual acceptance each has given the other. He suspects she is as comfortable and generous of spirit to most people. "I imagine you are just what idle, retired, wealthy golfers need. You might light a fire under such people."

Embarrassed by the compliment, Anne looks down at her hands. "I'm sure that I'm unfairly stereotyping golf communities. I'm also sure that they have lots to offer. No pun intended. I used to golf with my mother and loved it. I simply can't afford green fees and high homeowners association dues. And there are other sports I prefer. I only golfed because it gave me special time with Mama. If she were still alive, I would still be golfing.

"What I really want is to be in a small town where everyone knows each other and where I can be a part of the daily life of the community. I want to be close enough to walk or ride my bicycle to a shop or restaurant. And I want to find a market for my paintings."

"You mean like an artists' co-op?"

"Possibly, or I suppose there are art galleries up and down the coast where I could take my work."

Paul returns to his scaling and filleting. "Of course there are, but if you don't mind a change of subject, Anne, I'm curious. How did you feel teaching a culture other than your own?"

"What do you mean?"

"Did you feel like an outsider? Did you experience the other side of prejudice?"

"Sometimes. We had a few white students, and I found myself watching out for them because they were the minority—especially in the early years. I didn't think of myself that way, since most of my students and each of the faculty went out of their way to make me feel accepted. When I first took the position, my friends were sure I would be mugged and raped, or raped and murdered—but always in their minds, rape seemed inevitable. I have learned that prejudice and ignorance are best friends. But I imagine that as a Latino, you've experienced some of that yourself." He says nothing. "Of course your English is so perfect, I'm guessing your family has been here for generations."

The priest studies Anne a moment, satisfied with his character probing. She fears that she has assumed and said too much, and she notices even in the shade of the tree he still squints, as if trying to see her more clearly. He rinses his hands with the water from the hose and washes off his scaling knife and board. "I need to refrigerate these fish. I'll only be a minute. Then I want to show you something. By the way, if you aren't Catholic, what are you?"

"I guess I'm not anything, yet. I'm still becoming."

"Becoming what?"

"Spiritually found, sound, complete. I don't know if there's a word for it. But I'll know when I get there."

"I assume you've studied?"

"You mean have I compared religious philosophies? Sure. In fact, I've taught it. But it seems the more I read what man has written about God, the less I know about Him. Belief was so much simpler when I was a child."

He begins to speak, and then changes his mind. It has been a long time since university and seminary. He has missed challenging minds, intellectual conversations, and discussing his own conflicts with certain Catholic doctrines. But that can wait. There will be time. *Besides*, he thinks, *she had me at ignorance and prejudice are best friends.*

While he's gone, the two stray dogs timidly approach Anne. She pets them and they reward her by wagging their tails and licking her face. The priest returns with two cold cans of lemonade. "Do these dogs have homes?" She scratches behind the ears of the older black dog while the buff colored puppy with a white blaze on his face leans against her leg.

"Oh, yes. But they'll make you think they're starving for food and love." He now wears glasses that slide down his nose, and he pushes them back up with a freshly washed finger. They change him from looking like a construction worker to looking like a casually dressed professor. He smiles. His squint is gone, but the lenses magnify his eyes and expose his compassion. "There is something I would like you to see. It's not far."

Again, Anne walks with the priest, and the dogs shadow her. "How long has your culture been a presence here?" The priest picks up a stick and throws it. The dogs chase. A whistle is heard, followed by the distant laughter of children and joyful barking.

"My people have been in Pearl for over sixty years. I came here as a boy to live with my uncle and aunt after my parents' death."

"English isn't your first language? I'm impressed. You sound like an anchorman on the news."

Father Paul smiles and looks down at his feet as he walks. "That's how I practiced my English, imitating news reporters. I suppose I sounded pretty funny when I was thirteen."

"Kids can be cruel. Why did your uncle immigrate?"

"There was a rift in the family. My father was in love with my aunt. His betrayal was killing my mother and dividing the family. My uncle and aunt left in order to restore peace. I know, it sounds like a soap opera. Anyway, he came here and purchased all of this property, using some of it for the church, which he built with his own hands. When my aunt died, my uncle moved back to Mexico. I was in Vietnam at the time. After the war, I went to school at Uncle Sam's expense and then studied for the priesthood. I served in several large inner-city parishes before asking to return here to my home." He pushes his straying glasses. "I also sail and fish as often as time allows."

"Old Mr. Time." She laughs. "He has far too much control." She hadn't expected him to share personal information, but she had hoped. Now that he has opened the door, she can't stop herself from entering. "You don't look old enough to have served in Vietnam."

And why did you become a priest? And how could a man that looks like you give up the opportunity for romance and love and family?

"I was eighteen; it was the end of the war. And I prefer not to talk about it."

After an awkward silence, she changes the subject. "Your uncle must be wealthy to own this much coastal property. Is he still living?"

"No. He died several years ago. He had inherited an income that allowed him to purchase this land, when it cost very little, and a shrimp boat that he worked until arthritis made it too hard to pull up the nets. He was my mother's older brother."

"Who owns the land now?"

"His heirs."

"Does that include you?"

"It does, but I put my inheritance in a charitable non-profit company that will assist the people of Saint Angelica."

"I see. And is there a large presence of Mexican Americans here?"

"Several families came with my uncle in the forties after World War II. Others have come since then, but most of the Latinos here are not from the sizable migration of recent years. There isn't enough work in Pearl to support a large influx of migrants."

"That's odd. A waitress at the restaurant where I ate breakfast suggested that I come to Pearl. But she said the Mexicans here are men without women, and she implied that they're illegals."

The priest shakes his head. "As you said, prejudice walks hand in hand with ignorance. She probably saw the men at the bar. They don't take their wives there. The Latinos here are mostly of the traditional school of behavior, at least the older ones. The girls are starting to revolt against the old ways, so changes are taking place. Although I think most of the young people go to other towns to party and to avoid their elders. I suspect your waitress hasn't been here in a long while."

They pass a well-kept graveyard with a hundred or more headstones. Fascinated with old graves, Anne wants to stop and walk the paths, read the markers, picture the people below and the loved ones left behind. It isn't morbidity but a curiosity about the past and the undefeatable spirit of humankind. But the priest has a destination, and she can't presume on any more of his time or waste any more of her own. They continue another thirty yards with wind-blown oaks on the right and the bay below on the left. Beyond the last clump of trees, the road turns into a bricked driveway. At the end of the driveway is a carport attached to a tan stucco house. *Click. Bold texture and clean lines.*

As they approach the front door, she turns and is captured again by the view of water and sky, harmonious blues, white of seabirds, and wisps of blending clouds. In her blue shirt and white pants, she feels like she also blends in, as if she could flex her knees and push up, lifting into the sky, joining the birds. *What peace! What freedom!*

Below is a wooden staircase that leads down the bank to River Road. Cascading beside the stairs are low-growing wild pink roses. Across the road is a short dock at the water's edge with a bright blue sailboat tied to it. A pelican rests on a piling. Anne's eyes search the grasses and sky for a heron but finding none, brighten when she suddenly realizes this house on the bank, overlooking church, land, and water, has its back to the wall. *It's like a fortress—no surprises from intruders.*

The priest puts his hand on her shoulder. The weight brings her back. She says a small prayer and then turns to him. Instead of knocking, he has unlocked and opened the door.

For a moment she is overwhelmed by the dust and dirt. She controls a desire to flee to the clean outside. But slowly her painter's mind takes over and eliminates the grime, revealing the room's potential. It is large with an impressive fireplace. They walk without speaking through the house. Three doors open to two bedrooms and a bathroom. On the other side, a wide arched doorway reveals a dining room and kitchen. The floors are tiled and the walls stucco and at least ten feet high. The bedroom closets have curtains instead of doors. All the windows are arched. Bits of furniture, are old and

43

in need of attention. There are no cabinets in the kitchen, just two shelves that circle the entire room. But a curtained pantry/laundry room is large enough to replace a multitude of cabinets. Behind the kitchen is a roofed porch, the full width of the house. Beyond the porch is a walled-in courtyard with untended gardens. At the end of the courtyard is a shrine, the one thing that has been kept clear of moss and decay, clear of weeds and vines.

Almost afraid of the answer, she asks, "Who lives here?"

The priest looks timidly at her, pushing his glasses up once again. He clears his throat. "No one at present. You, if you wish."

Anne whispers another shorter prayer. "Thank you."

That evening, sitting in her motel room, Anne is reluctant to call her daughters until her decision is made without their influence. *This has to be my decision,* she thinks, but she knows it always helps to write her thoughts. So she does.

EMAIL TO NOAH:

Leaving the house for the last time was hard. I walked through each room and said goodbye as unexpected memories rose up and washed over me, mostly images of the girls growing up. Not sad— just the realization of the end of an era.

Thank you for wanting my stories. Writing them brought an understanding of the past I never expected to find. But I've had my fill of looking backwards—only forward movements and thoughts from now on.

I spent a couple of days with Greer and her family in Hickory. The boys wore me out, and we all cried when I left. I drove south, through Charlotte, and then over to the coast to begin house hunting. Once again, as in my gypsy childhood, everything I own fits into my car, and it has been a sweet freedom.

After a three day search, all the things I imagined I wanted in a house left me today. I found something lesser and better. And I already have two friends, an irascible old woman who sails her own boat and a Vietnam vet turned Catholic priest who competes with her in sailing and loses, probably on purpose. The priest made the house available to me. Like your purchase of my house, though, the offer comes with strings. A new phase of my life has begun and I don't think it is called retirement.

However, before we sign papers, I need to go to confession and tell him about my divorces. I feel like the house is a trust, almost a gift, and I don't want him to feel betrayed by my sin of omission. I don't think he needs to know everything, just the basics. After all, he is one of my two new friends, and I don't want to shock or offend him. Would a man of the Jewish faith know whether a back-sliding Methodist woman with Buddhist leanings may go to Catholic confession? Please advise.—*Always, Anne*

Chapter 3

A Silver Basket & An Iron Armadillo

NOAH LEVINSON LIVES the belief that a man's reach must be higher than his grasp. He demands perfection of himself and expects it of his employees. His perseverance, intuition, and ambitions have brought him success in publishing and disaster in his marriage. The death of their son might have brought them together for comfort. Instead, it drove them apart. Unable to decrease their own level of pain through sharing, they each isolated, closed ranks, and built a wall of defense. He lost himself in work; she simply lost herself.

With nothing to unpack except their clothes, Noah and Elizabeth have inhabited the new old home filled with borrowed things. Their emotional baggage, overstuffed with memories of their son, waits by the front door.

Elizabeth had resisted the move, but her husband's determination finally won, and she reluctantly conceded. When she first looked through the windows at the island, dock, and water, he saw a light in her eyes brighten and then dim. Now she waits for the medical procedures to fill the empty spaces abandoned by hope and kindness.

Today, Noah watches with troubled eyes as the great blue heron makes its ritual visit, floating down, landing with the awkward grace of legs too long. Wings fold behind the crane's back as if holding a surprise. He searches for his familiar audience, finding instead the man figure behind the glass door.

The two males lock eyes, the bird curious and wary, the man admiring and perhaps envious. Yes, definitely envious. He physically aches for the freedom of independence and flight, envies the heron's years of sharing this peaceful space with the mystical Anne. He hasn't opened her email about the priest and a house purchased with strings and commitment. He supposes she is still searching the Carolina coast for a new home, new waters, a new place to spread her own wings and land.

The bird waits, patient. He waits for the woman, the one who imitates his sounds, the one who enters his great space and small memory. She does not appear. A movement behind the glass startles him away.

Noah's wife shifts and clears her throat, impatient. He turns from the door, a human caricature of the bird, the leather-bound secret held behind his back. The red journal—his unorthodox gift, is soft and warm in his hands. He is delaying the dearly purchased moment, not for the element of surprise, but from fear of rejection.

"Are you comfortable, Elizabeth?" *Am I hiding the stories,* he wonders, *protecting them from your laser tongue? Or am I hiding Anne from your laser vision?* "Do you need more pillows?" he fumbles, unable to separate his thoughts from her perceptions.

"I'm supposed to be saving my strength for the first chemo bout, and this is wearing me out," she warns, leaning back in the well-cushioned willow chaise. "But if you delay any longer, I'm going to think there's more to this than hearing the work of a new writer-in-the-raw. The whole idea is beginning to seem too contrived." Fearing the truth, she pretends disinterest, "So, what's going on? Are you having an affair with this southern belle? Are the two of you plotting against me?"

47

I am contriving and plotting my butt off, he thinks, but he sighs and speaks the agreed upon lie. "She tells a good story. I thought it might amuse you and you might choose to guide a new talent—something to do while we're here."

"Is it fiction? You know how that bores me."

"No. It's memoir. She tells stories from her own experience, but each one is related to an object in the house." No response. Nervous, and fearing Elizabeth might recognize Anne through her comments in the introductory information, he decides to jump ahead. "All right, I'll skip the prologue and go straight to the first story." He clears his throat, trying not to seem too eager or to betray the significance of this effort to capture her imagination, and then—more importantly—her will.

As usual, Josh is near, this time sitting on the floor beside her chaise, his curly dark hair pillowed on her leg. But Josh will not listen. His presence is merely to remind his father of past and future loss. Noah reads.

QUEEN BESS

At last, the Queen Bess has a proper mistress. When my parents first moved to Wales, they rented a large old house on a street where every home had a plaque on it with a name. My mother, who always lapped-up the culture of each town, state, or country they lived in, decided to name their house Queen Bess, and she promptly hired a local sign-maker to carve the name on a piece of wood and hang it by the front door.

I assume she chose the name from the old film, *Young Bess,* a movie she had cherished as a young woman. It was about the early life of Queen Elizabeth I. As soon as neighbors saw the plaque, they went to my mother in alarm and told her that one cannot use the name of royalty without royalty's permission. Her independent American attitude would not allow her to go permission seeking, so she sent it to me—to the Great North State where it now hangs beside your door and truly represents the lady within, at least in name. That's not your first story. It's just a first connection, and it leads to the origin of the first object.

Somehow, Queen Bess fits my mental image of you. I picture you in the willow chaise with Noah at your side, playing the jester—no, never the jester, rather a suitor, entertaining you by reading my foolish stories in an attempt to win your favor. Is he trying to win it, I wonder, or am I? I'm not sure. Nevertheless, the first object, the silver basket, came from a land once governed by Young Queen Bess, but is the remnant of a marriage not half as noble as your own. I know. We never think of our own lives or relationships as perfect, but since I have obligated myself to honesty about my stories, and may never meet you and know yours, I choose to idealize you and your marriage in my own mind—a sort of bubble that can't burst. It is interesting that I am trading you truth in exchange for fantasy.

Elizabeth frowns. Noah asks, "Do you want me to read on?"

"I don't know. It's hard not to function as an editor. 'The bubble that can't burst?' Is that our marriage or her mind? Or is she saying that our ideal marriage is a fantasy?" She stops. *Did I just speak our truth, or did she put the words in my mouth?*

"Maybe she is saying that no marriage is ideal."

"Maybe you *are* plotting against me. Or my meds are making me paranoid. Is that part of the plot?" She runs her fingers through her heavy dark hair, lifting it in a pile on her head to cool her neck, making her look impossibly young and vulnerable. She closes her large hazel eyes and laces her fingers together across her chest, a woven fence between her heart and this intruder.

He closes the journal. "I can throw this all away." But he thinks, *No, I can't!*

No, you can't! She broods. *Stop being a bitch; you promised to give it a chance.* Her lips curve upward in a slight smile. *But you can make him work for it.* "Tell me again how this came about. Tell me about her."

"Where do you want me to start?"

"How old is she?"

"I really don't know." *A woman's question—good!* "She's a grand-mother."

"Ha! We're in the South. She could be a grandmother at 25; her daughter could be her sister, and her grandchild could then also be her niece or nephew."

Noah clears his throat, and drags out a crooked half-smile. "She has an advanced degree and just retired as a university professor, so I don't think she was prepubescently pregnant by her father. I would guess she's in her late forties or early fifties." *Or she's ageless.*

"Does she look my age?"

"You're not even forty and don't look your age; so how can I compare you? By the way, Queen Bess, mistress of all you survey, why do I hear jealousy in your voice?"

"I guess I'm looking for ammunition." *I don't know if I want her honesty.* "It's one thing to hear her personal stories. It's another for her to get personal with us." *What if her truths make our own lies stand out in relief, naked? I don't want to face an exposed three-dimensional reality of us.*

"But it sounds like you are preparing yourself to listen."

"All right, my 'noble suitor, never a jester', read on. But first," she replies, still caught between sarcasm and interest, "let the queen examine the royal object."

He places a delicately filigreed silver basket in her hands. "It looks antique." She turns it upside down and reads the trademark. "It's English. How would it have originally been used, to receive calling cards, perhaps? And how did Ms. Writer-in-the-Raw use it?" Only Noah bears witness as Josh smiles up at his mother, his eight-year-old face bright with encouragement.

While Elizabeth rearranges pillows for greater comfort, Noah looks through the window at the small island, remembering his first view of it, remembering the taste of those damn cookies.

Cursing himself for skipping ahead, Noah decides that Anne's choice to speak personally to Liz, to lead her comfortably into the stories was good—much better than giving Liz's imagination free rein to distort reality and close doors. He runs his fingers through his hair and says with measured care, "I think I'll back up and read her prologue. That might answer some of your questions about Anne."

Elizabeth pulls her legs up and circles them with her arms, eyes open but still resisting Noah's will. *Why didn't you do that in the first place—don't want me to know her?* She waits, silver basket on the table beside her.

Noah takes a deep breath and begins again.

PROLOGUE TO MY STORIES

Elizabeth, you have such a pretty name, and although your family and friends may have shortened it to Liz, Beth, or Bess, the schoolteacher in me wants to say your whole name. I have followed your sweet husband's request to tell the stories of various items in your new home. I will use a stream of consciousness writing style, resisting the temptation to edit. Anyway, computers make personal editing too easy. I have learned that in writing, you may reveal truths hidden even from yourself, and then slice them out for the sake of propriety, pride, or grammar. So, Ms. Editor, like it or not, the following is uncensored and uncorrected, except maybe for spellcheck (the teacher in me again).

Noah said you want real stories, not fiction. The stories are real, but what is true to me may be false to someone else. And if they will be true, they must also be honest which means they won't always be pretty.

First, let me introduce myself. I am a southern woman, originally from Texas, and call all children and some adults 'honey' or 'sweetheart'. I have just retired from the faculty of a historically black university, so a little African-American southern slang may also find its way into my conversation. My swearing is regular, but limited to damn, bitch, and hell, which I use separately or all together, depending on the depth of my aggravation. I have an overactive tendency to empathize, which brings me excessive joy as well as pain, and I have an over-developed extra sense about a few things—mostly about babies and romance, occasionally about death. I seem to know when a woman is pregnant, sometimes before she does; I often know when someone is having an affair, obviously not before he or she does. I'm not a psychic or a student of the paranormal. I honestly think I'm just in tune with natural instincts, kind of like a dog. Unfortunately, my instincts don't help me avoid disaster in my own relationships.

My father was a pipe-fitter for various construction companies that built oil and chemical refineries. So we travelled, following jobs around the country, but living mostly in Texas and in towns along the Gulf of Mexico. We moved our few belongings in our car and rented furnished places—thirty-eight houses, in twenty-seven towns, in twelve states, and three Canadian provinces. But who's counting?

I moved to North Carolina as an adult and have been here ever since. After my marriage, I lived in only two houses, and have accumulated many things. They have perhaps become too important to me. So my hope is this exercise will also be an exorcism. As I tell each story, I hope to free myself of the physical and find greater comfort and perhaps understanding through the relinquishing of memory.

Noah pauses and looks up. "Does that tell you enough about Anne Gray?"

"She is less gray. Read on, my *sweet* husband."

THE SILVER BASKET

I was a twenty-three-year-old virgin when I met my first husband. A walking, talking Pollyanna doll, I believed I had found the perfect man and would be the perfect wife in a perfect marriage. Don't laugh!

My parents raised me to believe I could do anything I set my mind to do. It took years of denial, shame, and frustration to finally face the fact that there are some things that even a Type A personality like myself cannot accomplish or change.

A mutual friend arranged the first date with Robert. When I opened the door, he introduced himself and without missing a beat said, "I hear you're a nigger lover." Whenever I hear the N word, my skin creeps on my bones. I should have ended our date, but in spite of his crudeness, I was polite, and granted him the first of a thousand second chances.

I quickly learned that Robert always said the unexpected for shock value—possibly to get attention or, as I eventually learned, because of his own insecurity. He had just completed his doctorate and contracted to teach at the University of North Carolina at Chapel Hill. I had just completed my Master's degree in Theatre and begun my own teaching career at North Carolina Central University, a historically black campus. He was also working with Head Start, screening underprivileged children, mostly black, for hearing impairments. He was not a racist.

Rather than seeing him objectively, I viewed Robert as refreshingly witty and wicked. He took pleasure in appalling the southern religious sensibilities of my friends while I blushed and twittered, thinking his innuendoes revealed a real man's man. His conversation usually included the human anatomy and/or a memorable sexual experience, and ultimately led to my anatomy in bed with him, experiencing sex. I was tired of being a virgin. I had waited so long that I was overwhelmed by the feel, sight, smell, taste, and sound of naked bodies touching. I believed this physical exchange somehow became an emotional and spiritual connection. Choice disappeared. I belonged to him. I was in love. Still don't laugh!

When I began facing reality, I realized his raw social behavior was embarrassing, and the sex wasn't all I hoped it would be. But the Pollyanna in me, still alive and well, knew everything would improve with a wedding band and legality. Now you can laugh!

A few months after our wedding, we visited my parents across the Atlantic, in Wales. Daddy had risen from being a pipe-fitter to plant supervisor, and now travelled internationally instead of just in North America.

It was the Christmas season, and a Welsh couple who worked for my dad gave a party honoring us, the new bride and groom. Like my dad, I was modest and shy while Robert, like my gregarious mother, loved center stage.

A particularly pretty and voluptuous woman at the party was drinking too much and flirting too heavily with my all-too-eager new groom. I walked to the room where music was being played and stood in the doorway watching said groom and slut dancing as obscenely as the other onlookers could encourage them to do. Another woman joined them, creating a shuffling ménage a trois. At that horrific moment, my mother came up behind me and shoved me into the middle of the room.

As luck would have it, I tripped over someone's foot and fell into the dancing orgy. As we hit the floor, we brought a few bystanders into the melee. Blinded by soft tissue, that felt alarmingly like someone's boob, I squirmed out of the human pile which seemed to be growing.

Still on all fours, my face red with shame, I crawled out of party hell and into the hall where my progress was blocked by a pair of sensible shoes. Above the shoes was a pair of thick calves, and above them, the smiling face of our hostess. She laughed. "You Yanks play the silliest games." She pulled me to my feet and took my arm, walking me to the kitchen and chattering about the Christmas holidays and her children. I sat on a stool and cooled my hot face with a drink she handed me. Then she placed a wrapped package on my lap. "We love your father and wanted to find something very special for his daughter. So we looked in every antique store, in all the surrounding towns, until we found this. And now that I've met you, I know it is perfect."

Considering how she had found me—crawling on the floor, I opened the gift expecting to see old knee pads. Instead, I found the beautiful silver basket I hope you are holding as you read this. I am not knowledgeable about antiques, and know nothing of this one's personal history, but it has been a treasure to me. It has held the thoughtful expressions of all my family and friends in the form of greeting cards from holidays and birthdays. Every New Year's Day, I look once more through its contents and then throw them away and begin again.

I suppose that's what I did that Christmas Eve, all those years ago, when I got the courage to put aside my embarrassment, walk back in to that God-forsaken room, and ask my already forgiven husband to dance. It was the first of many setting aside and starting-over incidents for us. Two children and several years later, I learned the overt sexual talk and behavior was just a disguise Robert wore to hide the real *man's* man.

"So what do you think?" Noah closes Anne's journal, barely breathing.

Elizabeth smiles at the silver basket and then raises it to her husband's waiting hands.

"I think it's a pretty basket."

"I mean the story."

"If you're asking what I think of her as a writer, I would have to say there's something familiar about her writing. She seems very comfortable with verbal expression. It's like talking to a confidant who is willing to expose herself and laugh at her own mistakes. She is introspective, maybe searching for her truths as she writes. Can she make a book of her personal stories? Can she write anything beyond memoir? I don't know, yet. I'm not sure I care. But I am curious. Did she say *first* husband?"

"Yes. That surprised me, too. Maybe she expects to have a second husband—someday. What do you think about Robert?"

"A guess—he's a sensitive man hiding under a cloak of bravado?"

"I don't think you were listening."

"You must be right. You always are."

He looks at her for a long moment. He tests. "How would you describe me if we were divorced?"

"I wouldn't." Hurt at his bringing up the subject, she pauses and then adds, "However, I'd appreciate the lack of irritation in my life, and if you were gay—as you're implying Robert is—at least I wouldn't have to feel jealous about the women you'd schtoop after I'm gone. Does that answer your question?"

"We have an appointment."

"Wrong." Elizabeth rises and walks away. "I have an appointment. You used emotional blackmail to get me here. I've agreed to try it, but don't even start to think it's a 'we' thing." She resumes her retreat into the bedroom, away from him, rejecting his need to share what he cannot. "But when it's time for me to die, we'll do *that* together and maybe we'll each be only half-dead." She closes the lace-curtained door.

The following evening, lacking an appetite, Elizabeth pushes her plate away and droops in her chair. She has already lost five pounds she couldn't spare, and the chemo treatments haven't even begun. Noah folds his napkin and places it beside the plate of Italian take-out.

"I'll clean up the dishes. Why don't you go into the great room and relax. Maybe we could watch the news on television and then play some cards or dominoes or something."

"Will you stop, Noah? I am sick of the doting husband routine. It doesn't suit you. I am not an invalid. I can do the dishes, and you can get on your computer. You haven't worked all day, and I'm sure it's killing you. Or do you think I can't do the dishes properly? Now that you've taken on domestic skills, I imagine you think you can do them better than anyone else on the planet. That would be more in line with your M.O."

"Actually, I hate doing dishes," Noah admits, "although I have developed a good routine for the task." Elizabeth groans. "I have come to appreciate all the things you used to do around the house in addition to your full-time job. Most of them aren't fun or satisfying."

"So why don't you hire a maid?"

"I'm thinking about it. And I do have to spend some time on the computer. Jack is a good man, but he can't run the company by himself."

"He did when Josh was dying."

"Liz, please." *Stop now!*

"Do you talk about him to other people?" she whispers, leaning on the sink. "Or is it just me you can't talk to about our son?" *And now I'll watch you retreat!*

"I'm going to take a drive." Noah rises from his chair and reaches in his pocket for his car keys. "Do you want to come?" *Say no!*

"No."

Almost out the door, he stops, unable to go any further. He returns to the dining room where Elizabeth is slowly gathering the few dishes from the table.

He offers. "Why don't we do them together?"

"Not a chance," she replies. "You'll try to teach me to do them your way, and I'll have to break a plate on your head. Go on and talk to Jack on your computer, or phone, or whatever you need to do." Regretting the bitchiness that has become automatic, she relents. "Afterwards, I think we could try another story."

"You don't have to sit on the chaise, Liz. You can sit in the rocker or on the couch."

"No thanks. Queen Bess reclines on the chaise." Josh emerges from the shadows and takes his place beside her.

Noah hands the object of the story to his wife. It's a linear sculpture of an armadillo. Elizabeth has noticed several representations of armadillos in the house. This one is a metal rod that was heated and bent to form an outline of the unusual creature. A hooked rod hangs on the bottom. She lifts the rod and strikes the form. A pleasing bell-like sound rings clear. She smiles and strikes it again, several times. Noah sits on an ottoman beside the chaise, wishing she would stop.

"Ah ha!" she says. "A dinner bell. Or perhaps it's a bell to call my faithful subject to attend to my every whim. By the way, why are you so faithful, Noah? I have been quarrelsome and resistant to your every demand. And it can't be the sex."

Shaking his head and smiling, he asks, "While we're on the subject, why is that? You act so jealous of other women and yet you clearly don't want me for yourself."

Her sarcasm spent, she runs her hands over the shape of the armadillo, buying a moment while she tries to find a response for an unanswerable question. "I wish I knew. Sometimes I think that whenever either of us reaches out, the other is unavailable."

"And sometimes I think you are trying to make our relationship as frustrating and undesirable as possible. Do you want me to leave?"

Fear and then sadness grip her. "I'm the one who'll leave, whether I want to or not. Maybe I'm just trying to make it easier so you won't miss me."

A break in his already tense features suggests the pain of her words. He retorts in defense. "What's to miss? The Elizabeth I knew has been gone for a long time."

"Since when, Noah?" Silence. She answers for him. "Since Joshua died. Right? You focused on your work; I focused on mine at the hospice center, trying to find Josh in other dying children. And every night, while I tried to self-medicate against the day's pain, you buried yourself in more work and buried me with your criticism. When I tried to reach out, you were unavailable."

"You wanted to relive Joshua dying with each of those children, and I couldn't share that with you. I couldn't watch any more dying. And I couldn't talk to you about him. I had all the pain I could absorb; another drop and I would have crystallized."

"Ah, like Lot's wife, if you had looked back, Shazam! A pillar of salt. Poor Noah. And now you have me to watch. I'll give you the most honest answer to your question I can. Consciously, I simply don't seem to feel desire for sex, food, or pleasure of any kind. Maybe I should simply say—I don't *feel*. Subconsciously, maybe I'm refusing to feel because if I open myself to being vulnerable again, I would have to experience the sadness as well as the joy. Sometimes I wish I believed in an afterlife. Then I would believe that Josh is waiting for me. That would give me something to look forward to."

"He isn't waiting for you. He's with you. You just don't see him."

"I don't share your faith."

"It isn't faith, Liz."

"Read the story, Noah."

An Iron Armadillo

Armadillos are one of the critters associated with Texas, my home state. I'm not sure why, because I believe they come to Texas from Mexico, on a migration that takes them across the southern Gulf states to Florida. But if that's true, what happens when they get there? Do they just walk into the ocean? I can relate to their being defenseless, in spite of their armor. But I choose to control my direction and destiny.

Anyway, you've probably noticed, there are several armadillos in the house. Each has a story.

The dillo dinner-bell was a gift from Robert. He brought it here for Christmas last year. We've been divorced for sixteen years now, and have finally found a way to mend our breach with a delicate friendship.

People never seem to understand why I didn't recognize earlier that Robert was gay. Ignorance was the main reason it took me so long to even consider the possibility. Then denial took over—denial that our whole life together was a lie. And I probably kept myself ignorant in order to nurture the denial. Deep down inside, where instinct and intuition live, I knew the truth almost from the beginning. But I thought I belonged to him, and I believed I could somehow make it work. If he had come to me with honesty, I would have reached down to that internal knowledge and turned it into understanding.

In the early years of our marriage, I tried to get his attention by reinventing myself. I read *The Happy Hooker, The Joy of Sex,* and other books with suggestions, positions, rituals, or anything else that might initiate passion between us. Sometimes my efforts worked. This was not easy for me because I had grown up modest and inhibited. However, my determination to explore and step outside my traditional attitudes and behavior in order to save our marriage, turned out to be our undoing. The more sexual I became, the more aware of my frustrations I became, the more aware of the interest of other men I became.

I think unhappily married or divorced women must emit a spore that is detectable by all men. I lost faith first in my marriage, and ultimately, in the whole institution, as husband after husband pulled me to the side and suggested a discreet relationship.

Since I shared our beginning, I'll also share the end. While planning Robert's thirty-fifth birthday party, I received a phone call from California. It was a friend of his who wanted to join us for the celebration and bring his wife and son. Of course I invited them with enthusiasm. Robert had mentioned meeting him at a conference and how much he liked the whole family. We picked them up at the airport and the moment his friend looked into my eyes, I knew he was Robert's lover. My legs could barely support the weight of my heart as we walked to the car, and they shared small talk. I was simply trying to continue breathing. After the party, while Robert napped on a couch, his friend sat me down and told me about his relationship with my husband. He was living in an 'open marriage'. His wife knew everything, and they both thought I knew as well. I drank while they talked. All doubt benefits erased, I crawled into my younger daughter's bed, by then too depressed and too drunk to talk with Robert about the present, much less the future. He found me and carried me from Summer's bed to our own. I pounded on his chest, begging him to leave me alone. As he fed me more lies, I continued to push him away. The next morning, I asked him for a divorce.

After the separation, my daughters and I became a strong unit, and we learned together about financial realities. North Carolina's no-fault divorce law calls for equal distribution of assets. I didn't think that would be a problem and agreed to equal distribution of debts as well. The debts surprised me. I used my half of the assets to buy the equity in the house you have now. It was the smallest, meanest house on the block. Even the movers were appalled and didn't want to unload our things and leave us there. But we tightened our belts and learned to live with non-necessities while I slowly paid off the debts. And after a time, the house began to grow and smile.

I'm not a homophobe. After a lifetime in the arts, I have as many gay friends as straight. It wasn't his sexual preferences that destroyed my feelings (although it didn't help). The real betrayal was the lies and pretenses. In fact, I still can't delve into all the anger and negative feelings that followed me for years.

One day, when my seven-year-old daughter was window-shopping with her dad, shortly after our divorce, she turned her head to the side, gazing at something unusual in the display and said, "How queer!" After a moment, she looked at her gay father and said with great seriousness, "No offense, Daddy."

Good-humored Robert dropped to his knees, fighting the urge to smile. He hugged her and replied, "None taken, sweetie."

He later told me the story, and we shared a rare moment of laughter. But after he left, I suggested to Summer that she not use the term which had strangely become a popular word for grammar school kids that year, probably because it got a rise from adults. I offered the word 'odd' as a substitute.

"Does that mean Daddy's odd?" she asked, hoping the answer would be, "No". She was always part of a group and deeply committed to fitting-in. And although Robert and I had told her together that he was gay and that queer was an unkind term to use, she had no understanding of the contemporary meaning of those words.

So I said what she needed to hear. "No honey, he isn't odd." It seemed too complicated to explain the dynamics of language, much less human sexuality to a child. So I took the coward's way out and changed the subject, using the words 'odd' and 'different' about things, not people, until I heard my little parrot mimicking me.

The evolution from then to now has not been easy. Throughout her high school and college years, Summer hid her father's sexual identity from friends and associates. When she finally decided to tell Tamara, her college roommate and friend since the third grade, she had a few drinks first—and still couldn't tell her. So her older sister Greer, who had accepted her father's lifestyle without question, told Tamara who said, "Oh, well that makes sense."

Summer eventually found the courage to tell her boyfriend, who is now her husband, and whose response was, "Huh!! Well that's cool." With Joe's and Tamara's acceptance, she gradually released the fear of people knowing that her father wasn't just like all other fathers. She was able to love him for who he was and not regret what he wasn't.

Sorry for the long aside about Summer's relationship with Robert, but I warned you I wouldn't edit. For years, I could not remember anything good that had passed between Robert and me. I tried. But all I could bring to mind were the hurts, the lies, and the cruelties. I wonder if that's true of all divorced couples. A few years ago, I was walking on the track at the gym with Summer, and remembered something good—the story of her conception.

Robert and I had wanted a second child, and one morning we came together with that express purpose in mind. There was a window beside our bed. After we made love, I began to fall asleep, but I felt Robert roll me over so the sunshine coming through the window was on me. It was as if he were willing the sun to nurture the seed he had just given me. I had learned to appreciate small kindnesses against a field of larger hurts. It was the first good memory in the negative replay of our marriage. The day I shared that story with Summer was the beginning of forgiveness.

Forgiveness is a concept we sometimes speak of lightly, as if it were a simple act. I think I had to forgive myself before I could forgive him. I had to forgive my ignorance, my unwillingness to face reality, my very bad choices in men, my use of alcohol as an escape, and my anger towards myself for all of the above. In time, I began to understand my behavior and the sequence of events propelled sometimes by innocent mistakes. Someone once said to me that wisdom is the result of unwise choices. I don't regret the choices

I've made, however unwise. I've learned from them.

Two years ago Robert asked if he could share Christmas with us. His parents had both died, and although he has a life-partner, he feels the need to be with his children, especially on holidays. Last year, we had our second Christmas together. Each visit gets easier. I remember more of the good times we shared in our marriage, but I also still remember the bad. I guess the children and grandchildren are our bridge, well above the unforgotten where forgiveness is a continuing process.

After our divorce, I considered moving back to Texas where my dad and stepmother were retired. But I didn't want to take the children away from Robert. Coincidentally, a few years later, he moved to Texas where he still lives. Each of his gifts to me is a reminder of my home state, and it's usually an armadillo.

"You know" Elizabeth muses, "I've never thought of armadillos as cute before. But I love this one. I also like the way she described them as being armored but defenseless. I wonder if that's how she sees herself."

"She did bring up some interesting thoughts," Noah agrees. "What is forgiveness, anyway? Is it forgetting a trespass, setting it aside as if it never happened?"

"No."

"Or is it understanding the cause of a trespass, and thereby removing or reducing or even sharing the blame?"

Elizabeth thinks before she responds. "Maybe, sometimes. Or maybe it is both—an acknowledgment of a trespass with a conscious decision to remove it from a relationship's indebtedness. Perhaps it is also recognition of the role each of us plays in creating an emotional debt."

"We are waxing philosophical."

"No, Noah, I think we are just exercising our editing muscle, trying to develop her thought for her. We should leave it alone. She may develop it herself in a later story."

"I don't think we were editing. I think we were talking about ourselves."

"And I think Anne Gray is a witch."

"Why would you say that?" Noah laughs as he rehangs the dillo dinner-bell.

"Although these are supposed to be stories about *her* life, so far each one seems to speak to us about *our* life and *our* issues—like she has a supernatural knowledge of us. Maybe the objects are her familiars and pass on information to her," she adds, conspiratorially.

"Except, my darling, the stories were written before we moved here. And after all, sex, forgiveness, and marital struggles are universal topics. Probably anyone could relate to them."

"Of course, but I prefer to think she's a witch."

After Elizabeth goes to bed, Noah tries the willow chaise. *This is weird. It doesn't fit my body, and I feel unwelcome.* He moves to the couch and opens his computer to find the messages from Anne. Warmed by her desire to share confidences and experiences, he responds.

EMAIL TO ANNE:

Liz thinks you're a witch. She won't admit it, but she likes your stories. Even asks for them. And they do seem to hit every nerve in our dysfunctional relationship. Did I tell you too much? Or are you in fact a witch? I don't know if I can dance without you to guide me, but if the opportunity arises, I'll try. Your heron tolerates us; but he never stays long. I think he's looking for you.

By the way, where are you? I don't like the sound of the priest selling property with strings attached. I didn't think priests were supposed to own property. Just tell him you're divorced. He has no right to more of your personal information. I sound jealous.

We've met the neighbors on both sides. Barbara is lovely and kind. In my opinion, Ben is a Neanderthal. He doesn't like being around sick people, so he leaves offerings of garden vegetables at the door. Weird.

And speaking of guys being weird, I don't even *like* many men, so I can't relate to your ex-husband being gay. On the other hand, I *love* women, so I can easily understand women loving other women. Does that work both ways? Obviously, your stories have made me feel too comfortable with you. And also obviously, I've run out of conversation.—*Noah*

To Noah's surprise, Anne's response arrives while he's constructing an email to his office.

EMAIL TO NOAH:

You're right about your neighbor, Ben. He is a Neanderthal. But he avoids Elizabeth for a reason. His wife died from cancer twenty years ago.

I don't think I'm a witch. When I was nine or ten, another child pointed at my hands in shock and said, "OOOh, she has witch's hands." I kept them out of sight as much as possible for years. Now I like my witch's hands. They serve me well. Read into that what you will.

About same-sex relationships—don't know exactly how to answer your question. I'm an old-fashioned girl thrust into a new morality. I have never felt sexually drawn to another woman, but I do like women. When I was a child, I was a tomboy and thought other girls were useless wimps. I have learned to respect women and myself as one of them. If I found myself attracted to another woman tomorrow, would I respond? I don't know, but probably not. Old attitudes are hard to break.

So, back to your question, does loving men make me okay with men loving each other? I would like to think at this time in my life, I'm okay with anyone loving each other. Barring children used by adults—a lot of that in the news lately. I know men are reputed to like seeing two women together. Rest assured, I don't want to watch two men together. And by the way, I'm in Pearl. You probably can't find it on a map, but you can Google it. I believe Father Paul wears a white hat—in addition to a white collar. Good night.—*Always, Anne*

Chapter 4

Confession

EVENING, AN IMPLIED TIME of evenness, a time for retrospect, and if one is very lucky, tranquility. Following a day of unexpected people and events, Anne soaks in the bathtub at the motel and recalls each person and each moment: June the waitress, Marjorie Hester, Father Paul, the conversations, and the verbal agreement to purchase the priest's house. Not the house she was looking for, it's more—not more in size, but more in character. Her scene designer's eye immediately saw a palette of earth tones in the kitchen, using a Venetian faux painting technique, transparent colors overlaying each other, undulating with texture and glaze. The palette could drop one color and take on another in each additional room, giving them continuity and harmony as well as individuality. She envisioned traditional Mexican accents of wrought iron, deeply stained wood and woven rugs over tile floors. But all of that was window-dressing. The more important impressions were those elicited by Father Paul's stories.

They had sat on the porch of his uncle's home in the still cool morning, while Father Paul told Anne the history of the house and the adjoining land which had been entrusted to him. For years, the family home had been rented. The rent paid the taxes and insurance and minimal upkeep. The land that included the church, the small house behind it, and the graveyard had been willed to the Catholic diocese. Part of the remaining land was a trailer park with rent based on the cost of maintaining the property. His Latino parishioners could not afford to live elsewhere. Developers had wanted to buy the full parcel, but he had refused to sell because he feared the destruction of the trailer park and the flight of his own people.

"Then hurricane Floyd created enough damage to provide government assistance," he had explained. "There was relief money to repair and renovate my uncle's house, the church, and the house behind the church where I live. Very little has been done cosmetically, but the houses and the church are sound, and the damaged trailers repaired or replaced.

"The last renters left the outside of my uncle's house to weeds and the inside to dirt and insects. I've maintained the shrine in his garden, but I don't have time to fulfill my duties as a priest and be a janitorial landlord . . . and fish," He laughed softly like one who knows and accepts himself.

"I've known that I need to sell the house. But I've been stalling, in search of a plan that will make maximum use of the land, or the profits from selling the land, in a way that would benefit the community. A local lawyer and I have been developing an idea for a limited liability company that would invest its income in the town with the ultimate goal of bringing jobs to Pearl. I knew the sale of the land beside the church would have to be the initial investment, but I hadn't decided what to do with my uncle's home until today."

"I am overwhelmed, Father Paul," she responded. "Your price is very low, very generous."

"This isn't a tourist town, Anne. Land prices here, even on the water, are not yet inflated. We need people like you to help restore the town to what it once was and should have become. The county maintains the road, but you would be responsible for the maintenance of the staircase down to it and the boat dock across from it. They both need work. The house only needs cleaning and painting unless you plan on some major renovations. The roof doesn't leak yet, but it hasn't been replaced in many years, so you should include that in your budget."

"Is there a problem with erosion?" She looked down at the grooved bank where plant roots had not been sufficient to hold back mudslides from heavy rains and wind. New growth clung tentatively in those deep crevices.

"Floyd beat it up pretty badly, but it has held its own since then. Another hurricane could cause more erosion. Your house wouldn't be affected, but the church might be."

"I think terracing, supported by stone retainer walls, could solve the problem."

"Stone walls sound like a beautiful, but expensive, solution."

"Well . . ." She paused, wishing she could stop herself but unable to resist. "I've done some stone wall building. Don't ask. It was personal therapy."

"Physical?"

"No, psycho."

Father Paul smiled. "We're talking about a lot of stone wall here. How much therapy do you need?"

"The therapy would have to be shared. Any lunatics in town, other than Marjorie Hester? I couldn't do it alone, but I could supervise workers willing to learn a trade at minimum wage. Afterwards, they could set their own prices and make a salary as stonemasons for the wealthy folks in Shallotte or Wilmington. I could also replace the wooden staircase with stone steps. This could be a permanent solution to the erosion problem as well as to decaying stairs. Built properly, mortared stone walls need no maintenance."

Father Paul slowly pushed his glasses up on his nose and smiled. "I could provide all the helpers you want. But what would this cost?"

"Well, to keep the costs down, we would have to get contractor's prices for mortar, sand, stone, and rebar. And unless you have an over-abundance of strong cheap labor, we would also need a small cement mixer and a trench digger. Some of the work requires skill with fitting rocks, but not super strength."

"Lentamente, Anna. You sound like you're ready to start tomorrow."

Anne hesitated, struck shy by the way he said her name, as if she were family. "Hurricane season seems to begin earlier every year, Father. I can't give you a dollar figure without a lot more information. But it would certainly be a solution to the erosion problem as well as improve the value of this land and make it very appealing to a buyer, if you must sell it. Even with terracing, though, we would need to plant in order to hold the soil. I would suggest natural or ornamental grasses with splashes of color from native flowering plants and maybe some hardy domestic perennials. You would also want some low growing shrubs with deep roots. And I would keep the wildflowers, like those roses by the steps down to the road." Anne stood and paced, measuring for height and length of walls with her eyes.

Father Paul leaned back on his elbows and laughed at her growing energy. "You see? You're already fulfilling my expectations." *And building fires that will make people jump.*

He looked away from her to the water and sky. "I have a suggestion. Why don't you go have lunch. I'll tell you a good place to eat not far from here. While you're gone, I'll shower and then take you on a tour of Pearl and its environs. There are two trailer parks and two gated developments with new homes. The people there could improve the economy of this town if we had anything to offer them here. Instead, they go to Shallotte or Wilmington. It's a Catch 22: They could help us if we could help them, which we would do if they would help us."

Enveloped in the warm bath, Anne knows Father Paul sent her off to give her time to herself, and time to think through this decision. If it was not what she really wanted, she could simply keep going, and she did consider that possibility. But she hadn't been able to resist a tour of Pearl.

Now she weighs her decision as she remembers and soaks. She wants an active part in a community, but she doesn't want another full-time job. She spent years teaching in an environment where she was an outsider, a minority presence. No matter how close she felt to many of her students and colleagues, and no matter how hard they tried to make her feel accepted, the effort was often more obvious than the result. And there were always some who simply distrusted and disliked her because she was white. Of course it did make her appreciate what they had lived with all of their lives, and not just in their workplace. Does she want that again, this time as a protestant Anglo in a Catholic Latino environment? *And do I really want to build more stone walls?*

Anne sinks beneath the water and shuts out the long day and the questions. A la Scarlet O'Hara, she'll think about it tomorrow.

Following a night of little sleep, Anne nervously prepares for her meeting with Father Paul at Saint Angelica. She wears a summer dress and a soft straw hat with a rolled brim to cover her head in the church. In spite of the long night spent thinking and sketching, she feels alert and ready for the day.

On the way, she retraces the route they had driven following lunch the previous afternoon. She begins upriver where he showed her the new housing developments with mostly wood frame construction and vinyl siding. She follows the winding River Road to the trailer parks with mostly Mexican families, lively and noisy with children and barking dogs. She drives through town, remembering his detailed histories of the various shops and restaurants, mostly closed.

The third from the last shop on Main Street is a shell of the once busy clothing store owned by Marjorie and her husband, John. She pictures the way the town was when its economy was better and wonders if the cultures lived so separately then, the Anglos and the Latinos. She hasn't yet seen any African Americans. It reminds her of the Dark Ages of Europe, when people lived in isolated groups, fearing strangers that might bring the plague and of her childhood in Texas before integration. Finally, she arrives at the church, the only place the priest did not show her yesterday.

As Anne enters Saint Angelica, she sees Father Paul sitting with someone at the front. He's wearing his collar. She is glad for the formality. It will make her confession easier. Perhaps it will also make it easier for him to withdraw his offer if he decides her past doesn't meet his papal or moral expectations. She stops at the entrance to the nave and looks around at the clean white interior with the richly stained wooden pews, pulpit, and altar. From her humanities class, she remembers the traditional architecture of a Catholic church—in the form of a cross. There are no other worshipers here now, but Anne senses a presence of countless souls who brought their faith and sorrows to this basilica and its priest. The sparse simplicity moves her. She has been in magnificent churches and cathedrals that awed her, but did not give the spiritual comfort she feels now.

Father Paul sees her and calls. "Anne, come join us. I want to introduce you to Kente." Kente Jackson is tall, young, and black. *At last*, she thinks and is reminded of the ultimate kinship she feels for African-Americans. His smile is genuine and bright as he takes Anne's pale hand with his dark one. *Click. Contrast—startling, beautiful contrast.*

But he immediately teases her. "Please tell me you didn't wear that adorable hat because you're in a Catholic church."

"As a matter of fact, I did."

Father Paul smiles. "That's no longer necessary."

"Paul tells me you are considering purchasing the Casa Blanca."

"Oh my! I'll have to honor Bogart and Bergman and paint it white again. He tells me that you're drawing up the contracts. Be kind. The price is so fair, I keep expecting an 'Oh, I forgot to tell you' clause. But when we last spoke, he did ask me to sign over all remaining funds and agree to indentured servitude on stone walls for the rest of my life. Seems like a good deal, but does it have to be in the contract?"

Kente rolls his eyes to Father Paul. "Will she go to Hell for lying in church, Father? Or just spend eternity in Purgatory?"

Father Paul grins. "It's a bit exaggerated but close to the truth."

"That reminds me, I'm here for confession." Both men turn to her, waiting for the punch line.

"I'm serious. But do we have to do it in a box?"

They respond in unison. "A box?"

"Well, a booth, a tiny room with a window. I remind you, I'm not Catholic, but I've seen them in movies, and I'm a little claustrophobic."

"Since you're not Catholic, Anne, I guess we can talk wherever you would like. And we don't use the tiny room here."

Kente whispers in her ear. "We use a torture chamber in the basement instead."

"Sounds charming. Before Kente goes on with the contracts, though, I have an idea to toss into the think tank. But before that, I need to tell you more about myself and make sure you are comfortable with selling to me."

"Why don't you tell us your idea first, so Kente can go on to his office?"

"You work on Saturday?" Anne asks.

"Only on Father Paul's pro bono shit."

"Well, I don't mind confessing in front of Kente, considering he's going to keep me company in Purgatory for *cursing* in church. Anyway, my life is literally an open book."

Sensing that she's serious, but still wanting to protect her privacy, Father Paul says, "No, you and I can talk later. Have a seat and tell us your idea." She sits in the front pew, and Kente sits beside her. Father Paul finds a chair and sits on it, facing them.

Anne takes a deep breath and begins. "I had an apartment on the second floor of my home in Durham. I renovated it from a large studio space in order to meet increased mortgage payments. In addition to helping me pay bills, it also raised the value of my property."

Kente turns to her. "Why did your mortgage payments increase?"

Father Paul clears his throat. "That's none of our business, Kente."

"Point taken, just my legal side speaking."

"Anyway, the price of your uncle's house will leave me with enough money to complete renovations and cover most of the cost of two apartment additions, one on either side of the house. They would actually be more like townhouses. I could rent them by the season to retired couples or singles, and that would make the mortgage, insurance, and tax payments."

"Why would you take out a mortgage if you have the money to purchase and renovate?" Father Paul looks disappointed in what seems to be a plan to simply increase her personal wealth.

"That's none of our business, Paul."

"Yes it is, because the low purchase price is based in part on having leftover funds to invest in the limited liability company."

"Exactly!" Anne agrees. "But if I leave the house as it is—sans dirt and critters—I would have to hold back some of the leftover funds for a new roof, regular maintenance needs, emergency health expenses, etc. I retired early, so my benefits are minimal. If I follow this new construction plan instead, I can take out a mortgage on the improved property and use *that* to invest in your company. I can get a much larger mortgage for an income-producing tri-plex than for a single-family dwelling. So my investment money will be significantly increased. I even drew a picture of what the front would look like and some undetailed floor plans. I think the property lines will allow for this much addition." She opens the sketchpad they hadn't even noticed her carrying.

Kente whistles. "Are you an architect?"

"No, I was a scene designer. I didn't bring my drafting tools, but I never go anywhere without graph paper. So the measurements aren't accurate, but they are close. An architect, or a savvy builder, would have to draw in or plan for incidentals like plumbing and air conditioning ducts, etc. This is an approximation of the current ground plan of the original house. Since I need to replace the roof anyway, I would like to build a loft above the existing living room. On either side, with a carport between, is a two-story, two-bedroom apartment. Is this Spanish style with stucco and plaster expensive to build?"

"Actually," Kente says with a touch of admiration, "it's not, and we have men with experience in this type of construction and finish work. They can also roof and lay tile, and they need the work. They drive to Wilmington now, for minimum wage. We would need to bring in a heating and air conditioning man, but we can provide the foundation, framing, and finish crews. You're right, Anne," he continues, "this idea would dramatically increase the value of your property, and it would then qualify for a significant mortgage for investment in the company. I like it, Paul."

"What about your privacy, Anne?"

"Shouldn't be a problem, Father. You can see each unit will have an enclosed garden and patio. There's a double carport on both sides of the original house to provide parking and a buffer for sound, and there's a roof deck over the carports for each townhouse unit."

"Is this a balcony that also serves as a roof over your front door?" Kente asks, and before Anne can respond he continues. "And it looks like the balcony leads to the loft which includes a master bath and bedroom. It also looks like the renters' roof decks are behind your balcony, maintaining your outdoor privacy as well as theirs. Wow! Don't let my wife see that."

A wife? Well, you're too young anyway. What's the difference? Why do I have to keep reminding myself that I'm not looking for a man?

Father Paul whispers. "Your lips are moving."

Anne whispers back. "Shut-up! Oh dear, sassing a priest. Is that another year in Purgatory?"

"As I was saying . . ." Kente covers concern with a smile as he hears what sounds like flirtation between his priest and this stranger.

"It still sounds like a risk." Father Paul interrupts, rising to distance himself from the fresh scent and presence of this woman who appeared without warning, and with seemingly unlimited ideas. He circles his chair and leans against the back of it. "Do you think there'll be a market for rentals like that here?"

"Oh, yes. I'm sure of it. I could set up a website and advertise them as seasonal rentals only—minimum three months. Retirees from the cold states and Canada would jump at the chance to winter here. And when they aren't rented, I have plenty of family and friends who would love to visit."

"You're right, Paul, she's a thinker, and I believe we could expand on this idea. I'll crunch some numbers and get back to you. Welcome, Anne." Kente offers his hand again, but she reaches up and kisses his cheek.

"Thank you, Kente. I look forward to meeting your wife."

"Maybe you do; maybe you don't. Just please do not show her the drawings."

"We wouldn't enjoy this in August," Father Paul says, sipping on iced tea under the tree, the place where he had cleaned fish the morning before.

"Is there usually a breeze like this?" Anne is nervous, afraid that all the talk and planning will be for nothing if her confession destroys Father Paul's respect for her.

"Often, but this is actually still spring. Summer is warmer and then you'll want to be on the water, catching the wind."

"I heard you're a sailor."

"Since I was a boy."

"Well, I guess I could make small-talk all day, but I really came here to fill in some gaps in the information I gave you yesterday."

"You have a cheerful mask that doesn't cover the many conflicting emotions I hear in your voice. You don't have to do this, Anne. I really don't care what your past includes as long as it is the past."

"I think I could become very dependent on your friendship, Father. So I want to make sure there are no surprises that might test the friendship later." Before he can stop her, she rushes ahead. "I'm divorced."

"I assumed that, or widowed."

"Twice."

"Twice? Well!" He laughs self-consciously. "I guess that was unexpected. You still don't owe me any explanations, and I'm not here to judge you. But, if it would make you feel better to talk, I am here to listen. Okay, I'm also curious. I hardly know you, but twice doesn't fit."

"I have come to terms with my choices and the results of them, so I'm not trying to rationalize or justify. And I'm not really asking for absolution. I'm not sure that I even believe priests have that power."

She sits forward in her chair as if her posture would add clarity. "My first husband, Robert, is gay. He's a good father and grandfather, and we've found a way to make peace."

"The church would have annulled that marriage. And the second?

Anne hesitates, looking for the right words, and then says them in a rush. "His name is Steven. He didn't want the divorce, but he also didn't want to live with me. And I couldn't continue living with him. He has remarried."

After a silence, Father Paul encourages her. "That's a little unclear."

Tears well, but she blinks them back. Her voice grows husky. "He tried to let me die. I have trouble saying he tried to kill me. The whole thing still seems surreal. I guess a court might have called it depraved indifference. I know that's confusing, but I don't want to go into details. When he knew I might be dying, he refused to give me help, and then tried to prevent me from getting help elsewhere. Our marriage had already begun to disintegrate, but he didn't want to give up half of what we had in a divorce settlement. So he took advantage of an emergency situation. Afterwards, he acted as if nothing had happened, but I feared what he might do if another opportunity arose that would give him a clean escape with all the goods and a fat life insurance payoff. It took time for me to accept that a second marriage had failed, but eventually I filed for divorce."

Anne is so used to Father Paul pushing his glasses up, that she is surprised when he pulls them lower on his nose and peers above them at her. After a moment, he says, "I spent years at a parish in the slums of Detroit. I've heard and seen much worse. In fact, I've heard worse from abused women here in this parish. But I didn't expect to hear such a story from you. This act was not the result of drugs, or passion, or anger, or ignorance, or poverty. Even if it wasn't planned, it was more subtle, more controlled, and, similar to many white collar crimes, somehow more evil. And by the way, I would call what he did depraved but not indifferent, not after he decided to prevent you from getting help."

"I didn't really intend to tell you this much," Anne continues. "The stories I wrote for the couple that purchased my house helped me put most of the dramatic/traumatic moments of my life into perspective, but I didn't include that one. I have told that story to only two other people."

"Why?"

"I suppose it's the same reason few people know, at least from me, that Robert is gay."

"Not the same thing."

"I was in denial about the seriousness of the situation until I told my sister-in-law the story. Just saying it aloud was enough to give me the courage to walk away from a second marriage."

"And the other person?"

She smiles sadly and tells about the choice she regrets. "I learned he had been seeing someone else, even before our separation. They married as soon as our divorce was final. I felt an obligation to tell his wife. Even though I believed she would negate the idea at first, she would perhaps be on her guard and not let the same thing happen to her. And by the way, she is very wealthy."

Unable to continue sitting while these memories churn inside her, Anne rises and paces, finally leaning against the tree. "Not long ago, I had a dream about him. We were at some outdoor event in a small town. Somehow, the story had reached every ear, and there was a frightening sense of anger and revenge in the air. He and I were walking together, trying to talk through our marriage and the problems in it. He was full of humility and shame, and I forgave him. But it was too late. The townspeople had created a mob that attacked him and beat him, all because of what I had told his wife. I woke up when they were about to lynch him. Anyway, I decided it was time to put aside my own anger. I didn't tell the story again, and was sorry I told his wife."

"I understand your concern, but if anything suspicious happened to her, you would feel responsible if you hadn't told her. You never pressed charges?"

"No. I could have, but by the time I had faced reality, I thought it was too late. In spite of his intelligence, Steven is careless. He will initiate his own downfall, and I don't want to be involved. I take equal responsibility for the choices that led to the consequences in both marriages, and I've forgiven myself for all of it. Now I'm working on forgiving them. I just wanted to assure you that I don't marry or divorce casually, and I don't walk out on a commitment unless it's the only solution."

"I think you're taking too much responsibility on yourself, Anne. In a way, you also give yourself too much credit. You may be a strong woman, but you aren't strong enough to make a man gay or to turn a man into a killer. And although you may have made mistakes in choosing to marry them, those were mistakes, not sins. And I'm sure you didn't know what you were getting into. Right?" When she doesn't respond, he adds, pacing his words, "And nothing you could have done made you deserving of that treatment. Some things you cannot blame yourself for, and shouldn't. You just accept them as being beyond your control and move on."

"You're letting me off too easy. I wasn't a perfect wife to either of them. Actually, I don't feel a need for annulments or absolution. After all, I wouldn't be here, talking to you now, if I hadn't married and divorced twice."

"Anne, if it was your fate to come to us, other less painful circumstances might have brought you here. It's very clear you are comfortable with who you are, but you're understandably concerned about how others perceive you. I think your biggest problems may be an inappropriate sense of guilt and a habit of resolving problems by accepting blame."

Surprised by his insight and tolerance, and not sure she agrees with him, Anne returns to her chair and sits in silence.

Paul moves his chair closer to hers and leans forward, peering into her lowered face. "First of all, I want very much to be your friend, Anne, and I'm not your priest, so I want you to call me Paul. May I have Kente move forward with the contracts on Casa Blanca? I can introduce you to a very good builder who can organize a crew for your renovations and additions. He will give you a reasonable price."

"Could I stay in the house during the renovations?"

He grins broadly. "I forgot to tell you, Marjorie Hester has offered for you to stay with her until you close on the house and are ready to move in. And by the way, you don't confess to me; you come to me as a friend, and I hope you will visit my church."

Anne's smile begins and grows. "So, do I have to genuflect, or is that only for bonafide Catholics?"

He laughs aloud. "Do what makes you feel comfortable." He pauses and then adds, "You do not have to mortgage your new home and invest in the company unless you want to; that is not a condition of the sale and certainly won't be in the contract."

Anne pulls her hat off, letting the breeze catch in her hair. She sees the two dogs from the day before, running and playing. She whistles for them. Then she turns to Father Paul, "Can I move ahead with planning the stone terracing and staircase? I could still use a little therapy."

"Yes, and I'll start looking for your crew."

Click—harmony—in the shape of his smile, his eyes, and the worry lines that hold stories of a painful past he tries to hide. Oh, Anne, you're still vulnerable to men, and (as usual) the wrong ones.

As she walks away, Father Paul releases a long cleansing breath.

Anne checks out of her motel and drives to Marjorie's home. She leaves her suitcase in the car and walks up to the front door. It opens before she can ring the bell. Marjorie is standing in the doorway, hands on her hips, wearing a t-shirt that says: "There are Lessons to be Learned in Life. Fear Is Not One Of Them".

"So, you're goin' to keep me company?" she asks.

"Yes, but only if you'll allow me to pay you. I may be here longer than you expected when you made the offer. Lots of renovations."

"No rent necessary."

"I know, but I don't want to be a guest. I want to help out. How about I buy the food and pay the utilities?"

"How 'bout you buy half the food and pay half the utilities?"

"How about I pay half the food, utilities, taxes, and insurance?"

"Whew, you're a tough cookie. But can you cook?"

"Yes ma'am!" Anne grins. "I'm also a good gardener. Not so great with housekeeping, but I'll do what you ask."

"We may need to hire a maid then, 'cause I'm the same. But we'll get along. Now get your suitcase and let's have us some sun tea. Your room is on the right, beside the bathroom."

Minutes later, they are sipping sun tea, seated on Marjorie's screened-in back porch, which overlooks the river. Marjorie sits in a wicker rocker and Anne curls up on a wicker chaise. A table between them holds their glasses of tea and a plate of brownies.

"I've been dying of curiosity, Marjorie. I've heard of the Red Hat Club but know nothing about it. Is it a formal organization?"

Marjorie slaps her knee and laughs. "It's women, honey. I can't say we're organized. We just get together every once in a while and wear our red hats and visit. Sometimes we meet in Shallotte for lunch."

"Are you all friends, or is there another common denominator? And why red hats?"

"You're sure full of questions. Well, let's see. Some of us used to come together just because we were friends, and we helped each other through losses—husbands, children, divorce, death. Course some of *them* are dead now, too. We don't have a common denomination. I guess we're all Christians, but some of us are Baptist, some Methodist, and a few are Catholic. We're not *against* other religions, you understand. There just aren't any around, not that we know of. I guess it's a sort of support group. There's a book, *The Red*

Hat Club. Never read it, but it was like a model for other clubs that popped up around the country. I do like the red hats we wear. Some of them decorate their hats outrageous. Makes us look like batty old women. Guess that's probably right. I don't care. We have fun."

"How many of you are there?"

"Depends. Sometimes only three or four show up, sometimes ten or twenty. Some of 'em aren't so old. We meet on the first Wednesday of every month. Wanna join?"

"Maybe. But if sharing losses is a requirement for membership, I'm not sure I qualify. I have two wonderful happily-married daughters and three beautiful grandchildren. I am a very fortunate and blessed woman."

Marjorie leans back in her rocker and smiles. She knows that Anne will eventually share her real reasons for leaving Durham—her own losses. *Maybe I'll tell her about my John, and my girl Sissy. Maybe I'll even tell her about Paul.*

"So, which church do you attend, Marjorie?"

"Ha! I go to all of 'em, Catholic on Friday night, Methodist on Sunday mornin', and Baptist on Sunday evenin'."

"Covering all the bases?"

"Naw! I'm just pesterin' His Honor."

After several days of meeting people involved in Paul's and Kente's plans, Anne finally unpacks her computer.

EMAIL TO NOAH:

I've always been willing to risk what I have in hopes of improving my personal or financial condition. I think that's called gambling. This time, I'm risking what I don't have in hopes of repaying it and improving the human and physical condition of this town. It's a joint effort between a priest, a lawyer, a looney old lady, myself, and hopefully some other citizens of Pearl.

Between Father Paul and Marjorie, I will learn to sail. They're a strange pair. They race their boats; they hardly speak; and yet I sense a real connection.

I hope Elizabeth's treatments are going well. I pray that my stories are helping. Does she still let you read them?

I only whistle when I'm very frightened or very happy. I have found myself wanting to whistle lately, for the latter reason.—*Always, Anne*

Chapter 5

The Wooden Box

"I HAVE AN IDEA." Noah sips his coffee and chews a bagel two days before Elizabeth's chemo is scheduled to begin. She is annoyed by the way he looks this morning in his lounging shorts, t-shirt and uncombed curly hair. *Too good.* Her own hair is pulled up and fastened with a large clip for coolness. Her attention wanders, but he tries to reclaim it.

"I imagine—no, I *know* you're dreading the side effects of chemo—not just the nausea and weakness, but also the hair loss."

"Noah, there's nothing I can do about it. I'm not looking forward to it, but I guess it helps that we are essentially strangers here and I won't have to deal with friends and their reactions."

"Do you want a wig?"

"God, no!" She pushes her own half-eaten bagel aside and gets up for a refill of coffee, then leans against the counter.

"The clinic will probably have someone to consult with about head coverings and other alternatives. But I was thinking, why don't we take control?"

"What's this 'we' stuff again? Are you going to take the chemo and lose your hair with me?" *Or do you simply want to control me?* "All right, I hate it, but you're intriguing me. What?" She sits again, her elbows on the table, propping up her chin in an exaggerated pretense of interest.

Good. "You have beautiful hair. You have always worn it long and in the same style. That's probably my fault because I like it that way, and I'm not very good with change."

"Remarkable insight."

"Nevertheless, it's a significant part of what you look like. But it's not who you are. Look in the mirror, Liz. It's also not the only thing about you that's beautiful."

"Noah, if this is going to be a series of compliments and clichés, you've lost my interest. Let's get back to you being incapable of change."

"I've read about cancer treatments and the strategies some women take for emotional health."

"Oh my God, Noah, you're reading women's books. That's beyond gay."

"I'll ignore that. Some women shave their heads before their hair starts to fall out. By doing this, they're taking control of at least the order of things, and they get it out of the way before they have to deal with the nausea and other side effects. They're a step ahead."

I feel like I'm a mile behind and you want me to be a step ahead. "So, you're suggesting I go shave my head now? Somehow I don't see that happening." *I don't even believe we're having this conversation.* She rises and walks from the kitchen into the great room. Noah follows.

"No, this is just the preliminary setup."

"You're wearing me out, Noah." She sits in a rocker, facing the view of the lake, trying to ignore and discourage him.

"I bought this magazine of hairstyles." He lifts it from his briefcase on a side table. Ignoring her sideways glance and derisive grin, he continues, selecting his words carefully, trying to maintain at least the appearance of a positive attitude in the face of her sarcasm and resistance. "Pick out a medium length style that you've always wanted to try. We'll go to a hair salon today and get the cut. Then we'll go to lunch and celebrate your new look. You need to see yourself looking different."

What I need! Oh Noah, what do you know about what I need? She closes her eyes and rocks.

Noah moves between her and the window, willing her to see him and the pictures of different haircuts. "Tomorrow we'll go back and you can try a shorter cut. Then tomorrow night, or whenever you're ready, you can shave it off. Instead of going from long hair to no hair, you can go from the current lovely, to cute, to sassy." He reads the descriptions from the magazine.

Elizabeth finishes for him. "To cue ball." A long silence fills the space between them while she ponders the alternative, another endless day. She softens as she considers his efforts. "All right, anything to get away from your hovering. Have you picked the salon, too?"

"It's not far, just a mile down Highway 54. Sue, the woman that used to rent the upstairs apartment, suggested it. She swears that Ian is the best. She also recommended a jazz performance we could take in this evening, if you feel like it. A little release time from here."

"Do you talk to Sue often?" *And was this your idea or hers?*

"No!"

"Is she coming with us?"

"To the hair salon?"

"No!" *Bastard!* "To the jazz performance!"

"Not if you don't want her to!" *Bitch!*

At noon, they walk into the hair salon. Ian, a Scotsman with the build of a weightlifter, leads Elizabeth into his cubicle. Noah watches as she leaves, her long legs bravely walking as if she owned this place. The hands he would hold, if she would let him, reach up and lift her shining long hair, letting it cascade in a dark billowing fall, knowing Noah is watching. She is giving him a last look that chains her, as she is now, to his memory.

Ian speaks with a soft Scottish burr as their eyes meet in the mirror. "Now, darlin', what do we want today, a trim?" She shows him a picture in the magazine.

He frowns at it. "A bob? And bangs? Sorry, love, that just doesn't suit you. If you want change, what about this one—long layers, a sort of gypsy look?"

"Nope, too dramatic. I'm here for shorter, but not too short, and cute."

"Ah, this hurts my heart, but whatever you say. Just relax and put yourself in my hands. I'll transform classic into cute."

An hour later, she emerges into the reception area to find Noah also wearing a new cut, shorter and more casual than his usual slicked back power exec look. It works well with his khaki shorts and knit shirt. He puts his magazine down and walks around her, admiring. She tosses her head and her hair swings with a new lightness. "I'm a different woman, and I've never felt cuter. You're clearly a stranger. Who is this laid-back California kinda guy?"

"I have no idea. I feel like I'm on drugs—like I'm standing back, out of my skin, looking at two people I don't know."

Ian walks up to them and beams at Elizabeth. "How do you like it?"

Charmed, Noah laughs. "I love it—always wanted to try cute. Don't tell my wife. We'll see you tomorrow."

"You'll what?" He immediately goes to the desk to look at the appointment book and an equally confused receptionist.

At a Mediterranean deli, they share a gigantic Greek salad with a side dish of hummus and fresh pita. Elizabeth flirts with the waiter and continually moves her hair with her fingers or a twist of her head. She feels ten pounds lighter and ten years younger. The blushing waiter is slowly backing and slightly bowing as he leaves their table when Noah looks at him and broadly winks. He turns and walks rapidly to the kitchen. Elizabeth giggles into her napkin. "Noah, what is becoming of my ramrod straight husband?"

"I'm just living up to your expectations, my dear. You suggested I might be gay; I'm trying it out." He leans across the table at her and says softly, "But it is hard to look at anyone else in the room with you acting so outrageous and looking so cute."

The waiter returns with a tray of Greek desserts and lowers it to Elizabeth, carefully avoiding looking at Noah. "Oh my, I *love* bak-la-va." Elizabeth moans, drawing out the word as if she were savoring the taste.

The waiter smiles. "My name, pretty lady, is Bak-la-va." And Elizabeth laughs brightly, a little too brightly, keeping the mood rolling. After serving her, the waiter turns to Noah. "And you, sir?" he says, with a broad wink. Noah almost spits out the salad he is finishing and sputters. "No thank you." They both hold their breath until the waiter is gone and then try to muffle an outburst of laughter.

"Well, I think you just gave your secret away, Noah. You're a hopeless hetero." She sighs deeply and smiles. "This was a good idea. Thank you."

Falling back in his chair, almost tipping over, he sputters in a stage whisper. "Stop! I'm used to haughty and sarcastic. I need more time to adjust to both cute and kind." He relaxes, taking in the full view of his smiling wife with her new hairstyle and the soft green summer dress. Then his face begins to slowly sag, the unexpected weight of pleasure too heavy to hold.

"What's wrong?"

"Maybe he doesn't recognize you, either."

"Who?"

"Josh. He's not here." And although he sees her emotionally back away from him, he can't stop. "He's usually with you, you know. Every time I look at you, I see him—in your lap, beside you on the chaise, on the floor with his head or hand touching you. He's always with you, but looking at me."

Elizabeth is stunned. For moments, she doesn't breathe. Noah has not willingly talked to her about Josh since his death. She sucks in a ragged breath. "What do you mean, Noah? How can you *see* him?"

Unable to look at her, he responds. "I don't know. I'm sure it's my imagination. I'm just putting him where I remember him always being, in your arms or beside you."

87

"He was with you as well. You were a good father."

Finally, his gaze meets hers. "But I couldn't save him." Tears glisten in his eyes, but don't fall. "He always looks at me as if he is saying, 'Why? Why didn't you do something?' I know we did all we could, and nothing else we might have done would have saved him. But I feel guilty because I'm alive. I look at you and I feel guilty because I'm healthy. And when I see the two of you together, I feel you're fading into his world, and I'm losing you both."

"I didn't know. I thought you couldn't make eye contact because maybe you were hiding something. I assumed it was an affair." She releases a bitter laugh. "I thought you could at least wait until I was dead." Noah winces, and Elizabeth regrets, silently berating herself.

"When you were unable to talk about Josh at first, after the funeral, I thought it was simply your way of dealing with grief. I thought that eventually we would talk of him and you would help me shed my own guilt for passing the disease to him through my genes, for causing the death of your son."

"Liz, when Josh was conceived, you had no way of knowing that your family would be riddled with cancer. My God, do you think he ever wished that he had not been born?"

After a long moment, Elizabeth smiles through her tears and says, "No, not Josh. He loved every minute of his life—until he got so sick that he just focused his love on us, waiting for us to fix him. Maybe that's why you see him looking at you the way you described." *I remember every expression, every detail.*

The restaurant is crowded, and although their conversation is softly spoken, diners at adjacent tables are clearly affected by the emotion nearby. Studiously focused on their meals, they glance at Noah and Elizabeth then back to their food.

Southerners are kind, Noah thinks, *but nosey.* A large African American man passes them on his way to the men's room, briefly touching Noah's arm. *That was meant as a pat on my shoulder. Okay, we're out of here.* "I think we should leave before someone offers us a contract for a soap opera, or refers us to a counselor."

"All right" She agrees, self-consciously dabbing at her eyes with her napkin. "But I'm taking my baklava."

By evening, Elizabeth is exhausted from more exercise and more emotion than she has allowed herself for weeks. No jazz tonight, but at her request, Noah prepares to read another story, placing the object of the story on the table next to her. Elizabeth pats the foot of the chaise for him to sit on and takes his hand in hers. She doesn't want to lose the ground they gained at the restaurant. She wants Noah to talk about Josh. "Didn't you, at some point, feel anger at me for Josh's illness? Didn't you think, 'If I'd married someone else, I would have a healthy son'? It's okay to say yes. Believe me, I would understand."

"I think we both went through every emotion available to us, and as you have pointed out to me lately, I do look for someone to blame when things don't go my way. I guess I've always known that about myself. I don't handle imperfection or failure, in myself or others."

Elizabeth fakes shock, throwing her arms up. "Hey! Luckily, the chaise is sturdy or I'd be on the floor."

"But the reality is this: only your mother and sisters developed cancer; your nieces and nephews have grown up with no trace of it. I'm no geneticist, but if Josh's disease was inherited, it wasn't a product of your gene pool alone."

He hesitates, searching for the right words. "I can assure you of one thing. You are the only woman I ever asked to marry me. I was too engrossed in my work to even consider the complications of marriage, until I met you. And I did spend a number of years in the eligible bachelor scene."

"Until you met me, Spunky Girl Editor."

"Until I met a classy woman who had the insight and instinct for working with writers and words, a woman who was both casual and formal, sexy and demure, assertive and modest."

"I sound like a walking contradiction."

"No, she was the best of all things. Whatever happened to her?"

"Thanks." Stung, she releases his hand and returns his fire. "You know, Noah, our marriage wasn't perfect. It was a constant battle for control—of me. It was fun being my defiantly independent self when I was simply your employee. Even when we began dating, you had such a reputation for short-term relationships, I never expected it to last. And so I never gave myself entirely into your keeping—not until we married. I don't know if it was old tapes from my mother that kept playing in my head or if it was you, trying to mold me into your twin, modifying my tastes, behavior, looks, everything that had previously set me apart. Whatever it was, I felt myself submitting, becoming my mother, and hating it. I was in a constant battle with myself, gravitating from the woman I had been to the malleable wife my mother had prepared me to be."

She takes a deep breath, looking through the window, and then back at Noah. "When Josh was born, everything changed. Both of us turned our focus on him, and I was able to be myself again. Because of Josh, we all flourished. After he died, the things you once admired in me quickly eroded."

"Why?"

"I didn't have the reason or the strength to maintain the *me* in us."

"Are you trying to say it's all my fault?"

"Finding fault is not my obsession. It's yours. You seem to thrive on criticism and control. That's why I finally resigned from my position, not because of Josh's illness or death, or even the discovery of my own cancer. I just didn't have the strength to deal with all those losses at home and work. Without your presence, I could look for my own answers."

"Did you find any?"

"No, just a desire for the cancer to hurry."

"That was probably clinical depression. I should have arranged counseling for you."

"More control. If you remember, Noah, I suggested we go to a counselor together. But you refused. You said I was the one with problems, not you."

"Even I can see now how stupid that was." He laughs bitterly. "I'm the one who sees my dead son and can't talk about him except to strangers. Maybe that's why I talked to you about him today, and I'm talking to you about him now. I hardly recognize you."

"Ditto. But it has been better here, at this house. You seem more relaxed, more in touch with both of our feelings, less controlling. I guess that's not entirely true. You've chosen my doctors, my treatments, my surroundings, even perhaps the author of our salvation. You even chose how I should deal with losing my hair."

"Elizabeth, that's small stuff."

"Sorry, Noah, that was not fair. I do understand that lately you've had to make choices because I wouldn't. You've also encouraged me to take back control, at least over my willingness to fight the cancer and my desire to live. Maybe that's the only arena where I have had some control, and I am in the habit of resisting you."

"Haven't you noticed? You have all the control now." He turns away from her, unable to make eye contact as his own sensitivity leaks out, leaving him unprotected. "You obviously don't see me as a reason to survive the cancer; you also obviously don't care how I would survive without you." Anger and hurt begin to creep into his voice. "Your death from cancer wouldn't be nearly as devastating as your death by choice, as an escape from life with me. Talk about criticism and blame! You're *crushing* me with guilt!"

Noah slumps forward, his eyes closed and his fingers rubbing his temples as if he were holding back a migraine. Then he turns to Elizabeth, covers her limp hands with his own, and takes a deep breath. "Here we are, finally being honest with each other—brutally honest. Does that mean that we no longer care enough to temper honesty with kindness? I probably shouldn't tell you this, but I had reached a point, before we came here to Durham, that all I could think about was getting you well so I could let you go. Today, when you stepped out of the salon, it wasn't just your hair that was different. I almost felt like I was betraying you with another woman. And then I realized that this new woman I was with was in fact the beautiful friend I married. The stranger is the woman who's sitting here now, waiting for death."

He pauses. "I'll see a counselor; I'll do anything you want. I'll be anything you want if there's a chance it will bring us back to who we were."

"Thank you for your honesty, Noah, but we'll never be exactly who we were ever again. We can't go backward. And even though an objective third person might help, I don't have enough strength or courage for analysis right now. So, a temporary truce—don't push me, and I won't push back." She looks around and sighs. "Do you see Josh now?"

"No."

"Good. He didn't need to witness all that."

"I'm sure he's just a manifestation of my own guilt and grief."

"Probably. But the next time he comes, tell me so I can try to sense him. There's enough guilt and grief to share. Right now, I'll settle for a story. We need a little distance from ourselves. But if this story is about criticism and control, I'm calling for a witch hunt."

Noah picks up the journal from the couch and then hands Elizabeth the box that has been waiting on the table beside the chaise. It is the simple wooden box he saw on Anne's dresser on his first visit. Elizabeth opens it. "Ah, Anndora's box."

"Anything alive?"

"Only in her memory. There are pictures, very old pictures." She turns them over and sees that they are numbered and dated with names on the back. "And here's a woman's sport watch. I don't recognize the brand. Mido?"

"I know that name. I think it's German, probably expensive. Find picture number one."

"Here it is. It's dated 1910—a formal portrait of a couple and a boy. Look at how austere the man is and how crippled his hands are with arthritis. He seems old, but the woman looks young and very gentle."

"Yes, the 'bury your head in her bosom and block out the world type'."

"You freak! Read!"

Noah moves to the loveseat beside the chaise and finds the next story in Anne's journal. Looking up, he sees Josh settle into the crook of Elizabeth's arm. She sees his gaze and leans back, smiling and closing her eyes to listen while she holds her son.

THE WOODEN BOX

One day, when I was about nine years old, Daddy helped me build this box. I stained and varnished it, then lined it with gold velveteen fabric. I loved this box because we built it together, and I've always kept special treasures in it. Some of the child stuff has been replaced by adult stuff. Funny I chose the word 'stuff' instead of 'things'. Maybe there's a reason.

The first photograph was taken around 1910. The President was William H. Taft; the popular songs that year were *Shine on Harvest Moon* and *Give My Regards to Broadway*. Ah, nostalgia!

The photo is a portrait of Mama's parents and her oldest brother. The last of seven children, Mama told me that Uncle Tom left home when she was a baby. He left because of a rift with their father, joined the Infantry, and fought in the Great War. Afterwards, he moved to California where he stayed until he was an old man. When his wife died, he moved back to Texas. My brother and I were teenagers, and formed an instant connection with this childless uncle who turned out to be a kind and loving version of Grandpa.

A Texas Ranger in his youth, Grandpa married late, became a successful businessman in east Texas, then sold his business and bought a burned-out cotton farm in south Texas. From the stories his children tell, Joseph Franklin was a hard man, insensitive to family. Born just before the Civil War, too late to own slaves, he made slaves of his children. There are many stories about Grandma's kindnesses and just as many about Grandpa's cruelties. Mama told me that he killed a black neighbor over some meaningless dispute. Probably because of the accepted racism of that era, he was never charged with the crime.

Grandpa supervised while his six older children worked the farm. Mama was too young for fieldwork, but she remembered riding on the cotton bags her older sisters pulled between the long plowed and planted rows. By the time she was born, Grandpa had softened a little. Like Uncle Tom, she had inherited her father's tall, slender body, high cheekbones, and brown eyes, winning her his meager kindness. She never learned to hate him. Ah, the luck of timing and genes!

Noah grins, as Elizabeth mouths the word 'witch'. "Look for a card."

Elizabeth finds a card with the picture of a babe in a manger and opens it. "It's a Christmas card for Anne, and it's signed 'Love, Grandpa'. Look how shaky his handwriting was. He appeared old and arthritic in the photo taken when his first son was still young. Maybe the arthritis kept him from working with his children. He must have been really old by the time Anne was born to his youngest daughter. An evil man wouldn't have sent this card to a grandchild. I guess no one is all bad. What does she say about it?"

"Nothing. Maybe she wanted us to draw the conclusions you just did."

"Hmmm! Read on."

Grandma, on the other hand, was considered by her children and grandchildren to be a saint. She never displayed a moment of racism, and she taught acceptance without judgment to her children—in spite of Grandpa. Her own grandparents had brought two hundred African slaves from Georgia to Texas. Some 'stuff', huh? An aunt told me that when Grandma was a young girl, a doctor was in love with her, but she chose Grandpa instead. The doctor inquired about her health and happiness for years, apparently still caring for her. Whatever made her choose Grandpa? Perhaps she interpreted his fierceness as romantic and dramatic. Girls have always gone for the bad boys.

One spring, Grandma was trying to bring in their workhorse from the winter pasture, and he kicked her in the face. She nearly died from blood loss. The doctor who had courted her saved her life with a direct blood transfusion from Mama, who was sixteen at the time. Grandma's face must have been badly scarred, but I don't remember ever noticing any imperfections. She left Grandpa after Mama married, and then lived with one family member or another until her death. Since my brother and I were the youngest grandchildren, she spent much of her final years (my first six years) with us, and so I remember her well. She taught us *The Lord's Prayer,* and every night I brushed her long silver hair.

Daddy's parents were the opposite. His mother was an unbending religious fanatic, and his father was a gentle, strong man whose looks as well as personality reminded me of Gary Cooper. It's too bad we can't cut and paste people in life the way we can cut and paste text in our computers. I would put Mama's mother and Daddy's father together. He wouldn't have noticed her scars either.

The second photo is of Mama and her siblings. The boys are sitting on a fence while the girls stand in front. Franklin D Roosevelt was President; *Porgy and Bess* was on Broadway; and the popular music where they lived was Texas swing. Mama's sisters married to get away from Grandpa. Ultimately, her brothers stood up to him and then left. Mama stayed until she married Daddy, but her marriage was not an escape from her father.

I think a great deal about the choices we make and the opportunities to choose that sometimes seem unbalanced. We are the product of choice. I guess it's not where we are, but how we got there, and what we do with ourselves afterwards that validates our existence. That's the only way to level the playing field and get past the fact that life isn't fair.

"Do I have to say the words?"

"No, I think you may be onto something, Liz. She may be a witch. Shall I go on? Do you need more proof?"

"I don't, but her family is interesting. Read!"

The third photo is of Daddy in his Navy uniform. It was taken in 1945. I'm sure you know what the headlines were then, and of course the President was still Franklin D. Roosevelt. The popular song was *Sentimental Journey,* and *Carousel* was on Broadway. Daddy was barely more than a boy.

He and Mama met on All Saints Eve (Halloween) in an orange grove. South Texas was called the Citrus Valley. If you walked in the country, as they did that night, you were either next to a cotton field or a citrus orchard of some kind. They were each with friends, wandering around, looking for trouble, and stealing oranges. She worked her magic, and they were married on New Year's Eve.

Daddy once told me that Mama's sisters didn't like him because they thought their baby sister, the only one to finish high school, had the good looks and intelligence to marry up. When Mama and Daddy met, he had a job delivering milk. They were never rich, but ultimately he had more professional success and made more money than any of his or her siblings. As they moved from one state to another, then from one country to another and one culture to another, they traded their ignorance and biases for knowledge and understanding. They were never in one place long enough to call it home, and that had its own consequences. But the adventures they experienced enriched them both beyond money or property.

The fourth photo is of my brother Earl and me standing in the sand on Galveston beach, holding hands. We were about five and three. Eisenhower was president; Elvis Presley was just beginning a career that would influence the music world for decades; and *Damn Yankees* was on Broadway.

In the photo, I was only a toddler, but Earl was already my best friend and protector, and still is. Moving as much as we did with limited possessions caused us to rely on each other and our imaginations for companionship and play. We were both athletic, and our family didn't own a television, so most of our play was outdoors.

There are too many stories to tell, some of them funny, many of them scary.

In Washington's Puget Sound, we hiked on cliffs overlooking Deception Pass; in Ontario, we dove off pilings into Lake Huron where the water was too shallow, and we had to time our dive to hit the water just as a wave crested; we lost the car keys in the snow while hunting pheasant in Alberta and learned how to hot-wire a car. Before I went out on my first dates, Earl made me hit him so I would feel comfortable using force against groping boys. He coached me in algebra, my worst subject, and taught me to drive a stick shift.

Our recurring challenge was water. He was always swimming out to a destination, and I always followed. He often had to pull me in because I would get tired of swimming and simply quit. I gave up so easily because I was a very spiritual child with no fear of death. Many kids have an imaginary playmate. Mine was God, and I talked to him non-stop, walking with one foot on earth and the other stepping toward heaven.

When we were about the age you see in the picture, we were riding on the ferry from Galveston to the Texas mainland. I had pulled myself up and was leaning over the side of the ferry, watching the porpoises play in the water. Earl had hold of my legs to keep me from falling overboard. I think his fear of losing me to water began then. He still has trouble letting go. And I have yet to tell him that I'll be relocating to the coast.

The small velvet pouch was found in my mother's jewelry box after her funeral in 1978. One of my female students attempted suicide that year, but failed; one of my male students attempted and succeeded. My mother's death was another, slower form of suicide. The President was Jimmy Carter; Mama's favorite song was *The Gambler,* and mine was *Macarthur Park.* Among the many shows on Broadway were *The Best Little Whorehouse in Texas* and *Evita* .

Daddy told me to go through Mama's things and take whatever I wanted. Inside the pouch, you will find a lock of baby-fine red hair tied with a blue bow. Mine. I was touched to find it and to know it had travelled with her to so many places for so many years. My

97

mother and I had always seemed like opposites. She was tall, beautiful, and always said exactly what she thought, never censoring her words. She was bold and brassy. People responded to her with absolute acceptance or rejection. There was no in-between. I shyly vacillated between embarrassment and admiration, as I clung to her shadow. I like to think that today I'm a little more like her.

I used to believe she was a witch because she seemed to know when I was doing something wrong. But after I entered puberty, she thought I was always doing something that I shouldn't, and I was not. Her lack of trust crushed me. We both lost faith in each other and never quite recovered it.

Our best time together came when she stayed a week with us after Greer was born. She was drinking and smoking steadily, from dawn to dusk, although she never seemed drunk. One day she casually commented that she wished she could be around to watch Greer grow up. I thought she was referring to the fact that they travelled so much and were currently living several states away.

A month later, she died in her sleep. For a year after the funeral, I dreamed about Mama every night. Each dream had its own set of circumstances, but they all had the same theme: we thought she was dead, but it turned out to be a mistake, and she was still alive. I'm not sure why the dream was so persistent. I used to think it was because I refused to go to her wake or to look at her during the funeral. I heard relatives, hungry to witness grief, whisper in shocked tones when I passed by her coffin with my head turned away. I couldn't look at her because I was pissed. I was so angry with her for dying. I had learned, since her death, that she knew she was sick and would have had to change her style of living in order to prolong her life. I didn't remember that she had tried to tell me, and I had ignored her. She knew the alcohol and tobacco were killing her. And even though I was an adult, I held on to the childish belief that she didn't love us enough to live for us. Ignorance isn't bliss; it's simply ignorance.

"Don't say anything, Liz." Noah warns, knowing what she is thinking.

"I was just going to say . . . ."

"Don't, please."

The watch you see was a gift from Daddy. The President was Lyndon B. Johnson; the war was in Vietnam. The music that year, 1964, was all Beatles: *I want to hold Your Hand, Can't Buy me Love*, and many more. *Funny Girl* was on Broadway.

Daddy had just returned from a year in an oil field in Arabia. He brought many gifts. The sport watch he brought me looked large on my skinny twelve-year-old arm. The watch worked until a few years ago. I used to jokingly tell people if the watch stopped, either my Dad or I would be dead. And that's pretty much what happened.

I was sitting in my office at school, grading papers, when the phone rang. It was my brother, Earl. He said that our stepmother Marie, who had been sick for a long time, had died earlier that morning.

A student came to my door with a sheet of paper signed by my design class. She said, "We thought you weren't coming. Everyone's gone."

I looked at my watch and argued, "It's not even time for class yet."

The student replied, "It's 11:30." My watch had stopped.

To make a long story less long, I flew to Detroit that afternoon, met my brother and sister-in-law, and we drove to Texas. On the second day, we had breakfast in Austin, and called Daddy's house to let him know when we would arrive. Our parents' oldest friend, Alice, answered his phone and said, "Go straight to the hospital. Your dad's had a seizure." The drive to Corpus Christi seemed to take forever, but I already knew what we would find. We arrived at the hospital a few minutes after he died, in time to formally identify his body.

He had gone to the funeral home with Marie's children to finalize the arrangements for the burial of their mother. He had even made the last payment on his own gravesite (beside my mother's) and his own funeral service. On the way home, he suffered a seizure but managed to pull the car over to the curb. My stepsister rushed him to the hospital where he hemorrhaged and bled to death.

Even though the watch had stopped running, I hadn't removed it. For some reason I couldn't make myself get it repaired. I certainly couldn't throw it away. But each time I look at it now, I feel such a longing for his presence.

One day, when I was a preteen, I was drawing a charcoal portrait of Daddy, and Mama walked into my room. She sat on the bed beside me. "You know, honey, it's a sin to love a man more than God." I didn't respond because I didn't know what to say. How could you tell someone to put limits on their love, or to organize it in a specific hierarchy?

I know she loved Daddy; she followed him all over the world. Among family and friends, their love was legend. But married love is more complex than the love between a parent and child. Looking back now, I wonder if her comment was a result of her own childhood. She didn't hate her father as her siblings did, but I don't think she loved him either. Consequently, I think she never understood the unconditional love my brother and I felt for Millard Gray.

A friend said that I dreamed about my mother because I wouldn't look at her at the funeral and, therefore, I hadn't emotionally accepted her death. So when Daddy died, I insisted on identifying the body, and against my brother's wishes, I insisted on an open coffin. I took every opportunity to look at him during the wake and the funeral. My eyes couldn't seem to get enough of looking at him. I wanted to remember him at peace, not struggling to come back to me in my dreams. I let him go, as I should have let her go, and I did not dream of him.

I understand now, however, that it was my anger at having to live without her after we were just beginning to get close again that made Mama haunt my subconscious. It was my need for more time, time to resolve old issues and put them to rest. It was also my disappointment in her unwillingness to make the choice, to take control.

Of course, there was also the guilt, the knowledge that my brother and I had become so independent and didn't let her know we still needed her, the knowledge that she had always been lonely in her travelling life, lonelier still after Earl and I grew up and left. Did I say that love between a parent and child is simple? Wrong.

Once again, you two have pushed me to new levels of thinking. I don't know what will be left of the old me when I have finished my stories.

"Hmmm, so Anne uses her maiden name. She called her father Millard Gray."

Noah shifts uneasily and clears his throat. He worries that if she figures out who Anne is, a former author under her editorial guidance, she might feel duped and so bothered by their subterfuge that she rejects Anne's remaining stories and loses whatever ground has been gained.

But Elizabeth smiles as she closes the lid and hands the box to Noah. "A lot of *stuff* in there. The stories of her family help me know and perhaps understand Anne so much better. I wonder how much our genetic past influences our present, and what our own genealogies would uncover. I'm sorry, Noah. Since you were adopted, you'll never know, will you?"

"Not important." He smiles at her. "I know just enough."

"Well, at least she came by her witchcraft honestly. She inherited it from her mother." Elizabeth stretches. "Let's see. The stories included a critical and controlling grandfather; people who did or didn't take control of their own lives; a mother who chose to die quickly rather than take control of her addictions; lots of stuff about choice and control. Empirical evidence—she's a witch!"

"I'm glad that, as Jews, we'll have closed caskets. I don't like the idea of people looking at me when I'm dead. I would rather they remember me alive."

"Don't forget, Noah. I want to be cremated."

"I know, fighting Judaism to the end."

"Beyond the end! And I don't want you keeping my ashes."

"What do you want me to do with them, Liz?"

"I don't know. I just know that I don't want you hovering over them."

The next day, Ian greets Noah and Elizabeth at the door of his salon. He again shows Elizabeth to the cubicle, and she again points to a picture in her magazine. This time, the style is very short and spiky.

Ian barely looks at the picture. Then he pulls a chair next to hers and sits, taking both of her hands in his. "Lovely lady, what is going on?"

"I want to look like a risk-taker, dangerous."

"What happened to wanting to look cute?"

"That was yesterday. Today I'm living on the edge."

"The edge of what?"

"Tomorrow!"

"What happens tomorrow?"

"Chemo!" She watches his face, daring him to show shock, pity, or embarrassment.

"I thought so. I actually work with many clients who are undergoing chemotherapy. You have several options. Following this mutilation of your beautiful hair, you can choose to shave it rather than wait for it to fall out."

"That's plan A."

"Good! Healthy choice! What about a wig?"

"No!"

"Good choice again! It's summer. Wigs are too hot. You have great bones and a well-shaped head. Fabric wraps would be stunning on you. I could also advise you on makeup. You're looking a little sallow."

"You're the man, Ian. Let's do it all."

"Before I dry your hair and style it with all the mousse and spray, I would like to demonstrate a wrap that I think would look smashing on you. All right?"

"Sure." *Am I ready for this?*

After the cut, he pulls a scarf from a drawer. It's an East Indian fabric with a batik print in blue, lavender and cream. He tries several styles of wraps, each of which has a very different look, and he suggests earrings that would complement each style.

"Will I lose my eyelashes and eyebrows?" Her eyes well with tears. *I don't remember noticing that on my mother and sisters. How insensitive. Maybe I thought if I didn't notice the cancer, it wouldn't notice me.*

"Some do, some don't, but makeup is next. I'll show you how to fake them. Here's a tissue. I warn you, if you cry, you'll have me blubbering right beside you."

With the hairdryer and mousse, Ian actually turns the cut into a feathery frame of her face with just enough outward spikes to add interest to the shape.

"I look like a surprised owl."

"You look like a movie star."

She smiles at her reflection and his and says, "You did make a potentially ugly style look pretty good. You're a magician. But I like hair that moves. This hair will stand its own in a tornado."

"It's just a transition. Your hair will come back. And maybe then you'll opt for the gypsy look. I think you're very dramatic."

When she emerges from the cubicle, Noah is again waiting for her, and he too has a shorter cut with moussed spikes. "That's not fair. I look psychotic; you look sexy."

This time, Ian circles Noah, evaluating his style while Liz tries to hold back laughter. He proclaims the complaining Noah still handsome. "With the right frock and some orange and green hair paint, I might find him a date for the ball. I might even wear my kilts and take him myself."

On impulse, Elizabeth hugs Ian and promises to return when she needs help with the wraps. "Come visit me," he says. "You don't need an appointment."

At lunch the mood has changed from forced flirtation to depression, and conversation is strained.

In the evening, Noah reads the story of *La, the God of Good Lungs*, the story that had sparked the idea for Anne's journal. At the end, though, instead of saying she would be ready for God's call if her two daughters were gone (as she had told Noah), Anne had written the following:

I was married to my second husband when the lung problem occurred. I haven't mentioned him before. We were divorced not long ago. I don't like to think about him. I also resist admitting to multiple relationship failures.

When I made my deal with God for more time with my children, I never even considered Steven's needs. I didn't feel responsible for him; nor did I think he would have difficulty recovering if I were removed from his life. He would have fought for any money or material goods I left behind without any regard for his step-daughters. He might even have convinced himself that he was lost without me. But I had already caught him in one indiscretion a few months before my illness, and later there were others. He would not have been interested in raising the girls; nor would I have wanted him to be their guardian.

I married Steven because I wanted out of the fast lane of the single life. My careless use of myself and others during that time had eaten away at my self-esteem. And, right or wrong, I chose him because I knew he had done far worse than I had and, therefore, would never judge me. He was also attractive and a good lover. I didn't realize that I was only temporarily down. I simply needed some healing time outside of a permissive social life, time to find my way back to myself.

Steven, on the other hand, was who he had always been, in his own words: anybody's boy. A natural musician and actor, he was also a chameleon, willing to change into whatever persona would get the most reward. I thought we would help each other, but we simply enabled our opposing faults.

The girls reluctantly accepted him as a part of our lives, but he never fooled them the way he fooled me. We were not easy partners. Our attempts at loving were, at best, bi-polar. They bounced from extreme sexual passion to irrational disgust and loathing. We lived with high highs and low lows; there was nothing in-between. No, I'm wrong. There was an in-between place for me. There was a boy in Steven that was insecure and needy and cried for my approval and love. I couldn't resist that part of him. Men usually want to hold me on their laps; I always wanted to hold him on mine.

I did try to end our relationship before we were married. I was still terrified of unwittingly marrying another gay man. Steven had done pirouettes in my kitchen, paid more attention to his hair than I did to mine, and was a magnet to gay men at concerts and bars. So I invited him to walk around the lake one day. I tried to explain my inability to trust and suggested a break from our relationship. He had just showered. His face was flushed and his clean blonde hair fell across his forehead, making him look young and incredibly fragile. He asked for more time, and I couldn't deny him. When we arrived home, he cut his longish hair, and began sitting and walking like John Wayne. The chameleon simply changed colors.

I sincerely tried to love Steven, but in retrospect, I'm not sure I have ever been in love. I've thought I was several times. I probably let the best man in my life go, or rather ran him off. Following my second divorce, your new neighbor, Ben, introduced Logan to me. We had so much in common—not just our interests and activities, but more importantly we shared the same values and beliefs, the same moral ethics. He was a competitive bicyclist and participated in hundred mile rides up mountains. His friends described him as leather and bone with white hair and attitude. I was terrified by our immediate connection, afraid of making another unwise choice. So I pushed him away. I think he loved me more purely than I have ever been loved before, but I could not return his love. I simply wasn't ready. In addition to that, I was embarrassed. After striking out twice, a third time at bat seemed to be tempting fate. So I flawed this blameless man and fled.

When I was in college, I sometimes assisted Mrs. Sanders, the campus gardener. Her husband was on the faculty and they were both quite elderly. While we were working one day, a girlfriend of mine and her fiancé passed us and spoke. After they were gone, Mrs. Sanders leaned on her rake and said, "Which of them loves the most?" I thought she was crazy. Why would she assume that one person must love significantly more than the other? But she insisted that one always loves more. I still don't know if that is necessarily true. After all, how do you measure and compare one person's capacity for love to another's? But I knew that I didn't want to be the person who loved less, or worse—insufficiently. So I let Logan go. He is retired now and building a log house in the mountains, still cycling.

I also wasn't ready for love or marriage when I met Steven. So I suppose I did him a disservice—I used him. And so perhaps, in a way, I deserved the catastrophes that ultimately happened. If wisdom is the result of unwise choices, I'm deserving of an honorary doctorate in the field of men and marriage.

What have I learned from these experiences? As I read my own words, I know that you can't force love, but if you are so lucky as to find it, it is well worth fighting for and living for, even if the fight is between you and your fears. I once caught a glimpse of the love that a man named Noah felt for his wife, a woman named Elizabeth, and it broke my heart for lack of the same.

Elizabeth's eyes are closed, and she sighs deeply before opening them. She looks at Noah. "Is he here?" she asks.

"I told you. He's a manifestation of my problems."

"Does his presence help you?"

"Sometimes I feel sadness; sometimes I feel comfort. At this moment, I feel exhausted."

Realizing she is just postponing the inevitable, Elizabeth sighs, "I need to finish what we've started. I really hate this haircut. So I guess it was a good last choice."

"Do you want my help?" *Please say no.*

"Absolutely not. But thanks."

In the master bathroom, with the door closed, Elizabeth takes the electric clippers Ian loaned her and begins the ritual she will practice daily until no hair grows. Her heart is filled with contradictions and frustrations. The time here in this new town and new home has brought new hope. It was easier to prepare for the inevitable and to let Noah go while she carried anger and resentment towards him. Now he's forcing her to feel again, to remember their beginnings and their love and to want it to go on. But it's too much to digest in such a short time. And at this moment, she has to deal with the stupid hair thing.

Why does hair seem so important? She was raised to think that her hair was her most feminine attribute—until she grew breasts, of course. She considers her mother and her sisters and the multitudes of women who struggle through cancer, losing their breasts as well as their hair. Some give up their uterus, their womb, often before a child is born. *I'm only giving up my hair. So far, not such a bad deal. And after the chemo, it will grow back. What a whiner I am!*

When she's finished, she looks at herself, steeled against shedding a single tear. *Not something I want to get used to.* Then she showers and uses a lightly scented moisturizing lotion all over. She slips on a large t-shirt and then starts to open the door and stops. She has already grown a little accustomed to the way she looks, but she isn't ready for Noah's shock and false compliments. So she turns out the light, opens the door, and then crosses the darkened bedroom to slip quietly into bed. *I'll face him in the morning,* she thinks, and because of the emotion of the day and the dread of tomorrow, she sleeps.

In the guest bathroom, Noah finishes his own ritual, one that he will continue for as long as it helps Elizabeth. Then he showers, dries, wraps the towel around his waist, and walks to the bedroom, turning off lights and checking locks along the way. As he expects, she is already in bed, sleeping or pretending. He knows she will not want him to see her yet. But the shower has revived him, and as he slips into bed, her scent arouses feelings long forgotten.

These few days of preparation for tomorrow have been filled with emotional release and upheaval, leaving Noah raw and exposed. But, as he looks at her delicate image in the dim light, he knows that however much he tries to share, he can't go where she's going. He can't take the chemo for her. He touches her shoulder and gently runs his fingers over her shorn head and over her face, feeling each shape and indention. He rolls her towards him and as she slowly awakens, he kisses her lightly on the lips, her throat, and then her breasts, all the while continuing to touch every part of her, remembering and awakening her body, remembering and awakening desire.

Elizabeth slowly becomes aware of Noah's touch and caress and is mildly surprised by her own lack of resistance, by her own responding need. She feels his lips on her breast and the t-shirt pushed up, in her face. So she pulls it off and then strokes his neck and head which is smooth, as smooth and as hairless as her own. She gently pulls his face up to hers so they can see each other. "My love, you didn't have to do this."

"Oh yes, I did. I will do what little I can to keep you from feeling alone. Besides, this just gives us more skin to touch. Think of it as virgin skin."

Elizabeth smiles and pulls him closer. She kisses him, slowly and deeply and then moves down to his neck and then to his chest, taking her time, twisting and turning so that all of her newly shorn scalp caresses every part of him, every inch of his skin. He stretches full length, allowing her passage. She turns in their bed, moving down, and as she reaches his feet, he catches hers and brings them to his lips, beginning his own journey around her skin, around her bones, lingering only where memory holds. Finally, they are face to face again, kissing again—lips and eyes and tender skin. Her fingers gently trace swirls, like pools of water on his back and hips, stirring and tantalizing until he moans his need, and their bodies meld, moving like a wave, at first gently rising and retreating, then pushing and spreading, growing in height and magnitude until it crashes, leaving them drenched and drained and breathless.

They lie apart, too sensitive to touch. After a while, he asks, "I couldn't tell, were you in control or was I?"

She doesn't even open her eyes, but she smiles.

Later, after Elizabeth falls asleep, Noah goes to the guest room and emails the woman with whom communication has become an addiction.

EMAIL TO ANNE:

I'm almost afraid to write it for fear the words will break the spell, but we may be finding our way back to each other.

I can't say that she's fighting the cancer, but at least for the moment, she's no longer fighting me. Your stories take us outside of our own problems and yet address them from a different perspective. You're better than chocolate, even if you are a witch.

Your stories of Steven, however, are different. You hint at things that cause me concern. —*Indebted, Noah*

Chapter 6

Therapy, Land or Water

ANNE RARELY SWEATS, but the humidity and heat of Pearl in July has her clothes soaked and her face dripping. In spite of the temperature, she wears jeans to protect her knees from the rough ground, and a long-sleeved thin shirt to protect her skin from the sun. She has tied a bandana around her head to keep the salty moisture from her eyes and added a wide brimmed straw hat to protect her face. She pauses in her work to put on sunglasses. *I wonder what it's like in the mountains today, in the shade beside Logan's creek. This therapy is killing me.*

Anne and her assistant, fifteen-year-old Juan, are scraping the almost dry mortar, recessing and smoothing the rough surface. During the early weeks of construction, people often slowed almost to a stop as they drove by, making encouraging remarks or asking questions about the long stone retainer walls. Anne sometimes paused in her work to engage in conversation. But now they are striking the mortar, scraping it with wooden tools before the mortar becomes too hard. They work quickly. She doesn't even notice when a pickup rolls to a stop.

"What 'cha think, Billy?" Loud words by the driver, meant to be overheard.

"I think I'm seein' a white woman workin' like a nigger 'side a spic. I guess that makes her a white nigger in bad company."

The driver nudges Billy. "I wouldn't mind workin' 'side her, or in front, or in back, but definitely on top." Guffaws follow his insinuating remark. Anne stiffens but ignores them.

Juan, too young to know better, stoops and picks up a rock of throwing size. Anne grabs his hand, removing the stone. "Let me, please."

"Why do you get all the fun, Miss Anne?"

She laughs as she turns, tossing the rock in the air and catching it. But instead of the response she had hoped for, the passenger door opens and a large man unfolds, stepping out, enraged by her threat.

She lowers her pitch, trying to sound tougher than she feels. "I'm not kidding. If you touch either of us, I'll crack your skull with this." While she speaks, Juan stoops again and picks up another rock. The man laughs.

"Are you here to see me, Billy?" A voice from behind her draws the attention of all four. Father Paul walks past Anne, taking the rock from her hand and giving a warning look to Juan who reluctantly drops his weapon. "Are you here for confession, or did you want to volunteer your services to Ms. Gray and Juan?"

Anne's mouth is dry from the fear she felt when the door opened and the huge man emerged. Father Paul's arrival brought short-lived relief, but her tension returns as he approaches the men. Billy seems to shrink from the tall priest. He backs up, turns and moves quickly to the pickup, slamming the door closed, surprising Anne with his retreat. She wonders if they've had conflicts before. If they did, she's pretty sure who won. The pickup pulls away, scattering gravel. Father Paul watches until it's out of sight.

"It's very hot out here. Why don't you two stop for the day? In the future, Juan, if these men come back, call me immediately. Don't challenge them. They're bullies, and they're bigger than you."

"Yes, Father."

"He doesn't have a cell phone, Paul, and I don't wear mine when I'm working. It keeps accidentally calling people. If they come back, I'll whistle. That'll bring you and all the dogs within hearing." She is trying to bring levity to their close encounter of the redneck variety, but no one laughs. "We'll finish this scraping and then you can go home, Juan."

"When you're done, stop by my office, Anne." Father Paul turns and walks to the church.

Juan picks up his scraping stick, muttering curses in Spanish. Anne sighs and joins him. "Do you know this Billy character?"

"Si."

"Tell me about him."

"He's a very mean man and a drunk. His friend who was driving the truck is named Ed. Billy calls him Mr. Ed, and it makes him angry. I don't know why. They're both loco."

Anne continues scraping. "There used to be a TV show about a talking horse named Mr. Ed." Juan laughs and then giggles while he scrapes. Anne stops and looks at him. "If you don't stop giggling, we'll have to use a chisel to finish this mortar." They both laugh while they pick up speed.

Later, on the door to Father Paul's office, Anne finds a note. "Shower and meet me at my boat for a sail, Superwoman. You need to cool off."

He was right. A shower followed by a sail makes the perfect physical and emotional release following a long day of hot sun, hard labor, and threatening rednecks. Anne's hand trails in the water while she goads him for more and more information on her newly found love, and perhaps a much better therapy.

"Ok, Father Paul, while it's calm, help me out. I keep forgetting which side is port and which is starboard. Are there any tricks for remembering? Like, you always hold a glass of *port* in your *left* hand, or the *stars* are always *right*, or something?" Anne ducks as the boom swings over her head, the calm ended.

Father Paul laughs. "Try this: *Starboard* really means steering board which used to be attached to the right side of a boat. Consequently, whenever a boat came into a port, it had to do it on the left to keep from damaging the steering mechanism on the right."

"Thanks, but that's a lot to process should you yell, 'Schooner on the starboard; turn to port NOW!' Never mind! I think I can remember 'the stars are always right'. Well, I don't know all the words, but I think sailing is the most natural thing I have ever done. It was the same with fencing. The first time I picked up a fencing foil, it seemed like an extension of my arm. When the instructor positioned his sword and tried to tell me how I should respond, I just did it before he could get the words out of his mouth. It happened again and again, much to the irritation of the instructor. It was instinctual. I feel the same about sailing."

"You are a natural sailor, Anne. Already, you could sail by yourself, as long as there were no other boats in the water. However, without the words, you might be more of a danger than a help when you're crewing with another sailor—especially if you encounter an emergency."

"All right, tell me about emergencies."

"Emergency number one is man overboard. What would you do if my head was turned when the boom swung and it knocked me into the water?"

"I'd pray very fast, Father, while throwing you a line."

"What if the line isn't long enough? And the wind is carrying you away from me?"

"You're making me nauseous. Obviously, I'd have to turn the boat and sail into the wind to get back to you. Tacking, I guess. But wouldn't that take a long time?"

"It might, especially if you've never done it before and never under stress. If the boat is moving slowly enough for me to catch a buoyant cushion or swim to it, I would want you to throw one tied to a line. If you are moving fast, just throw a cushion without a line. It would give me something to hold on to until you can sail back and pick me up. We'll try it out on a calm day, but not now. The wind's up and we'll be tacking back to the dock, so move to starboard and get ready for life on the slant.

"By the way, Billy O'Brian is a coward, but he's also a bully and is a real danger to anyone smaller than himself. If you had ignored him, they would have given up and driven away. But when you tossed that rock, you might as well have been holding a red cape in front of a charging bull. You've made an enemy, Anne."

"Sorry, Father. What's his story, anyway?"

"He was raised by an abusive man who ended up in prison. I think he is abusive in turn."

"Is he married?"

"Unfortunately. And I've asked you before, please drop the Father. It's just Paul."

"Okay, but people will talk."

"Now's a good time to come about. Hard a'lee; watch your head. Most of the people who grew up with me call me Paul, especially if they aren't Catholic. And no one will talk unless you call me sweetheart or honey, like you do everyone else."

As the wind fills the sail, it captures their joined laughter. Anne leans out across the water to keep the *Espirita* balanced as they tack to port and begin the journey home. She is already thinking about her email to Noah, wanting to lift his spirits as her own soar. Several pelicans fly beside them, low to the water, catching an updraft. She calls to them, and they answer.

EMAIL TO NOAH:

I vacillate between exhaustion and elation, building stone walls and sailing. Don't worry about my unexplained history. You and Elizabeth know more about me than any other human being—or will when you've finished the stories. Will you finish them, or are they becoming boring? And how is the chemo going? I'll write more in the morning when I'm revived.— *Always, Anne*

Chapter 7

To Teach or Not

CHEMO IS CHEMO, Noah thinks. He would like to visit Anne, see her home and the town of Pearl, and go sailing with her. *And yes, I am jealous of the priest and the old woman and the camaraderie the three of them have.* He envies their seeming freedom and fearlessness. Because they are single, they can sail into the ocean, unconcerned even for their own safety. He wonders if Logan is aware of what she's doing—even of where she is. He wonders if her brother Earl knows she's in the water without him.

By mutual agreement, Noah and Elizabeth's oncologist have only discussed the first phase of treatment with her. If she knew the full regimen, she probably wouldn't submit to it. Surprisingly, she doesn't even ask. Noah is already exhausted from watching her physical and emotional rollercoaster rides. The induction chemotherapy is intense and will last a month. The second phase, the consolidation therapy, is also intense and lasts four to eight months. Then there is a third, and possibly a fourth phase, unless or until there is remission, and all her leukemia cells are destroyed.

The bad days are miserable and simply survived while the better days are, comparatively speaking, good. Noah and Elizabeth resolved to make up for the last two years by making the most of those good days. They feast on rich foods and each other. When she is suffering, he makes chicken soup, poached eggs, whatever she can tolerate, and then he sleeps in the guest room to avoid disturbing her.

Noah also loses weight. When they go for her chemo treatment, people see his thinness and shaved head and for a moment assume they are both sick. But one look in his eyes tells them the truth. Other healthy partners seek his company, as if they share a kinship. One woman even suggests he call her after her husband is gone. He begins wearing sunglasses and bringing a newspaper to further hide behind. He feels like a spy.

Noah is in the guest room now, reading Anne's latest email about her sailing adventures. He writes back, telling her how he has started a running regimen early each morning before the heat and humidity of summer in Durham drive him inside. It not only tones his muscles and strengthens him physically; it also clears his mind and infuses him with the energy to face each day. He began with one mile; now he's up to five.

Alone, he thinks about Anne's life, how purposeful and how rewarding it sounds. He feels guilt over the wish that he could share in it. His passion is wrapped tightly around Elizabeth. So it isn't a sexual longing. He doesn't want Anne, but her stories make him feel part of a long enduring friendship. He admires her objectivity about herself—her willingness to expose her own weaknesses and bad choices in life and to take responsibility for them. In spite of her self-deprecation, which could lead to self-pity and bitterness, she is instead resilient and upbeat.

No, he simply wants her company, and he wants a break from his life.

"Noah," Elizabeth calls and then comes to his door. He guiltily closes his laptop. "I can't sleep. How about a story?" She looks at the computer and sighs. "I'll meet you in the great room."

Noah joins her, bringing the journal and the object, and sits at the foot of the chaise. Josh no longer appears unbidden, so Noah purposefully imagines him on the floor, reading his own book, leaning against the leg of the chaise.

It's a chemo transition evening, somewhere between good and bad. Elizabeth doesn't bother to cover her head at home, and Noah has learned to love the sleek contours of her head and the focus it gives to her great profile and her beautiful eyes—eyes that look less sad and less angry than before.

The object is a small figurine of a girl and a younger boy sitting on a bench with a book. Noah hands it to Elizabeth. "I wonder," she says, "is she reading to the boy or is she teaching him to read?" Her perceptive question is quickly answered.

To Teach or Not to Teach

The object is a gift from the cast of a play I directed. The play was *Steal Away Home*. It's a children's play, about two young brothers escaping slavery. Among the many people they meet on the Underground Railroad is Will, a boy who teaches the older brother to read. Because we had no white boys audition for a role, I asked Greer (then ten years old) to play Will. I didn't realize how thoroughly feminine she was until I saw her trying to walk, talk, and gesture like a boy. So we changed Will to Willamina. Thus, a figurine of a young girl teaching a boy to read was the perfect representation of the production and the perfect gift to the director. It also represents my life and finally chosen career.

A Korean friend of mine once told me that I am a blessed person. In his culture, this title is given to one who loves his work. Considering the number of hours, days, and years of our lifetime we spend working, I think it is an appropriate sentiment. One who loves his work *is* blessed.

I never wanted to teach. I never even considered it as a career choice. Years after I became a professor in higher education, I looked back at my life and realized I had been teaching since I was a child. I used to gather neighborhood children and put on shows for our parents. They were invariably variety shows, using the talents of each child. For those without a performance skill, I would create an act that usually included acrobatics or recitations which I taught them. Even then, I was the enabler, not the performer.

I have held several non-teaching positions, but during each of them, I somehow became the teacher, writing manuals or leading workshops. I even wrote a textbook for a training program I was in because the instructors were inadequate, and there was no text. After college, I went to graduate school because the opportunity was there, and I didn't know what to do with my degree in speech and theatre. I was never comfortable on stage, but I have always loved the production process—seeing the various aspects of a play being developed, then pulled together for technical rehearsals, and finally presented to a live audience.

During the last summer of graduate school, my undergraduate professor, asked me to teach two summer classes while he took a play on tour. I agreed because I needed the money. So I taught the classes and discovered the calling I wouldn't acknowledge for years. Before this, teaching had always been incidental to something else, a means to an end. That hot summer, in a classroom without air conditioning, I found that teaching about the theatre was the most satisfying experience of my life. I didn't feel the hook, but it was set.

Like many young people at that time, I had planned to work my way around the world with a friend before settling down to a real job. But the friend backed out at the last minute, and I wasn't brave enough to go it alone. My professor returned from tour and found that his colleague was resigning and moving to California. After receiving good reviews from my summer students, he offered me a one-year contract. My travel plans had crashed, so I agreed.

During the second semester, I applied to the Peace Corp, took the language exam, and was accepted. Unfortunately, I had developed a chronic ulcer problem, and my doctor refused to sign a medical form. I was offered another contract. Once again, I gratefully agreed . . . for one more year. That fall I met Robert and stopped trying to leave. I never intended to teach, but I spent over half my life doing it professionally, and all of my life doing it—in one way or another.

One day, at the end of my last year, as I was cleaning out my desk, I received an email from the School of Education asking me to make a list of students who graduated in the last five years with a degree in the Theatre Education Program.

Unable to remember the names requested, I looked through my grade books at class roles for the previous five years. It was a difficult journey. All the names were familiar; some brought faces to my memory, and some brought personalities and relationships, some joyful and some sad.

When I was through and had emailed the names, I knew that I wanted to go back and read through all the grade books, beginning with the first year. So I bought a Diet Coke from the machine in the lobby and sat down at my desk. Tears ran freely as I scanned the pages. Many images and memories blossomed in my mind, but some stood out from the rest.

During my first years, Abraham, James, and Samuel worked on scenery, lights, and even silk-screening the posters for the productions. One afternoon, we had worked through lunch to complete some part of the scenery before the evening's rehearsal. I had brought a carrot cake for the printmaking instructor to thank him for helping us print what would be the first of many poster designs. He had already left for the day, so I brought the cake, a knife, and some paper towels into the theatre. We all sat in a circle on the stage floor, breaking the no food or drink rule, and ate the entire cake. At some point, James ran across the street to a small grocery and bought a quart of milk. We had no glasses, so we just opened the carton and passed it around. It was an initiation ceremony that made me feel the beginning of acceptance by this wonderful culture.

I was lecturing in my Drama Appreciation class one day when I heard someone in the hall screaming, "Stop him! Get him!" Samuel and James were sitting near the back of the classroom. When they saw me run through the door at the front of the room, they jumped up and ran through the door at the back. Everyone else remained seated. The hall circled the theatre that was in the center of the building. They ran one direction; I ran the other. We met at the front of the theatre, following the sounds of the desperate screams. Outside, a woman had fallen. I went to her while Samuel and James chased her assailant. Another faculty member, coming from the opposite direction, helped catch the fleeing offender and escorted him back to our building, handing him over to a security officer.

The victim had broken the heel of her shoe in pursuit of the young man who had not attacked her or snatched her purse, but had peeked under the stall in the women's bathroom and stolen her dignity. If she had caught him, she would have avenged her loss. She hobbled away, following the security officer and the lucky peeper—lucky because she didn't catch him. We returned to the classroom to find fifty students, quietly waiting. I continued the lecture from where it had been interrupted, grateful I had not led Samuel and James into harm. And now, considering the school violence of recent years, I am even more grateful.

I saw another name that brought a special memory. It was Avery, a student who went to jail for drug dealing. I saw him once after he was released and then never saw or heard from him again. The first time I saw him, he was in an acting class in the front lobby, blindfolded. It was an exercise on sense memory. The instructor motioned to me to come over and put Avery's hands on my shoulders. He asked, "Who is it?"

Avery, said, "Well, your shoulders are not large and you're not tall. I'm guessing you're female." His hands released my shoulders and paused for a moment in air.

The instructor quickly inserted, "No touching below the shoulders." Onlookers had collected, and all laughed. He touched my neck, felt of my necklace, and then the back of his hand brushed my long hair worn down that day. He stroked it and then crushed some of it in his hand as a slow white smile widened on his dark face.

"I know you," he said. "You're that redhead. You paint scenery." Everyone laughed again.

I punched him lightly and said, "Right. So when are you going to come help me?"

This time, he laughed and said, "I'm an actor," as if that distinction released him from manual labor. I wish we had both known then what his future would be. Perhaps I could have diverted his path through some healthy backstage assignments. I hope he learned from his choices and has made a good life for himself. More realistically, I simply hope he's alive.

Another name that made me pause was Tamona. She had been a student with little interest in her education. She came to my office once with a black eye covered by sunglasses and, after swearing me to secrecy, told me about her boyfriend. I advised her to go to the police or to tell her mother, who happened to be a bail bondsman. Tamona was afraid of her boyfriend and had no faith in the legal system. I felt frustrated by my promise of secrecy, but a few days later, a friend of hers called her mother who immediately took care of the problem. Her mother was scarier than the law and certainly more effective.

The following spring, Tamona was helping me on scenery one day and confided what I already knew. She was pregnant and afraid to tell her mother. Looking forward to being a grandmother myself, and knowing that many of my students were unmarried mothers, I encouraged her to have faith in her own mother's understanding. She came to summer school and told me the pregnancy was terminated. She said her mother wanted her to have a career, not be tied down by the needs of a child without the help of a husband. Once again, it's hard to stand in someone else's shoes and understand their choices. I wasn't sure whether to feel sad or glad for her.

The next year, when she was a senior, she called me at home one night around ten o'clock. She was crying, and between sobs, told me that she was sick and in pain. I knew she was pregnant again. I asked where she lived and then drove to her apartment and brought her to my home where she spent the next several days, resting and eating chicken soup.

"Ah, chicken soup!" Noah interjects. Elizabeth kicks him in an unspoken demand to continue.

I couldn't make the nausea go away, but she was comforted by the company and the mothering. She said her boyfriend wanted to marry her. I asked if she wanted to marry him. She said, "No!" We spent hours talking. She said it was her third pregnancy and she didn't want another abortion. So I encouraged her to keep the baby. She went home for the Christmas holidays and came back with an empty womb.

That spring, she decided to focus on her studies because she realized she was about to complete her curriculum while learning as little as possible. She became my apprentice and my shadow, soaking up every bit of information and every skill she could in the time she had left. She was my assistant designer for two productions and took the full responsibility of mounting the scenery for an unscheduled third production. I never heard from her after graduation.

Of course there were negative experiences—students that cursed me in class, or in the hallway, or in my office. One student, angry about his grade, screamed obscenities at me across the street in the middle of campus and then later set fire to my office door, where the offending grade was posted. Some wanted me for their mother; some wanted me dead. A few of the hostile students eventually became my friends.

One morning when I was monitoring an exam, I looked at the bent heads in my large Arts and Humanities class. They all seemed so intense and beautiful. I suddenly felt a great warmth and affection for each of these young people with such possibilities but so many dangers.

After Logan and I ended our relationship, the classroom and even stage work lost their appeal. So I began inquiring about retirement.

Sometimes I lay awake at night remembering all the things I did wrong—every time I was unnecessarily critical or judgmental and every time I abused my position as a role model. I was always proud of my profession, but I wasn't always proud of myself. I can only hope that I never did significant harm to any student's self-image or limited any student's professional growth. I wasn't as aware of the awesome responsibilities of teaching when I began as I am now that I'm through.

I didn't mean to go on so long about teaching, but it has helped me understand something that I have thought about a lot. A friend once asked if I believed we are destined to do the work that we do, or if it is all by choice or chance. I couldn't answer. I know that I never planned to teach; I tried to do other things, but always found myself teaching, with or without a classroom. So it seems that, for me at least, my work was my destiny.

Elizabeth stretches. *And now I know who Anne Gray really is—or was—she's Anne Marshall. I knew her writing style was familiar. I wonder if Noah knows, and why he didn't tell me. I'll have to think about that.* "Well, she posed a good question. I wonder if we all ultimately do what we were intended or fated to do. I always knew that I wanted to do something related to literature, because I loved to read. My mother used to call me a bookworm and forced me to go outside and play. But I was also shy, and I think I used books as an escape and a protection from the frightening world of real people and real life."

"Listen to the non-believer talk about fate. Funny, though, I never saw you as shy," Noah says as he replaces the carved readers on the bookshelf. "I always thought of you as strong and independent."

"That was forced bravado that kept people at a distance, unable to see the fear."

"Maybe we'll look back on this experience one day as a blessing." Noah takes her feet onto his lap and massages them.

"Hey, easy for you to say . . . Oh God, that feels good."

"I think it has given us time to reevaluate our priorities. But most of all, it has allowed us to reconnect." Noah pauses and continues softly, "I don't think I've ever loved you as much as I do now."

She takes his hands and pulls him toward her. He tries to gently lie above her on the narrow chaise, keeping his weight on his elbows. "Would you like to ravish me right here, Genghis Noah Khan?"

"Yes, Bookworm Girl, but it might be safer if we finish this fantasy in a real bed." He's not afraid of hurting himself; he's terrified of hurting the increasingly frail body beneath him. "Honesty time, Liz, do you really want to make love?"

"I honestly wish that I wanted to."

"It's been this way for a while, hasn't it?"

"It seemed so important to you, and I didn't want to let go of what we've found again."

Noah rises from the chaise and gathers her into his arms. As he carries her into the master bedroom, she pulls his face down and kisses him, trying to recapture the moment.

"It's okay, Liz. I can wait."

Later, in the guest room, he opens his laptop and wishes Anne was there to talk to.

EMAIL TO ANNE:

So, you think you're through teaching? Last I heard, you were teaching stone masonry to a crew of unskilled laborers. There's also some learning going on in the old Queen Bess that you continue to influence. You're a good person, Professor Gray. I suspect your successes far outweigh your failures. Sleep well.—*Noah*

Chapter 8

Sissy

AFTER A DINNER OF broiled flounder, Anne and Paul sit at his kitchen table, relaxing with a glass of wine. "Tell me about Marjorie." Anne speaks tentatively, knowing she may be treading on private soil. "At first she seems like 'what you see is what you get'. But the more time I spend with her, the more I appreciate her and the more complex I've begun to realize she is. I know her husband died years ago and that he was a semi-prosperous clothing retailer in Pearl and Shallotte. They had two stores and one daughter who died when she was a teenager."

Paul leans forward in his chair, looking incredulous. "That's what she told you?"

"That's what I deduced. There's a room covered with dust and there are Barbie dolls on a high shelf where a young teenager might have put them. A woman would have packed them away. She doesn't talk about it. I don't want to pry, but she has seemed depressed lately. She's always talking or muttering to God. Or as she calls Him, His Honor the Judge. I sense emptiness in that frail body, an emptiness that keeps her feet about three inches off the ground. I worry she'll blow away when we're on her boat."

"Ha! Marjorie has her feet on the ground more than any of us, even more than you, who pretends to be totally together. By the way, you do that very well."

"And you seem to carry a burden that would break an ordinary person's back. Your feet can't possibly get off the ground. I know why you sail. The boat takes the weight from you. If you were a man overboard, you'd sink straight to the bottom and I'd have to jump in and probably drown trying to save you."

"Especially if the boat sailed away while you were in the water 'saving me'. Anne, promise you won't do that. Is that your last glass of wine?"

Anne gets up and rinses her glass in the sink, then turns to Paul. "It's my only glass of wine. I know my limits."

"You can't drink?"

"Oh, I can. I just don't remember much about it."

"You have black-outs?"

"Unfortunately, or maybe it's fortunately. There are some humiliations I probably don't want to remember."

"Did you join AA.?"

"No, I got a divorce." She walks back to her chair and sits. "That and some self-analysis and close friends took care of my need to drink. I was never a continuous drinker like my mother. Near the end, she drank a fifth of vodka a day, beginning when she got up in the morning. Her early death became a warning to me. I only drink after dark, not every night, never alone, and never to excess. As long as I limit myself to one drink or one glass of wine, I'm fine. If I allow myself to be talked into one more, and then just one more, I forget to stop. That hasn't happened in a while. However, you have managed to get me to talk about myself again. What about Marjorie?"

Paul takes a deep breath and looks at Anne as if making a decision. "I was there."

"Where?"

"It was our senior trip at the end of high school. We were going to graduate in one week. We went to Linville Falls, in the mountains."

"I know the place."

He pauses before continuing his story and refills his wine glass. The look on his face tells her he's not sure he wants to open this door, but he begins. "Our senior class was small. We had separated into several groups on our hike into the gorge. There are overlooks that extend out to afford a special view. Each has a short wall, built to protect hikers from falling over the precipice. Being kids, we were all over the walls, taking pictures or posing for them." Anne can't breathe. She fears she already knows what he's going to tell her.

"Sissy had studied photography every year in high school. She was the photographer for the yearbook. She even submitted pictures for the local newspapers and competitions, and often had them published. She was very talented, very smart, and very pretty. She wanted to be a photojournalist. Anyway, she stood on the wall— like every other kid in our class had done—and leaned out to catch a shot of a friend hanging from the limb of a tree." While he talks, Paul folds a paper napkin like an accordion, then smoothes it out and folds it again—each time into thinner, tighter folds.

"Everyone says they don't know how they survived their childhood because of all the dangerous, stupid things they did. Some of us didn't; some of us were simply lucky, or maybe God intervened to save us for another purpose." He pauses, takes a sip of wine and continues. "Anyway, Sissy took the picture, then turned her head. It was enough to unbalance her, and she fell. There were no cell phones then. While some went for help, three of us climbed down to where she had fallen. Rescuers arrived. They did what they could for her and then assisted in an airlift to transport her to a hospital in Asheville."

"Dear God. She survived?"

He balls-up the napkin and tosses it into a wastebasket. "A tree branch broke her fall and her leg. More branches and then rocks tore and scraped her face. I made a tourniquet for her leg which was a compound fracture and bleeding badly, and I tried to cover the open wounds on her face."

"But, I thought you were telling me about her death. Sorry, I don't mean to sound casual about a broken leg and face wounds."

"It wasn't the end of her life, just the end of her life here. The leg was bad. There were many surgical procedures, and she refused plastic surgery on her face. It was also an end to the Sissy I knew. More than her body was broken. When she left the hospital, she went to college in a distant city and stayed with relatives.

"For Marjorie, it was another in a series of losses. They rarely saw each other. But oddly, it was the beginning of our friend's recovery. She had spent so many years inside her head, talking to the dead in her family." Paul pauses while memories rush through him. "Anyway, Sissy's accident brought Marjorie back to reality. The teacher who was with us when the accident happened told her about it. She said a noise from behind startled Sissy and caused her to lose her balance."

"Is that what happened?"

"Not exactly. I didn't like Sissy being up there on the wall, leaning over so far. I reached up to hold on to her. Maybe she saw my hand in her peripheral vision and turned to me. She looked away when she lost her balance."

His hands are on the table, this time picking up a pencil and then putting it down, over and over, making a rhythm of tension. Anne wants to cover his hands and stop the sound, but she controls the urge and slowly sits back in her chair. "I'm so sorry, Paul. Did the teacher tell Marjorie that you made the noise that unbalanced her?"

"Yes."

"I'm speechless."

He smiles with contradictory sadness. "So was I, for a long time. I couldn't talk to anyone. Silence has always been an escape for me."

Anne starts to speak and stops. *And was the priesthood also an escape?*

"After graduation, I went into the army and was shipped to Vietnam. While there, I was able to talk to my confessor. I have replayed it in my mind a million times, but never out loud, until just now. You seemed to know what I was going to say before I said it."

"Just intuition. Marjorie doesn't talk about her. And apparently she understood and didn't blame you. She obviously thinks the world of you."

Anne grabs the annoying pencil when Paul reaches for his wine. "We have a tenuous peace, Marjorie and I. We don't discuss Sissy. When we race our sailboats, always her idea, by the way, I'm a little unsure of what is driving her to beat me, but I always let her win. Of course you are now sworn to secrecy about that little detail."

"No problem. What happened to the teacher?"

"She died last year. Originally, she might have reported exactly what she believed happened or wanted to believe."

"But she didn't have to put the blame on you, an eighteen-year-old kid."

"After I returned here as a priest, she came to me and asked for my forgiveness, which I gave. I knew that as the adult in charge, she just wanted the blame to go to someone specific so that she would not be considered negligent."

"She was negligent, letting kids stand on dangerous precipices."

"Actually, she wasn't even there. She walked up just as Sissy fell."

"Then she was certainly negligent." Anne pauses as a realization comes to her. "Paul, did her arrival cause the sound that made Sissy turn her head and lose her balance?"

"I honestly don't know. But she thought that maybe it did, and she carried that burden for twenty-five years. I told her it was my fault. There was, after all, no need in both of us feeling guilty."

"But you weren't guilty."

"I failed Sissy before she ever got on that wall, Anne. We take risks for reasons. We dare God to take us. Anyway, I have worked at forgiving myself and accepting what I can't change. Maybe I'll be granted understanding one day."

Sure that she knows the answer, Anne asks anyway. "So, is Sissy still living?"

"I'm surprised you haven't noticed her gravestone. Her given name was Sarah."

"I have seen a marker with Sarah on it. No last name, no dates. Why is that?"

"I placed the marker there when I returned to Pearl five years ago. She had been cremated and the ashes scattered on the river. The stone simply gave me closure."

Anne decides against asking more. *He placed the marker when he moved back here. I don't understand, and maybe I don't want to.*

"After her fall, she refused to see me in the hospital, and after she was released, Marjorie refused to tell me where she was. Since the passing of her husband, Marjorie had been in a deep depression. As I said before, I think Sissy's accident brought her back into the world, but her daughter never came home, at least not while I was here.

"Is that why Marjorie calls God 'Your Honor'? Does she think her husband's and daughter's deaths were some kind of judgment on her?"

"Perhaps. But she called Him Your Honor before they died. She had lost several baby boys before a daughter was born and lived beyond infancy. She seems stable, but she's emotionally fragile. Be careful about pushing her."

"I will. Her story gets more and more tragic. But I never bought into the notion about God's will. It's like blaming Him for everything that goes wrong."

"She's not blaming Him; she's blaming herself. She was so overwhelmed by John's death she was unaware of her grieving daughter. She thinks that if she'd taken better care of her husband, he wouldn't have died. And I believe she thinks if she had been more aware of her daughter's needs, she might have saved her."

"How could Marjorie's awareness have made a difference in what happened at Linville Falls?" She curses herself for encouraging him to tell her more. She doesn't want to know more. His pain and what he has already said is burden enough.

"It's a more complicated story than I've told you." He stands and stretches. She gratefully sees the change in his eyes. He's through looking back. "Let's go inspect your house, see what they finished today."

"Good idea. But one more question. Is this why you became a priest?"

"No."

As they walk to the construction site which was once his family home, Paul says, "I am pleased that you and Marjorie have struck up a real friendship. I've taken great pleasure in watching the two of you ride by on your bicycles. Your laughter carries all the way to the church, and lifts my own spirits. You're very good for her. I haven't seen her so lighthearted in years. And she's started wearing her hair in pigtails again. It makes her look a little less nuts than when it's flying around in a mass of curls." His voice falters.

"There's a black and white photograph at Marjorie's of a girl with blonde braids. I assumed it was Sissy."

"I know the picture. It's Marjorie. They were look-alikes, except Sissy's features were a little rounder and softer, and her hair was straight while Marjorie's curled. That's why they wore the braids. It made them look more alike. And when they took their braids out, their hair was wavy. That was when they were prettiest. John was so proud and protective of the two of them. Marjorie was very feminine, and very stylish, and kept a perfect house. I had a little crush on her when I first came to Pearl."

"No Fear Marjorie, feminine and a good housekeeper? That's hard to imagine."

"I know. But she was also reclusive then, rarely left the house. Now, she's rarely in her house. Her garden and boat don't leave much time for dusting and cleaning. She never sailed until she lost her family. The *Peli* belonged to Sissy. John built it for her."

"I guess being alone has toughened Marjorie," Anne says, wondering if it has had the same effect on her. "Have you seen her latest t-shirt? It says, in very bold letters, 'The Meek Shall Inherit Nothing'!" They both laugh until tears come.

"Gracias, Anna, I needed your humor. You know Marjorie goes to church every time there's a service, but she's a bit irreverent, in her own charming way."

Anne feels her whole body clench and then release, as it always does when he calls her Anna. Just then, the buff puppy arrives and licks Anne's hand and pushes against her leg with his paw as if he wants her attention. He whines softly. She bends down to pet him. "My, you're growing. What's your name?"

"Juan calls him Tio."

"Do you mean the Juan on my stone-wall crew? And doesn't tio mean uncle?"

"Yes. Juan's Uncle Hosea died a few months ago, before Tio was born. Maybe he calls him that because he misses his uncle; or hopes he's Hosea's reincarnation."

"I can understand that. He does always seem like an old soul, always trying to express something. And he is so affectionate. Was his uncle a lecherous old man?"

"No, he was young. But he did like the girls."

"And I like you, Tio. Tell Juan if he gets tired of you, you can come live with me." Tio barks, and they both laugh. As they continue the walk to her home, Tio follows and Anne updates Paul on the construction. "I begin painting tomorrow. Carlos is loaning two of his crew to help me while the rest pour concrete in the foundations for the adjoining townhouses. Did you see the modifications in the floor plans? No, I'm sure you didn't. You were out of town at your Catholic thing when we made the changes. They are now two-story and upside-down."

"What?"

"That means the bedrooms are on the lower floor and the living spaces are above. The entrance is raised and has two short staircases: one goes down to the bedrooms; and the other goes up to the living room, dining room, and kitchen. And there are French doors in the dining area that open to the deck over the carport."

"And you made them upside-down because?"

"It improves the view for the main living spaces, and of course is a better entrance to the deck above the carport. A lot of houses on beach property are built that way."

"It's an adjustment in thinking, but I like it. When do you antici-pate moving in to your home? That's still right-side-up, isn't it?"

"This weekend. And, yes, it is still right-side-up. I won't have much furniture. Carlos's sister is reupholstering several pieces, and I'm refinishing the rest. I've had to give away or throw away very little."

"I hope you threw away the beds."

"I did. I bought a new one in Shallotte to be delivered on Satur-day. My kids are coming down the following weekend. So I'll have to get two more beds before they arrive and an air mattress for the children. We're celebrating Bradley and Ray's birthdays while they're here. You're invited."

"I look forward to meeting your family. Of course I'll come. If you want to serve fish, I'll be glad to provide you with fresh catch. I could also smoke some blue fish from the freezer."

"The smoked blues would be great for appetizers. But Bradley and Ray have already requested fried chicken for the main dish. I'm fa-mous for it. Joe, Summer's husband, has asked for macaroni and cheese, another famous dish; Tommy wants my biscuits. They're terrible, but he likes them. And Lindsay wants guacamole and crab dip. She'll eat anything if she has a sauce to put it in."

"And what about your girls?"

"They don't ask. They grew up somewhere along the way. They *bring* things. Greer will bring her famous cheesecake, and Summer will bring her famous banana pudding. Oh, and by the way, Sum-mer's expecting another baby."

"Congratulations! When is she due?"

"I don't know. She hasn't told me she's pregnant yet."

"I see . . . I guess. Well, anyway, it's nice to know that all the food (except for the terrible biscuits) will be famous. Who else have you invited?"

"Marjorie, of course. And I want to invite Celita and Carlos and his crew. What do you think?"

Paul laughs and says, "I think that's a lot of chicken. Were you go-ing to include their families?"

"Sure. Wait. How many are there?"

"Carlos and Celita live with their parents. Tomas has a wife and three children. Mano has a wife and two children. The other four are single."

"So that's seventeen, if they all come, plus my kids, you, Marjorie, and me. It's a total of . . . twenty-seven to thirty-one, if the single men bring dates. I love it. It's a party."

"You're serious?"

"Yes. Do you know where I can find a piñata?"

"I'll talk to Carlos. They'll bring the piñata and some food. They wouldn't dream of coming empty-handed. You just make lots of chicken and mac-n-cheese. The crew and I will add to the meal and to the desserts. And by the way, I think it's a wonderful idea."

As they enter Anne's new home and look around at the space, noting the minimal modifications downstairs and the refurbished brass and wrought iron fixtures, Paul says, "It's so clean. Did you hire a crew or clean it yourself?"

"I guess I'm still not used to hiring others to do my work, and I'm still afraid that I'll suddenly find I'm out of money, so I do everything I can. I scrubbed the walls and even the ceilings before I took a scraper to the floors."

"Except for the need for fresh paint, it looks like new, Anne."

"You obviously did a good job of renovating it after the hurricane. There was only a layer of grime everywhere. The big change was in raising the roof to build the loft for my studio and bedroom."

"Yes, that and the roof over the porch that's also a balcony. I've noticed that you seem to think that way. You design individual things that serve several purposes. That's a good skill."

"You're right, I do that—probably a result of my years as a scene designer with a modest budget."

"I haven't seen the balcony since they finished it. Can we go up?"

"Sure." Anne leads the way up the iron and wood spiral staircase to the loft where she shows him the large bathroom with a solid door and the closets that will have curtains.

Paul wanders out to the balcony and looks at the stunning view of the sunset over the water.

Click. Click. Click. Paul's profile in the foreground and the panoramic view in the background. Too bad my visual memory isn't wide-angle.

As if he could read her thoughts, Paul asks, "Do you paint waterscapes?"

"I will. Obviously, I can't live here and not try it."

"Will you do one for me?"

"I will, and I'll put you and your blue sailboat in it." She joins him on the balcony.

"That might spoil the image of what God made."

"You don't think God made you and your boat?"

"This isn't the proper ecclesiastical answer, but I made my boat, and I fervently believe that we all make who we are; God just gives us the opportunity."

"You aren't an ordinary priest, are you?"

"No, I've been called a renegade priest. I think chance brought you here and perhaps it is fate that you have stayed. But chance and fate aren't building the stone terraces or painting this house tomorrow. Anne Gray is." He pauses, and turns to her. "You have so much to give, Anne. Don't you miss being married?"

"Is this your idea of divine intervention?" She is stunned and irritated at his comment, but realizes that what she says doesn't make sense. And that adds to her anger. "Thanks for letting me know what I'm lacking. I'll just run down the street looking for yet another opportunity at emotional, financial, and physical devastation. And thanks for the lack of belief in me as an independent individual, but don't bother wishing a husband on me!" She sputters. "Marriage has not treated me well!" Anne turns to leave the balcony. Paul catches her arm.

"I'm sorry. I forgot that marriage is a word that pulls your trigger. You have proven that you can exist on your own, my friend. Many people can achieve a certain contentment based purely on the memories of a good love, one that gave joy and fulfillment. You have never had that." She loosens her arm and walks away from him. He follows. "What I was trying to say is that you would make the right man so very happy, and you deserve to have that same happiness returned. There is sensuality in you that tells me you still want this for yourself as well."

She whirls on him. "I don't know whether to be embarrassed or angry. Maybe angry isn't the right word. I don't like my frustrations held up like a sign in front of my face. I am aware they exist. I'm not sure the right man does."

"Forgive me, Anna. I know that I'm speaking much too personally. But I look at this house and I wish you had someone to share it."

Flustered, Anne pulls out a response even she didn't expect. "I've only met three men who appealed to the sensuous part of me in the last I-don't-know-how-many years. And they're all married. The first to his bicycle." *I didn't mean to mention him.* "The second to his wife." *I shouldn't mention him either.* "And the third to the Catholic Church." *Good, I made him blush.* Paul pushes his glasses up and keeps his hand there, between his eyes, masking his own expression. Anne realizes that she has possibly said too much.

Timidly, she continues. "Anyway, I'll settle for friendship. Two failures at marriage have made me gun-shy, and that's probably good. Friendships don't carry nearly the amount of baggage as husbands. And friendships can be just as fulfilling, in a non-sensuous way."

"I can't imagine you settling for anything, Anna, but I do treasure your friendship." Paul takes her hand and turns it over in his own. He runs a finger over the calluses worn there by mortar and stone. "These little hands do so much." He turns her hand again and traces the protruding bones and veins. Anne's face warms, this time in shame for her ugly hands. "They speak so clearly of the woman you are. They should be painted, or at least photographed."

Shame is replaced by another warmth, one that spreads from her head down to her knees. "Give me back my hand, or I'll forget you're a priest. You win. I do want more, but not now."

They walk down the stairs and out the door in silence. At Anne's car, she turns to Paul. "So, since you brought up the subject of sensual needs, what do priests do to keep their vow of chastity or denial or whatever it's called?"

Paul shakes his head. "You do say exactly what you think." He leans against her car. "When I was in the military and when I was in college, I tried very hard to find someone to fill the emptiness in my life. It never lasted. And sex without love is just exercise, pretty good exercise, but not a replacement for love. I've never agreed with the church's stand on celibacy for priests and nuns. I also don't agree with the ban on birth control or the concept that lovemaking should be reserved only for procreation. I think it flies in the face of human nature. Most Catholics ignore both. And, as the media likes to point out, many priests do not live up to their vows. I just take each day as a gift and hope I get through it without completely screwing up."

Noah reminded me I am a woman, and you remind me that I do indeed want more. Naturally, more is not yours to give. Aloud, she says, "I know you are a man as well as a priest, and I am a woman as well as a friend. Can we continue this casual closeness without screwing up?"

"Do you want to?"

"Yes. I don't want to burden you or scare you, Paul, but you are one of the main reasons I'm here, and I don't want to lose whatever this is that we have."

Anne arrives at Marjorie's home to find her friend reading at her desk. Anne sits in a chair near her. "I just left Paul. We sailed again today, and then he made me some broiled fish. I hope you got the message that I wouldn't be here for dinner."

Marjorie notes that Anne did not say Father Paul, and so she reminds her, "He's a priest, you know."

"I know. He's also a man." *I hate secrets. I won't keep any that I don't have to.* "He told me about Sissy."

"Naw!!! He never talks about her! What did he tell you?"

137

"He told me about her fall and how it changed all three of your lives."

"We don't talk about it. If we got started, we'd say a heap more'n we should. Sorry, I've been down lately. As my momma used to say, I'm so far down, I'm sittin' on the bottom with my feet hangin' off."

"What's wrong?"

"It's the birthday of someone I can't even send a card to."

Assuming she is talking about Sissy or her long dead husband, and not wanting to encourage more confidences, or more pain for herself through empathy, Anne changes the subject. "What happened to your husband's stores? Was he leasing or did he own the property?"

Marjorie moves from her desk to a rocker and relaxes a little. "We owned 'em. After he died, I found out the profits from the store in Shallotte had supported the store here for a long time. Before John's heart attack, the store in Shallotte was failin' too. The doctor said it probably added to John's stress. It turned out he'd had a bad heart all along. We just didn't know it. His daddy died young, too.

"Anyway, I sold the shop in Shallotte to pay the bills. John's family had always been land rich but money poor. Nobody wanted to buy the store here, so I sold some of the property people did want—river land. It used to belong to John's family. Along with his life insurance, the land sales provided enough income to keep Sissy and me goin'. I wanted to make somethin' of the business here, but I was so depressed, I just let everythin' go, includin' my girl."

"What do you mean?" *Go ahead; get it over with! This must be a gut-spilling day.*

"One day she just up an' got gone. No one knew where she was, not even Paul, who had been her boyfriend since she was twelve." Anne's mouth falls open. "They split after spring break. He kept callin', but she wouldn't talk to him. Then she up an' disappeared. After a few days, she telephoned me, said she was all right, just needed some time to work things out. She said she'd come home when she was ready and not to look for her or she'd never come home."

"How old was she?" *Paul and Sissy were a couple?*

"Sixteen, goin' on thirty."

"How long was she gone?"

"Four months. She come back at the end of summer. She was real smart, so they let her make up the work she missed, and she started the new school year a senior. By Thanksgivin', they were datin' again."

"Did you approve?" *Of course not. Paul and Sissy were in love?*

"When they were little, I didn't think much about it. I thought it would blow over. When they started maturin' and were still together, I wasn't so sure. John didn't like it. He was afraid Paul, bein' Mexican, would have less opportunities in life and would hold Sissy back. Keep her from livin' her own dream. They seemed too young to be in love, but it was clear they were. I thought she run away because they broke up. I should'a guessed. I hadn't paid attention to her for a long time 'cause of my own grief. When she come back, I tried to keep her away from him. But you know how it is. Love's strong. Stronger'n anythin' in the world."

"So there was a baby?" Anne asks, still overwhelmed by the revelation, but resigned to hearing the whole story.

"I didn't say nothin' about a baby! Why do you say that?" Marjorie demands, an edge to her voice.

"Sorry, I didn't mean to upset you."

"I'm not!" Marjorie stands, straightening her No Fear t-shirt, as if to remind Anne or herself of something.

After a moment, Anne continues, softly. "Believe me, I'm not trying to pry, Marjorie. It just seemed like maybe you wanted to tell me. I have a kind of sixth sense about babies."

"Well, you're right!" She sits as all her gusto dissipates. "And you're the only soul in the world that knows this. You can't tell anyone, especially Paul."

Oh God, another secret. "He doesn't know?" No answer. "Did she have an abortion, Marjorie?"

"Naw. She become a Catholic because Paul was a Catholic. So she couldn't get an abortion. She had the baby and give it up for adoption."

"So she told you?"

"Not at first. But a mother knows. After she healed from the fall and then left, I had to do somethin' to keep from goin' crazy—again. So I found the place she run away to that spring. It was a home for unwed mothers in Raleigh. Course they wouldn't tell me nothin'."

"Later, I found Sissy's diary. Everythin' was in it. She run away 'cause she knew Paul would want to marry her and she thought his life would be ruined. He had such ambitions in those days, and he was so smart. She thought he and the baby would have a better chance at life if she'd give 'em up."

"Both of them?"

"She didn't think he would ever forgive her. She didn't credit him. When they started datin' again, she wouldn't see him alone for a long time. They dated in groups and she came home early. He was studyin' hard to get into college and he accepted her rules."

"You mean no intimacy?"

"Yes. I thought he was so glad to get her back that he agreed to whatever she asked, assumin' they would eventually marry and belong to each other."

"You thought?"

"Yeah. I didn't read the diary all at once. It was too painful. One night I had some wine to give me courage, and I read the rest of it. Just before Christmas that year, Paul came to her with a plan for them to marry after two years in college. He had it all worked out, part-time jobs and everythin'. She couldn't let him plan their future until she told him about the baby. She was afraid that if he ever learned the truth from someone else, he would leave her."

"How did Paul take it?" Anne asks, wanting to understand her friend, both friends.

"He cried. She wrote in her diary that he cried like a baby and kept askin' her to forgive him. And he cried for his son. She made him promise to never make contact with the boy. I remember it was just before Christmas because that was when her diary ended. It was one of them five-year diaries. She never wrote anythin' else."

Tears spring to Anne's eyes. She opens her mouth to speak and then closes it. *People don't write their thoughts every night for five years and then just quit. Stop, Anne. Some things should remain private. You're just here to listen.* And so she listens, overwhelmed. This story was suddenly too real and immediate—not just something from someone's past.

"So it was a boy, and Paul knows." *And I know why he didn't tell me. He wouldn't burden me with his sorrow or this long protected secret. And maybe he knew I would have held him. He's far too brittle to be held.* "So why did you ask me not to tell him if he already knows?"

"Because he might try to bind me to his promise—keep me from tryin' to find my grandson."

"Your grandson must be nearly thirty years old now. Is that why you're sad? Is today his birthday?"

"It is to me. I tried to guess when he was born by when she come home. I wish I knew somethin' about him, the kind of man he become. I understand that adopted kids can look up their real parents, but not the opposite."

"Actually, I'm not sure about the rules, but I believe the parents' privacy is protected as well. I think they have to let it be known that they are open to being contacted. I imagine there's a website for initiating this."

"I wouldn't know a website from a homesite."

"Does Paul know that you know about the baby?"

"Naw. By the time I found out the truth, he was in Vietnam. Then he become a priest, and I didn't want to interfere with his life. When he come back here, to Saint Angelica's, I just waited to see if he would bring it up, stupid old woman that I am. Of course he won't. He probably thinks he's protectin' me from the truth. And how would his church flock feel about him havin' a illegitimate son? So I haven't brought it up. I just race him in my sailboat and wait for him to get the courage to tell me I have a grandson. In a way, I guess it keeps me goin'."

They sit in silence for a while, Anne's mind reeling as she remembers Paul's words about the memory of a good love and about trying to fill an emptiness, an emptiness that grows within her as she grasps the meanings of all he had said that evening.

"Maybe you could do that website thing and let my grandson know that I'm willin' to be contacted."

Anne goes to her friend, kneels beside her chair, and hugs her.

"You know what?" Marjorie's smile begins and grows. "I think that maybe His Honor sent you to me. I was so sad, and now I could dance a jig."

"But can you shag?"

"You bet your butt I can."

Anne goes to her newly purchased CD player, puts in her favorite beach music, and turns to behold the Marjorie she never knew existed. *Oh for a video camera. Look at you, you miracle of life, out-dancing the dancer.*

As Anne prepares for bed, she thinks about this evening of revelations. She wonders how Paul can resist the desire to find his son. *Is he simply trying to keep the promise he made Sissy so many years ago? And what was all that crap about me needing a husband? I DON'T!!! I just need someone like him. But what does he need? Certainly not me and my world of baggage, even if he were free of his vows. Well, he did love, and he still does, and there is no freedom for him.*

EMAIL TO NOAH:

Sometimes I take men for granted. I expect too much toughness, too much strength. Sometimes, like tonight, I am reminded that your sex is perhaps more vulnerable than mine, and I am ashamed of the many times I have said and done insensitive things to any one of you. Please forgive.—*Always, Anne*

Chapter 9

Wednesdays with Nana

"DO YOU FEEL LIKE a story tonight?"

"It doesn't matter, Noah. I'm too weak to move, and I'm bored with television. Food tastes like crap. I don't have the energy, mentally or physically, to participate in anything short of sleep. But if I fall asleep now, I'll wake-up at midnight. It's strange, but what I've been missing lately is the feeling of satisfaction you get when you're dog-tired—tired from hard physical labor. Tired but with a sense of accomplishment, like when you clean the house, or create a garden, or take a long hike." She pauses to laboriously push herself into a more erect sitting position. Noah hands her a silk wrap which she drapes around her head and shoulders. Her skin has become overly sensitive to anything coarser or warmer than silk. Physically adjusted, she gazes through the large window at the lake and sighs, accepting the moment. "All right, read me a story. Where's the object?"

"The object is this little journal. It's titled *Wednesdays with Nana*." Noah hands the small black spiral bound book to Elizabeth who simply lets it lay in her lap as she continues to stare across the water to the trees and then up to the sky. Noah's eyes darken with concern before he lowers them to read from Anne's book.

Before he can begin, she rolls her eyes at the little journal. "I hope it isn't like *Tuesdays with Morey*. Not up for that."

WEDNESDAYS WITH NANA

When Summer went into labor with Lindsay, her husband Joe called me to come to the hospital. It was late, close to midnight. I stood outside the labor room in the quiet Women's Clinic, awaiting word of her progress. I was surprised when Joe invited me into her room.

Summer had received pain medication and was smiling in relief and gratitude for respite from the discomfort of contractions that were coming hard and regularly. I held her hand and kissed her cheek. Joe, the ex-Marine and ex-football player, was pacing the room with enough energy for everyone. The doctor, a young attractive East Indian, swept in, as though he had just left one battle and was ready for another. He sat in a chair at Summer's feet which were already in stirrups.

"Aren't you impressed?" the nurse asked.

"I'm very impressed. It looks like you're about to have a baby. I think we're ready to push on the next contraction."

I watched my own baby, grown to womanhood, take on the role of birthing with all the instincts and fervor of a lioness. I was sent to the foot of the bed where I would have a good view. Only a very strong willpower (Summer's) kept me there. I wanted to go back to holding her hand, but the nurse was on one side of her, and Joe was on the other. Every time I tried to move away from this frightening view, Summer told me to stay at her feet where I could see. So I did. And I saw.

As Lindsay's face emerged, that's all I saw. I knew she was a girl because Joe kept saying, "It's a girl; we got our girl." I just continued to stare at that beautiful, peaceful face. I will never forget that moment.

Two months later, when my other daughter's second son was born, I wasn't able to be in the room because I was taking care of his older brother, Bradley. When Ray called, we rushed to the hospital and Ray lifted Bradley up to look at his new sibling through the nursery window. Ray said, "Who's that, Bradley?"

To the amusement of all the family and friends looking at the array of infants, Bradley responded, "That's my brover. He has a penis." My number of grandchildren had risen from one to three, and I couldn't help thinking of Steven missing it all—no children and no grands.

Summer stayed home on maternity leave for three months and then went back to work three days a week. Lindsay was at a daycare two of those days, but she spent Wednesdays with me. I had arranged all of my classes to be on Tuesdays and Thursdays, and I worked on scenery on Mondays and Fridays. I kept a journal on those special Wednesdays with my granddaughter. It is written from Lindsay's perspective.

Because the journal represents a baby girl's voice, I think it might sound silly coming out of Noah's mouth. So I suggest that you read it yourself, Elizabeth. Don't feel obligated to read the whole thing. It is, after all, nine months of Wednesdays. I've put the first pages in my book for you because I didn't want to commit you to such a long read. Enjoy.

"Are you too tired for this?" Noah asks.

"I'll read a little just to keep myself awake a while longer. She writes it from the baby's perspective? Has someone done that before?"

"Yes," he says as he places Anne's book on top of the smaller journal, "before your time. Dale Evans, Roy Rogers' wife, wrote a book called *Angel Unaware*. It was about their daughter who was born with a terminal disease. The baby tells her own story. And there are probably others. While you're reading, I think I'll do some computer work. Okay?"

"Go, go, go."

WEDNESDAY, APRIL 25, 2001

Mommy and Nana keep walking around and around—walking and talking, walking and talking. Nana calls it exercise; Mommy calls it therapy. I call it bouncy, and it doesn't feel so good when your head is in the birth canal.

Mommy doesn't know I'm about to make the big move two weeks early. I guess the first big move was when the Daddy part of me swam ahead of all the other wigglies and got to Mommy's egg first. I've been in training to be a track star ever since. STAR! I like the sound of that. I think I'll be a star. But right now I need to rest. Mommy and I have to work hard tomorrow.

Hours later—OOOOOh! coolness; hands on my shoulders; I'm sliding. Choke! Gasp! Wow! Air, lights, cute doctor, Nana with her mouth open, and Daddy yelling. "It's a girl! We got our girl!" Hmmm, Daddy's a hunk. Mommy stops breathing and looks at me with so many feelings on her face. I can't describe them all (probably the pain meds. I liked that too). In fact, everyone's looking at me. Of course, a STAR is born!!!

INTRODUCTION

My name is Lindsay. You can call me STAR or Princess BABA or Lindy, or Sweetheart (that's what Nana calls me). This is my journal. Nana is writing it for me because I'm only three months old. She tunes into what I'm thinking and writes it down. She says she'll put in some extra stuff that I'll appreciate later.

I go to daycare on Tuesday and Thursday and spend Wednesdays with Nana. She works at a university and she thinks keeping me one day a week might help her keep her sanity. Just think about the responsibility for such a little kid. Oh well, I may be small, but I'm loud. And after all, I am a STAR.

FIRST WEDNESDAY, AUGUST 1, 2001

Early morning arrival, Mommy to Nana. I'm a little unsure about the program, and I test her a lot. She moves me, from rocker to crib, from crib to swing, swing to floor pad, back to rocker. I'm dizzy, but I'm not bored. She also sings to me. Why does that make me want to sleep? Sometimes her eyes are wet when she looks at me. But she doesn't make the great noise I make when my eyes are wet.

It's a tiring day, being moved so much. I think Nana is also unsure about the program. The best time is at the end. Mommy comes back and holds me. I love the way she smells and feels and sounds. She seems happy to see me, too.

"Noah, come here a minute."

"Is something wrong?" When she doesn't answer, he closes his computer and comes into the room to stand by her side.

"Look at this. It's a drawing of Summer and Lindsay. Anne must have drawn it. Look at the caption: 'Sometimes I'm not sure where Mommy ends and I begin.' And she has indeed created a sort of seamless representation of the two of them. I think Anne and her daughters must be very special. Lindsay has no choice except to be the same. I wonder how Greer's boys will fit into this strong woman-thing. Interesting."

"Really?"

"Yes. I wish I could know them all, and know them in the future and see what becomes of them." Elizabeth draws her legs up, providing room for Noah to sit.

"You miss your family, don't you?" he asks.

"Of course I do. But it's not the same. Reading about Anne and her girls and grandchildren makes me realize how little happened in my own family relationships. My parents stayed together in spite of the division between them. But there was more tension than love in our home."

"You mean because of the religious differences?"

"Yes. I'm sure Mother believed she was being a good wife when she converted to Judaism for Dad, but she never really accepted it, and she just got tired of all the effort. I'm sure she was sincere in her desire to believe as he did. We all went through the rituals because they were so important to Dad, but even he had difficulty being inspired, surrounded by our doubts."

"Your dad understood, Liz. We talked about it once."

"He understood her difficulty in changing her beliefs after a lifetime as a Catholic, but I don't think he ever realized what their silent division did to us, their children. Mother couldn't make us into good Catholic girls without destroying Dad. So she pretended to herself that she was raising us to think for ourselves by teaching us about all religions, hoping, I suppose, that we would ultimately choose Catholicism on our own. What she really taught us was to question all religions, and we ultimately had none. Why is it that some families get closer because of struggles while others move further apart?"

Noah has heard this story before, but he knows she is reexamining it in light of Anne's family. "Sorry, Darling, that's an easy one. Anne and her daughters pulled together, sharing common problems. Your parents pulled you and your sisters apart, each trying to win you to a different side. It was subtle. They probably didn't even realize it. But it happened. Unwilling to choose between them, you went in your own directions—away from each of them and each other. I had the opposite situation. My parents rejected religion, and I embraced it."

"But it didn't drive you apart. You were the only child, and you were adopted. Your parents worshiped you instead of God. I think I was closer to your parents than to my own." She smiles sardonically and adds, "We shared a common deity."

"Okay," Noah says as tension replaces concern and a shadow crosses his face. "I think I hear the rumblings of psychoanalysis mixed with sarcasm. Maybe you should get back to Lindsay's journal." *Or something you know more about.*

"Because of you, Dad thought I was his only real daughter. He thought that I had come back to the fold because I married a Jewish man. I was a coward; I couldn't tell him that I still didn't believe as he did."

Noah caresses Elizabeth's shoulder but stops when he sees her wince from the pressure. "You weren't a coward. You just didn't want to hurt him. What would have been the point in hitting him over the head with something neither of you could change. He had some good times with you and Josh . . . and me."

"He loved you. I'm so glad he died before Josh became ill." Elizabeth leans her cheek against Noah's hand. "You're the only one I have left. And I feel that for the last few years, we've been hit-and-miss. I've made more effort at sabotaging us than pulling us together. Was that because of my family?"

Noah reaches for her hand and pulls it to his lips, then smiles. "I think we've concluded that it was largely because of me, and you're being too hard on yourself. I've never doubted that you love me, Liz. Granted, sometimes you've had an odd way of showing it. But with your history of loss, maybe that's understandable."

"I know what it is, Noah. I'm going to lose you, too, sooner rather than later, even though I'm the one that will be leaving. And I don't have the faith to believe that we'll ever be together again. I just don't believe in that heaven in the sky."

"I don't either, Lizzie, but don't limit your imagination."

"What does that mean?"

"I'm not sure I can put it into words. Just please don't give up on us or the future."

"All right. That's enough of this maudlin talk. Go back to your computer. You need to read this when I'm through. It's cute. I wish she had more drawings. It would make a great adult storybook for new parents and grandparents, at least the concept would work. The story itself may be too personal. Or hell, I don't know, maybe that's what *would* make it work. I'm not sure I'm objective enough about Anne to be her editor. Go away!"

Laughing, Noah retrieves his laptop from the dining room and sits with it on the couch near the chaise and Elizabeth. Josh sits on her lap, reading with her.

"By the way," Elizabeth adds. "I've known almost from the beginning that you weren't serious about me evaluating a new talent by reading Anne's stories. Her stories weren't meant for the world; they were meant for me. I just can't stop thinking like an editor—and actually one or two of them might be worth developing." She doesn't look up to see that Noah is smiling and nodding while he scans his emails. But she senses that he isn't breathing—afraid she might have discovered Anne's true identity.

WEDNESDAY, AUGUST 8, 2001

It's that day again. Nana overslept and looks pitiful. She feeds me, rocks me, and I don't remember what happened next.

When I wake up, she looks better. My naps are good for her, too. We visit the neighbors, Mildred and Ken. They're older than Nana, but they aren't as lucky. They don't have any grandchildren, so Nana shares me with them. I give them smiles, but they have to work for them. I'm getting smarter. I have found that smiling, as a grown-up control tool, is easier than wailing.

I have also discovered that I can tell good people from bad people. I can, for example, tell who really wants to hold me and who doesn't. I think Nana calls it instinct. I don't like pretending people. I think my dog, Berkley, has it too—instinct. So I scream when the wrong people try to hold me.

Aunt Greer and Uncle Ray and my cousins are coming next week. Baby Tommy is only three weeks old. I'll have to show him the ropes.

WEDNESDAY, AUGUST 15, 2001

Nana's starting to relax more—she knows my wants and needs—and her response time is improving. Berkley is with me today. My face is licked a lot, but I feel protected. I sleep in short snatches, keeping an eye on Nana. She sometimes talks in numbers. She says that I was born 04/27/01. She says that adds up to 32. When I'm 32, she'll be 82 because she's fifty years older than me, and Papa Logan will be 91. She says I'll be the captain of my universe. Doesn't she mean *the* universe? She says that when it's 12/13/14, I'll officially be a teenager, and Daddy will be locking the windows and doors. What does that mean?

"Wait a minute," Elizabeth whispers. "This was written in August of 2001." Unable to wait, she skips ahead to September.

WEDNESDAY, SEPTEMBER 5, 2001

Nana got the courage to take me for a drive today. We went to her school. She wanted to show me off. She tried to do some work. I guess she forgot that's not allowed. It's my day, and how can I keep her sane if she isn't paying attention to me? I have a responsibility.

We went to the Academic Counseling Center to her friend Sara's office. When I turned my head from Nana's shoulder and looked at Sara, I saw the blackest woman maybe in the world. She had a good smile, but her black skin startled me and I jumped and cried. Nana was embarrassed, but Sara seemed to understand. She had lots of pictures of babies on her wall. I wanted to hold her and she wanted to hold me, but I just held on to Nana because I was confused. Some of the women at my daycare school also have darker skin than mine. But Sara is special. She has the most beautiful blackest skin I have ever seen. Nana says that people are all different in lots of ways. She says different is okay. Lots of our family and friends are more different than most, and that just makes them more interesting. Nana teaches theatre, so she's used to different people. She thinks she's normal. I'm not so sure.

WEDNESDAY, SEPTEMBER 12, 2001

Boring TV—all day. I have trouble getting Nana's attention. I don't know why she's so upset. Nana said people will remember the year of my birth because of what happened yesterday. Two airplanes crashed into the World Trade Center in New York City and one into the Pentagon in Washington, DC.

The planes were taken over by terrorists. They think thousands of people are lost. How can you lose thousands of people? They are still looking for survivors. I didn't know there could be so many hiding places.

A fourth plane went down in Pennsylvania. The passengers must have turned on the terrorists. I would have done that.

All in all, I am in a lousy mood. I think I will practice the way I would drive a terrorist crazy—by screaming! Nana keeps sticking a bottle in my mouth, but that isn't what I want, so I'll just keep up the noise. There is fear and anger and sadness in the air. I don't like it.

Hey, we're outside. It's a pretty day with lots of things to look at, much better than TV. This is how I take care of Nana.

WEDNESDAY, SEPTEMBER 19, 2001

I like the sound of the sewing machine. Nana is making curtains for scenery for an opera. She says she'll teach me to sew when I'm older. She started sewing when she was ten years old. She made a gathered skirt. My great grandmother made all of Nana's clothes. She got her first store-bought dress when she was fourteen. She said she loved it, but it wasn't made as well as the clothes her mother made.

Nana made Mommy and Aunt Greer's clothes, for special holidays or events. And she made her own clothes, including her wedding dresses. Why did she have more than one? Did she change in the middle of the ceremony? She doesn't have time to make clothes anymore, but she promises to make a dress for me.

Daddy's brother and sister worked at the World Trade Center. Uncle Matt wasn't there when it was attacked, but many of his friends were, and they're still missing. I just don't know where they are; I wonder if they do. Aunt Judy was evacuated before her building fell. Nana says Daddy's family has a busy guardian angel.

WEDNESDAY, SEPTEMBER 26, 2001

We're planning a trip to Grandma and Grandpa's in New Jersey. They're going to take me to church, and I'm going to wear a pretty white dress.

Nana and her friend, Papa Logan, gave me a wooden cross for my room. She says I'll understand its importance when I'm older. She says it's a gift that symbolizes the greatest gift ever given. Wonder what that could be!

They have stopped looking for more people in the Twin Towers. They call it Ground Zero now. Nana says that they found some, but many are still missing. They must be very good at hiding. Maybe one day, they'll jump out from their hiding place and say, "Boo!"

WEDNESDAY, OCTOBER 3, 2001

The church thing was okay and, as usual, everyone was looking at me—the STAR. I don't understand why the man put water on my head, but he seemed determined and everyone looked like it was supposed to happen. He also seemed nice. I got lots of gifts and lots of people held me. I held some of them, too.

It was also my first airplane ride. *Very* cool!

Daddy whispered in my ear that I'm Catholic now. I don't want to be Catholic. I want to be ballet. Mommy sits with me and watches *The Nutcracker* on television. I like the way they dance. Mommy calls it ballet. I want to be ballet.

153

Nana and I are at the library today. It's pretty boring and smells funny. I tried a book, but it tasted terrible. Daddy likes to read. Nana said that Mommy didn't like to read until she grew up. She said Mommy made a book report on the same book, year after year. She must have really liked that book. Nana said that Aunt Greer read all the time, but Mommy preferred playing softball or football.

By the way, I sit up a little now. I like that.

WEDNESDAY, OCTOBER 10, 2001
Nana was sad today because she lost her cousin, Richard. There must be lots of lost people wandering around. She said Richard's son just got out of prison, and the police are looking for Richard's daughter. I wonder if she's lost too. And I wonder if the lost people are with the missing people. I kind of like that idea. Maybe the lost and missing people can make their own place. I don't know where—obviously not where we can find them, because then they wouldn't be lost anymore. It's a kind of hide-and-seek. But we can't find the lost people until we are lost also. And then we'll all be together.

Nana says that when she played hide-and-seek (when she was little), the kids who couldn't be found would run to home-base where they would be free. Maybe the people in New York that are missing got to home-base since no one could find them. Maybe that's where all the lost and missing people are. I'll bet I would get to home-base if I got lost, and I would see Nana's cousin there and Uncle Matt's friends. But I think I would rather be found.

Elizabeth puts down Anne's book, picks up Lindsay's journal, and reads the remaining entries that ended in May, 2002. Finished, she sits for a long time, staring into space.

Noah has been aware of Elizabeth's occasional soft laughter and other sounds of response to words that are clearly enjoyable or moving. He turns off his computer when he realizes how much time has passed. He looks at his wife who is smiling with tears in her eyes. She looks back at him. "I want Anne's email address."

"For what?"

"I can't talk about it yet. I can write it down, but I can't say it out loud. Don't worry. It's good. I just need to contact Anne and get permission to use something of hers."

Realizing her mood is delicate, Noah doesn't press her for more. He hands her the laptop, Anne's email address already typed in, hoping this connection will not cross boundaries that have been respected for months.

EMAIL TO ANNE:

I just read Lindsay's journal. How she will treasure it. It gave me an idea, and I need your permission to use your concept. I want to tell Joshua's story—from his perspective. I haven't thought it all out yet. He loved superheroes, as do so many children. I thought there could be eight short books—one for every year of his life. On the realistic side, they would chronicle his illness and his upbeat attitude in spite of it. On the fictional side, there would be some kind of adventure in each chapter and he would be the hero of the action. Since it is for young readers, there would be many illustrations and minimal narration.

The first goal is to provide sick children with their own special role model, someone who suffers as they do and still lives a fulfilling life, making the most of the time he has. The second goal is to help parents of sick children. The third goal is for Noah and me to work through our grief and create a tribute for Josh.

I know you don't have a copyright on the concept of speaking through a child's voice, but I want to use the part about the missing and lost people. It truly touched me. That's uniquely yours, and of course I would give you credit for it in the acknowledgements.

What do you think?—Elizabeth

A short time later, Anne finds the email and responds.

EMAIL TO ELIZABETH:

You go, girl. I can't wait to read it. Let me know if I can help in any way.—*Always, Anne*

Chapter 10

Gifts

THE DAY IS OVERCAST, easier on the eyes, easier on the skin, but so far, no rain. Clouds and a stiff breeze help cool what might have been a sweltering August day. The *Espirita* cuts smoothly through the waters of the inlet, and Anne feels the exhilaration of the ride. She thinks of the journal she wrote for Lindsay and how it has impacted Elizabeth. Noah's emails ring with the relief this distraction has brought them. *When Lindsay is older and I give her the little journal, I'll tell her about Elizabeth and Joshua.*

"Your lips are moving, Anne. Have I gone deaf, or are you talking to yourself again?"

"I was thinking about family. So, how do you like my sons-in-law? I know you love my daughters. What choice do you have?"

Paul laughs and points ahead. "We're going to circle that buoy. Be ready. Joe's a ringer. With him on board, Marjorie's *Peli* might beat the *Espirita*, without any help from me. And this is one time I could try to win."

"Because it's not a competition between just you and Marjorie. Answer my question."

Paul grins at her mother's pride and is once again amazed that this happy smiling woman has been through so many difficult passages. At rare moments like this, there's no mask of cheerfulness. Her joy is real. And her daughters seem to be cut from the same cloth. He wonders if, like their mother, they shelter emotional damages that one day will surface and have to be addressed. "I talked with Ray last night, and watched him with his sons. He's a very impressive man. It's good your grandsons have a strong male role model."

"Why do you say it that way?" She fears he is referring to her first husband and exposing an anti-gay attitude.

"Anne, you and your daughters are a force. It's good they chose strong men."

"Oh!" She relaxes. "I agree, but sometimes it feels like a tug-o-war. There's a lot of mental and emotional muscle between the four of them. What do you think of Joe?"

"I don't know. He isn't very forthcoming. He's a Catholic and I'm a priest. Maybe he doesn't approve of our friendship. He looks like a mountain. Your daughters definitely both chose macho men."

"Yes. They love their dad, but I think they consciously made sure they weren't making the same mistake I made."

"Well, macho doesn't necessarily equate straight. Now act like a sailor. The *Peli* is gaining on us."

Marjorie and Joe have found the perfect positions for wind and sail. They cut through the water beside Anne and Paul, trading insults as they pass. Paul turns tightly around the buoy to gain time, unaware of the remnants of a gill net caught on the barnacles of the buoy. The net snags Paul's rudder and holds just long enough to throw the boat out of position. For a moment in time, everything that could go wrong, does. The *Peli's* bow crosses *Espirita's*, pushing it down. The *Espirita's* sail waffles. Anne moves from starboard side, where she was balancing the boat, to keep from being hit by the *Peli*. Without warning, the combined elements of wind, a gill net, the *Peli*, and Anne's change of position cause the *Espirita* to go over, her sail ripping on and hooking around the buoy.

A short flight ends abruptly with the impact of water. Anne instinctively ducks as the *Peli* crosses over her, slipping from her life jacket to escape the deadly buoyancy that would trap her under the boat's hull. When the shadow of the boat has passed, she resurfaces.

Joe is hauling in their sail to stop progress away from the site, all the while looking wildly around until he sees Anne. Marjorie has already found her and is poised to throw her a line. Anne swims to it and then looks around for Paul. He floats from behind the buoy, and they all three see him at once.

Joe dives in and swims to him as Marjorie pulls Anne to her boat. After she climbs into the *Peli,* she looks back and sees blood on Paul's face. She starts to dive back in but Marjorie grabs her shirt. "You can help better from here."

As Joe swims with Paul to the boat, Anne sees the blood is coming from a single wound on his forehead. *Could be serious, could be nothing. Please God, let it be nothing.* Joe holds on to the side of the boat while he pushes and the two women pull. The still unconscious Paul is dragged aboard. Joe treads water and waits.

Anne slips a cushion under Paul's head, and calls his name while she checks his pulse. "He's alive!" She takes a cloth from Marjorie to wipe the blood and examine the cut on his head. "It doesn't look too bad." *Thank you, God.* "Head wounds just bleed a lot."

Paul's eyes open, and he gradually remembers what happened. "Where is *Espirita*?" are his first words and concerns. Marjorie and Joe both cross themselves, whispering their separate prayers, Marjorie's beginning with, "Dear Your Honor" and Joe's beginning with, "Thanks, and no sharks, please".

"Just like a man, even if you are a priest!" Anne stammers in relief. "The damned boat is on its side. You and I are alive. Which is more important?"

He smiles up at her. "You are, my dear friend. But I see and hear that you are well. Let me be concerned for my only worldly possession."

Still in the water, Joe tries to evaluate the *Espirita's* condition. "The mast looks all right, Father Paul, but the sail is torn. Do you want me to cut it loose?"

"Yes. And please, just call me Paul."

"No can do, Father. I went to Catholic school," Joe says as he accepts the knife from Marjorie. "Then you'll have to tell me how to right it. Do you have a trolling motor?"

Marjorie answers, "Yes. We both do. Let's get her up and motor back. You might need a stitch or two, Paul."

"Holy Mother of God," he whispers, trying to sit up. "I hate needles."

Joe swims to the fouled *Espirita* with the knife between his teeth, every inch the Marine. Paul chuckles and then groans in pain. "I think he's enjoying himself."

Anne positions herself behind Paul, sitting on the bottom of the boat. With her legs on either side, he is able to lean back against her and not have to support his own head. Of course he is now trapped within the sound of her voice, and he groans again as she says, "I'm sure he is. All right, now that you are injured and can't move and you aren't distracted by wind and sails, tell me what you think of my grandchildren."

Paul looks pleadingly at Marjorie. "Is there any wine on this boat?"

Anne grins. "And by the way, does this count as our practice session on man overboard emergencies?"

Marjorie looks at her old friend and her new friend, the image of her daughter replacing Anne, and blonde hair, instead of red, blows softly around Paul's injured face.

That evening, Anne and her daughters prepare for the next day's party while Joe, Ray, and Bradley clean up the *Espirita,* making lists of the salvaged gear to help Paul determine what was lost. Marjorie rides her bicycle down to the dock to see the results of their efforts.

"How's Father Paul?" Joe asks, smiling at her new shirt which has "Life Is A Contact Sport" on the front.

"He's fine, just eight stitches. He wouldn't let them deaden it, said he preferred the pain to the Novocain needle. It's so close to his scalp, the scar won't even show."

Ray notices his son's disappointment. "What's the matter Brad?"

"I think scars are cool. I wanted to see it."

"He has lots of scars, Bradley. Most just don't show. Did your daddy take you out on one of the piers?" Bradley nods, and Marjorie continues. "They're Paul's epiphany. I think that's what he calls them. He invested the profits from the sale of Anne's house into the Company and said it was money for buildin' a marina. Some of the boat slips will be used by the folks that rent the places they're buildin' over there below the church. The whole bank is goin' to look like a Spanish village with all that stucco. I think it'll be a beautiful sight. And they'll all be white, like Anne's house and Saint Angelica."

Ray smiles at her enthusiasm. "How many houses will they build?"

"Just four, but each one'll be a triple thing like Anne's, three houses in one. And they'll all be upside down. Has she told you about that?"

Joe stows the last of *Espirita's* gear while he answers. "The bedrooms will be on the bottom floor, and the living spaces upstairs. So there will be twelve rentals, fourteen, counting Anne's?"

"Yep. Paul planned one boat slip for each of them and one for each of the partners in the company, about twenty all together. The rest will be rented by other people in town. And there's a couple developments upriver, where the water's too shallow for boats of any size. Those folks could keep a flat-bottomed johnboat up there and motor down here to a larger boat. It's also safer from hurricanes and tropical storms here than on the Inlet. So people who live closer to the beach, and those that just live here in the summer, could winter their boats in the marina. It's a way to get back the money for the piers and finance other projects in Pearl."

Joe wipes his hands as he stands, finished with his work. "But, if Father Paul's family owns the property that was the original investment, won't the profits all go to Mexico?"

"Naw. Paul's family don't really need the money. They inherited it from his uncle, who wanted to leave it all to Paul. He wouldn't accept the money for himself, so they asked him to use the money to help the people here, especially the ones who come over from Mexico."

"So, legally, it belongs to Father Paul?" Joe asks, looking surprised.

"It's invested in his family's name as part of the LLC."

Ray raises his eyebrows. "If I remember my one business course, an LLC is a limited liability company. So that means his family is a partner in the company?"

"Yep!" Marjorie says, her voice filling with pride, "and so are Anne and me and a few others—all partners. It's kinda confusin', but we have a lawyer that put it all into contracts. The money made from rentin' the boat slips will be used for the community. Anne and me and a few others mortgaged our homes to build the triple house things, and we'll take half the profits from rentin' them to pay back our loans and reinvest the rest in the Company."

Ray whistles in appreciation. "So, even if the investors take little in profits, your own property value will grow as a result of these improvements and your investment will continue to grow! It sounds like a win/win."

"It is." Marjorie beams. "We employed every man, woman, and child that wanted to work this summer. We had to hire a barge from Shallotte to put in the pilin's for the piers, but mostly local labor did the rest, includin' helpin' Anne with the stone walls up there."

Bored, Bradley hangs on his dad's leg. "So what's next?"

"Whew! It's hard to see that far ahead, young man." Marjorie ruffles his hair and Bradley shyly slides to the ground, writing in the dirt with a stick. She follows his movements with hungry eyes.

"What's it called, Miss Marjorie, the LLC?" Bradley asks.

"That's just the kind of company it is, Brad. We just call it the Company—no real name yet."

"Nana's house is called Casa Blanca."

Marjorie stoops to Bradley's level. "Do you know what that means?"

"Yes!" Bradley jumps up, and Marjorie falls backwards. "White House! Does that mean Nana's the President?"

As everyone laughs, Ray helps Marjorie to her feet and Joe grabs his nephew and tosses him in the air. "What do you think they should call their company, Brad?"

"Look at me, Daddy!" Bradley shrieks as Joe tosses him again. "I'm a bird. I'm flying." And as he grabs his uncle's neck to prevent being tossed yet again, he says, "Call it White Bird. There's lots of white birds around here."

"How do you say white bird in Spanish?" Ray asks.

Carlos joins the small group. "Pajara blanca or ave blanca."

"How do you say seagull?" Ray asks.

"Gaviota. The words for seabird are ave marina." He turns to Marjorie. "Where is Father Paul?"

"He's sleepin' at my house tonight. I'm supposed to keep an eye on him. He has a minor concussion. Course he wanted me to check on his boat. He'll appreciate all you fellows have done. And course I'm thankful to you for savin' him, Joe. He's like family to me." She picks up her bicycle and walks it up to the road, muttering. "He *is* family. I like Ave Blanca. The White Bird Company and the Red Hat Club. We can get along. Maybe I'll put a white feather on my red hat. Whatta ya think, Your Honor?"

"You saved somebody, Uncle Joe?" Bradley asks in awe.

Joe watches Marjorie cycle away, her gray braids flying behind her. "If I hadn't been there, Bradley, Miss Marjorie and your Nana would have saved him." His eyes darken with concern knowing neither of them could have gotten him into the boat alone.

A piñata is being raised on a tree branch the following evening. Anne finishes frying the chicken in her kitchen while whistling "Yellow Bird", a tune from *Man of La Mancha*. She pulls a large pan of macaroni and cheese from the oven as Paul enters, carrying its twin.

"A whistling woman. You know what my mother used to say about that?"

"If it's about whistling girls and crowing hens, yes I do know."

He finds a hot pad and sets the casserole on the table. "More mac-n-cheese. My oven's not great but your recipe is. I confess, I took a small bite from the corner."

"You are forgiven, my son."

He smiles at her irreverence, and sits in the closest chair. "Most of the smoked blue fish is gone. I'm still overwhelmed every time I walk into your house. These are the same walls I grew up with, but your painting technique has given them so much . . . I don't know, character I guess. The colors are subtle and rich at the same time, especially here in the kitchen. I feel like I've walked into an old painting."

Anne finishes transferring the last of the chicken onto a platter lined with paper towels. "Fine praise. Thank you. All right, that's done. Seven chickens. Do you think that's enough?" She turns off the oven and burners and crosses to Paul. "Are you all right? You still look a little pale."

"I'm fine. Please, sit for a minute."

Knowing that will make him rest, she joins him at the table. "By the way, Kente called. He's out of town and won't get back in time to join us."

"It may be that his wife doesn't want to come, Anne."

"Why is that?"

"Ayesha's a mixture of good business and bad attitude. She's happy to sell houses to whites and get the commission, but she doesn't bring them home to dinner."

"Too bad. That must be hard on Kente. Well, I'm not going to let her attitude spoil tonight's party."

"Agreed! This will be a feast, Anne. With your food and all the other dishes, there will be leftovers for everyone to take home."

"Hmmm. Maybe I won't have to cook tomorrow night."

"If you'll bring your family to Mass tomorrow morning, I'll cook fish for your dinner."

"Okay."

"That was too easy."

"We planned to come to Mass anyway. So your bribe wasn't necessary, but we'll take it."

Anne removes her apron and Paul whistles in admiration at her beautiful traditional style Mexican peasant dress. It's black with colorful embroidery, a full skirt, and a low neckline. "Where did you find that?"

"Celita, Carlos's sister. She's a wonderful seamstress. Have you seen the furniture she reupholstered for me?"

"You mean the old stuff from the house? I've been meaning to tell you how I appreciate that you didn't throw it out. It would have probably been less expensive to just replace it with new stuff."

"Stuff is right. I couldn't replace it with the same quality. I did all the wood refinishing, and Celita probably doesn't charge enough for her upholstery time. So it wasn't very expensive. I saw a picture of your uncle sitting in the armchair she just finished. I want you to have it. I don't want to make a melodramatic presentation. I just want Joe and Ray to bring it to your house tomorrow."

"I should protest, but I won't. Sissy took the photograph," he says in a changed voice. "I would love to have that chair as a reminder of him and my childhood. He was a father to me."

Just then, Lindsay, followed by Bradley, followed by Tommy, run into the kitchen, giggling and shrieking. Paul catches the little girl and lifts her up. "Lindsay, I heard something about you," he teases, grateful for the lightening of spirits caused by the three sprites.

"What?" She laughs all the way from her belly, her whole body shaking.

He pushes her strawberry blonde hair off her brow, damp from playing with her cousins. "I hear you're going to be a big sister."

"Yes!" She sobers. "Is that your boo-boo?" She carefully touches the bandage on his forehead.

"Yes."

Lindsay looks directly into his brown eyes with her blue ones.

"You'll live!" she declares, and wiggling out of his arms, chases after the boys.

"Did she really say, 'You'll live'?" Paul laughs as he watches her run away.

"Yes, I imagine she's been told that many times."

"Is she only three years old? Or is she a short teenager in disguise?"

"Can you imagine what we'll have on our hands when she *is* a teenager?"

"You'll have entertainment. All of your grandchildren are happy and pretty and smart, but I think I like Tommy best. He says very little. He would be a good fishing buddy."

"I'm ignoring the hidden insult. Want to lay any bets on football being in Tommy's future?"

"No, I think you would win. Any bets on people outside being hungry for your famous fried chicken?"

Anne rises to pick up a pan of chicken and Paul carefully stands, still feeling a little weak. She turns to him. "Thank you for tonight and for yesterday and for tomorrow. Since I met you and Marjorie and Kente, my life has been a blur of blessings."

Their eyes meet and crinkle, and they both burst into laughter. "A blur of blessings?" they say together.

Anne forces a serious face. "See, I'm no good at sentimental talk. Grab the rest of the chicken, and we'll go whack a piñata."

Earlier in the day, tables were created with sawhorses and plywood borrowed from Carlos's construction materials. Anne covered them with sheets, and Marjorie brought vases full of late summer blooms from her garden. Now Christmas lights strung throughout several live oaks reflect on the gaily-colored piñata hanging from one branch, tantalizing the children.

An awkward shyness prevails as people join those already gathered. But they warm quickly, and a festive atmosphere develops. Carlos's family and crew brought enchiladas, steamed fresh tortillas, and some dishes that Anne has never tasted. And in spite of the quantity, the food disappears. Paul and Carlos mingle, making sure those with little English are engaged in conversation, and serving as interpreters where needed.

Following dinner, while people are still eating their desserts, Greer passes out poppers to the children. She is kneeling down, showing a small girl how to open one when she overhears two young women speaking in irritable tones. One whispers. "Why is she wearing that dress? Is she a Latina woman-wanna-be?"

"I think she's a Father Paul's woman-wanna-be," the other responds.

Greer is tempted to say something equally unkind to them but doesn't, because she can't really blame them.

Anne had stipulated that although this was to be a birthday celebration for Bradley and Ray, there would be no gifts. After the children break the piñata, Bradley shows his sweet nature, making sure all of the children have a fair share of candy by giving away most of his own. Carlos's sister, Celita, watches and then leaves.

Guitars and violins fill the warm night with music. Anne talks Greer into singing, and Marjorie accompanies her with simple strumming on her mountain dulcimer. Greer's voice is lilting and clear, reflecting years of training as well as experience in her high school performing chorus. She surprised all of her family and friends when she majored in engineering instead of music. She sings two mountain folk songs of Scottish origin and then melts into the background. Another musical group is forming when Celita returns and calls for attention.

"All right everyone, we want our birthday men from the mountains to feel welcome here, so I brought a gift from all of us to Bradley and Ray." From behind her ample back, she brings forth two sombreros. Cameras flash as she places a hat on Ray and kisses his cheek to the cheers and howls of onlookers. Then she puts the smaller hat on Bradley, whose head disappears. He lifts the brim of the hat enough to see she is going to kiss him and turns and runs for all he's worth. Joe leans down and points to his cheek.

"I'll take Bradley's kiss," he says.

"Make sure it's on the cheek," Summer warns, good naturedly. And to the laughter and applause of the crowd, Celita plants a very long sensuous kiss . . . on his cheek. The music resumes.

Greer approaches Anne with a tray of cheesecake slices on small paper plates. "Mom, will you pass these around for me? I think I heard some requests from those girls over there in capris and crop-tops." She points at the young women overheard earlier. They look embarrassed when Anne approaches them. She assumes they are wives, girlfriends, or daughters of someone invited. She introduces herself and spends time trying to get to know them while insisting they try her daughter's cheesecake. They are soon laughing and joking.

Later, Anne finds Celita and thanks her for the gifts. "Please tell me you didn't make those great hats."

Celita laughs. "No, I have been collecting some things from Mexico when I go for visits to family. I hope to open a gift shop one day."

"Really? Do you have a lot of things?"

"I don't know what you would consider a lot, but not quite enough to fill a shop. I have hats and pottery and ponchos and tablecloths and rugs. It's just a beginning."

"Ponchos are very popular this year. Have you thought of using one of the shops in town, one of the closed ones?"

"Sure, but if I sold all I have, it wouldn't pay for the overhead. And I wouldn't have time to do my own work. I have a long-term plan, but a rich husband would help."

"Don't marry for the wrong reason. Believe me, that's no solution. I may have an idea. Let's talk about it tomorrow, after Mass."

Anne sees people looking at watches and beginning to collect dishes and children. She finds Paul and speaks loudly enough for others to hear. "Father Paul, some people are starting to leave. Will you please thank everyone for me in Spanish and then in English and give us your blessing?" She too has seen the looks and cool attitudes toward her friendship with Paul. She wants to dispel the concerns and rumors by openly treating him like a priest.

He smiles at her and holds her gaze a little too long, destroying what she was hoping to accomplish. And then he does as she asked.

Anne puts her head down to hide her blush. *I have to talk with him. Damn! Why do we make our lives so complicated?*

His blessing spoken, Paul looks up, a flush of anger and embarrassment on his own face. He turns away and leaves. A man stops him and after an angry exchange they leave together.

Later, Anne finds Marjorie at the serving table, clearing the last of the dishes, and mumbling to The Judge, as usual. "There you are. I haven't seen you all evening."

"I've been with the little people. I'm guessin' your granddaughter is a Leprechaun. She's pure magic. She and Tommy make the perfect pair." She licks her finger after using it to wipe up the last of the mac-n-cheese. "She talks enough for the both of 'em. I hope Tommy stays the way he is, kind of laid back and quiet. I didn't see much of Bradley; he was playin' with the older boys. You're very fortunate, Anne."

"By the way, I didn't know that you played the dulcimer. Where did you grow up, Marjorie?"

"I guess you can tell it wasn't here. I talk different, for one thing. I was born and raised in the Blue Ridge Mountains."

"I thought you'd been here forever."

"Durin' the war, World War II, my girlfriends and me used to go over to the Marine base for parties. That's where I met John. We saw each other every chance we got until he was shipped out. The day before he left, we were married. This was his home, so after the war, we come here. I'm livin' in the house he was born in.

"Anyway, Anne, you did a good party tonight, and you did a good thing. Most Gringos couldn't have pulled it off. They would've been too busy pretendin' and condescendin' to be real. Any fool could see you were exactly where you wanted to be and with the people you wanted to be with. I'll admit, I hid out with the kids 'cause I wasn't as comfortable as you."

"I was just thinking about how we make things so complicated for ourselves. Why can't life be simple and kind? Why do we have to question motives or even have motives? Anyway, as you said, it was a good party and I am a fortunate woman, in many ways. You know, sometimes you are sort of addled, and sometimes very insightful and succinct. I like both parts of you."

Marjorie puts a friendly arm around Anne. "I believe you because you aren't very good at tellin' lies or even hidin' truths. That's good and bad. I have two bits of advice: don't play poker, and don't look into Paul's eyes in front of his people. He don't hide much either. And here's a third bit, no charge. Don't confuse pity and carin' with desire."

"I guess it's my instinct to mother a man in need, and maybe I give mixed signals."

"It's our hormones, honey. They're frustratin' when we got 'em and more frustratin' when they're gone."

"I think you just changed the subject from mothering to meno-pause. And tell me something, when do the hormones go? I keep thinking mine are gone, but they just seem to be in hiding, and jump out at the most inappropriate times."

Marjorie's attempt at lightheartedness is betrayed by her con-cerned face. She whispers to Anne. "I suppose you noticed that Juan wasn't here tonight." Anne nods, feeling suddenly worried. "Did you also notice that Carlos and a few others left early?"

"I thought they were just avoiding the clean-up. What happened?"

"I didn't want to spoil the party for you, but you're going to hear about it anyway. Juan was riding his bicycle here, later than the rest. Someone in a pick-up run him off the road. He's bruised and scratched, but he'll be all right. His older brother found him and come up here and told Carlos."

"Was it Billy O'Brian?"

"Carlos went to the bar and found Billy braggin' about it. Now Billy's busted up, and so's his truck. Several Mexicans and white men are also sportin' black eyes an' bruises."

"Dear God. Is that why Paul left?"

"I think he went to Billy's house to see if he's all right an' to make sure he don't hit on his missus."

Anne sinks to a chair and wonders if this was her fault for tossing that rock. She's the one Billy should have gone after.

At the conclusion of Mass the next morning, Father Paul steps from behind the podium and walks to the middle of the aisle. He stops there and turns a full circle, looking at each of his small congregation. He notes that some look battered but proud.

"Something happened this weekend that reminded me I am surrounded by people of courage. I'm sure you've all heard about my accident and those who saved me. We always note the bold acts of heroism, but I think we sometimes fail to acknowledge the courageous choices taking place around us in our daily lives because we forget that there are many kinds of courage."

"There is the courage to leave the country or house you call home and begin again in a new place as a stranger."

"There is the courage to let the child or parent go when it is time for them to leave for a better place."

"There is the courage to give up or risk personal security in order to improve the lives of others less fortunate."

"There is the courage to walk away from a destructive life or relationship and be willing to open your heart again and risk more disappointment and pain."

"There is the courage to rebuild when everything you have has been taken away."

"There is the courage to live *on* when everyone you lived *for* is gone."

"There is the courage to face yourself, to accept responsibility for the deeds that bring you shame rather than looking for someone else to blame."

"And after facing yourself, there is the courage to forgive yourself, because only then can you begin to forgive others who have wronged you."

"There is the courage to walk away from revenge and seek instead, justice."

"And finally, there is the courage to resist the temptation of an easier road when the road you have chosen is hard but is the right road for you."

Paul opens his arms to his congregation. "I have the privilege and responsibility to know much of your suffering, some of your shame, all of your courage. It is your courage that gives me the strength to fulfill my own purpose, my own chosen destiny." He speaks the traditional words of benediction and then exits the church to a beautiful, unseasonably cool August day.

Anne sits in her pew, collecting her thoughts, knowing that, among many other things, he has just told his people and her that he will not betray them or his vows. *I guess we won't need to have a talk. He has said it all. Thank you, God. I need this friend.*

After her family leaves, Anne takes her computer to the balcony and watches a sunset while she reviews the weekend and her confusing feelings for Paul.

EMAIL TO NOAH:

Why am I drawn to unavailable one-woman men? Is it because you're so safe, because you've already found your one woman? Am I purposefully sabotaging my chances at a real romance for fear of making another mistake? Or am I simply, as Marjorie said, confusing compassion with passion? Is it possible for two needy but attractive people of the opposite sex to be good friends without good sex? I ramble. Good night.—*Always, Anne*

Chapter 11

Sex & the Egg

NOAH BREATHES DEEPLY, controlling his own reactions as he hears Elizabeth try to conceal her physical as well as emotional weaknesses with a business-like tone of voice.

"The baby books are in Josh's room on the top shelf above the chest of drawers. Please ship them overnight. Insure them and have them delivered with signature required. Use lots of packing materials; these are precious and fragile. There are also some albums on shelves in the family room. I only want the ones in green binders. Oh, wait," she adds, pausing and then continuing in a softer voice, "there's a framed picture of the three of us in the master bedroom. Please pack that. In fact, include all the pictures around the house that have Josh in them. Thank you, Sharon. You were always the one I depended on. You still have a key, don't you?

"What? . . . Oh, I'm fine . . . Yes, really. I'm still in the midst of treatments, but this second phase of chemo may be over soon. I look like an alien, thin and bald . . . No, I hate wigs, and even silk irritates my scalp. So I stay in a lot. My immune system doesn't need to be around other people anyway. Noah's lost weight, too. Only he, of course, looks better for it. He runs every morning . . . Yes, he's sexier than ever." She winks at her husband sitting in shorts and tennis shoes, and he lifts the newspaper to hide his disappearing composure.

"I hear you choking up, Sharon. Stop it! I want Josh's things because I'm working on a project, and I need his images and our memories of him to surround me. It's good, not sad. Now, I want to talk to Shuching. Please tell me she isn't in Singapore. Oh, good. Can you connect me? Actually, my energy is failing. Please call her for me and see if she can clear her schedule to come here for a couple of weeks next month. I want her to illustrate the project. So she should bring whatever portable art supplies she needs. We'll buy the rest here. Make her travel arrangements. Noah can pick her up at RDU. It's only minutes from here." Elizabeth smiles at Sharon's response. "I miss you, too, but I'm too weak to travel, and you're afraid of flying. I have to hang up, Shar. I'm exhausted. This is the most energy I've expended in a while."

Noah lowers the paper. He hasn't heard such enthusiasm in her voice in years. But he worries this project could overwhelm her. After all, she's tired from just talking on the phone. She's been working on the outlines of the books for two weeks now. She can only write for an hour at a time and then has to lie down or take short slow walks. Her strength is diminishing, but the light in her eyes tells him she is regaining focus and will. When this project is finished, he'll find something new to hold her, maybe something less emotional.

"I'm all right, Noah. I just don't have the psychic energy to talk to friends whose sympathy makes communication painful on both sides. However, I am hungry. Is there any homemade chicken soup left?"

"There's always chicken soup." Elizabeth follows him to the kitchen where he fills two bowls and heats them in the microwave. She gets silverware and crackers while he continues his thought. "Remember the Korean roommate from college I told you about? We liked to compare cultural practices. I told him chicken soup was the Jewish mother's remedy for every ailment. Then I said probably all American mothers do the same. He laughed at me and said, 'Korean mothers, too.' We found during our time as roommates, many behaviors, beliefs, and practices cross international boundaries. Underneath, we're the same."

"I agree, but I'm interested in those characteristics unique to a culture, things that give it identity. They used to call America 'the melting pot'. In the end, everyone was rewarded if they were able to blend in, no added spice. Thank God that's changed. I love walking down the street in Chicago and seeing different cultural clothing and hearing different languages."

"I agree." *Wow, we're on a roll. We're actually not talking about her disease, our relationship, or Josh.*

"Let's eat our lunch on the deck, and then will you take me on a canoe ride?"

"I'll take you anywhere anytime," he says, putting his arms around her and nuzzling her neck.

"Not that kind of ride, Noah."

"I know. I'd better shower. Running makes me horny."

"I wish I could run with you."

"Well, my love, maybe after your chemo is over, we should get a couple of bicycles. That would be easier on our joints."

"Are you thinking about Anne's friend, Logan?"

"Yes, he's in his sixties and rides in two hundred mile races. I think he's my hero."

"I think he's Anne's also."

The next morning, two large packages arrive from Chicago. They sit unopened, through two difficult chemo days. On the third morning, Elizabeth rises early, showers, and before Noah joins her, slowly unwraps the history and images of their son. Her heart races, and she has to control her breathing as the memories flood through her.

After moments of deliberate calm, she places the framed photographs around the great room, the space where she is most comfortable and where she will work. She purposefully keeps the rest of the house free of him, knowing she may need those rooms for escape if remembrance becomes too hard. There's a danger of being immersed in the past, and she's again amazed at Noah's insight in bringing her here, away from Chicago. She lifts the last album from the box and finds a small wrapped package below it.

Inside is a knitted hat of the sheerest, softest fiber she has ever felt. She puts it on. "Gossamer," she whispers. It has a small rolled brim that she can lift or lower to cover as much of her head as she wants. The color is a deep violet. She peers in the bathroom mirror and to her surprise thinks. *A few of Ian's makeup tricks, and I might look human again. I'll have to email Sharon and see if she can get me a red one for Christmas. And I'll have to send Noah out to find a North Carolina gift for her . . . maybe some pottery. Maybe I'll wear this and go with him.*

In the days that follow, Elizabeth finds her thoughts are continually on the books. She mumbles, daydreams, and rarely hears Noah when he speaks to her. In the middle of a conversation, she will pick up her pen and notepad (always nearby) and begin writing.

The first book practically writes itself. She finds the non-fictional increments easily written because of the baby books. She knows it will get harder as Josh ages in the stories and becomes ill. But she finds relief in the fictional superhero content which includes humor that lightens an otherwise stark landscape. For this, she uses characters she and Josh created during his story times. But now those same characters take on depth and personality without her conscious control. She was an editor and had heard of this experience from her authors, but she hadn't fully understood it until now. She will begin a line of dialogue, and suddenly the character is saying things Elizabeth had not consciously thought about, and the story changes. She feels a need to corral her words to keep them on track. But she loves the ride, and sometimes it takes her to a better place than her imagination had originally conceived.

She attempts to explain it to Noah. "It's almost as if the characters and I, or maybe Josh and I, are collaborating. I try to get into his head, to imagine the kind of adventure that would have thrilled but not terrified him. And suddenly I find myself in unknown territory, but still writing." Then she returns to her notebook without hearing Noah's response.

At dinner, after a long silence while Elizabeth stares at her half-eaten food, Noah says, "A penny for your thoughts." She doesn't look up. "Or fifty bucks for your ATTENTION!" Still nothing, as he feigns exasperation.

"Give me fifteen minutes to write something down before I lose it. And then make me a virgin Margarita, sans salt."

"No tequila and no salt. You mean a lime-aid?"

"Yes, in a Margarita glass, please."

Fifteen minutes later, Noah brings their drinks to her chaise and suggests they have them on the dock, but only if she promises to talk about something other than the books. Elizabeth carries the drinks, and he carries two lawn chairs across the bridge and the island, to the end of the dock. He pulls a paper bag from his pocket.

"Snacks?" she asks.

"Not for us. I went by the farm supply store down the road and bought catfish food. Next-door-Ben says they'll come to you like pets if you feed them." Noah takes a handful of the small round pellets and throws them up high and away from the dock as Ben had instructed. Each pellet makes a plopping sound as it lands on the water's surface. They float, then disappear, followed by concentric rings of tiny waves, and here and there . . . a splash.

Noah speaks in a whisper. "They're around." He tosses another handful, this time closer. Plop, plop, plop they sound as they land.

"Underwater morse code?" Elizabeth whispers back, trying not to laugh.

Another toss, this time at the edge of the dock, and Elizabeth gasps as hungry mouths break the water's surface. The smaller fish are skittish, staying six to ten feet from the dock, splashing their annoyance as the larger fish slowly and fearlessly swim around and under the dock, sucking in the majority of pellets.

"Look at that big one. I'm sure he's over five pounds. I'm going to call him Ben in honor of our neighbor. And look at the orange one. Is that a koi or just a three pound goldfish? She's pretty; I think I'll call her Princess."

Noah stops tossing pellets and turns to Elizabeth. "How do you know that one's a male and the other a female? Maybe I should get you a job in a carnival, guessing people's weight and sex."

"I'll bet you're down to one hundred and fifty pounds, and I'm pretty sure you're a he."

"And you're probably down to ninety pounds."

"Shut up, Noah! I'm a big one-ten."

"And that would be fine if you were five inches shorter."

"Really, shut up! Why don't you go and get Anne's journal? Maybe the fish would like a story. It's so nice out here, and I need to think about something other than the books."

"Okay, but you just mentioned you-know-what."

"Sorry."

"Remind me, when is Shuching coming? And when can I read you-know-what?"

"In two weeks, and not yet."

Noah leaves Elizabeth feeding the fish, and retrieves Anne's journal from the house. He brings a pillow for her back and then settles into his own chair with his feet on the nearest dock piling. He groans. "I forgot the object to go with the story. I'll be right back."

"Wait! Let's trick the witch. Instead of reading the next story, let the book fall open and let fate decide which story we'll read."

"All right, but we may be playing with magic." He does as she asked, pretending fear and covering his eyes.

Elizabeth leans forward to read the title. "Yikes! This may be X-rated. Go away fishes; you're too young. I'm not sure I want to know what object goes with this story."

Noah looks at the title and laughs. "I'll be right back."

A few minutes later, he returns with a down-filled throw to cover Elizabeth's legs. She has become less able to tolerate the cool fall evenings. After he wraps her legs, he reaches into his pocket and pulls out a hand-blown glass egg. Inside the egg is a flower. Noah reads.

SEX AND THE EGG

Don't you love the title? It makes me think of a romantic comedy from the fifties with Doris Day and Rock Hudson. See, even Doris Day didn't know a straight guy from a gay one. Not funny, I guess . . . poor Rock.

However, the glass egg with the trillium inside is a gift I bought for Logan and never gave to him. If you aren't familiar with the Blue Ridge Mountain flora, a trillium is a native wildflower. Besides cycling, Logan's other obsession is propagating wildflowers, especially trilliums and terrestrial orchids.

I have never formally studied sexual behavior, but I have been an interested observer since I was fourteen. I was a very late bloomer. I could see flirtation taking place between classmates and even adults, but I didn't know how to make my own voice, lips, eyes, or body do the same. When I was in college, I went out a few times with a very hot drama student. My roommate asked if he had kissed me. I shamefully admitted he had not. She said, "Make him want you."

Make him want you. The concept I understood; the process, I did not. It was simply not natural to me—at least not then. Batting my eyes, saying sexy teasing things, and sensually rolling my hips seemed silly and embarrassing. I would probably end up batting my hips and rolling my eyes. I suppose that's the same reason I'm not an actress. I'm no good at pretending or being anyone but me. I wanted to be touched and kissed, but I didn't feel comfortable with touching or kissing him. More simply stated, I felt desire but didn't yet feel the freedom to express it. So I certainly couldn't initiate it. I was also shy and rarely made eye contact. I later learned that eye contact was key.

Years later, Robert and I were in an airport with our two girls, one in arms and one a toddler. We were waiting for a delayed connecting flight. An attempt to distract and entertain Greer, while Robert held Summer, turned into a game of follow-the-leader. I walked, then hopped, then spun. She imitated my movements behind me. Soon other bored children followed her. We made a long train, hopping and dancing through the aisles, past relieved and equally entertained parents. I remember I was wearing boots and a long skirt and must have looked like a crazed Mary Poppins. My long hair, which was pulled up in a twist held by a clip, began to fall. The stewardess announced it was time to board. The children dispersed, and I swept my laughing daughter into my arms just as an attractive passenger, with briefcase and overcoat in hand, walked up.

"I enjoyed the Pied Piper," he said, looking into my eyes.

My face was flushed from the exercise, and as I pulled my loosened hair back, I looked up into his eyes and felt the current of electric desire pass from him into me and back again. I was late getting there. I already had two children, but I had finally arrived.

From that time forward, I knew how to make a man want me—not by being a Pied Piper, but by unashamedly being myself, releasing the physical, emotional, sensual me. That gets a man's attention and eye contact pulls the trigger. However, it is still largely subconscious and isn't something I remove from a bag to use as a tool.

Back to observations. Sex is a force neither exclusive to humans nor limited to interaction within a species. I had two large dogs when I met Logan. Spur was the male, and Robin the female. They were an important part of my life and each has a story, but not to be told now. Spur loved and followed me everywhere. When I left the house, he sat by the window and watched me drive away, remaining there until I returned. Even when I showered, he would lie beside the closed door and wait for me. When Logan embraced me, Spur would moan and groan as if he were being tortured.

Robin in turn loved and followed Spur everywhere. After his death she transferred her loyalty to me, but it was no more than that. I was her provider, and she was my protector. Logan was her real replacement for Spur. She would jump on the couch beside him and lay her head on his leg, rolling her eyes and looking up at him adoringly. When I entered the room, Robin's head would come up and she would give me an evil look as if to say, "Back off, girlfriend, he's mine."

Spur was buried in a garden in the front yard where I could talk to him and keep his memory near. There's a large stone beside an azalea to mark his grave. If you go there, say "hello" for me. When Robin died, I called Logan even though we were no longer seeing one another. He had also cared for her, and I wanted him to know. He came immediately and asked if he could bury her on his lot in the mountains. She had travelled there with us, and her arthritic joints had become young again in the cool high altitudes. So it seemed like a good place for her to rest.

Another example of love between humans and other creatures happened when a perfect stranger who had heard that a variety of animals had been in my keeping brought me an African goose. She thought Charlotte would be happier in a home on the lake where she could live a more traditional goose life (whatever that is).

Charlotte was beautiful. She had brown, black, and white coloring, and her head was at least three feet from the ground. This was before Steven and before Spur and Robin. When she was out of her pen, she walked beside me. When I stooped to plant or weed in the garden, she would gently peck my shoulder. Cars would stop while both adults and children watched in wonder as a woman and goose walked and talked together.

One day while we were out in the yard, my neighbor Ben came over. Charlotte was in front of me and the moment she saw him advancing, she lowered her head, spread her wings, and ran straight for him. Her beak closed on a very delicate part of his anatomy and twisted. Ben dropped to his knees, his face drained of color. The story spread, and no men were willing to step in my yard while Charlotte was out and about.

She wasn't friendly to my daughters, but she seemed to be of no danger to them. Fearing she might injure a young boy, I found a home for her on a farm with a pond. The couple had two sons. I warned them of her behavior, but they were proud of their ability to handle varied animals, and promised to wear cups for protection.

A few months later, the new owners called to say Charlotte was the proud father of eggs about to hatch into goslings, and he was no longer attacking anyone. Because Charlotte did not lay eggs, they had wondered if it was possible that she was a he. So they bought a female goose, and the question was answered, the problem solved. Charlotte is now Charlie.

Charlie had claimed me as his mate and had protected me from other males. Maybe I should have kept him.

Sexual desire held its power over me for a number of years. It dominated my ability to relate objectively to men, and interfered with my peace of mind. When early symptoms of menopause began, I was ending my life with Steven, before it ended me. Sex was stuffed away in a closet.

After Steven, I didn't want another relationship, but I didn't like the loneliness. The girls were busy with their careers and marriages. Never alone before, I'd had roommates, a husband, or my children since I had left the care of my own parents. Intellectually, I knew I would adjust eventually, but I hated it.

So one day, I asked my goose-shy neighbor if he knew any single men. He did. One was a dentist, divorced for several years; the other was a botanist who taught with him at UNC and was in the midst of a divorce. I opted for door number one, and after a few dates closed that door. By spring, a few other nameless men had briefly entered my life.

The botanist, Logan, didn't call until May. He had waited until his separation was final, and he had been in his own place a while. He asked me to dinner, and after comparing calendars, we finally found a Saturday in mid-June. With such a tight schedule, he seemed safe—no time for a real relationship.

I wore my most feminine dress and was pleased when he arrived in a sport coat and tie. We went to a modest Thai restaurant with fabulous food. Like me, he was born in Texas. We were both university professors, gardeners, and athletes. We both liked country and western music and built stone walls. Best of all, we spent the evening telling stories about growing up in Texas. And we laughed.

I think Logan decided I was the woman for him on that first date. It was too quick for me. I had layers of barriers to break through before I could trust someone else of my own species. Dogs and geese were simpler and limited to adoration. I encouraged Logan to date other women, but he didn't.

Eventually, when I couldn't drive him away, I embraced us. We were like two eagles, sky dancing—spinning above the ground, locked together and lost in passion, then releasing and falling to earth, weighted by doubt. At the last moment, an updraft of wind and spirit would lift us, allowing us to soar together again. But I couldn't get past the past.

After Lindsay was born, I focused on my children and grandchildren and my teaching. It gave me enough separation from Logan to look more objectively at us. I felt trapped once again, but knew it was my own fault. Robert once told me that when we kissed, he felt like he was suffocating. My immediate thought had been, *So why don't you breathe through your nose?* But now I finally understood. It was emotional, not physical.

When Logan had been gone from my life for a while, I realized he had done nothing wrong. He had offered love in expectation of it being returned. Instead, I turned him away, told him the magic was gone. It wasn't gone; it was simply smothered by my fears.

Logan retired and left for the mountains to build a log house, his boyhood dream. I felt hollow and found less and less pleasure in my work. Life went on for another year, and then the university system created an opportunity for early retirement. I took it.

Logan had shown me that increasing age and hormonal changes in no way eliminated my desire for or enjoyment in physical love. It was simply no longer all-consuming. Maybe that's why menopause is sometimes referred to as the change. Your passion doesn't go away; it merely changes from an overwhelming blinding need to a delicious dessert after a fabulous meal. In other words, it can still be hot, but it's a controlled burn.

I bought the egg with the trillium inside for his birthday. We went our separate ways before that day. So now it is a reminder of something good behind a door I slammed shut.

"It sounds like Anne knows she made a mistake letting Logan go. Why hasn't she gone after him?" Elizabeth muses.

"I think Anne learned a lot about herself when she wrote this journal for us. Maybe she didn't recognize her mistake until it was too late."

"You mean maybe he has already found another woman?"

"I can only answer based on what she has told us about him, Liz. He sounds like me; he wouldn't give up easily. He also sounds like a loner. I imagine he would rather be alone than with someone purely for the sake of company. If he truly loves Anne, there won't be anyone to replace her."

"Is that how you feel about me, Noah?"

He lays the journal carefully on the dock, sits for a moment watching the light growing dim, and then whispers. "Come here."

She moves to his lap, bringing the down-filled throw and the glass egg. He wraps his arms around her as she pulls the throw closer to her neck for warmth. Noah kisses her ear. "Can I feel you up, lady?"

"Don't you dare!" She glances at the houses across the lake. "I'll bet there are people with binoculars, leering and drooling."

He slips his arms under the cover and says, "Not unless they have x-ray vision." And they remain there, on the blue heron's dock, holding and caressing one another—both painfully aware that the days of intimacy and rediscovery have ended, as Elizabeth's body has become a war-zone between cancer and chemo. Unable to think about or even daydream about the future, steeped in disease and decline, her mind escapes to Josh's books. Unwilling to think about a future without her, Noah's mind escapes to Anne.

"Faaarark!" startles them both as the blue heron soars by, low to the water, and scoops a small fish for dinner.

EMAIL TO ANNE:

Your damned heron scared us half to death this evening. When will you be in town? I need to talk to someone outside of the world I live in before I go insane. In answer to your earlier question, you are drawn to one-woman-men because that's what you want for yourself. Wake up and smell the roses. Go see Logan!—*Noah*

P.S. In your stories, you continue to hint at very dark experiences with Steven. Are you safe? Did you leave Durham because you're afraid of him? This isn't nosey. This is concerned. One more thing, who is your exterminator? I know you had the house treated before you left, but he forgot the attic.

EMAIL TO NOAH:

I happened to be online when your message arrived. I'll be in town after Thanksgiving. Thanks for the advice and concern. I'm not afraid, just careful. By the way, how would I find out if someone has a life insurance policy on me? Probably accidental life. Wouldn't I have to agree to that, even if that other person is paying the premiums?

My exterminator is Harris and Sons. Sorry you had a problem.— *Always, Anne*

Chapter 12

Purple & Red

AS ONE SPARK CAN KINDLE a flame that grows to a warming fire, one suggestion can prod memory into tentative desire.

Anne makes plans to visit Logan. But Celita's gifts of hats at the August party ignited another idea which has to be explored before a trip to the Blue Ridge Mountains.

Instead of her usual jeans and t-shirt, Anne is wearing tan slacks and a cream colored blouse as she walks her bicycle down the bank to the road. She turns to look up at the progress of the massive construction project. She wonders if it pleases Paul, or if this reshaping of his childhood landscape is a loss that saddens him.

From River Road, looking up, Anne's house is above and to the left of Saint Angelica, and the four new sites are growing below and on the right, dotting the bank with white stucco, in a diagonal flourish, caught in place by parallel lines of stone walls. It looks more like a painting of a seaside village in Spain or Mexico than a riverbank in North Carolina. Kente and Carlos, unable to visualize the end result, rejected suggestions from Anne about where to place the four triplexes. So she planned the terracing in a way that led their decisions. And then she happily gave them credit for the sweeping design.

Carlos hired ten additional men to keep the multiple projects in motion. For the first time in many years as a laborer, he has to limit his work to supervising, while three crews work simultaneously on different structures. The foundations for the four triplexes are already poured. Anne and her apprentices have almost completed the stone walls and have finished planting the grasses and shrubs everywhere except in the construction zone.

She walks her bicycle past Carlos and calls out to him. "Don't overwork my crew. And don't drive over my new plants with your machinery."

"Your crew asked me for a break from you, Anna. They said keeping up with you is killing them. Where are you going to so clean? You are so clean, you sparkle. What did you do, run yourself through the dishwasher?"

Anne smiles. "It's a dusty day, isn't it? Well, by the time I get to the Baptist Church, my sparkle will be gone."

"Ah, yes! I forgot about Miss Marjorie's meeting. Be careful on your bicycle. Remember what happened to Juan. And why do you want to go to this silly woman thing, anyway? You're a builder of walls. Marry me, Anna," he jokes, "and I'll let you build all the walls you want."

"Thanks, Carlos, but besides you being closer to the age of my daughters, I think my wall-building days are over." She taps the new rearview mirror on her bicycle handle. "This will tell me if I need to get off the road. I got one for Juan, too. But if you want a wall-building woman, you know Maria is my best apprentice."

"Maria scares me," he whispers. "She's stronger than I am. Anyway, tell my baby sister good luck."

In a classroom of the Baptist Church, Marjorie calls the meeting of the Red Hat Club to order. She wears a purple print cotton dress that has been in her closet for the last thirty years and a red cowboy hat with a white feather in the band. The noisy conversations continue.

Wacko, Anne thinks, sipping hot tea and eating shortbread cookies. Her visual memory is clicking away, logging-in the wonderfully picturesque ladies in their red and purple. Ten members and several guests have arrived, a large showing, spurred here by phone calls from Marjorie. Anne, not yet a member, sits hatless beside Celita. "My head feels naked." Anne whispers to Celita, who smiles nervously.

"We're not here to visit today!" Marjorie's raised voice causes the loud conversations to soften and finally end. "Although there's nothin' wrong with visitin'. Just save it 'til after the meetin'. Today we have business to discuss. Most of you know Anne. She brought her friend Celita Ramirez with her to tell you 'bout her idea. More like a dream, I guess. Before Celita talks to you, though, I'm goin' to answer a question that might get in the way of you listenin' to her. You know my Johnny's business has been closed for over thirty years. It just sits there gettin' more dust and spider webs and generally bein' useless. So I've decided to let Celita use it for her dream. But before she speaks, I want to remind those of you old enough to remember, that I used to be a sorta' recluse. Now here I am talkin' in front of everyone. What I'm tryin' to say is, with a little determination, anyone an' anythin' can be improved."

Celita pats her face with a handkerchief and rises to face the membership. "Buenos dios. I mean, good afternoon, senoras, I mean ladies." Flustered, she takes a deep breath and continues. "A few weeks ago, I told Anne about my dream to open a gift shop with goods that I bring back from Mexico: sombreros, dresses, rugs, baskets, and other crafts. Everybody knows it takes money to make money. I couldn't afford the overhead of a shop or the cost of advertising. And I couldn't leave my regular job to sit in a shop in a dead town that nobody visits, no offense intended. Of course, shop rental in a larger place, like Shallotte, would be even more impossible. So I thought I'd have to find a rich man to marry in order to make the dream come true." Kind laughter urges her on.

"But Anne and Miss Marjorie, were worried that I might be serious about marrying for money, so together we came up with this idea. We want to clean up Miss Marjorie's store and paint it. It already has shelves and display cases and a counter. They only need to be washed. It won't cost much money, but it will take a lot of labor. Then we want to invite people to bring in samples of their art. Anyone whose work shows creativity and good craftsmanship will be accepted into the co-op. That's what we want, an arts and crafts cooperative."

Celita skips a beat and then continues after a sharply dressed stunning woman arrives late and stands at the back. "I'm not an artist, but I will bring arts and crafts from Mexico. Each item will be signed and will include a biographical sketch of the artist that made it. Anne is a painter and will submit some of her work for consideration. I know at least six artists—potters, weavers, and painters—from the Latino community. I have heard there are many others in the new developments upriver, and some of you are artists as well."

A freelance newspaper reporter asks, "Would you include photography? And what are the details on the business end?"

Celita looks to Anne for help. She rises and walks to the front. "Yes, we want art photography. Your costs will be ten percent of your sales to be used for shop overhead, and another ten percent will go to the Ave Blanca Limited Liability Company. Your commitment will be your assistance in getting the shop ready for use and time spent in the shop, selling to customers."

"How much time?" someone asks.

"That depends on how many artists are involved. One half day a week is our current goal, with two workers in the shop at all times. That means we're hoping to get at least twenty-four artists in the co-op."

A disgruntled member stands to speak. "Why would Ave Blanca get ten percent?"

"I can answer that." A small gray haired woman, in what Anne guesses is a purple square-dance dress and a red ribbon in her hair, responds as she stands. "I'm a partner in Ave Blanca. Our sole purpose is to rebuild Pearl and make it a thriving town again, not just a bedroom community for Shallotte and Wilmington. The money that comes to the company is used to begin new projects such as the one they're describing right now."

"How much of the Ave Blanca profits go to the partners?" And more disgruntled mumbling follows.

The square-dancer patiently continues. "Each of the partners either emptied their savings or mortgaged their property or both in order to invest in Ave Blanca. When the rentals beside Saint Angelica, are finished, each member will get a portion of fifty percent of the rent profits, based on the amount of their original investment. The other fifty percent will go back to the company to support another Pearl project. Eventually, if this is as successful as we hope, our original investment will be paid back and we will each begin to see a small income. Of course I'll probably be dead by then, so my children will inherit my share. But that's only fair since I hocked their inheritance in order to be a part of this wonderful project." More laughter follows as she sits.

"What does this have to do with us? We're not all artists."

Anne takes a deep breath and then plunges into the next idea. "That brings us to Phase Four. Phase One is the marina, already completed. Phase Two is the triplex rentals. Phase Three is the artist co-op. And Phase Four is the most ambitious because it involves so many people. We want to clean up the remaining closed shops and empty houses on Broad Street and find a use for them. One of the ideas we've considered is to turn all of Broad Street into a flea market every Friday and Saturday. Some of the empty shops could be used as restaurants sponsored by the three churches. They would be fundraisers for the churches, and provide food for the people that come to the market."

An intake of breath is followed by a simultaneous response. "Restaurants?"

"Not on a large scale, more like what you see at the State Fair. One church might have nothing but fried chicken, potato salad, and green beans. Another might have only baked goods, breads and desserts. The third might have only fried fish and coleslaw, or hot dogs and potato chips, or tamales and burritos, or soup and salad. Somebody stop me!" This time the laughter is long. "In other words, each shop would have a limited menu they could produce in large quantities, preferably ahead of time."

A young woman with a baby in her arms stands. "Why not limit the food to something we could become known for, like barbeque, or chili, or clam chowder? My kids won't eat any of that, but we could have something simple like corn dogs for the children. We could become known for our soups or barbeque, and we could freeze what doesn't sell."

"Or eat it," someone adds.

"What about barbeque and chili in the winter, and chicken salad and clam chowder in the summer?"

"Every weekend? That's asking a lot."

"Ladies," Anne calls, trying to calm the simultaneous eruption of questions and suggestions. "That would be up to you. You could chose to do one weekend every month with extra weekends during the summer when we're likely to get more visitors from beach tourism. A flea market includes everything from antiques, to junk from your attic, to vegetables from your garden. You don't have to be an artist."

"It sounds like a lot of work, a big job of coordinating people and space."

"What happens when it rains?" The questions and talk amongst themselves continues as Anne tries to get their attention again.

"We thought about a series of large tents," she says without enthusiasm. "I wish we could build something more permanent, but the construction crews are booked for two years just finishing the triplexes."

Another member Anne has never met rises. "Well Ladies, for you newcomers, I'm Donna. Not all of our husbands are dead or run off. My Dan can build anything. I'll bet we could get enough volunteer workers to build a long narrow one-story building. You could put booths in it and rent them to the serious sellers. The others could take their chances on the weather and set up their own booths or tents in the park at the end of town at no charge for the space."

"That would be wonderful," Celita says. "And we could use the building for other community activities when it's not a flea market. If we don't make permanent booths, we could have dances and all kinds of gatherings and activities there."

"We could make folding screens to use as dividers to separate the booths."

"And we could paint them or cover them with fabric."

Anne is thrilled to hear the sometimes timid, sometimes bold ideas being offered. She promised herself she would propose the idea and then turn it over to the group. She didn't want heavy involvement. But she can't shut her mind down. The solution to the permanent space seems so obvious, but she hasn't been able to lead anyone to it. She calls once more for attention. "There are two free-standing shops between the future art co-op and the park. That's where the flea market should be. I don't know who owns them, but they both seem abandoned. Maybe we could purchase them for back taxes and then renovate them. Donna's husband could build between the two shops, joining them and making one long building with entrances through the shops at either end." Overwhelmed by the enormity and yet obvious logic of the idea, the women are speechless.

"All right ladies. These are all good ideas, but we're gettin' ahead of ourselves. Now we're talkin' 'bout land and materials. I know who owns the buildin's between my shop and the park," Marjorie says, resuming the role of leader. "I'll look into the possibilities of purchasin' it. I think we need to talk this over among ourselves and with our families and come up with a plan after we have more information. Then we'll meet again after Thanksgivin'." She pauses for a moment and then continues, "Some of us are tapped out. We can't take on more debt. The co-op is very doable. We can start on that right away and continue brainstormin' 'bout Phase Four. Now who wants to be on the committee to get the ball rollin' on Phase Three, the art co-op?"

A timid woman with a small red artist's tam on her white hair raises her hand.

"Do you want to be on the committee, Dorothy?"

"Yes. But I also want to say that I like to paint murals. If we want to be identified as something new and special, we need to develop our own look. The triplexes at the marina will have a definite Spanish look. We could continue that. We could do murals on the outside walls of the co-op and on the walls of the shops used as restaurants. We could even do murals on the flea market building. The designs could combine Latino and North Carolina coastal images."

"I'll help you, Dorothy," Anne offers with a resigned smile. "I've painted scenery for more than half my life. In fact, everyone could help. We could create paint-by-number designs."

Still standing at the back, the late arrival asks, "What about the African American members of the community? They don't seem to be represented in this too-cute Anglo Latino plan."

There is a silence, and Anne notes that several members roll their eyes as if they expected this interruption in an otherwise united atmosphere. Thinking as quickly as she can, Anne responds. "Thanks for reminding us. Would you like to work with Dorothy and me in planning the murals?"

"I'm not an artist."

"But you can help us make sure that all cultures in Pearl are represented. Maybe you can also research some of the history of the area and find new ideas to include."

"I don't have time. Just be sure we aren't *excluded*." With that, she turns and leaves.

Angry murmuring follows and is interrupted by a soft voice. "Could I help paint?"

"Can you hold a paintbrush?"

"Yes."

"Then you can help."

"All right," Marjorie concludes, "like I said, we need a committee."

When the meeting is over, and the last member is gone, Anne walks to Marjorie. "Who was that gorgeous bitch with all the anger?"

Celita laughs as she ties the garbage bag full of paper plates and cups. "That was Ayesha, Kente's wife."

"Oh! I guess that explains some things. But to be honest, I'm amazed. I'm very sensitive to African-Americans. In fact, I usually gravitate to them when I'm in a culturally mixed social situation. Kente is the only black I've seen since I moved here. And his wife has turned down several invitations, so I assumed they socialize away from Pearl. And, until you told me, I wouldn't have guessed she was black in the first place. Let me carry that, Celita."

"She could pass," Marjorie admits as she sits, exhausted. "In fact she did for a long time. Her mama was white, and her daddy was light-skinned. He was Army and was killed in Viet Nam by what they called friendly fire."

"A prettier child there never was—not because she was light, you understand. She seemed to inherit the best looks from both worlds. When they moved here, she was in high school and her daddy was in Vietnam. She passed as white. It cost her lots of abuse in school after they found out she was black. She grew a chip on her shoulder you wouldn't believe, always in trouble. Then she and her mama disappeared. When she come back, married to Kente, she had a different name and a different attitude. The chip was still there, but she had sorta got control of it, and had decided she was more black than white and more African than American. So she called herself Ayesha 'cause the name her parents give her, Allison, was too white."

"She was definitely in control today."

"Yep!" Marjorie sighs. "That's Ayesha. But to answer your other question, there's several black families that live in Eula, a few miles west. They have their own school and keep to themselves. I once had some very dear friends there, but they were older than me, and they're all gone now. Miss Sarah was black as night and was my daughter's namesake. She helped me when John died, and even before that, when my babies died. People here have discouraged the folks there from buyin' property in Pearl."

"That kind of thinking and behavior should have ended forty years ago."

"I know, Anne, but as long as people live apart, change is slow."

"I assume they have their own church?"

"Oh, si," Celita says. "When we were little, my brother Carlos and I used to go there and sit outside just to hear their music. We thought we weren't allowed inside."

Anne puts her arm around her aged friend and nods to Celita. "I have to tell you two, I love the plans. I'm really impressed with the idea of using the food as a hook and specializing in chowders and chili. But there is a limit to how much time I want to commit. If we can't get general support from the community, I won't go beyond the co-op. I know the co-op can work. It would work better in conjunction with the flea market because that would bring larger numbers here with the intent of shopping. If the flea market materializes, I think we'll have to create two or three paid positions to take the responsibility for spearheading the business end of it. For that matter, the co-op will require some business knowledge just to manage it on paper. We've already used all of Kente's pro-bono time with contracts and other legal responsibilities for Ave Blanca. Do we have anyone with accounting and marketing skills in the Red Hat Club?"

Celita shakes her head as she rises and searches for her purse. "Anne, do you know what my real job is?"

Anne is embarrassed. "I assumed you worked for an upholsterer in Shalotte. I'm sorry, Celita. I guess I don't know what you do."

"I'm an accountant for a furniture company. I learned how to upholster and work the sales floor while waiting for a position to open in management. That's why I wanted to have my own shop. I'm not an artist, but I know how to sell and how to balance the books and pay the taxes."

"Well that settles it. We'll have to find a way to pay you so that you can be here full-time. I would argue about you not being an artist, though. You're a gifted seamstress and upholsterer. You could probably take orders for custom upholstery and sell original dresses if you wanted, as part of the co-op."

"Maybe. But oh, Anne, can you just picture the town with all the murals? Wouldn't it be beautiful? And it would stretch all the way to the marina. People could ride in their boats to the flea market. And we could continue your landscaping idea for the triplexes."

"You mean stone terraces?" Anne groans.

"No. I mean beautiful grasses mixed with bright colored flowers."

"Wow!" Anne laughs. "That would add even more continuity between the town and the triplexes. We could order large quantities of grasses to get the best prices and sell them to the whole community at cost to encourage more of the same."

"At cost, my grannie's panties!" Marjorie exclaims, slapping her hand on the table. "We can charge a gnat's ass less than retail, for the sake of competition, and use the profit to help with the costs of that gol'danged flea market."

"I'm sorry, ladies, but I'm on overload. This is moving faster than I can follow. I have to go tell Carlos. Gracias, mi amigos." And after a flurry of hugs, Celita leaves. Anne tells Marjorie she also has to leave to select some flat stones for topping the last terrace wall.

"Is that why your waist has gotten so small, all that bendin' over and fittin' stones?"

"I'm sure it helps," Anne laughs as she walks beside Marjorie to the door. "I've also been riding my bicycle more, thanks to you, and eating healthy, thanks to Paul. He provides me with so much fish, and has taught me a number of delicious ways to prepare it. I used to think the only way to eat fish was fried. I need to have you over for dinner."

"Yes, you do. Now, before you go, tell me what you meant about havin' limits in what you're prepared to do. You seem to be over-the-edge involved already."

"Yes, but each of the projects I'm doing right now will end. The terraces are almost finished. The co-op is ongoing, but I'll just be one of the members, contributing art and a little time in the shop each week. That's all I want. I don't want a full-time job. I have three grandchildren and another on the way. I need time with them." She gets on her bicycle, and then pauses before pushing on the pedals. "And I have some personal issues to straighten out."

"Personal, huh? Are you hidin' a man somewhere?"

"Sort of."

Marjorie's face falls. "Does he deserve you?"

"I think it's more a question of whether I deserve him and whether he still wants me."

"Hmmph! So are you just goin' to sit around and wait for him to make those decisions?"

"Well, he doesn't know that he has a choice. I'm going to Greer's for Thanksgiving. I may see him then. And to be honest, I'm not sure he *does* have a choice."

"He's in the mountains?"

"Yes."

"That's a long way from here."

"I know, and that's a part of my confusion."

"Okay. I'm beginnin' to get the picture, I guess."

"Marjorie, I'm so invested in this town and very attached to my home and friends. I'm not leaving. I just don't want to let my level of busy-ness interfere with my family and a personal life—if one exists."

Email to Noah:

This is all your fault. I'm going to see Logan. Glad my heron scared you—wish I could have seen that. I'll be in Durham next Saturday.— *Always, Anne*

Chapter 13

Phase to Logan

A CRISP BREEZY DAY begins the week of Thanksgiving. Anne tosses her bag into the Honda and pulls out of her drive. She sees Paul on the road ahead, fishing gear in hand. She feels conflicted, pulled between Pearl and the mountains—or is it between Paul and Logan? She slows the car to his pace. "I've been hearing a lot about the mercury in fish. You aren't supposed to eat fish every day, Paul."

"Too late, I'm addicted. Besides, your Lindsay told me I'll live. Remember? I'm trusting that she has insider knowledge."

"Will you be having Thanksgiving dinner with Carlos's family?"

"Actually, Marjorie asked his family and me to her home. She's never done that before, invited someone from the Latino community to her home for dinner. You continue to be a good influence."

"She's become very attached to Celita. And she cares more about you than you know."

"She does seem more relaxed with me than she used to be. Is that your influence again?"

"No." Anne stops the car. "I can't drive and talk without risking running over your foot. I'm occasionally a sounding board for Marjorie, as she is for me, and as you are for me."

"Will you get out of the car?"

Anne opens the car door. Paul puts his fishing gear down and opens his arms to her. She steps into them and they hold each other for a long moment. It isn't a passionate embrace, but rather one filled with warmth and caring. His voice is clear, not husky with need when he says, "I will say this only one time, Anna. Your presence has reminded me that I am a man. You have forced me to remember how it feels to want and love a woman." Anne starts to speak, but he stops her. "You are much like her, but you aren't her. Perhaps that's why I am so at ease with you. You are a safe haven. I think I am the same for you. If I weren't a priest, I would be tempted to take advantage of your kindness, but I would always be thinking of her. You deserve better than that."

He releases her from his embrace but holds her shoulders. "I am very grateful for our friendship. Give your family my good wishes. Will Summer and Joe join you?"

"Yes," she says, and steps further away. "It will be mayhem. I'm going up into the mountains for a day to visit a friend." Her eyes look away, unable to meet his. "I'll probably need a break from the little ones. They're easier one at a time than all at once."

He lifts her chin so she can't avoid returning his look. "Lucky friend. Now I am jealous. I love the mountains, especially at this time of year. Drive carefully and God speed."

Anne gets into her car and drives away before he can see the tears welling, about to spill. She is already missing Paul and Pearl, even as she escapes them.

The drive to her daughter's is long but beautiful. Anne rehearses what she wants to say to Logan, discarding each imagined dialogue until she decides this is something she can't preplan. She'll know what to say when the time arrives.

Why do I want to see Logan? Do I want to restart our relationship? There were reasons why we ended it. How can I build a life with him if he's in the mountains and I'm at the coast? Am I willing to give up my home? Would I ask him to give up his? Is this all wasted energy because he's found someone else? Am I opening an old wound for both of us because I'm lonely? She shakes her head in frustration, and then tries again.

I'm tired of having to carefully choose words around needy men for fear of misleading them. I'm tired of controlling my own needs or trying to turn friendship into something more. BUT! In spite of my friendships and a high level of busy-ness, I am lonely. I don't simply miss intimacy. Maybe I simply miss intimacy with Logan, not only the passion but also the companionship. I guess it's time to find out. BUT!

She turns on the radio and finds a political talk show, more rehashing of the war in Iraq, anything for distraction.

The day before Thanksgiving, a cold front arrives and settles on the foothills. As Anne and her grandson Bradley drive to where Logan is building his log house, she vacillates between reluctance and determination. She hasn't called, but even if he's not there, she wants to see what he's accomplished on the house and to find Robin's grave. She has brought Bradley for company, and to reduce the number of children creating havoc at Greer's house, and perhaps to ease the tension if Logan *is* there.

The leaves are still pretty in the foothills, but as they ascend to higher altitudes, little color remains, except for the evergreen hemlocks and pines. Although she appreciates the lavishness of the view in the peak leaf season, Anne prefers the barren trees with the Blue Ridge Mountains in the background, rising above their sometimes lacey, sometimes stark patterns of branches— much more interesting than the dresses of color they wore just a few weeks before.

"Where are we going, Nana?" Bradley asks yet again.

"We're going to the mountains. We're going to see Papa Logan. Do you remember him? He's an old friend of mine."

"Of course I remember him, Nana. He came to my house."

"Really? I mean, recently?"

"I don't remember when, but he came to see us one night. He played with Tommy and me."

"I wonder how much he's done on the house." Anne muses, not expecting a response from Bradley.

"He doesn't live in it yet. He lives in a tent. It's cool."

"Is that what he told you?"

"No, that's what I saw."

"Okay, someone's keeping secrets from Nana. So you've visited Papa Logan?" *And now I understand Greer's look of concern when I asked Bradley to come with me today.*

"We visited after church one day. Tommy and me played in the creek. We saw some fish."

"How long ago was this?"

"I don't remember. But I can tell time, Nana. It's 10:30 o'clock."

"You're a smart boy, and I'm proud of you. Do you remember what Papa and your parents talked about?"

"Boring stuff—the cabin, and flowers. There's lots of places Tommy and me can't step because of flowers, so Papa made a trail for us to walk on."

"Somehow, I can picture all of this. What happened if you forgot and left the trail?"

"He yelled, really loud!"

Anne's laugh is tinged with sarcasm. "Now it makes even more sense."

"Are we almost there?"

"Yes we are."

They turn off the highway onto a gravel road which narrows quickly. Anne was with Logan when he first looked at the lot and decided to buy it. He was so happy to find land on water—just a creek, but a wide and noisy one, full of boulders and rushing water. He thought it would be nice to sleep with the sound of the creek. It was. They returned to the lot twice to camp out and to plot the locations for the house, well, and septic tanks. She remembers to bear to the right as she passes driveways and side roads with several log houses that appear empty. She wonders if anyone lives here year-round, or if they're just summer homes. The road turns again, and she sees Logan's cabin at the end of it. She forgets to breathe. His dream is a reality of square logs with white chinking and black trim on the windows—beyond dramatic. She sees Logan's truck, and slows the car. She breathes.

Bradley squeals in excitement. "There's Papa up there!" Anne looks up and sees Logan on a scaffold.

"He's working on the chimney." Anne watches him anchor a large flat stone into the mortar he has spread." *Funny thing to have in common. We both like to work with stone. And neither of us knows we're too old for this kind of crap.* She can't resist taking a mental picture. *Click. Stone chimney, stone mason, stone man.*

Logan's so involved with his work he doesn't notice his visitors until he hears the car door slam. He twists his body to see the car but sees only Anne. He has imagined her coming here so many times, but in his daydreams, he is freshly showered and on his porch—not on a scaffold and covered with mortar and sweat. He puts his trowel in the bucket of mortar and climbs down the ladder tied to the two-by-four make-shift scaffold. By the time he reaches the ground, Anne and Bradley are walking down the front path, admiring his landscaping. Bradley is on the large boulders beside the path, leaping from one to the other.

"Don't jump on that last stone," Logan says, wiping his face and hands with a handkerchief. "My pet snake lives under it. He doesn't hear sounds, but he feels vibrations."

"Will he bite me?"

"No, but you might scare him away. I want him around. He eats mice and keeps away poisonous snakes. He's my friend."

"Your friend is a snake?" Bradley asks with exaggerated disbelief.

"No, the snake is my friend. There's a difference." And finally, he can focus on Bradley no longer. He lifts his gaze from the boy to Anne.

She's wearing black jeans and a green sweater. She's lost weight, making the bones of her face more pronounced. He had expected her to age in the year since he last saw her when he picked up Robin's body to bring back here for burial. But, if anything, she looks younger. She also looks fragile, but he knows better. Her hair, red-gold in the sun, is longer than he remembered, long enough to tuck behind her ears, long enough to catch the breeze and dance across her face. She pushes it away, extending her other hand. "Hello, Logan." He holds it in both of his.

"Hello, Anne. If I'd known you were comin', I'da baked a cake. Or at least taken a shower."

"Sorry. It was a sort of spur-of-the-moment decision. I didn't even know if you'd be here. But I'm glad you are." He looks thin to her, but he has always been thin. And, in spite of his weight and his age, he looks strong. He is tan and muscular and moves with the energy and purpose of a man half his age. His white hair has also thinned, but he still wears it in a flat-top, reminiscent of the fifties. He has always reminded her of the actor, Lee Marvin. His blue eyes probe her face and her green ones look back. She reaches up and brushes a leaf from his hair. His jaw muscles flex, but he forces a smile. She backs away, realizing her mistake—too intimate, too possessive, too soon.

"Come in and let me show you the house."

Anne had seen the floor plans for the house before they ended their relationship, so she thinks it will hold no surprises. She's wrong. The massiveness of the log walls and the beautiful detail Logan has brought to the construction are overwhelming. The kitchen, laundry room, and bathrooms already have natural stone tile floors. The living room and dining room will have hardwood floors made of hickory. The bedroom floors will be carpeted. The kitchen cabinets are already installed and made of hickory with a natural finish, and the countertops are made of large granite tiles. The master bedroom is downstairs and the two guest bedrooms, a bathroom, and a loft that overlooks the living room are upstairs. Counting closets and storage spaces, there are fifteen doors. Logan made each one.

Anne laughs softly. "I have four internal doors in my house: two for bedrooms and two for bathrooms. The other doorways have curtains or nothing."

"That idea could have saved me hundreds of hours of labor. You should have visited sooner."

"You wouldn't have been happy with curtains."

"Maybe not."

Bradley runs inside. "Can I go to the creek, Papa?"

"Sure, partner. But don't get on the rocks or in the water. We can watch you from the back porch." There are two Amish-made rocking chairs on the covered back porch which is larger than any room in the cabin. They rock and watch Bradley while Anne gives Logan the sincere compliments he needs to hear about his home and the hard work that created it. He knows she understands the time and labor. He also knows that if they had remained together, it would have taken him twice as long. He would have been back and forth to Durham and would have spent the rainy and cold weeks and months with her. But it would have been less lonely. He would gladly trade progress on the house for Anne's affection.

"What a beautiful fall day," she says, making conversation.

"It gets pretty warm in the sun, especially handling mortar and stone up on that scaffold. But it's always cool here in the shade. I see Greer and Ray now and then."

"I know. Bradley told me." There is a slight edge to her voice.

"When you and I stopped seeing each other, I had a hard time letting their friendship go, particularly hard since they live so near me. Ray and his dad have helped me several times when I needed an extra pair of hands. It's only in the last few months that I've visited them. I asked Greer not to tell you because I didn't want you to think I was keeping tabs on you or putting pressure on you in any way. Don't be angry at her."

"When have you seen me angry at one of my daughters? I'm glad you're still friends. And you don't have to keep your friendship a secret from me."

"I'm hoping we can be friends too, Anne."

"Of course," *Why does that irritate me? I thought, maybe hoped, he wanted more.*

"When the house is finished, we can do some things together. Things that friends do—like go on a bicycle ride, or on a picnic, or go fishing."

You do want more. But I can't encourage you unless I'm sure I want it as well. "You'll have to come to Pearl and see my home. I've learned to sail, and the fishing is great." *And you need to see that I have a life.*

"I'd forgotten how your lips move while you have a conversation with yourself. But I'm sure you remember I don't like being in water where I can't see the bottom."

"Every time I go out, I just put myself in God's hands, and I don't worry about it. In fact, I feel strangely safer there where I can see three hundred and sixty degrees around."

"I'm as bothered by big water as I am by tight spaces. Bradley! Don't step on that moss! It has flowers in it."

"I forgot. You're claustrophobic." *And I'm beginning to remember some of the things that used to bother me. Like controlling every step of a child's feet, or mine. Like . . . Shake it off, Anne! You're looking for excuses to blemish him.*

"I'm also afraid of heights, but I roofed this house, and I'm now facing the chimney with stone on a twenty-foot scaffold of questionable stability. So my neuroses don't stop me from doing what I need or want to do. In other words, Anne, I would like to sail with you sometime." They both almost smile.

"Speaking of stone, I just finished supervising the laying of two terrace walls, each of them thirty inches tall and five hundred feet long." She says it like a challenge.

"Big job. Did you trench and use rebar?"

"Of course."

"And did you make anchors to keep it secure?"

"Logan, I'm not your student. Stop grilling me. I even had an engineer look at the anchors before I covered them up, to make sure they were adequate. Are you doing your chimney the way it should be done?"

"Seems like old times. Me telling you what to do, and you throwing it back in my face. Sorry, Anne. It's just that we've had some problems here with people randomly changing the lay of the land, clear-cutting slopes where tree roots used to retain the soil, and filling in behind unmortared stone walls with tons of dirt. They're unstable, and I'm sure they'll turn into a disaster sooner or later."

"You mean a mudslide?"

"And a rockslide. And some of the rocks are huge boulders. You know hurricane winds and rain can make their way to the mountains."

"I know. Well, I'm sorry about your concerns here, but my walls at the coast will hold, and I'm sure your chimney will as well."

After a short silence, Logan asks the question he has wanted to ask since her arrival. "Why are you here, Anne?"

Good question. "I'm not really sure. I was in the neighborhood . . ."

"Right!"

"Okay. I was curious about how your house was coming, and I thought I wanted to see Robin's grave. I say 'thought' because now that I'm here, I'm not sure I'm up to it."

"It's a short climb across the road. The grave overlooks the house and the creek."

Tears surface and Anne sighs, "I mean that I'm not sure I'm up to the emotion."

Logan reaches over and takes her hand. "I'll ask you again. Why are you here?"

Afraid of what her face might expose, Anne looks away. She rises and calls, "Bradley! You'd better come on up here. We'll walk down the road to the fish pond." She watches the child climb up the bank from the water. "It makes me nervous for him to be down by the creek without us, even though we can see him."

"All right." He sighs, accepting that he will not receive an answer now. "So, you remember the fish pond? Unfortunately, a river otter reduced the trout population there. But it's still a nice walk. I need to cover the mortar in the bucket and the mixing box so it doesn't harden."

"We picked up some fried chicken and biscuits when we passed through Morganton. Would you like to picnic with us, our first thing that friends do?"

"That would be a treat."

Bradley's little legs finally get him up to the porch and his eyes widen. "Where's the chicken? I'm starved!"

"First, we'll use Papa's porta john."

"Cool!"

On the walk to the pond, Logan points out the various wildflowers to Bradley. He stops beside the trunk of a tall Mountain Laurel and bends over.

"Look here," he whispers to Anne. He lifts a large Maple leaf. She bends to see an unimpressive cluster of small green plants.

"*Shortia galacifolia*—wild and rare. I'm protecting these little guys during the leaf season so tourists don't dig them up. Most people wouldn't know them without their spring blooms, but I'd like to move them to a spot where they can spread, a place with less foot traffic. "

Anne wants to touch his shoulder. She loves this protective side of him—even though minutes ago she had complained about it.

During the picnic, they talk of children and grandchildren. Anne tells Logan about Summer's pregnancy, and he updates her on his family. One of Anne's concerns about Logan had been his reluctance to introduce her to his children. His divorce was recent, and he felt they would be too divided in loyalties to accept another woman in their father's life. Anne understood, but it sat sour on her stomach. She shrugs off the negative and tells him about Ave Blanca and Marjorie and Father Paul.

"It sounds like you are really entrenched there."

"I am, Logan. I think it is my destiny, the place I've always been seeking, without knowing it."

"I was just elected president of the homeowners association. I feel like I'm up to my neck in alligators, trying to finish the house and moderate the activities around here."

"Well, we've established that we're both busy in separate worlds."

"It seems that way. You also seem different, Anne, in a good way. I'm not sure I know the words to describe it. You seem less intense, more relaxed in your skin.

"In most ways, I am more relaxed. I've come to terms with a lot of my past, and I don't dwell on it anymore."

"What about *our* past?"

"I still dwell on that."

"Papa, is this a good walking stick?" Bradley asks as he runs up to them, excitedly waving a branch larger than he is.

"I can help you make it into a good walking stick." Logan pulls a knife from his pocket.

After their walk to the fish pond and picnic, they go up the bank across the road from the cabin. Logan leads them to the carefully selected place where he buried Robin. Anne catches her breath when she sees the mound covered with stones. Logan takes Bradley farther up the bank to a clearing where he has planted some rhubarb and a few fruit trees, leaving Anne alone.

"Ah, Robin, my old friend and companion," she says as she sits beside the grave. "I miss you and Spur so much. It still hurts each time I think of you, although it's a hurt that always brings a smile. Greer still has your son, Buddy. But he's getting older, too. You may see him soon. I let Logan bring you here because you loved it so, and because I knew I would be selling the house. I thought he would want you here, too. Remember when you came up here with us to camp, and you ran around like a puppy? And remember how you loved sleeping in the tent with us? Logan covered you with a blanket and slept in the middle with one hand on you and one hand on me. We seemed totally happy then. Why is it so hard for me to trust happiness? Why am I always waiting for it to end, or to be taken away? At least you were never without love, and you never stopped giving it. We could learn a lot from you."

She hears Logan clear his throat and she wipes her eyes with her sweater sleeve, refusing his offer of a handkerchief. "Don't be offended, but my sleeve isn't full of mortar. Your handkerchief is."

"Crazy Nana," Bradley laughs, and then stops when he sees her tears, "What's the matter, Nana? Are you crying?"

"I'm fine, sweetheart."

Logan offers her a hand, pulls her to her feet, and they walk down the path together while Bradley races ahead. At the foot of the slope, he says, "You haven't been without love, either, Anne—not since we met."

"Are we going home, now?" Bradley asks as he jumps the remaining feet to the road, and then runs to the car.

Logan's hands slide up to her shoulders. "I'll ask you for the last time, Anne, why did you come here?"

"I couldn't stay away. I've made a good life for myself, but I miss you. I miss what we had."

"I miss you so much, it's like a living thing that walks in my shadow while I'm working, and lies just out of my reach when I'm sleeping. I can understand your lack of trust in relationships, your general lack of faith in men. But, for the life of me, I don't understand why you let *us* go. Your husbands deserved to lose you. But what did I do?"

Anne lifts her arms to encircle his neck, leaving her body unprotected, exposed, waiting for his hands to pull her against him in the old way. She has always physically opened herself to Logan in an embrace of trust, with no hesitations, no holding back. And he has always accepted this offering with gentleness and gratitude, as he does now.

"It's not you, Logan. It's me," she whispers, stroking his cheek with the back of her hand.

He lowers his head to kiss her and finds her lips soft and eager. The kiss is passionate but brief. Logan is the one to release and back away.

"Forget the friendship crap. I don't want less than all of you, Anne. I don't want to just kiss you and let you go. And I can't go through losing you again." He takes a deep breath before continuing. "So unless you're ready to stay, you need to leave. You know what I can give you."

"Oh, Logan. Those are my choices? Leave or stay? I hate ultimatums. Don't you know that in the end, they never work?"

"I'm sorry, I said it badly. We can meet each other halfway. You know, I don't even like how that sounds. It sounds like compromise. Anne, I want all you have to give in exchange for all I have to give. And if it's not equal, that's okay. Relationships usually aren't. Didn't you tell me that?"

"That imbalance used to haunt me. And now you're telling me that it's okay."

"I appreciate your sense of morals and fair play, but we're not sitting on the scales of justice, Anne. I think we each have more love to give than anyone could measure. But you have to get the cobwebs out of your head before you can see that and believe it."

The car horn is honked impatiently.

"You can't just leave now," he says with frustration, pulling her close again.

"You already told me to go, and I think I'd better. I'll get a broom after the cobwebs and see what's left up there." She gently pushes away. "My card is on the counter in the cabin. It has my address and phone number. I would really like for you to visit. Don't give up on me, Logan, and don't fall off that scaffold."

As Anne drives up the gravel road away from him and his log home, she looks in the rearview mirror and sees Logan watching. He lifts a hand to wave, and she lifts hers to signal back.

After several miles of silence, Bradley asks for a song.

"What would you like to sing?"

"I don't know. You pick"

"All right. How about a song I learned when I was your age? It kind of fits what we've been doing."

"Visiting Papa?"

"No, walking in the mountains. It goes like this:

> 'I love to go a-wandering
> Along the mountain path;
> And as I go, I love to sing,
> My knapsack on my back.
>
> Val-derie, Val-dera,
> Val-derie, Val-dera-ha-ha-ha-ha-ha
> Val-derie, Val-dera,
> My knapsack on my back.
>
> Oh may I go a-wandering
> Until the day I die;
> And may I always laugh and sing
> Beneath God's clear blue sky.

"And then you sing the chorus again." Anne struggles to speak as she chokes up.

"That's a silly song, Nana."

Her eyes are blurred with tears, and she reaches for a tissue. A honking sound jerks her back to reality, searching in her rearview mirror, and then the side mirror. An SUV is trying to pass her on the left, crowding her to the right and the rail on the edge of the cliff. She looks forward and sees an oncoming truck, also honking. Fear fuels white anger as Anne pulls onto the shoulder, lightly scraping the rail, and stops. The passing car slips between. Adrenalin courses through her body, making her weak and shaky. She carefully pulls back onto the road, not wanting to see how close she came to dropping off the side of the mountain . . . with her grandson.

"Did you see the driver in the other car, Bradley?" she asks through clenched teeth.

"No. But I saw the truck driver. He looked scared. I thought it was cool."

Anne drives to an overlook with a view of Table Rock Mountain, pulls into the parking area, and stops. She leans against the steering wheel. Relief from the near accident that might have cost her grandson's life breaks through her wall of control.

Bradley sits for a moment, confused. But when her crying doesn't stop, he releases his safety belt and climbs up into the front seat. Not knowing what is wrong or what to do, he begins to cry also. "I'm sorry, sweet boy." Anne holds him while they both sob.

After a few minutes, Anne pulls her emotions back in check and finds a tissue, wipes her eyes, and blows her nose. She offers another tissue to Bradley who does the same. "I'm sorry I made you cry, Bradley. Let's go sit on the wall and look at Table Rock."

They sit together and Bradley puts his small arm around his grandmother's waist and leans his head against her. "Why were you crying, Nana? You scared me."

"We almost had an accident because I wasn't paying attention."

"Why weren't you paying attention?"

"Because I was sad."

"Why were you sad?"

"I don't know if I can explain it. I guess a lot of things just made me sad all at once."

"Like Robin's grave?"

"Yes."

"And the mountains?"

"Why the mountains?" Anne laughs through new tears.

"Because you were singing about them, and then you started crying. They look sad to me now, too."

"Why do you think they look sad?"

"Because their trees lost their leaves. They look cold."

A line by May Sarton springs to Anne's mind. "I read something in a book once. I believe it goes like this: 'When I think of the trees, I think of how gently they let go, let fall the riches of a season. How, without grief, it seems, they let go, and move deep into their roots for renewal and rest.'"

"I don't understand."

"It means that the trees don't lose their leaves; they let them go." Anne struggles to keep the tears back again. "They release their lovely covering because its time is over."

"You mean like some old clothes?"

"Kind of like that, like some warm protective clothes. And the trees do this without grief or sadness."

"Because they'll get some new clothes?"

Anne laughs. "Yes, they become quiet and still for the long winter, and they rest. Then when spring comes, what happens?"

"They get new leaves! I get it! They let the old brown leaves go so that they can get ready for the new green ones."

"That is one way to look at it. But I think the writer of the book wasn't just talking about trees. She was comparing trees and their leaves to people and their special friendships. She was thinking about the feelings people have for each other. Leaves keep trees alive by bringing water and sunshine into them. You'll learn about that in school. The old leaves are like friendships that people let go of because their lives change. It's nothing to be sad about; it's just what happens sometimes. And the people, like trees, take time to rest until the new friendships come into their lives."

"Don't they miss the old friends, Nana?"

"Sometimes."

"I'm glad we're not trees."

"Why, sweet boy?"

"Because I wouldn't want to be naked and cold all winter."

"Of course," Anne laughs as she stands and helps her grandson down from the wall. They pause before turning away and gaze together at the dramatic horizon and the changing light. "But sometimes when we do without comfort for a while, it makes us appreciate it all the more when we get it back."

"So you want your old warm clothes back?"

"Maybe." *Or an old strong man with brown leaves in his silver white hair.*

"I love you, Nana."

Loneliness is a hollow space that, even when full of loving family and friends, is still empty. It howls and echoes, drowning out their happy voices. Anne sits alone in her daughter's crowded household, and opens her computer.

EMAIL TO NOAH:

I'll be at Summer's house on Saturday. If you want to get together for lunch, let me know. I also could use an afternoon outside my own reality. Thanks for the advice, but seeing Logan was hard—at once too good and too frightening, ultimately a reminder of passion, failure, and doubt.

Have you found an answer to my insurance question?—*Always, Anne*

Chapter 14

Durham Revisited

NOAH KNEELS BESIDE his wife and kisses her cheek. He starts to speak and stops. She is lost in a photograph of their son.

"How mischievous he looks in this one. I want Shuching to capture the sparkle and sweet devil in his eyes for the adventure story in book six." Noah doesn't respond, so she looks up at him. "What's wrong? You don't agree?"

"It's perfect. I just had to pause for a moment to take us in. We've come a long way. We can look at his pictures and speak his name and there isn't a tear in sight."

"Sometimes a turn of a phrase in the narrative, or remembered words that he speaks in the dialogue will bring tears. We're still vulnerable; there's just less sadness. These books are difficult journeys, but each one makes me stronger. Now stop talking about it, or I can't guarantee the consequences."

He rises and gazes out the window at the Canada geese, newly arrived for the winter. The blue heron flies over them like a drill sergeant squawking commands. The comedy is a diversion. It's hard to look at Elizabeth without being overwhelmed by the shock of her deterioration that triggers his fear of losing her. The current chemo treatment has ended and a dark shadow of hair has emerged on her scalp. He turns back to her, remembering with a smile the exotic passion aroused by virgin skin and a reawakened sexual abandon. He shakes his head clear to stop his body's response to the memory. *I need to take a long run. Or not. It releases tension, but it also releases those pheromones.* Their first night of old passions seems like yesterday, but it has been months. And because of her ebbing strength, he hasn't come to her bed for a long while except at her request and then only to cuddle or to massage wasting muscles.

Elizabeth looks up from her photographs. "Sue called today. She suggested dinner and a jazz performance on Ninth Street. It would do Shuching good to get out. She needs some fresh air. I probably do too. Shall I call her back?"

"Do you want me to?" he asks.

"Yes. Please. I'll probably forget, and I want to focus on this right now. My chemo brain can't be trusted to remember daily things. Don't make it too late. I have trouble staying awake after nine."

"It's Durham, remember. People eat early, and the fun starts and ends early."

"When I'm better, we'll find some late Chicago-style parties. I'm sure they exist in Durham. Why don't you call Ian and see if he wants to join us?"

"Good idea. Three women are a lot for me to keep satisfied."

"Oh, please, Noah. Like Ian would help."

"He'd do anything for you—maybe even have sex with a woman."

"Stop. You're putting pictures in my head."

"I'll make the call, and then I have errands to run. Remember to take a fifteen-minute break every hour, Liz. Sitting on the chaise with your laptop is hard on your back."

"Get thee gone, control freak."

Anne walks into the lovely Thai restaurant between Durham and Chapel Hill where she and Logan had their first date. Pausing to breathe in the scent of Asian spices, she requests a table in the corner where she can sit with her back to the wall and still see the door. She orders hot tea, and removes her rust-colored cardigan. Layered clothing accommodates hormone temperature jumps, and she now owns tank tops in every color and fabric, from casual cotton to dressy silk. Today's tank is a soft beige knit.

Anne glances at the door each time it opens to a new customer. She hasn't seen Noah in six months, since they danced on her deck. His emails have been brief. Hers have varied from short notes to long letters, filling him in on news of Pearl, the Red Hat Club, her home, and her daughters, even Billy O'Brian. He said he was printing all the emails. If he runs out of stories, he'll just read them to Elizabeth.

There's an unspoken understanding that Anne and Elizabeth will remain strangers. It isn't about jealousy. Noah thinks the stories of another woman's struggles and survival might be more meaningful if the woman who wrote them remains a part of Elizabeth's imagination—her own superhero. Anne thinks Noah is wrong. But she's not comfortable around the sick and dying, so she accepts this condition to their friendship.

An attractive man in a tweed sport-coat, jeans, and a very short haircut enters and looks around the restaurant. He sees Anne, pauses, and then smiles and walks toward her. *This can't be Noah. But I think it is.* She rises from her chair to greet him with a hug.

"If it weren't for your red hair, Anne, I might not have recognized you."

"And your hair confused me. If you hadn't come to my table, I honestly would not have known you." She sits. "And it's not just your hair."

"I've lost twenty pounds. But you've also lost weight, and muscled up."

"That's not flattering. Sit down. People are looking at my muscles. I'm of the old school that thinks women ought to at least give the *appearance* of softness and femininity."

"Believe me, you don't look masculine—just healthy, firm, and energized. You look poised on the brink of an athletic competition of some kind."

"Is laying stone an Olympic event?"

"If it did this for you, it ought to be."

"Well . . . thank you." An unexpected blush confuses her. "So where are your curls?"

"I shaved my head when Liz started chemo."

"I understand people sometimes do that. It's a fine gesture, in many ways. How long has it been growing back?"

"Two months. When she could finally see the end of chemo, she asked me to stop shaving it. Hers is growing back also, but a little slower. Her body has to adjust to not being poisoned."

"For all its good, chemo is brutal, isn't it?"

"The next treatment is worse. She was putting it off until she finished the first draft of her books. Now the doctors are putting it off until she regains some strength. She's actually in the rewriting process."

"Eight books, isn't it? One for each year?"

Noah proceeds to describe the books, their chronology, and the choices Liz made in documenting their son's life with the joyful and courageous adventures of his imagination. "His character battles the arch villain, Creepy Cancer. His friends are Super Doc, Crafty-Chemo, and Radiation Man. You get the picture. As his health fails, he can't do ordinary things, so he uses his mind to do the extraordinary. They are stories that he and Liz made up together when he was alive. She wrote them down, and he drew pictures to go with them. Now she's incorporating their stories into her books, and Shuching is incorporating his drawings into her illustrations."

"It sounds wonderful. But how does she handle the fact that he loses the final battle?"

"She has written that chapter several times. At one point, she had him give up his earthly life to cancer in order to come back as a supernatural force to help other children fight cancer—sort of an angel with muscle."

"Could be dangerous."

"I know. She didn't want sick children to give up their fight in expectation of coming back as a winged hero. She's rewriting and refining, but that final chapter is still incomplete."

"As Josh's parent and as a victim herself, she is uniquely able to empathize about the disease and . . ." Anne stops, realizing she is about to say something that Noah surely can't discuss—Elizabeth's anticipation of her own final chapter.

"No offense, Anne, but can we change the subject? I live with this all day and all night every day and night. I'm here for distraction, lady. By the way, I like your hairstyle. It's longer and softer. It works."

"Funny, I cut it off after Steven left, but I continued to wear it short because it was Logan's preference. Even after we stopped seeing each other, I kept the same haircut because it was easier, and in my mind, I think I was still trying to please him."

"I'm only beginning to realize how often women do things like that—subordinate their own preferences to accommodate a man's."

"The last seven months have been good for me. It began with the stories I wrote for you. I think they helped me see myself more objectively and let me shed a lot of the garbage, even make peace where I needed to. I think I'm more my own person than I have ever been in my life."

"What about Steven?"

"That's not exactly resolved yet. You don't know the whole story."

"I know enough. One of the reasons I wanted to see you is to tell you what I learned about your insurance question. But first, tell me why you even asked about a policy. Did you know it existed?"

"After I nearly died from the lung disease, he pressured me into adding his name to the deed for the house and increasing my life insurance policy. Steven had always been poor, and he was afraid that if I died, he would once again have nothing. Actually, that explains a lot about him. So, what did you learn?" She holds her breath.

"There is still a policy with Providence."

"For how much?"

"It was five hundred thousand. Now it's a million. I had someone on my staff do the research, so I didn't see the details. But I assume he's the benefactor."

Anne laughs sarcastically and shakes her head. "What can I do? We've been apart for years and he still carries an insurance policy, even increased it."

She rubs her temples and reflects. "The memories of the bad times with Steven used to haunt me. If I wasn't dreaming about them, I was reviewing them in my conscious mind, moment by moment, trying to understand how and why they happened. That ended when I left the house. But there is still something wrong, something that makes me . . . well, uneasy is the only word to describe it. I'm not afraid, but I always sit with my back to the wall. The memory of the insurance policy reactivated that feeling of unease."

"Do you want to tell me what happened, why you finally divorced him?"

"No. It makes me feel worse to talk about the bad things, because they negate all the good ones. And there was some good. He was miserable with day-to-day humdrum; but he was great in a crisis. And his music was as passionate and as erratic as he was. No simple melodies to balance all the sounds of joy, abandon, or anger and resentment."

"What was he angry about?"

"I think he was angry about his music. It was never recognized, and he desperately needed recognition—and fortune. Because of his poor childhood, he wanted money even more than fame. He spent his adult life prostituting his talents and himself and looking for someone to blame for his misfortunes. Like a dog chasing his tail, his frustration only grew."

"Once again, you're almost telling me something more."

"Sorry."

The waiter arrives for their orders. Anne's appetite is gone, but she selects a remembered favorite and then focuses on Noah while he studies the menu.

More than his body and hair are different. His eyes are no longer evaluating and calculating, no longer hiding personal agendas. He has allowed himself to be exposed. But surrounding and behind his openness, I can still sense a tightly wound spring. She remembers that morning last May—how he arrived early, complimented her baking to get her off her guard, and then procceded to march around her house, quickly and efficiently determining if it fit his criteria, but keeping his creative mind open to new possibilities. Then he returned the next day with the idea and an offer she couldn't refuse—one that changed both of their lives. She had seen desperation and loss in his eyes that second day when he talked about Elizabeth and his son. And she had seen need in his eyes when he returned in the evening with contracts and a bottle of wine. But she had too often taken men into her arms and life because they wanted consoling and mothering. She did not do that with Noah. She would not do that ever again. *Tell me about your eyes, Noah.*

"Where are you, Anne, besides having a dialogue with yourself?" Noah asks after the waiter leaves.

"Remembering our first meeting. I don't believe in people changing who they are. I know we can modify our behavior, but we don't become different people. You, however, seem more than a little different. Maybe you've simply released the person that was always hiding under a tough negotiator exterior. It reminds me that I know almost nothing about you, and you know more about me than my own mother ever knew."

"We haven't finished the stories, but I do feel a kind of kinship. Like I really have known you forever."

"Someday, I hope to know more about you. And I know you asked for a change of subject, but please tell me about Elizabeth—not her books. How is *she* doing?"

"She's surprisingly happy. The books have given her a focus that keeps her going. That's why we haven't finished your stories. I'm saving them for when the books are done and she needs more 'Anne wisdom'. It's painful to look at her; she's emaciated. I don't know if that's a result of the disease or the antidote."

"What do her doctors say?"

"Their comments are guarded. They refuse to give a prognosis. I think they're amazed that she's still alive. Today, just before I left the house, she said something about how we can party when she's better. That's the first time she has spoken about the future with the expectation of improvement. Completion of the books has given her something to live for. They've also allowed her to purge all of her sadness and revisit the goodness of Josh and his life. I think she has looked deep inside our lives to find the words to encourage children to be proactive in their own recovery and survival. In the process, she has accomplished the same for herself."

"What about you?"

"I'm just taking it one day at a time. When she finally let me read some of her writing, I had to lock myself up in a room alone. I didn't want her to see me lose it. It was living the reality of Josh all over again—from his birth forward. She captured his spirit. She was always terrific at editing, at helping writers find and refine their voices. I always thought she was hiding a personal desire to write, but I had no idea she would be so good. Anyway, between taking care of her needs, and trying to provide her with a calm, supportive atmosphere, I've fallen into her world. I guess I've gained some of her new peace by osmosis and managed to find a patience and acceptance that I've never known before."

"Maybe that's why you seem different." *There's the answer. This laid-back self-control is something you've forced on yourself, for her sake. It isn't real.*

"I would have to say, though, running is possibly saving my sanity. It leaves me emotionally and physically refueled, and ultimately allows me to relax a little."

Then why are you so tense? "What's Elizabeth's next treatment?"

"A trip through Hell for both of us. They call it stem-cell replacement therapy. We'll be isolated for at least two weeks while they treat her blood and then wait for it to regain its ability to coagulate. She'll be completely open to infection, and I'll be her caretaker, so neither of us can leave the space." He pauses, looking down at his tea. "This treatment is even more dangerous than the chemo, and I think that's why she's pushing so hard to complete the books. We have our illustrator, Shuching, living upstairs and also wanting to be finished by Christmas so she can be in Singapore for Chinese New Year."

"Will the stem-cell therapy be done before Christmas?"

"I hope so."

"Can Shuching work without her?"

"Yes. At this point, she can."

"If Elizabeth begins to lose hope, or if you believe she is not going to make it through this therapy, there's a story I want to make sure you read to her. It caused me to do a 360 on my own feelings about death and loss."

Noah's face tightens and she sees him age years as he hears the words he and Elizabeth think but are no longer willing to say aloud. *And this is the source of his tension.* His right hand is tapping on the table. Anne covers and stills it with her own.

"I'm not saying you should give up hope, Noah. I'm only saying you should be prepared to help her and yourself if it becomes necessary." She smiles and adds, "It's easy for me to say. In the same circumstances, I would be useless. What I've written, I would not be able to say aloud. It touches me too deeply. In fact," she says, rubbing his hand while she tries to think of something to say to move the conversation away from death. "I spent two years of college in a pre-med program. I wanted to be a doctor and help people. It was a while before I realized I was totally unsuited to the profession. I feel other people's pain too much. It overwhelms me. Nursing my daughters when they were ill was different. I still felt every pain; I just hoped I was absorbing some of it, taking it away from them." She removes her hand, as if the disconnect will stop the powerful urge to hold Noah and absorb his fears.

"God, I only wish I could take her pain."

Anne leans forward, searching her mind for something to soothe his anguish. And, surprising even her, an idea forms from an old memory. "You can make it less important. I took a Lamaze class before Summer was born. It was one of the best things I ever did, and not just for childbirth. It taught me to allow pain to pass through me. The concept is this: by not resisting it or tensing against it, the pain is lessened."

"And how do you do that?"

"By controlled breathing and diverted focus. I've used the technique over and over to deal with various kinds of injuries and ailments. It always helps. I even taught it to my daughters." She sits back. "I'm sorry, Noah. I can't seem to stop being a teacher. Even the stories I wrote for you were often more like lectures." Anne smiles and shakes her head, as a slow blush rises again on her face. "However, a lecture is better than the alternative."

"And what's that?"

"Theraputic sex, which is almost always a disaster. So, this is an improvement for me."

He looks down, laughing. "According to who?"

"According to me. Sex is a temporary balm, but it can have long-lasting negative effects."

"You mean like a sexually transmitted disease?"

"No, idiot! I mean like low self-esteem and a screwed-up friendship."

"Well I could certainly use some TLC of the carnal type, but I guess I'm not willing to give up your friendship for it. Speaking of that, though, I've always considered you to be my guilty pleasure."

"What does that mean, besides eating high calorie food?"

"It means I live outside of cancer through you and your emails about Pearl as well as the stories about your things—our borrowed things. I think of it as my exit time."

"That's very innocent. You shouldn't feel guilty."

"I don't know if it's innocent, but it's very necessary. So keep those emails coming. You have no idea how I depend on you and your zany friends in Pearl."

Their food arrives and a feeling of calm settles around them as they continue to talk of Pearl and the latest events in Anne's life. After the waiter clears their table, Noah asks about Logan.

"I honestly don't know what to say about my feelings for Logan. He is so dear and so good and so aggravating—all at once. We have many things in common, but as retired teachers, we each want to do these things our own way. Perhaps because he is older and a man, he thinks his way is the only way. Most of the time I'm with him, I'm looking for an escape route."

Noah runs his fingers through his hair, thinking about her words and how Liz would relate to them.

"I'm not sure I want to go through the adjustment it would take to let someone into my life. Friendship is one thing; marriage is quite another—especially with a dominating personality like his and a stubborn one like mine."

"Sounds familiar, Anne. So don't marry him."

"He won't be satisfied with friendship. Neither would I."

Unable to resist, he teases. "Maybe you should relax and just let the negatives wash through you. Don't resist them or tense against them and the pain will lessen."

She throws her napkin at him and laughs. "Where did you get a stupid idea like that?"

"I'm not making fun of your advice. I appreciate it, and we'll try it. In fact, I'll drop by Barnes and Noble for the Lamaze book on the way home. However, Anne Gray, I'm sure you will figure out what is best for you. But I don't want to hear that you've taken Logan into your bed just to make him happy. And don't you let him take you into his bed just to make you happy. I can't condone that kind of mutual pleasure of the flesh. Humph!"

"Shut up," she laughs.

As Noah walks Anne to her car, she searches her purse for her keys, lost in thought about how to help him, and how to say good-bye without touching him. He's too fragile. A car turns into the parking lot, moving fast, the driver on his cell phone. Noah sees the car and stops for it. Anne, still looking for her keys, continues walking, directly into its path. Noah reaches out and pulls her back, into him, out of harm's way.

Anne feels herself being jerked backwards, almost losing her balance, just as a car passes, barely missing her. She drops her purse, and would fall if not for Noah holding her.

"Oh my God!" she breathes. "Did you see the driver? Did he have blonde hair?"

"Blonde hair? Anne, he wasn't aiming at you. You stepped in front of him. I doubt that he even saw you. He was focused on his cell phone." Noah's face drains of color. "Does Steven have blonde hair? Are you that afraid of him?"

"No! I don't know." When she is reoriented, she starts to move away, but Noah holds her and lowers his face to her hair.

"Damn it! Will you please watch where you're going?" He turns her around and, holding both shoulders tightly, he whispers, "I need you!" All the teasing has gone from his face. He pulls her to him again. "I need to feel life. I'm so tired of death and pretense."

Anne slowly relaxes in his arms and an old sad smile moves across her lips. *You aren't the man for me, Noah.* But she reaches up and touches his face gently with one hand and then strokes the back of his neck while the other hand pulls him closer. They stand in the middle of the parking lot, each absorbing the other's fear and need, holding back reality, holding on to exit time.

I am filled with him, so why this everlasting emptiness? I can't seem to get close enough, but it feels like I'm suffocating. They roll together in this unknown bed. She gasps for air as she pushes up from his chest, pulling her knees forward, then relaxing above him. His hands and the soft sound of jazz lead them back into their rhythm. As her breathing quickens, he pulls her down and she stretches out against his body, forgetting the loneliness, giving herself to the sensual unreality. They roll over again, and his thrusts become faster, more insistent. She moans, on the brink of orgasm, and opens her eyes, wanting to see him ... a blank face! She doesn't know him!

She pushes him away and sits up in the bed, in her daughter's guest room—alone.

In another part of Durham, Noah has thrown off the covers and uses the sheet to dry his face. *I haven't had a wet dream since puberty. I need a shower.*

Fifteen minutes later, Noah passes the master bedroom on the way to the guest room, wearing only his towel. Elizabeth calls to him.

"Are you awake, Liz?"

"Yes. I heard you in the shower. Are you all right?"

He lies. "I'm fine. I woke up in a cold sweat. Bad dream."

"Sounds more like a sexy dream."

Busted!

"Would you like to cuddle? I could use a back rub."

"Your wish is my pleasure, ma'am. I hope you aren't offended by my lack of clothing."

"I only wear this t-shirt of yours so my skinny body won't offend you."

"Nothing about you offends me. All right, I admit it," he says as he slips under the covers beside her and pulls her into the spoon position. "I just had a very erotic dream about you."

"You sure it was me? And you're sure it wasn't an orgy with Ian?" she says slyly. "I'm sorry I've been so distracted and unavailable lately, Noah."

He reaches under her t-shirt and begins to massage the connecting muscles down her spine. "No problem. You have priorities: big ones—like getting through each day, and finishing the books. I would be a selfish bastard if I put my needs above all that."

"I am feeling a little better each day," she says and turns towards him. "If you'd continue massaging just a little lower, I could probably prove it. But I'm not up to a passionate workout. You'll have to make all the effort."

"You're tired. Cuddling suits me just fine." He kisses her shoulder and draws her close. "Rest."

Anne looks at the clock. It's now four a.m. and she still can't sleep. She turns the bedside lamp on, picking up her latest book purchase and trying to read. Finally, she puts the book down and picks up her cell phone and punches in Logan's cabin number. She hears the ring on the connecting line and wonders what possesses her to call at this hour . . . and what she should say.

"Hello?" Sleepiness is replaced by alarm. "Anne? Is anything wrong?"

"Caller ID in your tent? I'm impressed, Logan. I'm sorry to call so early. I'm at Summer's home and everyone's fine. I just needed to talk to you."

"At four-thirty in the morning?"

"You're right. I'm sorry. I'll call another time."

"Dammit, Anne, don't you dare hang up! I was just concerned. The only other time you've called me in the last two years was to tell me that Robin had died. Since you're out of dogs, I was afraid it might be a human this time. I need a second to wake up and re-group." He blows out air and then takes another deep breath. "All right, why did you call?"

"Talk to me. I can't answer that question yet."

"Okay. Well, let's see. I'm not in the tent anymore. I'm on an air mattress in the cabin. It's not approved for occupancy yet, but it's warmer than the tent."

"Are you off the scaffold?"

"Yes, and more than a little happy about that."

"Congratulations! That chimney's a big accomplishment."

"You have no idea."

"You've done all this in only two years. I'm impressed."

"Well, I still have the antique cabin to erect for a woodworking shop and a wildflower propagation lab. And I still have lots of detail work to do in the main cabin."

"I guess you'll be glad to see the porta john go."

"I'll have a bon voyage party. Why did you call?"

"This seems like a replay of my visit."

"I'm waiting, Anne. I'm waiting to hear what you have to say."

"I had a dream about you—at least I think it was you."

"Was it a good dream?"

"Too good. I need a shower to cool off."

"Oh, Anne . . . you do know how to wake a man up. But why did you say you *think* it was me?"

"There was no face on the man. But I was doing things I've only done with you."

Logan groans. "So, you called to torture me?"

"I'm sorry. That wasn't my intent. But," she adds, grinning, "I'm glad to know that I can still get your attention."

"You have my fullest attention."

Anne pauses for a moment before asking, "Is there anyone in your life, Logan?"

"If you mean a woman, no. What about you?"

"If you mean a man, you know me, there's a multitude." Logan does not respond. "You want names? Let's see." Something even Anne doesn't understand begins to happen. She teases and tempts him, knowing she's being cruel. *Or am I trying to make you reject me?* "There's the priest, Father Paul. He'll never recover from a lost love, not to mention his vows. There's Noah, the married man whose wife's dying of cancer. There's Carlos, my builder, but he just needs me on his crew. And there's the lawyer, Kente. He's a bit young for me, but his wife's a bitch, so he's willing to forget the age and culture difference. And let's see . . ."

"Yes, let's see how well I know Anne Gray." Logan relaxes into the unpleasant game. "They are all real men you have met in Pearl. They caught your eye because you caught theirs—new girl in town. That's a no-brainer. The first two are probably serious concerns for you, men for you to mother. The rest are just thrown in to impress or confuse me. The first two—I swear, Anne, what kind masochistic magnet do you wear? A priest and a soon-to-be widower. They may

228

want you in bed, but you're much too smart to think you can compete with the Catholic Church or a fresh ghost. How am I doing?" *Damnation!*

"You're close. I met Noah before I moved to Pearl. He bought my house. Otherwise, you're pretty much right as usual."

"Where are you, Anne?"

"I told you. I'm at Summer's house."

Logan wants to ask Anne if she drove to Durham and saw Noah today, if the faceless man in her dream might have been him. But he can't. *I know that she might protect my feelings with a lie, and I don't want to hear a lie or the truth, if she dreamed about someone else. But,* he reasons, *she didn't telephone Noah in the middle of the night. Of course not—she couldn't—he's married!*

Jealousy is difficult for Logan. He has little control over his feelings for Anne and even though he has no hold on her, he still doesn't want her with another man, and he certainly doesn't want to hear about it. But he can't stop the question or his own responding cruelty.

"Did you call Noah first? Or are you waiting until a decent time to call, so you won't arouse his dying wife's suspicions?" There is no humor in his voice.

"I'm sorry Logan. I shouldn't have called you at all, certainly not at this hour. Please forgive me."

He hears the finality in her voice. "Don't hang up, Anne." But it's too late; she already has.

As Anne pushes the off button on her cell phone, she hears Logan's plea, and her heart contracts with pain for him and anger at herself. She turns off her cell phone so he can't call her back. *Why did I do that? I woke him up; I turned him on; and then when we were both feeling warm and fuzzy, I destroyed it. Was it because of Noah? Or was it just my usual approach and avoid syndrome?* She was surprised by his question, didn't expect his perception. And she wasn't ready to give him honest answers. Anne can't sleep.

Noah can't sleep. Elizabeth sleeps like a baby, secure in Noah's love. She had smelled the perfume on him when he came home. He had forgotten to call Sue and Ian for the jazz club outing, so they ordered dinner from a local restaurant. She was thoughtful during their meal, wondering what to say or do. Not wanting to hear a lie, but afraid of the truth, she kept her jealous nature at bay. After Noah's shower, she invited him into her bed to remind him that he still belongs to her, at least for now.

Elizabeth knew that another woman might have held him in her arms, but she had not possessed him. She also understands his need to be touched by someone who isn't a part of this slow dying—this life charade. But, in the end, she sleeps without dreams because she feels content with her choice to reassure Noah rather than accuse him. And she is grudgingly content in the knowledge that her husband will survive without her.

Noah slips out of bed. He goes to the guest room and opens his computer where he finds a message from Anne.

EMAIL TO NOAH:

I can't sleep tonight. When I try to, erotic dreams awaken me again. I wanted to think they were about Logan, but I suppose they are a result of today. We are all born of passion, and it is often our strongest comfort, a reminder that we still feel and are felt. It is human nature to reach out; it is human nature to respond to another's need. Sometimes we rise above our nature and reject passion in exchange for a greater inner-peace; sometimes we are less noble; sometimes we excuse our weakness as an attempt to give comfort. Sometimes we lie to ourselves in order to justify our true desires.

I have been without a lover for a long time. I miss the intimacy. But I know your passion is with Elizabeth. You are a good husband. Today, you were a good friend. I hope you are sleeping well tonight.—*Always, Anne*

EMAIL TO ANNE:

Sometimes you think too much. You definitely use too many words to say a basic truth. Yes, I am awake, damn you. Yes, I know, we are complex human beings, driven by passion, but capable of making choices. Sometimes, I think, the only truth is the passion; the choices are all lies.

When I held you in the parking lot, and later, I thought you were the one in need. Ultimately, I realized it was the reverse. For a time, we helped each other.

Back to sleepless in Durham: I also dreamed of you tonight; and I lied to my wife; and I held my wife; but what we share is not a lie.

So, you and I are back to focusing on our friendship. You said that you want to know more about me. How about information in installments?

I am forty-six years old, nine years older than Elizabeth. I was born in Raleigh. Part of my reason for coming to Durham was to introduce Liz to my home state.

I grew up knowing that I was adopted. My father was a very successful printer and publisher. His work took us to Chicago when I was nine. My mother had her own career in sales and they were both evangelical atheists. They were raised in the Jewish faith and both renounced it. My grandfather insisted that I receive the traditional training, and I loved it—all of it. So I am a practicing Jew but not orthodox. Liz was raised by a Jewish father and a Catholic mother and doesn't buy into any of it.

When my father died, I opened his lock box at the bank and found my birth certificate—with his name on it. There was also a contract relinquishing parental rights, signed by an unknown woman. I don't know if my mother had ever seen these papers. So I learned, just before my father's funeral, that my adoptive father was in fact my birth father, and my birth mother was a girl from his office. I later learned that when she told him she was pregnant, he talked her into having their child, and then took me home to Mother as an orphaned baby. Unable to have children herself, she was thrilled. I don't know if Mother ever learned the truth or questioned the simplicity of the adoption process. He must have concocted a believable story for her. She died before he did and was spared the truth.

I found and met my birth mother. She was married, had two children of her own, and didn't want them to know about me.

That's it—installment number one. Don't put on your psychologist hat. My scars did not come from my childhood, at least not any important ones. But, for whatever reason, I've never told Elizabeth, maybe because she was closer to my parents than to her own and didn't need to be disillusioned.

Thank you for today. Thanks for the dream. Go to sleep, my friend. We need to talk about that insurance policy, but not tonight.—*Noah*

Anne closes her computer, stunned by Noah's story. She thinks also of Marjorie and of Paul and Sissy's child. She remembers all the bad melodramas on stage and film that used a similar plot line, and that she once laughed at and found unbelievable. *God, life's the biggest melodrama. I need to go home.*

Chapter 15

A Pearl Christmas

TIO SITS ON THE PORCH STEP of Anne's house, leaning against her leg. Paul sits beside them. They gaze on the marina below with four long piers providing a total of sixty-four slips for floating real estate. Sailboats of various sizes, powerboats, and small fishing boats are already beginning to fill the spaces. Low lights attached to the pilings turn on with darkness, lighting the dock but not the night sky. Although there are more plans for the marina, it's the first project already in use.

"I'm still not sure whether to feel hurt or complimented that I haven't been included in preparations for the Pearl Christmas," Anne grumbles to Paul, as they sip hot coffee. "Have I been too pushy? Or is it obvious that my activity cup runneth over?"

"That's a complicated question," Paul says, grinning and leaning back on the top step. "The best answer is that the Pearl Christmas has been going on for years, since I came back to Saint Angelica's. There are many traditions already in place. It doesn't require your input."

"Then it was your idea?"

"It was just my desire. I wanted to bring the various churches together, and I thought, what better time than Christmas. We're all Christian, so why not come together to celebrate the birth of Christ? I just gave them the challenge, and they each came up with ideas. Unfortunately, their ideas were all very individual, just for their own church. So I had to stimulate them with some suggestions of ways to work together."

"Like what?"

"I want to surprise you. Using the marina as a final gathering place is new because it didn't exist last year. That was Marjorie's idea. And I like it. It's neutral."

"She does love the marina. She's there every day."

"I think the water and her boat help her cope with her personal tragedies."

Anne looks at Paul. For a moment she's afraid she might have accidentally told him that she and Marjorie both know about his son—Marjorie's grandson. He smiles back at her, and she is sure he doesn't know. Anne isn't comfortable with this huge secret, fearing she will betray one or the other of her friends. She understands why Paul hasn't told Marjorie that there was a baby boy. He promised Sissy that he wouldn't tell her mother, and that he wouldn't look for the child.

But I wish Marjorie could tell Paul that she knows. It would give them so much to share. I know she's afraid Paul would bind her to the promise he made her daughter and prevent her from searching for the boy—a man now, perhaps with children of his own. Marjorie might be a great-grandmother. How will Paul react if she finds his son? I'm looking at him and talking to myself—again.

"I know, my lips are moving. Back to my conversation with you, sailing is Marjorie's exit time—her exit from reality."

"Exit time, I like that."

"I heard it from a friend who uses his computer and email as exit time from his reality—a dead son and a dying wife."

"You're talking about the man that bought your house and your stories?"

"Good memory, Paul. I forgot that I had even told you about them."

"Does he email you?"

"Yes," She wishes she had not brought up this subject.

"Then, you're his exit time?"

She opens her mouth to lie, and thinks better of it. "Yes." *Might as well tell him the rest, or some of it. Maybe he can help me see it objectively.* "He also refers to me as his guilty pleasure."

"Why guilty?" Paul asks as he pushes his wayward glasses up.

"Because it is just between us. His wife doesn't know that we communicate regularly." *Much less that we spent a day together two weeks ago.*

"I'm surprised at you, Anne."

"It's not my choice, Paul. Noah thinks it's better if she and I don't meet. He explained it to me, but now that he isn't present, his logic escapes me. I think he just uses me as a relief from the death and dying that has surrounded him for years. My emails are completely innocent, usually about Pearl and Marjorie and Ave Blanca, and you. He says that when he runs out of stories to read to her, he'll print and read the emails."

"I hope he doesn't. That could hurt her."

"It isn't cyber-sex, Paul. The emails are just conversations between friends."

"But the friendship is a secret."

"Not if I know wives. I imagine she knows and isn't threatened by it."

"Why? Because she knows he loves her, or, more likely, because she knows she's dying? That might help her forgive him now, but what if she lives?" He pauses for a moment. "Don't encourage him, Anne. His pleasure *is* guilty. I can't say that I know women, but I do know men. No matter how innocent the conversations, you are the lifeline that makes him feel like a man. He'll come for you when she's gone. And what will you say?"

In that moment, Anne realizes he's right. Noah will come to her for comfort. *And what will I say?*

She puts her mug down and shakes her head in frustration. "Why is it like that, Paul? Why can't men and women be friends without hormonal interference?"

"Explaining that to you might be as tough as explaining the Holy Trinity to a Muslim. How can we speak of the Father, the Son, and the Holy Ghost and call ourselves monotheistic? Most people don't grasp the concept because the explanation seems abstract."

Happy to change the subject, Anne says thoughtfully, "I ran into that problem when we studied religions in my humanities classes. I have my own answer, but I never shared it with my students because it was too personal."

"Will you share it with me?"

"I don't know if I can express it in words. It was simply an understanding that came to me one night when I was in college, and a group of us had been sitting around in the theatre after rehearsal. It was near Easter, and we were talking about the crucifixion. The director had turned out all the lights except the ghost light, the bare bulb that prevents accidents in a darkened theatre. My mind drifted away from everyone else. I had not yet experienced being a parent or feeling the overwhelming love that comes with the giving of life and watching it grow. But somehow, that night, I felt it. I know this is blasphemy, but I tried to put myself in God's place in order to understand His choice."

"What choice, Anne?"

"We believe God is all powerful and therefore could have prevented the crucifixion, or He could have removed Jesus from the cross and from all that suffering. But he didn't."

"His son was there for a purpose, Anne—to save mankind."

"I imagined myself in a similar situation, in a crowd with someone calling for the sacrifice of my son. He was small, standing beside me, holding my hand. If I didn't give him up to a painful death, many others would suffer. Like any parent would do, I offered myself in his place, but the crowd only wanted him. How could I let him go? I couldn't. The only way I could allow him to fulfill his purpose would be to go with him—suffer with him, share his pain, give him strength."

Paul waits while Anne blows out a breath and takes another.

"That's what I believe God did. He couldn't be with Christ physically, so He sent His spirit."

"You know the words Jesus spoke from the cross." A statement from Paul, rather than a question.

"Father, why hast Thou forsaken me?"

"How do you explain that?"

"He came to us as a man. And as a man, he felt everything any man would feel. I don't pretend to have any answers. I just accept the bits of understanding that come to me and trust that eventually I'll know more."

"So, you would have gone with your son?"

"That night I believed I would."

"How old were you?"

"Eighteen."

A moment passes before Paul continues. "Do you condone suicide?"

"Suicide?"

"In your imagining, you chose to die with your son. But your death was not required."

"I think of suicide as an act of cowardice or weakness—an unwillingness or inability to face the future. What I imagined that night was an act of sacrifice, not suicide. I think there's a difference."

"What about the people you would have left behind?"

"I would have hoped they would understand."

Paul rises and walks down her steps. He sees a stone and kicks it. He sees another, bends over and picks it up, then throws it as hard and as far as he can. He stands for a while with his back to a confused Anne. *Is it possible? Did she push herself away from*

237

my arms reaching for her because of our son? In her mind, was it an act of sacrifice rather than suicide? She survived the fall but it changed everything, our plans for a life together shattered like her leg, forever scarred like her beautiful face.

He closes his eyes as he remembers her coming to him years later at the seminary, with her scared face hidden by a side wave of hair and a limp that couldn't be hidden. They had held each other for two days and nights before she left, telling him to finish his studies and become a priest.

A few years later, she had found him in Detroit, coaching a basketball team at a gym in his parish. The moment he saw her, he dropped the ball and went to the locker room. He showered, dressed, and then walked out, taking her hand and leaving. This time they disappeared for a week. He never saw her again. Seven years ago, he read about her death in a newspaper. She was covering a story on child abuse and was shot by a desperate father. He'd understood the circumstances of her death and had prayed for her killer. What he never understood was the choice made on the wall above Linville Falls, just before she fell.

When he finally turns back to Anne, his jaw is clenched and his face a mask. "How do you move from talking about hormones to explaining the scriptures?" He forces a smile.

"I didn't. I just told you my personal interpretation of the Holy Spirit. I don't expect anyone else to agree with me, especially a priest."

"It is perhaps the simplest, but most concrete, explanation I've ever heard. You just confirmed my worst nightmare but also offered me a way to make peace with it."

"I'm lost."

"Hardly, but back to your question about hormonal interference in friendships. Sometimes it isn't a problem. But when you are attracted to your friend physically or intellectually or emotionally ," he sighs, sitting again, "then it can be very difficult." Resisting the urge to comfort Anne or himself, he scratches Tio behind his ear. Tio shifts loyalties and leans against Paul's leg, looking up at him.

"Noah loves Elizabeth. He comes to me only for diversion. I could never replace her. And although I have a tendency to want to give comfort, it is just that—a gift, a temporary thing, not a commitment. I have confused the two in the past; I won't do it again." She realizes that she has said or thought these words a number of times lately. *Who am I trying to convince, and when will never again begin?*

"Good. Then stop misleading him. It's human nature to be drawn to someone you admire or empathize with, but you can choose to keep it innocent. Find the words to communicate the boundaries of your friendship without making him feel rejected. You can be his friend, and hers. But if you cause him to think of you instead of her, to wish he were holding you instead of her, to even want to talk to you instead of her, then you are causing Elizabeth additional pain and loss. And it doesn't sound like she needs any more of either. It will also cause him to feel guilt, which reduces him in his own eyes and limits his ability to make her feel loved—when she needs it most. Forgive me for sermonizing, but do you understand what I'm saying?"

"Of course I understand. I guess that's a trap I sometimes allow myself to fall into—perhaps for the wrong reasons. I excuse an indiscretion because I convince myself that it is just to give comfort, but it is in fact misleading and wrong."

"Ah, you scare me, Anne." Paul shakes his head as he leans forward, laughing. "I wasn't talking about indiscretions. I'm talking about the words you use, and your eyes. I always know exactly what you're thinking when you look into my eyes. I'm sure you don't do it on purpose. You're just being your natural generous self. And I don't want to change you; I'm only suggesting that you be more aware of yourself—particularly with him. He sounds very vulnerable."

"I hear you, Paul. I'll try to be more aware of my overwhelmingly sensual effect on the obviously weaker sex," Anne stretches the limits of melodrama, trying to lighten the mood.

He doesn't smile. "We *are* weak."

Anne sees the distant look in his eyes and knows he isn't weakened by her. She sighs, a part of her wishing it were otherwise, because his loss is so complete. His Sarah is gone. She turns and looks out at the water and the dark sky, slowly pulling herself—and him with her—to safer ground. "So, what's the finale? What happens at the marina?"

"The boats will be decorated with lights which will come on at the appointed time. And if that doesn't blow a breaker, we'll sing Christmas carols."

"You could have everyone armed with candles, just in case."

"Don't spoil my surprise, Anne."

A visual idea begins to form in Anne's mind. "I don't have a boat, as you know. So would you let me decorate yours? I'm sure you'll have enough to do without that."

"Good idea! *Espirita* isn't the largest boat in the Marina, but she will be the only one decorated by a professional designer. I would be honored. And we should look for a boat for you this spring."

Anne gives him a bright smile. She would like to hug him, but she knows that, at this moment, Paul is her guilty pleasure, and so she wills herself to follow his advice. She wraps her arms around her drawn-up knees and hugs herself for warmth instead of him. Tio whines and licks her hand. She includes him in her hug. The smile fades.

"I must go prepare for Mass." Paul reluctantly rises from the porch steps. "You and Tio look so small there. I feel like I could put each of you in a pocket and carry you with me." He puts one foot on the top step and leans forward to look in her eyes. His glasses slide down, and he pushes them back up. "You give so much of yourself to everyone else. You deserve to have someone who is free to give back."

"Maybe. Maybe I surround myself with impossible relationships because I don't want all the compromise and loss of self that comes with commitment."

"If that is your view of commitment, then run like a jack rabbit, my friend. A good relationship should not require that of you. It should be an intermingling of souls, not a compromise of spirit. If your friend in the mountains wants to absorb you into his life, into his ego, leave him in the mountains."

"For a man, you're very insightful, and kinda dumb. All men want to absorb."

"Yes, but some of us are trainable. Now stand up. I can't leave you here looking so forlorn. Why don't you come to Mass? I think you need company."

"Why do you have Mass on Friday evening?" Anne rises stiffly and dusts her backside. "I thought that was a morning thing."

"I schedule services to match the needs of the parishioners. Mass on Friday evenings is because most of the men here have construction jobs and are at work early every morning. It also detours those who would take their week's earnings and drink them away at the bars. After Mass, many are willing to go home to their families. Of course I don't get them all here."

"You know what you should do?"

"I'm sure you're about to tell me."

"Have a Friday night fish fry after Mass, or a Bar-B-Q. That will bring whole families in."

"Sounds like bribery. And how will the church finance this?"

"Everybody pitches in. It shouldn't be your responsibility. The women of the church can plan and organize it."

"Anne, you should have been a corporate idea-woman. It sounds like another job to add to my list—which is already too long. But if it can be delegated, it might have some merit. And it wouldn't have to be every Friday. It could be the first and third Fridays. We'll try it out after Christmas."

"Thanks for the invitation to Mass, Paul, but I think I would like to commune with God in my studio tonight."

"Are you painting?"

"No. I'm designing a Christmas boat—*La Espirita de Navidad*."

"*El Espiritu*," Paul corrects. "The spirit of Christmas is male."

"But your boat is female."

"Si, Anna." Paul kisses the top of her head, and ambles down her new stone steps and across a terraced walkway to his church. Tio follows.

241

It's Friday morning, two weeks later, and preparations for the Pearl Christmas have escalated. The marina is busy with owners decorating their boats. Anne has baked twelve dozen cookies to be served with a spiced tea at the art co-op, now named *The Brown Pelican*. The co-op will open for business on Monday but will have a preview opening with tea and cookies tomorrow as a participant in the Christmas Pearl festivities.

In one month, the Red Hat Club has painted the interior of Marjorie's old shop, made a colorful sign to hang above the door, and put a fresh coat of white paint on the exterior that will be enhanced with murals in the spring. The sign includes the name of the co-op and a logo design of North Carolina's well-loved brown pelican.

Anne has resisted taking a leadership role in renovating the space, deferring to the obvious need for a creative outlet for the members of the Club. She saw their timid enthusiasm, and didn't want to dominate it with her own ideas. As she enters the store, bearing tomorrow's cookies, she is glad she has kept a distance. The walls inside are covered with framed art, and the floor is littered with baskets containing varied objects de arte. A rack is filled with handmade ponchos, a revived fashion. The women of the co-op decided to make ponchos their signature item this year, and everyone who can weave or knit or crochet has been busy. Another rack holds t-shirts with the brown pelican logo silk-screened on them. Pottery, jewelry, and Celita's imports from Mexico help fill the few shelves and counters kept from the original store. It's a welcoming space, alive with color and texture.

Anne's contributions included designing the pelican logo and creating a graphic identity for the shop. However, she suspects that Marjorie spread the word that Anne is not to be assigned to multiple jobs. In fact, she has only worked on the tasks for which she volunteered. There hasn't been time for anything else.

"I'm so impressed, Marjorie. The store is wonderful. And the best part is that so many people have been involved."

"Well, the place wasn't in bad shape, just dirty and needin' paint. Course we had to get rid of lots of the shelves 'cause we wanted more room for hangin' canvases an' quilts n' stuff. How's the construction at your place? Have you finished paintin' the apartments or whatever you call them?"

"They're townhouses. Anyway, the first addition to the triplex is completed and the renters will arrive on January third. It's a retired couple from Toronto, Ontario. They'll stay through April. The second addition will be finished in February."

"Don't they call them snowbirds? How did you find 'em? Or maybe I should ask, how'd they find you?"

Anne raises her eyebrows and wiggles them. "Kente's wife, Ayesha, made the contact through the realty company she works for. She didn't have anything available in Shallotte or Holden Beach, so she offered the renters to me. Of course, they didn't come free. You know Ayesha. She claimed ten percent of the first two months' rent as her fee. In exchange for the fee, I gave her all the responsibilities of contracts, rent payments, etc. We're still negotiating. I'm afraid she sees me as an opponent. Luckily, we don't have to work together every day. The attitude and anger in her wears me out. I got that 'whites are not to be trusted' treatment from some of my students. Thank God for the rest." Distracted by words in nearby conversations, Anne mutters, " Damn, bitch, Hell!"

"Whoa, Anne, what'd I do?"

"Sorry but, speaking of prejudice, who are the two women at the jewelry counter, pretending to be busy?"

"Oh, the one in the blue shirt is Marsha's cousin. Marsha's the one that complained about everythin' at the meetin' when Celita talked about the co-op. The other one's her neighbor, Billy O'Brian's wife. They told me their names, but you know what my memory's like. Anyway, we never put 'strictions on membership, so when they showed up and said they wanted to help—I know, they're not really doin' anythin', but I couldn't tell them to leave."

"I'm not trying to hear their conversation, but while we've been talking, at least three 'spics' and two 'niggers' have come out of their mouths, loud enough for me to hear. Mind if I have a talk with them?"

"Have fun."

The two women are dusting the clean counter and rearranging an already nice display of jewelry when Anne introduces herself.

"I'm Marsha's cousin, Phyllis. Marsha's a member of the Red Hat Club. And this is my next-door neighbor, Sherry. We wanted to come see what all the hullabaloo was about."

"Well, what do you think?" Anne asks.

"It's pretty nice. Course, a lot of it looks like it swam the border." This is the grating voice Anne overheard. Her friend, Sherry O'Brian, looks timid and embarrassed.

Anne smiles. "Yes, some of the items are carefully selected imports from Mexico. The co-op's chief executive is Celita Ramirez. This whole thing is her idea." The two women exchange surprised looks. "The imports are her contribution. She's also a wonderful seamstress and will put in some of her own designs when she has more time. And of course, many of the other crafts are from our own Latino residents. Isn't it nice that the whole country likes Latin food, music, dances, and even some of the fashions, like ponchos?" Phyllis rolls her eyes at Sherry, who once again looks embarrassed.

Encouraged by Sherry's reaction, Anne continues. "We have an interesting variety of people in Pearl and we're hoping this co-op will help bring us together." *But for the moment, I need to divide and conquer.* "Which of you is better at words?"

"Words?"

"Who made the better grade in high school English?"

"That's easy. I did," Sherry says.

"Good. Then you can help me. Phyllis, Marie needs some help in the next room." Phyllis starts to protest, but Anne calls to Marie and says she has a volunteer. Then she takes Sherry's arm and leads her to the front desk. "You and I are going to write some guidelines for the members of the co-op. Since you're from this area and I'm not, you can help me phrase things in a way that will not offend anyone. We need to remind them of how to talk to customers and to each other so that no one in the shop feels unwelcome or disrespected. I'm so glad you can help."

Without warning, Anne's hair is roughly pulled backwards, causing her to fall against a body much larger than her own. In a moment's panic, she cries out, "No, Steven! Stop!" Shocked by the pain and overwhelmed by the smell of cheap cigars, alcohol, and a lack of deodorant, she freezes.

He sputters in her ear, "I ain't no Steven, and my wife ain't no part of this goddamn wetback bullshit! You been nothin' but trouble since you come to town with all your stupid ideas."

His words bring Anne back to reality and to the identity of her assailant. From her position of disgust and pain, she sees Sherry's face turn from surprise to fear, and in the reflection in the mirror behind her, Anne sees Marjorie raise a flag pole over her attacker's head and bring it down with a vengeance. The pole, never intended to be a weapon, snaps; Sherry's husband, Billy O'Brian, does not. Revived by Marjorie's action, Anne drives both elbows backwards into his ample gut. He gasps and contracts, releasing her hair. But as she falls forward, Anne's right eye makes contact with Sherry's fist. *Damn! Bitch! Hell!*

Billy unbends, grins and bellows, "That's my girl!" just as Marjorie's new weapon, a mop handle, strikes a sounder blow. The other women recover from their temporary paralysis and join Marjorie in holding the fallen man. Their efforts are unnecessary as he's now unconscious.

"Call the law!" Marjorie shouts.

While pressing her palm against a throbbing eye, Anne sees Sherry's frightened, shamed face and suddenly understands. *Shake it off, Anne.* "No, Marjorie. Let them go." Phyllis has come to her friend's side. Anne looks hard at her with her one good eye. "Will Sherry be safe?"

"I'll stay with her 'til he sobers up."

Anne purposefully lowers her hand so the two women can see the damage. "I won't bring in the law if you won't tell him that Marjorie hit him. I don't need to remind you that everyone here witnessed his attack and yours, Sherry. Tell him we're even now. No one else needs to be hurt." Her last words are a clear threat.

Sherry is crying now. "He's really not so bad. He's just drunk 'cause he got laid off, and it's Christmas."

So what's his usual excuse?

That evening, all of Anne's family and her first husband Robert arrive. It's a week before the actual calendar Christmas, but they wanted to share in the Pearl celebration, and Anne wanted to recruit their help in her personal project—Paul's boat decoration.

At Joe's request, they all attend Friday evening Mass, and afterwards the children open stocking gifts. Robert takes Bradley and Tommy to the newly finished triplex unit, and Summer lies down with Lindsey in Anne's guest room for story time. Joe and Ray wander down to the marina where they meet with Paul to talk boats.

Alone with Greer, Anne moves an ornament on the Christmas tree to satisfy her artist's eye. "Want to bet who'll be asleep first: your dad, the boys, Summer, or Lindsay?"

"Sucker bet." Greer laughs. "Dad and Summer will be out in five minutes."

"So, am I getting a mother/daughter talk? You've managed to get privacy in a recently crowded space."

Greer finishes wrapping a last gift to be opened in the morning, then looks closely at her mother's face. "The makeup hid your black eye pretty well at church, but the bruising is spreading. I don't know about tomorrow. Not that it matters. I think the whole town knows what happened. I still can't understand his wife hitting you."

"It's pretty typical, honey. That's why so many policemen are injured when they respond to domestic violence calls. And then the abused wife won't press charges. So the law changed. The victim doesn't have to press charges; the arresting officer can do it."

"You didn't press charges. You didn't even call for an officer."

"That's because I was afraid Billy would take it out on his wife later—or Marjorie, for hitting him. Sherry protected herself from him by hitting me."

"I wasn't talking about today." Anne's face changes. "I'm sorry. I almost brought up him-whose-name-is-never-mentioned. Maybe it needs to be mentioned. Marjorie said you called the brute 'Steven' before you even saw him." She pauses to take a breath before opening a subject her mother never discusses. "I was there, Mom. We never talked about it, but I'm not blind or stupid. I know what happened with Steven." Anne doesn't respond. "You were too generous with him, and you're entirely too understanding about those lowlifes that hit you today. But that's not why I wanted to talk to you. What about Logan, Mom?"

"Did Logan ask you to talk to me?"

"No."

"You're treading on very private property, sweetheart."

"I know. But someone needs to say something."

"All right." Anne sighs in resignation. "Shoot."

"You know that Logan has remained a friend, and that we see him from time to time."

"Yes. Bradley told me."

"I didn't like keeping that from you, but he asked us not to mention him. He was afraid you would think he was trying to get to you through us."

"I know, honey. He explained that to me when I saw him at Thanksgiving, and believe me, I understand."

"Have you talked to him since?"

"Just once. It was a bad idea."

"Mom, if you don't see any hope of a future with him, you should tell him—let him go."

"I let him go almost two years ago."

"I know, but for some reason, he believes you just need time—that eventually the two of you will be together again."

"Can we sit? I'm exhausted. There are many things I miss about Logan and me as a couple. But there are also many things about us

I don't miss. I don't miss being the woman behind the man. I did that for my whole adult life. Logan has a dream-fulfilling agenda that doesn't include time for any dreams of mine."

"I never saw you as a woman behind anyone. And I'm sure your students and your colleagues didn't either." Greer sits and Anne tosses her a down-filled throw, and then sits across from her.

"Yes they did. The directors as well as the students all depended on me to back them up, to facilitate their dreams, either as a designer or as a teacher. And that was fine. It was my job. But that time is over. Moving here and creating my own place in this community, was the most independent and personally fulfilling thing I have ever done. I love my home and my friends. I'm not willing to give it all up for him. Maybe that says it all. Maybe there just isn't enough love. Or maybe I'm no longer willing to sacrifice everything that matters to me in order to have his or any man's love."

"What is it that matters so much to you, your property? I thought you had given up the responsibility of *things*. And you moved away from friends when you left Durham."

"It's not the things, and not only the friends. It's how I feel here. I'm not sure I can explain it. And I don't mean to imply that this is all I want. I do want a man in my life. I do want love. But I don't have a very good track record with marriage."

"Daddy was an innocent mistake; Steven was a stupid mistake. I don't think Logan was either of the above. I think you're just afraid, Mom."

"No argument there. Why do you think women get married, Greer?"

"Well, I would have to say: sex, children, financial security, a free repair man, someone to do the tax returns, the fear of growing old alone, and, of course, love."

"I think many women mistake all of your first answers for love. I think love is actually least often the reason for marriage. I think some of those who marry for lesser reasons are lucky if a love develops over time. It's different with me. I find people very deserving of love and I find it easy to give love. But that's not the same thing as being in love. And I have learned that love shouldn't necessarily lead to marriage. I already have children and grandchildren. I can take care of my own financial security as well as household repairs and tax returns. I have lots of people to grow old with. Of course it would be nice to find someone whose presence supersedes everything else, someone who enriches my life without absorbing it. And it would be nice to have intimacy in my life again."

"No marriage is perfect, Mom."

"I know. Perfect is boring. I've invited Logan to visit. I don't know if he'll come."

"Why wouldn't he?"

"He doesn't like the beach, he's afraid of deep water, he'll probably never take a break from working on the log house and the land."

Greer shakes her head. "Ok, I'm beginning to see your point. But don't underestimate him."

"I appreciate your willingness to bring up a sensitive topic, Greer. And you didn't even flinch when I used the word intimacy. You knew I meant sex didn't you?"

"Yes, Mother," she says, rolling her eyes.

"Ah, you're growing up. And I'm becoming my own mother, enjoying your embarrassment. Okay, you're right. I need to talk to Logan. But I'm exhausted, and tomorrow's a long day." *And tonight will be another long night.*

As Anne anticipated, sleep for her is an elusive thing. Tossing and turning, covers on. Too hot. Covers off, pajamas off—ah, nice cool sheets. Too cool. Covers on. *Damn these hot flashes!* Finally, Anne resorts to the tried and true. She prays. She sleeps. She dreams of a great blue heron landing on her balcony. Large enough to bear her weight, he beckons, and they fly away—from pressures and expectations, from fear and indecision, from hot flashes and dread of age.

The next day, Anne prepares a large breakfast and then sends her daughters and grandchildren off to Holden Beach. The water is too cold for swimming, but the children run barefoot in the wet sand and shallow waves. Joe goes to confession for the first time in years. Anne thinks he and Paul are probably plotting a sailing trip for after Mass on Sunday. Robert and Ray offer to stay and help her decorate the *Espirita*.

The day is unseasonably warm. They load the boat with the materials they'll need and then motor downriver to Marjorie's private dock. The ride is pleasant but quiet. It seems strange to be sharing this activity with Robert. Although they have spent the last two Christmases together, it hasn't been completely relaxed. Each year gets better, but there is still a lot of carefulness in the way they talk to each other. Ray eases the quiet and the mild tension with questions and comments about the river and the history of the area. Raised by two public school teachers, he has an insatiable appetite for knowledge. Both men try to avoid looking at Anne's black eye, which is shocking in daylight, without makeup.

When they reach the dock, they unload the supplies and begin their task. Ray's electrical engineering skills are applied to the lights, and Robert's interest in sound technology is used to set up a speaker and microphone—all battery operated and all borrowed from a former student working at a theatre in Wilmington. They both help with the construction and by early afternoon, they're finished. Marjorie returns from decorating her boat at the marina, and brings them plates of fried chicken, potato salad, and rolls from the Baptist church fundraiser.

"What's happening at *The Brown Pelican*?" Anne asks.

"Craziness. They're all runnin' around like chickens with their heads cut off. They're openin' at two o'clock. I'm about to go change. They got games an' toys an' face paintin' for kids in the basement of the Methodist church at three o'clock. Get your grandchildren on over there."

"What happens after that?" Robert asks.

"A fish fry at Saint Angelicas an' then around seven o'clock, the real festivities begin. In the meantime, they got free clam chowder an' live musicians at the bait shop. It's supposed to get chillier.

Bring a jacket. All the evenin' stuff is outside. I gotta get ready. See ya there."

Robert shakes his head at the retreating figure of Marjorie Hester. "I love her, Anne. She reminds me of your aunts in south Texas, the ones that lived next door to each other. Remember the old toilet in the back yard with marijuana growing in it? Do you think they knew what it was?"

"I doubt it. Probably one of the kids or grandkids planted it."

"How are they?"

"Aunt Laura died a few years ago, and Aunt Martha is in her nineties and in a nursing home. Her neighborhood had become dangerous. A gang of kids was using her house as a place for meetings, and she was confused and just couldn't deal with them or with her own needs anymore. So her daughter put her in a home, and now she's not much more than a vegetable."

"I'm sorry to hear that."

"How old is Marjorie?" Ray asks.

"In her seventies, I think."

"Her face looks old," Robert says, "but her movements are young."

"Exactly. I tried to capture that in a portrait I did of her. But when she saw it, she said, 'Who is that old woman?' She didn't recognize herself."

"I understand that," Robert laughs. "I look much younger in the mirror than in photographs."

"I know what you mean. There's a different level of objectivity between a mirror reflection and a photograph."

"Well Robert," Ray laughs, "I don't think you or our brawler here are in danger of a nursing home. Anne would probably fight her way out. I just hope Marjorie doesn't end up in one."

"Me too, Ray." Anne nods, knowing she won't let that happen. "She wouldn't last long in confinement."

"If the boat's supposed to be a surprise, how do we get back to La Casa Blanca?" Robert asks.

"We'll leave the tools at Marjorie's house and walk back, so the chicken and potato salad don't become a natural part of my hips.

Thanks for helping, guys. And stop avoiding eye contact. My eye probably hurts you more than me."

Robert grins, and admits, "I'm just trying to keep from laughing."

Back from the beach, the children take a long nap. Lindsay wakes with a fever, and so she and Summer, now in her sixth month of pregnancy, are content to stay inside the warm house while the others join in the community activities.

Joe's help is enlisted for the fish fry, and Robert carries plates of fish, cornbread, and slaw up to Anne's house to share with Summer. Lindsay, limited to clear liquids, looks at her grandfather with glassy feverish eyes and claims his lap for the remainder of the evening.

Over two hundred people arrive at Saint Angelicas for the fish dinner. After everyone is served, Father Paul speaks, thanking them for coming and inviting them inside for Mass. Many follow, but after the pews are filled, the remainder sit on the church steps or on the grass to listen. Ray and Greer and their sons leave to dress for their part in the finale, as do Marjorie, Kente, Carlos, and Mano's older son, Marcello.

Anne sits on the stone terrace, looking at the stars, and wishing that Logan was here to see and understand. But how could he comprehend what she feels when she consciously or unconsciously destroys his feelings for her each time she sees them rising? She had tried to call him earlier that evening, but he didn't answer. She wonders if his Caller ID warned him, and he simply chose not to answer.

After Mass, Joe finds Anne for an update on his family. She has spoken to them on her cell phone, and they're coming to the balcony to view the finale. He leaves to join them. Singing is heard in the distance. The crowd moves down to the marina except for Paul and Anne, who stand on the top stone terrace where they have a panoramic view of the marina below. The combined choirs of the Baptist and Methodist churches walk into view, singing secular Christmas carols, from "Rudolph the Red Nosed Reindeer" to "God Rest Ye Merry Gentlemen". They each carry a lighted candle and a handful of unlit candles. As they meet the crowd, they hand out the extra candles and light them from their own. During this ritual, a third choir walks from Saint Angelica to the lower terrace. When all of the candles are lit, a strong baritone voice from the Methodist choir sings:

"Silent night, holy night,"

An equally strong mezzo soprano, from the Catholic choir, begins the song again in Spanish:

"Noche de pas, noche de amor,"

Then, much to the amazement of the listeners, the choirs join in and continue singing this beloved Christmas song as a round—one in English and one in Spanish. As the song ends, the decorative lights on the boats begin to come on, one at a time, until the marina is filled with light. Anne blinks back tears. The crowd cheers, but is hushed by a new song.

Slowly entering from the left is the *Peli*, with Marjorie in a robe and crown, operating the electric motor. Kente and Carlos are dressed as the other two kings, and of course they sing, "We Three Kings of Orient Are." The crowd applauds and joins the weak singers for the rest of the song. Marjorie loses her crown in the water, and there is scattered laughter. Anne pulls a remote control from her pocket, and moves down to the second terrace. Paul follows.

The *Espirita* emerges from the right in darkness. Anne operates the remote, and a large star at the top of the mast gradually fades in from dim to bright, and below, carefully hidden spotlights fade in to illuminate the faces of those on the boat. The crowd responds with soft applause and verbal ooohs and ahhhs. There is a suggestion of a stable roof created by fanned beams below the star. And beneath the beams, Greer sits, draped in a blue robe. An empty wooden manger is in front of her. Ray wears robes and looks down at his son, Tommy, asleep in his wife's arms. Bradley stands beside her, dressed as a shepherd. Marcello, also dressed as a shepherd, runs the electric motor. As the boat gets closer to the crowd, Greer, in a clear soprano, sings: "What Child is This?" Her sweet delicate voice is magnified by the microphone and reaches across the water and up the bank to Paul and Anne. There isn't a sound in the crowd.

Paul takes Anne's hand in his and whispers in her ear. "Gracias, Anna." She smiles up at him and he winces at the sight of her injured eye, making him draw her closer, wishing to comfort and protect her. She turns to her balcony, where Robert, Joe, Summer, and Lindsay watch. Summer gives her a 'thumbs up' and Anne returns it. When Greer's solo ends, the combined choirs and the crowd sing "O Little Town of Bethlehem" and then "Joy to the World".

Just as people begin to separate into family units, preparing to leave, more music is heard, and another group makes an even more dramatic entrance. The music is African; the players and dancers are African American. The crowd is uneasy, not sure how to respond.

Paul releases Anne's hand and quickly runs down to the road in time to open his arms and welcome Ayesha and her companions, dressed in Kwanzaa colors: black, red, and green. Father Paul raises his arms for attention and introduces the African American holiday to a crowd largely unaware that such a thing exists. He asks them to sing one of their songs and while they sing, several women dance. The movements are a combination of modern dance and African dance.

Anne is very familiar with Kwanzaa, a celebration of the history and future of African Americans as well as family and unity. She knows the holiday is scheduled for the week between Christmas and New Year's Day, and she hopes that, by this early presentation, Ayesha is saying she and her people want to be a part of the Pearl Christmas. She hopes Ayesha is not suggesting they were left out. Or were they? Perhaps this was part of Paul's surprise. Risking Ayesha's hostility, Anne walks down to the road and holds out her hands in a gesture of welcome. Ayesha smiles stiffly and nods in her direction. Kente has managed to get off of the *Peli* and to his wife's side.

"Will you teach us a Kwanzaa song?" Anne asks.

Ayesha looks at her for a long moment and then her smile softens. "All right—a traditional call and response."

She points her finger at a young man who begins the song. He calls, or rather sings, a verse and then the crowd responds with the same line. Drums enrich and complicate the beat. Then the dancers begin, adding still more rhythms. Young people of the several cultures represented join in, trying to imitate the movements. At the end, there is general applause and scattered shouts of enthusiasm.

The young will always teach the old. Anne refuses to note any disharmony or negative behavior as she slips through the crowd to help Greer and the boys get off the now docked *Espirita.* She sees Sherry who quickly drops her head in embarrassment. Billy isn't there. Anne makes a mental note to ask Paul about the presence of a women's shelter as she takes Tommy from Greer and carries him from the pier to the road where Joe meets her and takes the heavy sleeping child to bed. Anne hugs each of her performers. "You were all wonderful."

"Thanks for making me do it, Mom. You know how shy I am about singing in public. Oh, and here's the baby Jesus," she says, handing Anne a doll. "When Tommy started falling asleep on his feet, I decided to replace the doll with him. His shepherd's cloak made good swaddling clothes. He's a little big for the baby Jesus, but I don't think anyone minded. And actually, the wise men didn't find the baby Jesus right away."

"True, but do me one more favor. Ayesha and Kente!" Anne calls. "I want you to meet some of my family." Ayesha and Kente walk to them, holding hands. "You missed them when they were here in August for the birthday celebration."

"I would be happy to meet the daughter of the woman who took on Billy O'Brian and his wife." Ayesha grins. "I just wish I'd been there."

It's late in the evening, and everyone has gone to bed now except Summer and Lindsay, who Anne is now rocking.

"Her fever seems to be gone."

"Good." Summer hesitates and then adds, "Mom, did you see Logan?"

"I saw him at Thanksgiving."

"No, I mean tonight."

"Logan was here?" Anne stops rocking and looks at Summer. "Are you serious?"

"Yes. I saw him from the balcony. He stood off to the side by himself. After Greer's song, he disappeared."

"Well, why did he leave?"

"I don't know. But he might have seen you holding hands and whispering with Father Paul."

"Oh no! He was just thanking me for our nativity scene. Well, I guess Logan thinks I'm a total whore, now."

"I'm sure it's not that bad."

"I'm sure it is. He already thinks I have the hots for Noah. Now he thinks I'm getting it on with a priest." She rises from the rocker. "Sorry, sweetheart. I seem unable to do anything right with Logan. Your daughter's asleep; you should be also. I'll carry her to bed for you."

Anne kisses Lindsay after she covers her with a soft blanket. She and Summer tiptoe back into the living room. "Are all your presents wrapped?"

"Yes, believe it or not . . . Are you okay, Mom?"

"Sure. But I don't know what to do about Logan. I don't like to think about him driving all the way back to the mountains, especially if he's feeling angry or let down. I wonder if his cell phone is on."

"Be sure you know what you're going to say before you call him. Goodnight Mom, I love you."

"How did I raise such smart girls? You must have gotten it from your Dad. No, he's not very smart either."

"You're smart about everything but yourself, Mom. You'll figure it out. Meanwhile this baby girl is kicking the stuffing out of me. I'm off to pee and then to bed. I hope Lindsay sleeps."

"So, do you *think* it's a girl, or do you *know* it's a girl? Are you holding out on your old mother?"

"I *hope* it's a girl. I want Lindsay to have the same experience I had with a sister."

"That's nice, sweetheart. And if she wakes up, call me. I'll get up with her."

Anne hugs her daughter for a long moment. When she starts to let her go, Summer holds on. "In case I haven't told you lately, I feel very lucky to have you and Dad for parents. I don't feel like a victim of divorce. When I was a kid, I sometimes felt that way, but no more." Summer puts her arm around Anne and they cross to her bedroom door.

"Did I ever tell you what Dad did when he visited after Lindsay was born? Every night he slept on the couch instead of in the guest room."

"Why did he do that?"

"Because I had to nurse her every few hours, and I would go downstairs and feed her in the living room so I wouldn't bother Joe. Dad would sleep there so he could wake up and keep me company. He didn't want to miss an opportunity to visit."

"He's a good father. Thank you for sharing that memory." Anne pauses and then hesitantly asks, "You didn't see anyone else did you?"

"What do you mean? There were lots of people."

"I mean anyone else that didn't belong here." No response. "I mean Steven."

"Steven?" Her face shadows with anger and concern. "No, did you see him?"

"No, but I felt his presence. I've been feeling it since I moved here. I'm sure it's nothing."

"I thought you put him out of your mind, Mom."

"I thought I did, too." And for a moment, Anne considers telling Summer about the life insurance policy but doesn't. "Must have been the Ghost of Christmases Past. Goodnight sweetheart."

Anne takes her cell phone to the loft and sits on the bed. She dials Logan's number. It rings, but there's no answer. She considers leaving a message but can't. What would she say? She remembers too clearly the words used to end their relationship when she feared she was slipping into yet another commitment bound to end in disaster. Only this time she had held her heart back, not allowed herself to dive into the crest of the wave. She knew there was only hard, mutilating sand below and she might miss the mark—again. So when he began planning their future and taking her presence in it for granted, she told him one night that the magic was gone, that she no longer felt anything for him. He left without another word. She saw the stoop in his shoulders as he walked to his truck, and she sagged with the heaviness of his hurt. But she also felt a great relief, as if she had dodged another bullet.

Now she feels his pain again. He cared enough to come here—perhaps to surprise her and be a part of the family gathering. After all, she had invited him to visit, and this was just a family weekend, a family that still embraced him. She imagines he had Christmas presents in his truck, but she can't imagine what he must feel now. *I was home free, no longer responsible for anyone except my girls. Now I've opened a door that I don't know how to close, if I have a choice anymore. Stupid thought. Even tonight won't end Logan's feelings. He's a rare man. He offers all the love and goodness I could ask for; but I want to be the one that loves. Being loved is not enough. Maybe I could sort things out in a letter.*

After an hour of trying, and still unable to find the words for Logan, she turns to another form of writing with another man.

EMAIL TO NOAH:

I haven't heard from you in days. I assume Elizabeth's physical and emotional needs occupy your time. God bless you both. I know it's hard, but think of the stories you'll be able to tell when it's all behind you.

We had the Pearl Christmas today. It's a one-day celebration now, but I'm sure it will grow into at least a three-day weekend. I predict that one day, friends and relatives and maybe even tourists will come to participate. That almost makes me sad. There has been special food all day and activities for the children. The choirs from the three local churches sang carols and a fourth choir from Eula joined us, led by a would-be-militant black woman. There was a little tension that dissipated quickly. I hope it's a new beginning for local race relations. I know, Pollyanna rears her head to take another punch.

Summer told me a touching story tonight about her dad. It makes me realize how hard I was on him for years after we divorced—not mean, just cold. I think it's time to stop thinking about forgiving him and to ask for his forgiveness.

Are you there?

EMAIL TO ANNE:

I am here. I've missed our conversations. I know that's my fault. I've received all your emails, but haven't had the time, energy, or heart to respond. I keep waiting until I have good news, but it doesn't come.

Liz and I both practice your Lamaze. It helps us through the physical and emotional stuff, but hearing your daily activities and thoughts help more than anything else.

Maybe we'll have stories to tell one of these days, but I doubt it. There are some things you don't want to relive. Liz may feel differently. She has turned into a real optimist—embracing each day. I am the coward that can't bear to watch her struggle. She used to call me a control freak. Now she is the only one with any control. Why do I think I sound like a girl?

EMAIL TO NOAH:

Because you're allowing yourself to see through her eyes. You're trying to be her, to absorb her fears and pain. It's all right. You'll probably get back to your old macho insensitive self again. I'll bet you even have lots of hair now.

EMAIL TO ANNE:

I actually need a haircut. I want to say something to you, Anne. I want to thank you for that day in November. Thank you for meeting with me and for the parking lot and for afterwards. And thank you for allowing me to share some of your concerns for a change. I went home with made-up excuses, and Liz seemed indifferent. Later, she lured me into bed to remind me that I belong to her for as long as she lives. I probably should have told her that I met with you. I don't like the lies, but I'm in too deep to confess now.

EMAIL TO NOAH:

She would forgive you.

EMAIL TO ANNE:

But we would lose something.

EMAIL TO NOAH:

Yes.

EMAIL TO ANNE:

So thank you.

EMAIL TO NOAH:

Thank you, Noah. I needed your strength and support that day, but let's close and seal that door.

EMAIL TO ANNE:

Are you going to move on to Door #3—the Logan door?

EMAIL TO NOAH:

Are you psychic? Or is that a crude reference to my two failed attempts at marriage?

EMAIL TO ANNE:

God, no. I think you have room for three great loves in your life: your daughters and maybe Logan, or maybe someone you haven't met.

EMAIL TO NOAH:

You're sounding like a girl again. Maybe we can be girlfriends. Laugh, laugh. Seriously, I'm ready to try to go to sleep. Sleep well my (girl)friend.

EMAIL TO ANNE:

Wait. I'm not sleepy yet, and I haven't given you the second installment on the real Noah. I told you that I was adopted and that my grandfather raised me Jewish because my parents were practicing non-believers. I told you Liz doesn't know the truth about the adoption. I needed time to adjust to the betrayal myself, and she was already dealing with enough family issues. There never seemed to be a good time to tell her. Maybe I was more bothered by it than I admitted, even to myself. You're the only person I've told. So, what other secrets do you want to know?

EMAIL TO NOAH:

None. I am burdened with secrets. Tell me something ordinary, like how you got to be a publisher.

EMAIL TO ANNE:

My grandfather was a printer. He had a shop in Raleigh, and he printed everything from posters to newsletters to opera tickets. Eventually, he bought binding equipment and started printing books as well.

My Dad was drafted into the military and planned to go to college afterwards. But when he returned, Granddad was sick, and so Dad took over the business. He narrowed it to just books and began soliciting authors and learning how to market the books. Later, he had an opportunity to take his business to Chicago for a partnership in a small but impressive publishing house.

My father didn't teach me religion, but he taught me a love for books and the desire to bring new ideas and stories to the public's attention. After college, I joined him and worked from the lowest editing position up to CEO.

EMAIL TO NOAH:

What about your mother?

EMAIL TO ANNE:

She was all about family. Maybe because she couldn't have her own children, she made me feel like the most important person on Earth. Although she wasn't religious in the traditional sense, she was a devout follower of the Golden Rule. She believed we should respect and care for the rights and dignity of others simply because it was the responsible way to live—not out of fear of Hell and damnation, not out of pious self-righteousness nor out of humble servitude.

EMAIL TO NOAH:

She sounds like quite a woman. When did you lose her?

EMAIL TO ANNE:

Years ago. She died, and within six months, he did too. I've been thinking about them since I read your story about the antique flower vase. I haven't read it to Liz yet. I was afraid she would want to go gladly into the great good night.

EMAIL TO NOAH:

I understand. Go to sleep, Noah. I'm passing out.

EMAIL TO ANNE:

Sweet dreams.

Chapter 16

The Hobnail Vase

I**SOLATED TOGETHER DURING** her stem-cell rescue
in the Bone Marrow Clinic at Duke Hospital, Noah and Elizabeth
passed most of their hours watching television. Noah became a passionate college basketball fan, watching Duke, NC State, and UNC–
Chapel Hill games, but only while Elizabeth slept. When she was
able, they watched the news. Sometimes they compromised, and
she listened to the radio while he watched a game set on mute.

She is now home, in a prolonged state of recovery—not from the
disease, but from the treatment. The books completed, her only exit
time is reality outside of herself. Sick of being sick; tired of focusing
on her own body and her disease; wishing for distraction from the
never ending treatments and their devastating side effects, Elizabeth weans herself from the mind-numbing medications and becomes obsessed with the news. She listens to NPR, reads the papers
from cover to cover, and watches CNN. Isolated by her illness, she
develops a distance and some objectivity about all the information
she is able to collect and process.

Christmas is over. The Indian Ocean tsunami has destroyed the homes and lives of so many, and the war with Iraq goes on. In frustration, she rages. "Money is collected to help in the relief of victims of nature and war, but no one changes their style of living, or their use of the world's resources, or their contribution to the pollution problems, or their political allegiance. Everyone feels the rising cost of medical care and prescriptions, but everyone is afraid to challenge the profiteering backed by government."

"Relax, Liz. You're preaching to the choir. Save it for some non-believers, or at least a bigger audience."

"I think I can finally understand something about the German people—not the Nazis, the ordinary people who went about their lives as if the death camps for Jews didn't exist." Noah smiles at her fervor while he straightens the bedroom after helping her bathe and dress. She is back in bed, propped on pillows. "It's human nature to ignore or disbelieve what you feel powerless to change, and to focus on personal survival. But it's wrong!"

"So you say you understand the German people, but they were wrong."

"No, I'm saying we're all wrong. We used to blame the good Germans—the non-Nazis—for doing nothing to stop Hitler. But don't we all behave the same way? We allow ourselves to be led like sheep to the slaughter. We're so focused on our personal wants and needs that we don't see where we're going or what we'll leave behind for our children."

"I think you're over-dramatizing, Liz. Some people do speak out against the system. Some do fight for the rights of others. We publish books that focus on the need for change. We have two books being printed as we speak that address reform, one on the environment and one on health care. And you, my love, you have almost finished a set of books to help children and the families of children who are facing a life-threatening illness."

"I wrote about sickness and how to accept death, about how to die. I should have written about overcoming adversity, about how to live!" She turns, trying to get comfortable. "Noah, we have learned

264

so much firsthand about the flaws in the system for providing medical care. I am one of the privileged few who could afford to be sick and get the treatments and professional care I've received."

"I agree. In fact, if you remember, we gave some anonymous aid to two of the families we met."

"I know—guilt money! It's not enough."

"All right, Liz. When you're well, I'll hook you up with some health reform groups and you can be their poster girl."

"Don't laugh. That's not a bad idea. Not the poster part, but I would like to be involved in pushing for change."

Noah sits on the bed beside Elizabeth and takes her hand. "I'm glad to see you so passionate about something. In fact, you've got me aroused. Care for a tumble?"

Elizabeth laughs and kisses his hand. "Hey big boy, my brain's alert, but my body isn't. Give me a couple of weeks to get my strength back." She turns again, still seeking comfort.

"We've only been sprung from that blood clinic prison for three days. But I can't just lie here."

"How about a story? There's one that Anne asked me to read to you if things became hopeless. I read it to you when you were at your worst in the clinic. You were so doped up, I doubt that you remember it. In fact, I think I read it more for myself than for you."

"All right. Maybe it'll take my mind off the news. What's the object?"

"It's one of your favorites. I'll go get it and some ice water. Can you believe how warm the weather is in late January?"

"You mean it isn't summer? I thought I'd slept through winter and spring. What did you get me for Christmas, anyway?"

"The same thing you got me—nothing. They wouldn't even let me bring flowers into your room. We decided to take a long romantic vacation together when you're better."

Elizabeth smiles contentedly as he leaves, but when he's gone, the smile disappears and she begins her controlled breathing, trying to minimize the new pain in her back, the one she hasn't told him about.

A few minutes later, Noah returns with the journal and the fan-shaped hobnail glass vase. "Oh, that *is* my favorite thing here." *Breathe.* "I wondered if there would be a story to go with it."

"It's quite a story. I'm not sure how you will respond to it. I'm only reading it to you because your Irish is up. I think you're strong enough to hear it, and it's strong enough to calm you down."

"When did you get so analytical about my emotions? You sound like a girl."

"Ah, that again. It just proves how confident I am in my masculinity that I can share these thoughts with you."

"Oh my God, it gets worse," Elizabeth moans, covering her face.

"Shut up and listen."

THE HOBNAIL GLASS VASE

The hobnail glass vase was a gift from the daughter of Alice and Riley Anderson, my parents' best friends. They met after the war in a housing development in Galveston, Texas, built specifically for World War II vets. They remained friends for the rest of their lives.

A few years ago, the phone rang, jarring me from sleep. I shook my head and stretched my facial muscles in an attempt to find 'alert'. Late night calls are always frightening, and I'd had my share. I checked the clock—only eleven—not necessarily an emergency. Leaning across the empty space where my former husband had slept, I picked up the phone to stop the ringing.

"Anne Megan?" a voice asked in answer to my 'hello'. I knew it must be a Texas relative as they were the only people remaining on the earth who called me by my first and middle names. "It's Billie Rae. I just wanted to call and tell you . . . Mama's in her last days now. And there's something you should know."

My heart clenched at her words. Dear Alice, my mother's best friend from the time I was two years old, a second mother to me, was dying. Familiar snapshots of the tall big-boned woman with the hearty laugh, the loudest hiccups ever heard, and an always kind word pushed their way into my mind.

I'm sure I said something, but I can't imagine what. "I'm sorry" simply would not have been enough. But she continued as if I had said nothing. "People have been coming to her from the past."

"What?" I asked, confused, wondering what relatives would be visiting at such a difficult time. Of course, if my parents were still alive, they would be there, but Mom had been gone for over twenty years and Daddy (whose loss was still fresh) for four. They would have been beside her, holding her hands and giving love and support to her husband Riley and their grown daughters. They would have reminisced about the years of hardship and love and sharing. Daddy would have told about taking Alice to the hospital when their youngest, Susie Mae, was born because Riley was on a job in South America and couldn't be there himself. Mama would have remembered taking her and the girls with us when we evacuated Galveston during a hurricane, a terrifying trip across a flooded causeway . . . and the return trip, also frightening, not knowing whether our homes would still be standing. They would have laughed about the beans and cornbread dinners when money was low and we pooled our resources, and camping on the beach at Padre Island.

Billie Rae interrupted my reverie. "I mean people who have already passed have been coming to her to prepare her for . . . " At that point she had to pause and regain control of her emotions. While she excused herself to find a tissue, memories flashed like family pictures.

Daddy and Riley had met in Galveston, both working out of a local union as pipefitters for the construction of oil and chemical refineries. They were laying pipe together in a ditch when the infamous Texas City Blow-out occurred. A nearby ship full of chemical fertilizer exploded, and they survived because of being in that ditch. They spent the rest of the day carrying dead or injured men to rescue locations. Daddy eventually moved up to supervisory positions, but Riley never wanted to order other men around. They worked together in South America, Arabia, and of course all over Texas. But Riley didn't like leaving his home state, so they often worked apart.

Mama and Alice were equally close. They called each other El and Al. They were tall, pretty, and rowdy. But Alice was as practical and steady as the earth, while Mama was as exotic and changing as the moon. When money was short, they cooked beans or whatever was available and made us feel like it was a feast. They shared food, babysitters, laughter, and tears.

When I was ten, both families moved to Corpus Christi, and we often camped on Padre Island. We parked our two cars about six feet apart and stretched a blanket between them, caught in the car doors. That was our umbrella and our tent. We surf fished, seined, gathered oysters, and ate like kings. I have two strong memories of those trips. The first was running along the seine after it was pulled up on the beach and looking at all the amazing sea creatures it caught. There was everything from hammerhead sharks, to jellyfish, to red drum fish, to crabs and seaweed. They threw back whatever we couldn't eat. I'm not sure why we returned to the water after we saw what had just come out of it. The second memory was of sand in the crotch of my bathing suit.

Although our nomadic lives often took us to different cities and states, our families remained best friends, and Corpus Christi became the place we considered home. After many more years of moving, it was the place where both couples retired.

Mama died when she was only 50, Daddy flew her body from Robinson, Illinois to Corpus for burial. In a year, he remarried out of sheer loneliness. The marriage lasted only three years because she was an engineer—not a housewife who could follow him from job to job. Daddy had aimed to replace Mama and missed. He married again, this time to a Jewish woman named Molly. Riley and Alice had welcomed each woman he brought into their friendship without question and without reservation. In private, they would let me know how much they still missed my mother.

After only a few years of retirement, Molly died on a Thursday, and Daddy died two days later. He was buried next to Mama. Molly was buried in the same cemetery, but in a different location set aside for people of the Jewish faith. I don't know if a separate burial place for Jews is their religious choice or a result of prejudice. It bothered me. Of course, Riley and Alice were there, supporting us as they grieved for the loss of their friend.

Alice was a collector. At first she collected salt and pepper shakers, and later she began collecting hobnail glass vases. After Daddy's death, Alice, always the tower of strength, began a swift decline. Their older daughter moved home to help her dad and to nurse her mother.

Billie's voice again broke through my reverie. "I wanted you to know that she told me Eloise and Millard came to her. She said they were young, and they were holding hands. And they both looked so good and so happy."

I managed to mumble, "Thank you, Billie Rae." I'm sure I said something more about her mother and dad, but I was crying too hard to say much. I'm equally sure she understood. Alice died the next day. I spent weeks in a deep depression, grieving for Alice, for my parents, and ultimately for myself. I had been divorced for the second time and felt very alone and very selfishly aware that there would be no one waiting to hold my hand—at least no soul mate.

A year later, my brother Earl, his wife Emily, and I took a sentimental journey around south Texas, visiting relatives. Of course we went to Corpus Christi to see Riley Anderson. His daughter asked Emily and me to each select one of the hobnail vases to keep as a memento of her mother. I chose the fan-shaped vase that reflects pastel colors in the sunlight. Not long after that, Riley joined Alice.

I suppose most people would reason that Alice was a sick, elderly woman and might have been hallucinating. I think, in fact, that would be weak logic. Alice was always the sharpest mind of the four, and also very spiritual. I choose to believe she saw my parents, reunited and returned to their stronger selves. And even if they existed that way only in a dying friend's memories, it restored them to me in the same form—young, together, and happy.

Now I like to picture the four of them on Padre Island, Riley and Daddy surf-fishing while Alice and Mom walk the beach, sharing a beer, memories, and loud wind-filling laughter.

How comforted you must feel, Elizabeth, knowing you and Noah and Joshua will be together forever—that is, of course, if you believe that Alice's story was not the delusions of a dying woman, but a revelation of hope for us all.

Elizabeth takes the tissue from Noah and wipes her eyes and blows her nose while she looks around the room. "Where is he?" Noah doesn't answer. "Okay, why not?"

"Why isn't he here?" Noah asks, as he spots Josh in the corner, watching them both, relieved that she can't see him—and that Josh isn't there to help her leave.

"No, why not believe? It's so much better than the alternative." She sighs deeply and then says, "I want to meet Anne. I want to know her."

"Are you sure?"

"Very sure. That was the last story, wasn't it?"

"If you don't count the emails," he says, knowing he must.

She hesitates for only a moment. "Did you save them?"

"Yes."

"Will you read them to me?"

"If you want."

"I want. But first I want to email her. I need permission to use something of hers again. And then I would like some of the pain meds. I actually want to sleep."

EMAIL TO ANNE:

Thank you for your story of the hobnail vase. May I use it for the ending of my Joshua books? That's the title, by the way—*My Joshua Books*. There's time for one last re-write, and perhaps the ending will not be fiction but the truth. Josh could tell his readers that dying young does not prevent them from living happily-ever-after. No one does. It just means that they will come to the ever-after (home base) sooner, and that their lost family and friends will be there, waiting to hold their hand. Perhaps Josh's grandparents did come to him to help him through his last days or moments; perhaps Josh will be there for other children defeated by disease—to welcome them and to ease their way.

I want to meet you.—*Elizabeth*

EMAIL TO ANNE:

In response to your earlier question, Jewish funerals are steeped in ritual and tradition that is unique to them. And yes, I could tell you many stories of anti-Semitism especially towards my grandfather, but also towards my father and even me. And I could tell you stories about love and support from Christian friends. We never purposefully isolated ourselves within our religious community. My family always lived in the world. My grandfather is in a Jewish cemetery; my parents were cremated, their ashes scattered. There is no simple answer to your question about divided cemeteries. But don't automatically assume it is a result of Christian prejudice. There is a long history of Jews being buried in a separate space. For some, it is related to identification in the time of the resurrection. For others, it is merely tradition.

Thank you for the story of the hobnail vase. It was and is a comfort to us both. We're out of stories from you. She wants me to read your emails. I've agreed. There may be one or two that I'll accidentally delete. So if you have any more stories up your sleeve, email them.

Liz is slowly recovering from the stem-cell treatment. We don't know yet if it stopped the cancer. That's the layman's description of her current state of health. Sorry I can't be more specific. The doctors explain everything to me using all the appropriate medical technical terminology, and then I forget it by the next meal. Maybe that's on purpose. It translates down to 'not very hopeful', and I just want it all to go away—the words, not her.

She is living up to her promise to allow medicine to have its crack at healing her; she has even developed an attitude of positive intensity about life instead of resignation and negativity. I won't describe what she looks like now; instead, I'll attach a photo of her and Josh, B.C. (before cancer).

Don't you need to visit Summer? Liz and I want to see you.—*Noah*

P.S. Now that I can think about something besides stem-cells, I think you need to be proactive about the insurance policy that Steven holds. Since you didn't approve the policy, it can be cancelled, and he can be arrested for forging your signature. At the very least, he needs to be confronted and told of your knowledge of the policy. I think his wife should be told as well. But it's your life, and these are your choices.

Chapter 17

Valentine Pearls

ANNE SMILES EVEN BEFORE her eyes open, assured she is not dreaming. Logan is kissing her shoulder and rubbing her arm, then her wrist, and then her hand. He massages each finger and then her palm, taking his time, pulling gently on each of the joints. He has osteoarthritis in both hands; she has the beginnings of it. They used to laugh at themselves, claiming to be blue and white collar workers—both full professors, who found themselves using their backs and muscles as often as their intellect. Now their joints reap the rewards of years of physical labor, both on and off the job.

Logan gently lays her right hand on the sheet and reaches for the other hand that he brings to his lips before repeating the massage ritual. Anne shifts to accommodate the change and moans with pleasure. She had forgotten what it is like to try to sleep with Logan. His need to touch and stroke and be close seems insatiable. She reluctantly admits that time would probably change this. *At some point, we will have to get a good night's sleep—but not now. For now, this is just fine.*

Anne takes her turn and massages Logan's hands, following his routine, but giving special attention to his thumbs, which seem to suffer the most. She murmurs. "I love the pearl earrings. I haven't had a Valentine's present in a long time, unless you count the cards Bradley makes for me." Logan smiles but says nothing. "I don't usually like surprise visits—half the fun is anticipation and preparation. But last night was okay."

"Just okay?"

"The surprise was okay. In fact, it was good. Everything else was amazing, unbelievable, great! Do I have to go on?"

"Well, you could mention the kiss that started at your front door and lasted until we got to your room—which, by the way, was complicated by those damn spiral stairs. I'm not sure which of us was carrying the other."

"Carrying? I think it was more like pulling and pushing—and we took turns. I'm sure we could have won something on *America's Funniest X-Rated Home Videos*."

Logan grins, remembering. "Please don't schedule much for us today. I'm going to need a nap. I'm an old man."

"Yeah, right!" She finishes with his hands and rolls onto her side. He pulls her into the curve of his body. Anne smiles with contentment. How nice it is to be the comfortee instead of the comforter—to have someone sensitive to her instead of the other way around. She touches the pearl drops, the only thing she's wearing. "You know how fussy I am about jewelry. How did you know I would love these black pearls?"

"I know you better than you know yourself, Anne Gray—or at least I thought I did."

"What do you mean?"

"Let's take a bath. Will your bathtub hold two?"

"Yes. It's a big old-fashioned footed tub, came with the house." She rolls over and kisses his mouth, tugging gently on his lower lip.

"Stop," he says. "You know what that does to me."

"Ummm, there does seem to be a direct connection between your lower lip and your lower parts. There must be a sign along the way that says, 'go straight down; do not pass through the brain; resistance is futile'."

"Well, for this one time, there's a detour sign that says, 'Get out of bed; fill the tub; it's time to talk'." Anne groans, but knows it's true. She has stalled for two years. It is indeed time to talk.

She rises, not bothering to cover herself. Logan reaches for his glasses and watches her stretch as she slowly moves away from him. "If you could see yourself from my perspective, your internal camera would be clicking away, taking pictures for future paintings." She turns a dazzling smile to him and disappears into the bathroom, touched that this man chooses to be blind to her body's imperfections.

He sits up and looks around the room, now brightening with morning sunlight. He sees canvases stacked against the wall and one on the easel. There are several seascapes, a blue heron, a white egret, and one canvas with a sailboat and a man in it. *She's painting again.* He pulls on his shorts and walks downstairs to use the guest bathroom and to look again at what he only glimpsed last night.

The rooms are and aren't a surprise. They are a visual feast, a complex composition of texture and line, but warming and soothing in subtle and occasionally dramatic hues and values. Her home in Durham had been an attractive concoction of her past, the good and the bad. This space is like a dream bubble that burst, spreading itself on the walls, floors, and furniture, looking natural, unplanned, and perfect.

Surprisingly, it doesn't say, "Me, Me, Me!" There is history in the antique furniture, the plaster walls, and even in the dried honeysuckle vines and plumed grasses. There are stories in every nook and cranny. And the beauty is that they aren't Anne's stories. They are someone else's—just waiting for Anne to discover and find delight in them. Logan sees and feels it all. He knows she will not leave this place. And he also knows it isn't the house she won't leave. In the end, it's just a house. It's whatever or whoever has freed in her spirit the courage to express herself. He thinks of the flat traditionally painted walls in his cabin, and he can't picture Anne there. He feels defeated. Anne calls to him. He inhales deeply and then lets it all out. He will focus on the two things he can do and have: he can help Anne, and he can gain her trust.

Logan climbs into the tub of steaming water, audibly groaning in pleasure and opening his arms to her. "When is gravity going to pull on your butt?" he says, feeling her firmness as she settles between his legs, her back relaxing against his chest.

"When I stop cycling and doing manual labor, I guess" She laughs.

"Stick with me and we'll be cycling when you're ninety and I'm a hundred."

There is a pause. Anne tenses. *Stick with me*. And then, in a small voice, half teasing, she says, "Is that a proposal?"

"No," he answers. *Not yet*. He encircles her with his arms and she relaxes again. "Thank you for the letter."

"I wrote it at least a hundred times. It was pages long. So I condensed it to a few lines in a blue envelope that sat on my table for a week before I finally sent it."

"It sat on my table for a week before I finally opened it. And then I read it at least a hundred times. 'My Love, if my love you still will be,'" he recites.

Anne whispers the rest of the letter, a poem etched in her mind,

"You showed me
hiding places, wildflowers
found years before,
Gray's Lilies,
Blue-eyed Grass, and more.
You showed your heart,
and found mine.

Still I ran,
in need of air,
found a brush, mixed a hue,

painted empty.
I cannot lose myself in you,
but I can draw us
side by side.

Time provides a clearer view,
and we may find
a common grace.
Show me where
wild orchids grow;
show your heart,
and I'll find you.

Anne's chest tightens as she sits forward, giving him the opportunity to emotionally back away. She knows the romance of the night may have been just that—no more. "I felt like a schoolgirl, sending you a poem. And when you didn't answer for so long, I thought the poem was too little, too late."

"I would have come sooner," he responds, stroking her back, "but your past got in my way."

"What do you mean? . . . You couldn't forget the past?"

"No, I had to try to fix it. How do you feel right now, Anne Megan Gray?"

She thinks for a moment and then leans back into him again. "Safe."

"Good. That's how I want you to feel." He kisses her hair and then says, "Tell me about Steven. Tell me about the bee sting."

Anne's breath stops in mid-inhale. "How..." she stammers, trying to sit up.

"Doesn't matter," he responds, holding her tighter, not allowing her to rise. "Tell me."

She throws her head back in anger and he turns his head to miss it. "Ouch. That's my collar bone speaking. You have an issue with it?"

"No, I have issues with feeling calf-roped, thrown, and tied."

"Tell me, Anne."

Anne takes a deep breath and then lets it out. "All right. I'm sorry. Did I hurt you?"

"No." His arms loosen their grip and they both relax into the warmth again.

"I didn't tell you about the bee sting incident when we first met because I didn't want you to become my protector. I didn't want to bring you into my life just because you're a man."

"I think I understand that."

"I'll tell you now because I want you to know me."

"Are you saying we can't move forward without backing up?" he asks with trepidation.

"Can you play that on a guitar?"

"Moving on."

Anne blows out a long breath and begins the story that was a constant companion in her days and nights. "It's not as if he beat me or used a gun or knife on me. Some people would say it was all in my imagination."

"You're delaying, Anne."

"You want details? All right," she sighs, closing her eyes and returning in her mind to that long ago evening. "It was almost twilight—that silver sliver of time just before dark. I was alone in the garden. It was still but for the persistent humming of the bees. I felt an overriding tension and kept telling myself to shake it off, to focus on Summer's bridal shower the following day. There was a strong perfume of the flowers we raised for her wedding. But there was something different, an unusual scent in the air, a sickening sweet, riding on the weight of the heat and humidity." She sighs again.

Logan resists telling her to get to the point. *After all, the real truth may be in the details.*

"The Japanese beetle trap Steven insisted on was full of beetles—and bees. I hated the trap! I wished it drove them away, instead of drawing them. The trap was intended only for the beetles. I lived in a tenuous peace with the bees. They didn't bother me if I didn't invade their space. I'm allergic; I've learned to be careful." Another sigh as tension grows while she relives the betrayal.

"Without warning, a bee flew directly at me. I couldn't back away fast enough. It stung! I tried to shake it off—to make it fly away! But the stinger was sunk deep in my palm. I had to push it off! Hurrying into the house, I called to Steven to get the Epi pen!

"Steven snapped that he didn't know where it was. He was angry at my weakness and beyond angry with us. I found it where it always was and plunged the needle into my thigh. Lying back on the couch, I called for him . . . Silence . . . I called again. He finally came to the doorway. My skin was moist, and the itching had begun at the back of my neck, under my arms, on the bottom of my feet. The swelling had also started, mostly my hand and forearm, but spreading all over. My throat started to tighten. I didn't tell him. I didn't want to panic."

"Jesus!" Logan whispers through gritted teeth.

"With measured calm, I told him I needed the second dose. I'd never asked for seconds before. I was trembling too badly from the first injection to do it myself. He crossed to the couch and sat beside me, picking up the second syringe, looking at it meditatively, turning it in his hand, delaying. I begged him to use it, and told him my throat was swelling!" Too tense to continue leaning against Logan, Anne sits forward, wrapping her arms around her knees.

"He looked into my eyes, still not moving, and said I looked fine. Shock replaced panic. I could see the red blotches on my skin, and my arm swollen like a long rubber glove filled to the point of bursting. Headlights shone in the front windows. Greer had arrived to help with the bridal shower. Steven gazed at the circle of light on the shade, sighed deeply, and injected the epinephrine into my other thigh, then left the room."

"Anne, are you sure he was purposefully delaying?"

"I'm not finished, Logan. Greer walked in, saw me and knew instantly what had happened. She got an icepack for my hand and Benadryl with a glass of water. She sat with me and rubbed my itching feet, swollen round, waiting as the medicine worked. Her presence was so calming—her presence was everything.

"Still, my throat was tight and my voice raspy. I saw her begin to panic as she called Steven. He walked to the doorway, carrying the phone while he talked with a telemarketer. Shocked at his casual conversation with a salesman, Greer yelled at him to call 911. I felt myself slipping, not caring."

"Minutes passed, but gradually the tightness in my throat began to ease, relief slowly coursing. The reaction was over; the epinephrine had worked. We stopped listening for an ambulance. More time passed, and he stood in the doorway again, still unwilling to cross the threshold. Without asking how I was doing, he reported that the doctor on-call said if I wasn't better in twenty minutes, he would have to bring me to the emergency room. Neither of us responded."

Anne struggles to pull herself back from the intensity of the experience. "I wonder what would have happened if Greer had not come home and forced Steven to action. Without the second injection, would I have survived? He obviously did not call the doctor, or he didn't tell the doctor about my allergy to bee stings, much less about my throat swelling. With that information, no doctor would have said to wait twenty minutes before taking a thirty-minute drive to the hospital. So, to answer your question, Logan, yes, Steven purposefully delayed. I saw in his face the moment when he realized he had a choice to help or not help; the coldness in his eyes when he said I looked fine; and his resignation and disappointment illuminated by headlights when Greer arrived."

Logan reaches out to touch her, but she pulls away, reminded of the list of betrayals by men, reminded that she won't be taken unaware again. She saw the bee coming. She even understood the bee's anger at the death smell from the beetle trap. The ambush was what followed the sting.

"Why didn't you go to the police?"

"Because some people would say it was all in my imagination. And that's where I kept it—in the back of my mind. Summer was about to get married, and I didn't want my problems to spoil it for her. I also didn't feel threatened. I thought it was just a freak situation that he saw as an opportunity. It identified him as an immoral snake, not a murderer."

"I think more of my snake than of Steven."

"Okay, bad comparison."

"Did you ever find out what he said to the doctor—or if he even called him?"

"No. That would have forced me to face reality, and I was in another ostrich phase, the same one I retreated to when I knew, but didn't know, that Robert was gay. I kept the memory of that night just below my threshold of cognitive thinking until after Summer's wedding. When all the guests were gone except for my brother and his wife, Emily, I had a kind of mother-of-the-bride breakdown. Emily took me for a walk, and before I could stop myself, I was telling her about the bee sting. As I heard myself say the words, I knew our marriage was over. I knew I had to get out before he took advantage of another emergency or found the courage to create one. I was also ashamed."

"Why?"

"Because when I heard myself tell the story, I knew that only a very foolish or very frightened woman would stay in that situation."

"What happened when you confronted him?"

"I didn't ask for a divorce; I just told him we had problems we needed to discuss. He was clearly surprised when I told him that I knew he tried to let me die. I slipped that accusation in between many other problems that made our marriage a miserable place for both of us. He denied it and said he didn't want a divorce. I told him to think about it. A few days later, I asked him if he had thought about our discussion. He said he hadn't thought of anything else. He said that everything I had accused him of was true."

"He admitted it?"

"Yes, although I'm sure he wouldn't have admitted it in front of witnesses. Anyway, we began planning our separation. As you well know, North Carolina is a no-fault divorce state, and we had to divide everything equally, even the house I owned before I met him.

He could no longer look forward to inheriting my estate, so he hid assets and stole whatever else he could. He diminished the value of the property he wanted; and he inflated the value of the property I kept. I caught him at a few things and made him make adjustments, but basically, I didn't care. I just wanted him gone."

"How did the girls react?"

"They were jubilant."

"About the bee sting, I mean."

"I didn't tell them."

"But Greer was there."

"She saw that he was disinterested in my welfare and slow to call the doctor after he knew my throat was swelling. She thought he was an asshole, not a murderer. But, she was so upset that she called Summer and complained about him. She recently admitted that she knew there was more to it than simple negligence. Probably, because I said nothing more about it, they just added it to their list of negative experiences with Steven. They were relieved and grateful when he was gone."

"What else?"

"What do you mean?"

"What else did he do?"

"Who knows? If I allowed myself to get paranoid, which I can do, I would see a plot in everything he did. It doesn't matter anymore."

"Tell me about the life insurance policy."

Anne stops speaking. She turns around and faces Logan from the other end of the tub, an incredulous look on her face. "No, Logan! You tell me where you got your information. Did you call Noah, or did you hack into my email?"

"I don't know whether to yell back at you or laugh. Number one, I don't do underhanded things. I'm. Not. Steven! Do I have to get a t-shirt with that printed on the front of it? Number two, I'm a technological dinosaur, and you know it. I don't even have a computer." He pauses to calm his own anger and frustration. He wanted to come to her with love and assurance, *but here we are yelling—again. Seems like old times. What happened to last night—and this morning?*

"Number three," he says softly, "Noah called me. I'll explain why after you tell me about the insurance." He pulls a washcloth from the towel rack above. "And would you cover yourself while we talk? I can talk objectively to your bare back, not to your bare breasts."

"You won't have to." She throws the washcloth back at him and rises, stepping from the tub and grabbing a towel to wrap around herself. "This isn't talking; it's interrogating. I'm finished." She storms from the room.

Logan sinks into the tub, letting the water cover his face. *Why do I always say things in a way that triggers her defenses, and why is she so unreasonable?* He resurfaces. *I'm forgetting what she just told me. It's not that she doesn't trust me or men. She doesn't trust love.*

After showering off the bath water and shaving, Logan joins Anne in the kitchen where the smells of coffee and bacon draw his gnawing stomach. She puts a cup in front of him and apologizes. "I don't know what comes over me sometimes. I know you're only trying to help."

"I would ask about your hormones, but there are too many knives in this room."

Anne smiles a warning and puts the cooked bacon into the warm oven. "I'll wait on the eggs until we're through talking."

"Please, I'm starving. How about I make us omelettes while you sit, have your coffee, and talk to me?"

"Okay," she shrugs. "The milk and cheese are in the fridge and the eggs are already in the bowl. Anything else?"

"Do you have any salsa, or hot sauce?"

"Don't be silly. They're both in the fridge door. There's sour cream, too. Do you want me to chop some onions?"

"No, I'd worry about your fingers with a knife in your hand and Steven on your mind."

Anne puts an onion on the butcher block in the middle of the kitchen and then sits at the breakfast table with her coffee.

"By the way," Logan says as he peels and chops the onion, "I walked down here earlier while you were drawing the bath. It's a beautiful space. I've never seen anything quite like it. Can you imagine yourself anywhere else?"

"If that's a proposal, it's the feeblest one I've ever heard," she says, smiling and feeling a little unsure of them both.

"It's not," he says. *Not yet.*

Anne sips her coffee, then shrugs her shoulders in surrender and begins. "Steven and I were talked into huge accidental life insurance policies when we were planning a long trip to the Caribbean as part of a cultural arts study program. When we returned, we cancelled the policies, or so I thought. Steven paid all the bills and took care of the investments and other finances. One day I happened to look at the monthly bank statement, and realized the insurance company was still withdrawing premium payments. Thinking it was an oversight, I brought it to his attention. He said he would take care of it. I assumed he did what he said he would do, and I forgot about it."

"What made you think about it again?"

"I thought I had put Steven behind me, but memory of the bee sting has been gnawing at me for the last nine months or so."

"Since you sold your house?"

"I guess. Yes, it did start coming back to me then, a constant reliving of that night. And something else troubled me, but I didn't know what."

"Whoa! Interesting! . . . Sorry, go on." He pauses, shaking his head, then begins sautéing the onions, tossing in a few chopped mushrooms.

"When I left the Durham house, the nightmares ended, but the uneasiness persisted. Then one evening I was emailing a message to Noah, and all of a sudden I realized that I never saw any paperwork confirming that the insurance policy had been cancelled and that Steven never mentioned it again. Since they had been collecting premiums long after the time they were supposed to have stopped, he would have taken some kind of action to get a refund, and he would have bragged about it. Of course, he might have invested the refund in a private account."

"Or he might have continued the premiums instead of cancelling."

"Apparently, that's what happened. So, I think it's your turn to talk. What have you and Noah been up to? And by the way, how did you find out about the bee sting?"

"Why don't you set the table and pour some orange juice. The eggs will only take a minute. In fact, stick the plates into the oven to warm. Let's talk after we eat."

"Are you afraid I won't want to eat after we talk?" She steps beside him to refill their mugs with coffee. He turns her face to his and kisses her gently but for a long moment. He slips his hands inside her robe and holds her close. She sets the coffee pot on the stove and returns his embrace.

"The only thing I am afraid of is losing you because of your fears."

"I'm no longer afraid, Logan. I'm just cautious."

"That's probably true. But you are, or were, afraid of commitment. Your fear kept you at arms length when we were together and made you leave when you felt us getting closer. Your cautiousness makes you sit with your back to the wall. Your cautiousness makes you turn to men who are strong and loving—but not available. No expectations, no commitment." He sighs, resting his forehead against hers. "What do you feel with me, Anne?"

"Vulnerable," she whispers, as the last of her resistance slips away.

"Earlier, in the bath, you said you felt safe. That doesn't compute."

"Yes it does. I feel both with you. But safe is static; vulnerable is full of possibilities. I'm not sure how we got here. Such a short time ago we were so far apart." *Unfortunately, I know how we got here—pressure, pressure from my family, from Paul, from Noah, and now from you. Am I compromising again, giving in to someone else's need? Surely that isn't it.*

"You read my poem, Logan. I'm not the same person I was two years ago. My confidence and self-esteem are back, almost with attitude. I don't feel the need for a man to complete me or take care of me. I asked Noah if he could find out about the insurance policy because I was ready to deal with it instead of sticking my head back in the sand. I didn't need anyone to do it for me. I made love to you last night because I wanted you. Not just any man . . . I want to love you."

"And I want you to let me love you, Anne Gray, my love, if my love you still will be. Now hear this; this is a proposal. I can't write poetry. Unless I'm quoting you, I can only speak plain. Will you marry me? Can we spend the rest of our lives making each other happy?"

"Can you put up with a pre-menopausal woman?"

"Yes. But I don't think it's pre any more. There were a couple of times last night when I thought I was hugging a potbelly stove."

"Potbelly!" she squeals.

Anne tries to shove him away, but he holds her and stops her laughter with a kiss. "You haven't answered me."

"I love you, Logan, but I don't want to lose myself again."

"You won't. I know you don't want to leave this house and Pearl. We'll find a way to make it work. And we'll take our time."

"If I agree to marry you, will you introduce me to your children?"

"That is a little overdue."

"Yes," she agrees.

"Yes, what?"

"Yes, it's overdue." She slips her hands under his shirt and kisses his neck. "Let's do take our time, Logan, about everything but that damned omelette. I'm starving."

The kitchen, which looks like a painting, takes on a new sheen of translucent warmth as they watch one another through eyes blurred with acknowledged love. After breakfast is devoured and the dishes are washed and put away, Logan takes Anne's hand and leads her into the living room where they sit together, facing each other, under a chenille throw.

Anne begins. "Noah must have told you that the insurance policy still exists and has been raised in value. I already knew that. Is there more?"

"Yes. Are you allergic to wasps as well as bees?"

"Wasps, hornets, you name it. If it has a stinger, I'm allergic."

"That's what I thought. Last October, Noah brought Elizabeth home from a chemo treatment, and they walked into a house filled with wasps."

"Oh my God, were they stung?"

"Noah was stung twice, but Elizabeth wasn't. He isn't allergic. Who knows how a sting, or multiple stings, might have affected her with a compromised immune system? He took her over to Ben's house and called an exterminator. The nests were in the attic, and the attic stairs had been left down. He didn't remember going into the attic, and he didn't know what drew the wasps down into the house. But he didn't think much about it until Ben said it was a good thing you weren't there because of your severe allergy."

"Noah said you recently told him Steven had taken advantage of a life-threatening situation. He started putting two and two together and decided to call me."

Stunned by his words, Anne mumbles, "How did he find you?"

"He knew I was retired from the University, so he called the Botany Department, and my former assistant, Kitty, gave him my phone number."

"So he thinks Steven planted the wasps in an effort to collect on that insurance policy? And he might have hurt them, instead of me. That makes me nauseous." Logan holds her hands, wanting her to feel safe again. "Why did he wait so long to act?"

"Steven didn't do it, Anne. I'm just telling you how we drew the conclusion about what happened to make you finally divorce him and continue to be concerned about what he might do, concerned enough to ask about a life insurance policy."

"So, you didn't know about the bee sting? You were just guessing?"

"Actually, Noah guessed it."

"And you didn't come here to woo me. You just came here to protect poor little helpless me."

"Not that simple, Anne. I came here because I love you and, yes, I do want to protect you. Is that wrong? Apparently, Noah was also concerned for you and didn't want you to tackle this alone—or to just ignore it."

"He knows I care for you." After an internal debate, she adds, "I'm glad he called you . . . and I'm glad you want to follow up on this. I really don't want to see Steven or even speak to him. But I also know that something has to be done. All right, if you want to be my protector, do it. Just see that the insurance policy is cancelled and let him know that the whole story is in my lock box, and he'd better pray that an accident doesn't happen to me, because he will be the first suspect."

"It's already done. And don't push away from me. Please stay where you are. I have more to tell you."

A mixture of conflicting feelings of relief and anger course through Anne, but she overrides them and waits.

"When Noah told me that Steven had tried to take advantage of an accident—unplanned or not, that's attempted murder, Anne—everything suddenly made sense. Your inability to trust or to accept another man's love was finally, not only understandable, it was even logical. I didn't ask permission to help you, because I was afraid your pride and stubbornness would prevail. So I went to Greenville and looked him up."

"You found him?"

Logan pulls her close, holding her head against his chest and stroking her hair. "No, I found his wife."

Anne holds her breath, waiting for the rest, but already beginning to know.

"Steven's gone," they both say in whispered voices.

She sucks in more air. "When? And how?"

"His wife said he was killed last May in a drive-by shooting. It was classified as random violence."

"Dear God." Her eyes well, but she doesn't cry. She gulps air and pushes away from Logan, once again feeling suffocated. He lets her go, understanding her need for space to digest his news. "That was when I sold the house and couldn't stop thinking of him."

"Yes. His wife and I talked for a while. She didn't show any emotion. I asked her about the life insurance policy, and that seemed to surprise her."

"I'm sure," Anne murmurs.

"No, it didn't surprise her that it existed, only that I knew about it. She said that she had found the policy and had it cancelled in March, two months before his death."

"But the policy was doubled in March."

"Not that one. After talking to Steven's wife—her name is Karen, by the way—I contacted Noah, and his lawyer found out that she replaced your policy with one on Steven. His lawyer's assistant had originally just skimmed the information on the insurance policy, not noticing the changes."

"And she doubled it?" Incredulous, Anne struggles with the possibilities.

"I know . . . it sounds suspicious. Surely the police drew the same conclusions. But I guess there wasn't enough evidence to build a case."

"We're jumping to conclusions, Logan. It might have been random violence."

"Of course. However, when I left, I looked back at her house and a man was standing by an upstairs window, watching me."

Anne rises and moves towards the kitchen. "Stay here, Logan. I need some time alone." She goes through the kitchen to the back porch and her garden, almost barren in winter. It's mid-February, and a brisk wind precedes what promises to be a nasty day. She wraps her robe tightly around her, sits in the porch swing, and tries to shut out all the noise surrounding Steven's death.

Was it my fault . . . for warning her? Maybe not. But when she found the insurance policy, she must have realized I wasn't lying about him. She may have thought that after me, she would be next. Or it might have been a random shooting . . . but not likely.

Anne closes her eyes and focuses just on the memory of his face, and finally she finds the sorrow he deserves. Years of paranoia have fed negative feelings that can finally be released. She says a prayer for him and resolves that she will not close that door. Sometime in the future, she will revisit her life with Steven and she will consciously search her memories for each good thing that passed between them. It will be late, but she will find forgiveness. *No wonder I have felt your presence, Steven. No wonder it has troubled me. I'm so sorry.*

That afternoon, Logan leaves for his cabin to clean out some drawers and a closet for a long visit from Anne. He also understands her need for some space to think about her past with Steven and her future with him. On the way, he calls each of his three children and schedules a date for them to come to the cabin and meet Anne. He even tells them that she won't agree to marry him until she meets them. *Time*, he thinks. *We all need time.*

After he leaves, Anne opens her computer to give Noah a piece of her mind, but finds herself apologizing for the wasps and thanking him for calling Logan.

EMAIL TO NOAH:

How do you determine what is too much or too little involvement in a friend's life? In this case, you decided to err on the side of too much. Thank you. I suppose Logan shared what he learned about Steven and his wife. I will take responsibility and follow-up on the insurance policy. I want a letter from the insurance company, concerning the cancellation as well as all the data surrounding it that concerns me.

I'm too overwhelmed at the moment to say more. *Always—Anne*

Chapter 18

The Letter

THE WEATHER IN PEARL is cold and threatening. Anne drives to Marjorie's, wanting to tell her about Logan's visit and their fledgling plans. And because she needs to talk about him, she'll tell her friend about Steven. On the other hand, she's reluctant to talk with Paul. In spite of his insistence that she needs love, he's aware of her past misgivings and will not support this sudden decision. Anne wants to assure them both that she will not be selling her home or leaving Pearl. Actually, she doesn't know what she'll be doing. The morning's revelations replaced the warmth and passion of the night with a sad growing chill that blends into the miserable day.

The sky darkens, and the wind begins to pick up. Anne thinks about the fishermen and hopes they are all forewarned and safe at home, or at the docks tending their boats and nets.

She runs to the protective porch just as the first raindrops fall. Looking forward to coffee and company, she rings the doorbell. *How can I share my joy without diminishing hers? Can I get her to come up to the cabin to visit? Linville is very near where she*

291

was born and raised. The never-locked door remains unanswered, so Anne opens it and sticks her head inside, calling. There is still no answer. Thinking she might be on the back porch, Anne walks through the house. Not there. She can see Marjorie's car in the unattached garage. *Maybe she's sick,* Anne thinks. She goes upstairs. Relieved not to find her friend in bed, Anne returns to the front room. She forgot to look for Marjorie's bicycle. The bicycle is usually on the back covered porch. It's gone. She pauses to think.

Many places she could have ridden her bicycle to: the art co-op, one of her three churches, the marina. But there would be no protection from the weather there. Why am I worried? She's gotten along on her own for the last thirty years.

Anne notices an almost full cup of coffee on the table. She decides Marjorie will return soon, so she pours herself some from the unplugged pot, heats it in the microwave, and then sits at the table to wait for her. She notices an open letter beside Marjorie's cup. The salutation is to Mrs. Hester, a formal beginning for a handwritten letter. She sips the coffee. *Wow! Really bad!* Not intending to read further, Anne sees the words 'web search' in the first sentence. Both curiosity and dread fill her as she decides to forget her friend's privacy and read her mail.

Dear Mrs. Hester,

I recently learned of your web search for your grandson. He was my adopted son. He died of congestive heart failure when he was just eight months old. Your daughter came to the hospital after the authorities called her to get family medical history.

I asked her to leave. I didn't think she had a right to be there. I was angry and sad. I was not kind. I had waited so long for a baby, and finally I had a beautiful son. But he was sick. I blamed her. I thought she didn't take good care of herself during her pregnancy because she didn't want him.

She wouldn't leave. After he died, we went to sign some papers, and when we came back, she was holding him. Once again, I wasn't kind.

It took me a long time to realize how wrong I was. Please tell her I'm sorry. I don't know why she didn't tell you about his death since you obviously knew there was a baby.

If you need further proof, please contact Memorial Hospital in Chapel Hill where he died. Your grandson's name was Jonathan McKinnon. I understand this is hard news to hear. It has been an unending pain for me as well. Please do not contact me.

Mary McKinnon

Anne's hands shake as she lays the letter back in its original position. *Unkind is not an adequate description.* She empties, rinses, and dries her mug, then puts it away. She starts to pour out the pot of offending coffee and realizes it's stone cold. *It's bad because it's old.* Her concern grows as she telephones *The Brown Pelican*. No luck. Then she thinks of Paul. Maybe Marjorie's with him, telling him about his son. *Oh, dear God, I don't want to interfere in their time together, but I need to make sure she's there, not alone somewhere.*

She calls Paul. He's not at his house, but it's past time for Mass. She looks again at the envelope. No return address—not surprising. It was postmarked days ago. *Marjorie must have had it for at least two days. Why didn't she call or come by? Maybe she did and saw Logan's truck. She wouldn't have waited this long to tell Paul.*

Anne runs through the rain to her car. She drives to Saint Angelica's where she finds Paul, sitting alone in a pew, deep in thought— or prayer. She sits beside him and prays for guidance. Paul reaches over and takes her hand.

"Did Marjorie tell you?" he asks.

"I was going to ask you the same thing."

"I already knew. After the war, I broke my promise to Sissy and searched for him."

"And you never told Marjorie?"

"And give her someone else to mourn? I didn't know that she was even aware there had been a baby."

"How could a mother be unaware of her daughter's pregnancy?"

"You didn't know Marjorie then. She was so devastated by John's death, she was hardly aware that Sissy existed." He takes a deep breath and blows it out. "When Marjorie came to me yesterday, she was in denial. She didn't believe the letter until she talked to me. She thought it was an Internet prank."

"I don't blame her. The letter was cold."

"I know. I read it. I already knew that he had died, but not that Sissy had gone to the hospital." He removes his glasses and puts them in his pocket while he rubs his eyes, trying to remove tension.

"Not that it matters, Paul, but is he the reason you became a priest?"

"Indirectly. After I learned of Johnny's death . . ." He falters and has to pause to regain control. "Did you know his name? She had told me that she refused to hold him or look at him when he was born because she knew if she did, she would never be able to give him up. But she asked the nurse to tell the adoptive parents that her daddy's name was John, and would they please call him that. They named him Jonathan, close enough. As I started to say, after I learned of his death, I began to wonder if Sissy's fall was an accident . . . or a choice." Again Paul pauses, collecting himself before continuing. "I talked to my priest. His answers were unacceptable, so he suggested I look for the answers to my questions myself in the scriptures and in church theology. When I went to college, I majored in political science, but I took all the religion courses I could fit into my curriculum. By graduation, I had found my answers and was headed for seminary. I think that was Father Sam's plan all along."

He pauses again and then softly continues. "Since I read that letter, I can't stop thinking about her—about her holding her child for the first time, too late to help him and alone in that hostile environment. She might have let me go with her, but I was in Mexico that weekend. When I returned, she was distant."

"Would you care to share the answers you found?"

"Is that why you came here? Looking for your own answers? I saw the truck at your place. I assumed it was your mountain man's."

"Actually, I came here looking for Marjorie. She's not at her house. That's where I found the letter and read it. I know. I'll ask for her forgiveness later. Her car is there, but her bicycle is missing. I called the co-op. They haven't seen her. So I thought she might be here. You haven't seen her either?"

"No. I hope she wasn't caught in this rain on her bicycle."

Suddenly, Anne knows. "Oh damn," she spits. "Damn! Bitch! Hell!"

"Easy, Anne." And then Paul knows what she's thinking. "Marjorie's on the *Peli*—in this storm."

They both run to the church doors and look out through the rain at the marina. Beside Marjorie's empty boat slip is her red bicycle.

"I'll call the coast guard."

Anne is already punching 911 on her cell phone. She hands it to Paul. "I'll go get my rain gear and meet you at the marina."

Paul waves her on as he begins talking to the operator. After speaking to the coast guard, he calls Carlos. Then he runs to his house behind the church and puts on his own foul weather gear. He meets Anne on her way to the marina.

"Carlos is bringing his boat. He has a radio on it. I've written the information for contacting us on a piece of paper and left it on my desk in the church. The shore patrol has my phone number. They'll call if they find her, and then you can tell them how to radio us. If we find her, we'll radio them and they'll call you."

"Why are you making this so complicated? Can't we just use the radios? I want to go with you."

"I need you safe."

"This is all my fault. If I hadn't helped her search for her grandson, she would have never received that letter. I don't think I can stand to be alone. I can help you look."

Paul can't see her clearly in the driving rain and that alone tells him that he can use an extra pair of eyes to search for Marjorie. He reluctantly turns and signals for her to follow. They make their way to the marina where Carlos is already driving his boat into an empty slip.

295

Following Marjorie's usual sailing route, they motor in a zig-zag pattern to enlarge their search area on the assumption that the storm may have blown her off course. Paul's one comfort is that he's sure he didn't see her bicycle at the marina yesterday, so he thinks she's been out for only a few hours. There are no other comforts. It's cold and wet. The three searchers are protected by their waterproof pants, jackets, and hats. Marjorie is not. He's also concerned about her emotional state and how that's affecting her survival instincts. He remembers her last words to him and knows that she thinks His Honor has exacted His final judgment on her.

When they get to the mouth of the river, the water is much rougher, and the rain increases. They can't see the horizon. First Paul gets sick, and the sounds of his wretching cause Carlos to turn over the wheel to Anne while he runs to the other side of the boat, where he proceeds to lose lunch and then breakfast. Anne tries to shut out the sounds of their vomiting while she quells her own nausea. She rarely throws-up, but at this moment she thinks she would feel better if she could. She tries to see through the denseness, growing darker by the minute. The two men help with the search, but both are dehydrated and struggling to hold their heads up. Anne thinks of her brother and wishes he were here. At the same time, she's glad he isn't—even more glad that he doesn't know she's back on water and in harm's way.

When the motor sputters and Carlos has to crawl over to switch from the primary gas tank to the smaller reserve tank, he and Paul look at one another. They know they'll have to start back soon or become another casualty of the storm. Carlos radios the Shore Patrol to tell them their location and their need for fuel. The radio operator tells them the Patrol unit is nearby and will come to them.

Paul sits in misery and frustration, waiting. He looks again at the gray wall of rain and fog, trying to see through it, trying to will his old friend into view. As if Paul's will has power, the rain lessens, the constant spray caused by the wind ends, and the two men simultaneously see through the mist. A cross moves from side to side in the waves, and Carlos genuflects as Paul realizes it is not a cross, but the empty mast of a sailboat. They show Anne and she drives toward the boat, no one speaking until they see the small figure hunched and leaning against the base of the mast.

Carlos uses his flare gun to signal the Patrol boat. A short time later, Paul and Anne and Marjorie are on the larger and faster boat, being taken to the nearest medical facility. Carlos tows the *Peli* home.

An ambulance meets the boat at the dock and brings them to the emergency room at the Wilmington hospital where Marjorie is examined and treated. Paul and Anne sit in the waiting room, wrapped in blankets. Anne repeatedly walks to the desk, asking for information. She remembers arriving at the hospital in Corpus Christi, too late to see her father before he died. She wants to see and talk to Marjorie. She sits again beside Paul and puts her hand on his back, between his shoulder blades, gently massaging the tightly hunched muscles.

"How is she?" No answer. "Is she alive?"

"Yes," Anne whispers hoarsely.

"Is she conscious?"

"I don't know." Anne recalls how they found Marjorie, muttering non-stop, sometimes to Sissy, sometimes to John, sometimes to Jonathan, the mumbling interspersed with curses at His Honor. "Do you think she was mad at God because He took them?" she asks.

"No! She's angry because He left her."

Anne removes his glasses from her pocket, cleans them, and hands them to him. He gives her a weak smile, puts them on, and pushes them into place with one finger. That is her reward. She has learned to love this ritual and the self-conscious human quality it lends the too-strong man.

A few minutes later, an intern leads them into the ICU stall where Marjorie is receiving oxygen and fluids, looking pale and drawn, old and frail.

Anne breathes a sigh of relief. "At least she's sleeping."

The intern corrects Anne. "She's in a coma. She has pneumonia, and she's suffering from prolonged exposure. The attending physician will be back in a few minutes to give you the details." He looks harder at Paul. "Are you all right?"

"I'm fine. How is her heart?"

"Amazing. I believe you said she's eighty-three? Considering what she put her heart through, she should be in the morgue instead of ICU."

Anne looks at Paul and decides he needs to be sitting. She leads him to a chair and says to the intern, "Thanks for your help. We'll wait here for the doctor. Go work on your bedside manner."

Marjorie's hand moves slightly. They both search her face for signs of consciousness. The only change is the beginning of a smile.

Anne sits beside her friend and begins to unbraid her hair.

For the next week, Anne, Paul and Celita take turns sitting with Marjorie each day for four-hour shifts. Anne realizes for the first time that, although Marjorie knew and interacted with everyone in Pearl, and attended every church in Pearl, she had few close friends. And those few were her age and older, making their drive to Wilmington difficult or impossible. The big surprise is when Sherry comes by with a card and homemade cookies. She shyly looks at Anne's eye, relieved to see it has healed, and apologizes for the first time. Anne makes a mental note to get to know her and see if there's any way she can help with her home situation.

Marjorie's doctor tries to prepare them first for the unlikelihood that she will come out of the coma; second for the necessity of placing her in a nursing home if she does recover. Anne's response is, "I don't think so. She'd be a definite flight risk. We'll take her home *when* she recovers, not *if*."

Anne has the first shift, from six a.m. until ten; Paul takes the second shift until two p.m.; Celita relieves him and stays until six; Anne returns and sits with Marjorie until ten, bringing her computer and cell phone. When she's not talking to her silent friend, she sends emails or makes phone calls to Logan, Noah, and her daughters.

She asks Noah to contact officials at Memorial Hospital, a twenty-minute drive from his house, and find out what he can about Jonathan's birth certificate to make sure the child adopted by Mary McKinnon was born to Sissy or Sarah Hester.

In a surprisingly short time, Noah responds.

EMAIL TO ANNE:

I have an appointment to talk with a records person at the hospital tomorrow. But I took the liberty of finding Jonathan's adoptive mother today. I told her what happened to Marjorie, and she is appropriately ashamed of the things she said about Sissy in her letter. She is an unpleasant woman, and probably not because of Jonathan. I suspect anger and bitterness are her daily bread and water—with a lot of self-pity thrown in. Sorry. As you can tell, I don't like her.

But she did begrudgingly allow me to borrow some photos of Jonathan. I've scanned them so you can bring them up on your screen. I've also made copies of them and will put them in the mail tomorrow. Thanks for the assignment. It gave me a little time away from the hospital—which I needed.

We are back at the hospital because Elizabeth's doctor is concerned that the cancer has spread. New tests, new treatments. I don't know if her poor body can survive much more modern medical help. Even if she achieves a remission, I have little hope that it will last.

I should have told you about the wasps in the house earlier, but I didn't want you to think it was your fault. Apparently, the exterminator, the one you hired before you left, did not fumigate the attic. We thought there was a psycho in the woodpile. It was just human error. And it turned out that I did leave the stairs pulled down. I had moved packing boxes into the attic and forgot to raise the stairs. Mia culpa.

And speaking of the wasps, what a convoluted way to find out about Steven! When I finally guessed some of the history between you two, and I called Logan, his anger and concern took on a life of its own. I know what Logan told you was shocking, and you will need time to process it all.

It was a strange set of circumstances that brought you and Logan back together. The man loves you, Anne. I hope this frees you to love him in return.—*Noah*

P.S. Now perhaps you can relate to hospital duty and the importance of exit time. I hope Marjorie gets better soon.

Chapter 19

Luke

DAYS OF THE WEEK ARE LOST in driving to and from the hospital, in sitting beside Marjorie's bed. Anne has to look at the calendar to find her place in time. On Monday, Celita is unable to get away from work, so Paul stays additional hours with Marjorie. Anne is dressing to go to the hospital early, in order to relieve him. The doorbell rings. It's another cold day, so Anne opts for warmth and comfort. She pulls on a navy hooded sweatshirt as she runs.

She opens the door, smiling, expecting to see an apologetic Celita, sprung from her prison of work. On her porch stands a man Anne has never met, but has seen daily for months. Except for startling blue eyes, he is the image of Paul. She gapes. Her mouth open, she is all but drooling.

"I was told you would be friendly," he says, teasing and pushing his glasses up on his nose. "I'm trying to find Father Paul. He wasn't home. Someone on the road said you might know where he is."

With difficulty, she finds her voice. "Your father's at the hospital—with your grandmother."

The young man blushes and looks down. "I don't know where you fit into this, but I want to see them both. Can you direct me? By the way, my name is Luke."

"Forgive my staring, Luke, but I feel like I'm looking at a ghost. I'll take you to the hospital. I was going anyway. Did you come in response to a message you received online?"

"Yes. How did you know?"

"Because that message came from my computer. Before your imagination gets carried away, I'm not your mother."

"I know. She's dead. And the message didn't come from you. It came from a Noah Levinson."

"We'll be standing here tomorrow if we get started. Let's go to the car, and you can tell me on the way."

Delayed by the work and university traffic of Wilmington, Anne has plenty of time to hear Luke's story. He begins with his own questions about his parents.

"I know the answers to some of your questions, but you should hear your parents' story from your father's perspective—not mine. By the way, I love your grandmother and your father. They are both very fine people. If you want to ask me about them after you have met and talked, I'll be glad to tell you all I know. Now, tell me about yourself."

"Where do I begin?"

"How did Noah find you? We thought you died in infancy."

"He got access to hospital records concerning the death of a Jonathan McKinnon. He was adopted, so when he became ill, there was a search for family history in order to accurately diagnose his ailment. They found his mother, but it was too late. He died of heart disease. Her father had also died of heart disease. His illness might have been inherited, so the McKinnons informed the doctors that there was a fraternal twin—me. My own adoptive parents were contacted and they immediately had me checked for heart problems. I guess I got more of my father's genetic traits. My heart is fine."

"It's a good thing *my* heart is strong." Anne shakes her head as they pause in a bottleneck of traffic. "Paul doesn't know he fathered twins. I don't know if your mother knew or not. She told him there was a child. Why wouldn't she have told him there were two? Of course, in those days, women were often unconscious when their child was delivered. And an unwed mother was sometimes treated like a person with no rights. Since she said she didn't want to see or hold her child, because of the emotional pain that would cause, it's possible they didn't even tell her that she gave birth to twins. That sounds unbelievable, but I have two daughters, and I was awake to see the second one born. However, between my first and second child, the medical world changed its whole approach to birthing. I might have had triplets when my first daughter was born, and I wouldn't have known it."

She looks at Luke's profile, so similar to Paul's. The nose is perhaps a little sharper, and his coloring is a shade lighter, but otherwise they are the same. "Did you know you were a twin? Did you even know you were adopted?"

"My parents told me I was adopted when I was so young that it was never an issue. They didn't tell me I had a twin, probably because he died while I was still an infant. After I received the email from Noah Levinson, I confronted my mother and she told me what she knew—which was very little."

"She's still living?"

"Yes. She and Dad divorced not long ago."

"So, do you know anything about your natural family?"

"Oh yes. I've been watching them a long time, since I was fifteen. I'm pretty good on the computer. Except for having a twin, I probably knew more about my natural family than anyone else"

"In case there is still some confusion, they knew about your twin— not about you. But Marjorie believed her grandson was alive all these years. I know that's confusing, and it's a long story better told later. I set up a website at her request, for the purpose of getting the two of you together. Did you ever see it?"

"No. After college, I gave up on the idea of ever meeting them. I knew my mother was a photojournalist and my father was a priest. I didn't know what my grandmother knew of me. So I decided it was best for everyone if I stayed out of the picture. I never saw your posted message, because I had stopped looking for one."

"Unfortunately, the adoptive mother of your brother did see it. She sent a letter to Marjorie, telling her of Jonathan's death and of your mother's unwelcome visit to the hospital. That letter probably caused Marjorie to sail her boat into a gale in the middle of winter. She has pneumonia and is very weak. You can't just burst into the room. She and Paul would probably both have a heart attack."

They are silent for a moment. "Who are you?" he asks.

Just then, the traffic begins to move and Anne's attention is on driving. If it weren't, she would be trapped between laughter and tears. "I'm Anne Gray," she manages to say.

"Are you family? You knew me immediately."

"I have a gift regarding children. But even without that extra sense, I would have known you. I've painted your portrait—once on canvas, a hundred times in my mind. Except for your eyes, you look exactly like Paul."

"Are you in love with him?" he asks awkwardly.

"I do love your father and your grandmother, but there is someone else in my life." *Is he truly in my life?* At this moment, he seems so distant, more than a few hundred miles away. "It was probably fate that brought me to Marjorie's door and then to the steps of Paul's church, but it was the two of them that kept me here. They are both my best friends. I've carried each of their secrets, secrets they wouldn't share with each other, for too long. Now that you're here, that will thankfully end."

At the hospital, Anne sticks her head into Marjorie's space in the intensive care unit. Paul sees her and motions for her to come close. He speaks softly in a voice filled with defeat and acceptance.

"She's getting worse. She has a living will. She doesn't want any heroic means used to keep her alive. Anne, I can be her priest or her family. I can't be both. And legally, I'm not either. Help me."

"Paul, I have a surprise that's going to rock your world. She does have family. He's here, but he needs time to get to know her before we talk about pulling any plugs."

"I don't understand."

"Luke," Anne calls softly. The curtains on the other side of the bed open, and Paul sees his own reflection enter the sterile space. They stare at one another. "Time for you two later. Luke, your grandmother needs you."

Luke pulls a chair close to the bed and takes Marjorie's hand in both of his. Her long white hair is unbraided and spread across the pillow in tight waves. Her face is puckered, ancient. He kisses her hand and then speaks softly to her, telling her of himself and his twin, telling her of the boy who always dreamed of meeting his real family.

Paul sinks back into his chair on the other side of the narrow bed. He crosses himself and silently prays. Then he covers his face with his hands and leans forward, lost in emotion, listening to Luke's words. Anne takes Marjorie's other hand and gently massages it. She feels a resistance as the frail hand pulls away and reaches for Luke's hands. He holds them both and for the first time whispers, "Grandma."

Marjorie's eyes slowly struggle to open. Her mouth moves as if to speak, but can't. She finally relaxes her determined lips into a smile. Then her whole face slowly eases as decades of sadness and pain melt away. She looks younger than Anne. And through their tears, all Luke and Paul and Anne can see are her bright blue eyes and her loving smile. *This must be exactly the way she looked when she first saw her baby daughter, Sissy, all those years ago,* Anne thinks. For the first time, she can see the resemblance between her dear friend and the photographs of her beautiful blonde child. Stunned by her youthful appearance, Anne wonders if Sissy is also here, sharing this moment with her mother, eyes hungrily taking in Luke's face, hands clutching his.

Paul finds the words he knows Marjorie is thinking. "Your mother never saw you, Luke, or she would have never let you go. She would have looked at you exactly as your grandmother looks at you now, and she would have fought the world for you. She was trying to take care of us all. Your grandmother and I didn't even know that you existed. Until it was too late, too late to claim you or to save her."

Marjorie's eyes close and the translucent lids relax into what appears to be a peaceful slumber. Anne has seen this remarkable look of quiet and peace only once before. It is the face she saw when Lindsay slid into the doctor's waiting hands, the face that looked as if it knew it was entering a world where it would forever be loved and protected. The look on Lindsay's face as she was born is replicated on Marjorie's as she dies. *Don't click. Don't remember her leaving.*

For a moment, no one moves. They know the machines will bring the staff running, and they do. Paul rises and puts his arm up. "I remind you of her living will," he says with sad determination. "She asked that she not be resuscitated, that no artificial means be used to keep her alive."

"Living will, Hell!" Anne growls. "She had nothing to live for before. Bring her back! Luke, tell them!"

Luke hesitates, looking from Anne to Paul. "Please do what you can," he says, and moves away to give them room. The doctor looks from the tall young man to the look-alike priest, who merely nods his agreement. Paul pulls a chair away from the bed and sits again to pray, this time for his dear friend's deliverance—not into her daughter's arms, but back to her grandson's and his.

Anne steps from the cubicle to avoid watching the obscene things medicine does to keep the body alive, even when the spirit is willing to die.

Luke joins her in the hall and says in a small voice, "They asked me to leave. God knows, I wanted out of there. Did I do the right thing?"

"If it buys her some time with you, yes."

In what seems like hours, but is really only a few minutes, Paul finds them sitting on a bench in the hall.

"She's back. She's not in a coma; she's sleeping, and she's alive."

Anne takes several deep breaths before she can speak. "It's my turn to stay with her. You two go get some coffee or something. You haven't even spoken to each other. Check back in an hour. I'm sure she'll want to see Luke when she awakens."

"I want to look at her before we leave," Luke says. They all return to the curtained miracle room. A nurse tries to tell them that only one person can enter, but they ignore her. Marjorie's face reflects the trauma she has just been through. Peacefulness gone, she looks again like a wizened old woman with an attitude.

"That's my friend," Anne says, smiling through new tears. "God, I love that face." *Click.*

Anne sits beside Marjorie's bed and begins her own prayer of thanks while Paul and Luke leave. She hears them speaking softly to each other in Spanish and once again she is amazed, overwhelmed, and humbled by the events of the day.

For the next seventy-two hours, Marjorie is lucid. She is able to talk to Luke and Paul, who alternate sitting with her during the days, usually letting their visits overlap. Because she is weak, most of the time is spent with them both telling her their stories.

"I went to the library every day," Luke tells her. "Mom thought I was doing homework. But half of the time, I was researching my biological family. I went through all the local newspapers on microfiche that reported events in Pearl from 1960 forward, looking for your names. I found photographs my mother took that were published in the paper. I found the obituary about Grandpa's death. When I found the article about her fall from a cliff in the mountains, I couldn't eat for a week, and I couldn't explain why to Mom. Somehow, I knew the fall wasn't an accident. I thought maybe I had screwed up her life, and she wouldn't welcome a visit from me. Guess I was wrong."

"I found an article telling of my father joining the Marines and leaving for Camp LeJeune and then for Vietnam. There was nothing for a long time, so I changed my search and learned he had become a priest and was living in Detroit. I stopped looking after that. When my mother, your daughter, was killed, it made front page news in

Raleigh. She had been a well-respected photojournalist. I came to her memorial service and saw you, but I didn't want to intrude."

Sitting on the other side of the bed, Paul says, "Sissy didn't tell me of Jonathan's death. It happened while I was in Mexico with my grandfather. When I returned, she was despondent. Later, after I came back from Vietnam and learned the truth, I had to wonder if she had fallen at Linville Falls on purpose, to join our son. I almost lost my own faith, but gained it again in a search for answers. Of course it's possible that Sissy did know she delivered twins. If that's true, then the fall might have simply been an accident."

"Sissy came home now and then," Marjorie confesses, "but only after she checked to make sure you wouldn't be here, Paul. I think she forgave herself of everythin' because she believed you was happy."

Marjorie looks at the shining eyes of her grandson and says, "I want to hear more of your stories, Luke. I've dreamed about you for so long. What's the first thing you remember?"

And so Luke tells his stories, from his earliest memory to the present. He tells of how, after Sissy's death, he joined the Peace Corp and found it so fulfilling that he signed up for a second term, and then stayed abroad and travelled. He tells of his return to Raleigh and of trying to please his mother with a reporting job and a girlfriend. And at the end of the third day of talking, he tells of finding Noah's email.

"I have always wanted to know you both, but I didn't want to make trouble. I know Catholic priests have so much negative publicity to battle. I didn't want to be another problem for you."

"Don't be concerned about me, Luke." Paul laughs. "My parishioners know that I am human. They see it every day. I'm sure the news of you has already spread and many of them are shaking their heads and thinking they knew it all along. The older ones remember me as a boy and knew that Sissy and I were in love and would have married eventually. Some probably even guessed that she left home that summer because she was pregnant."

"Do your adoptive parents know you're here?" Marjorie asks.

"Yes."

"How do they feel about it?"

"My mother's her usual hysterical self. But I call her every night and reassure her that she's my only mother. It's a lie, but it's one she needs to hear."

"What about your father?"

"He's in this room."

"You know what I mean, your adoptive father."

"My parents divorced while I was abroad. It was one of the reasons I came home. Dad was never easy. Now he's making life a little harder for someone else, and of course she's half his age—only two years older than me."

"Don't be too hard on him," Marjorie whispers. "Their marriage troubles had nothin' to do with you."

"I know, and Mom wasn't easy either. She was always very nervous, about everything. It's funny though, instead of driving her over the edge, the divorce has calmed her a little. Maybe Dad was a part of her problem. At any rate, she's joined some women's groups, and they've given her more self-confidence than she's ever had. Of course she's still worried about me finding another family—worried she'll be left completely alone."

"You need to continue reassuring her," Paul says.

"I need to find her a man. It's hard, being someone's reason to live."

Marjorie pulls the sheet over her face. "You'd best get used to that." She giggles through the sheet.

Luke laughs and pulls the sheet back and kisses her cheek. "I didn't mean you, Grandma." And tears slide down from her tired eyes.

"You two go on and have your supper," she says, a little hoarse. "I need to rest. I'll be fine. Anne'll be comin' soon."

As Paul, in his turn, leans over to kiss her forehead, Marjorie whispers, "Stay."

"Go on outside and call your mother, Luke. You can't use cell phones in here. I'll be down in a few minutes." He sits again and takes Marjorie's hand. "I'm listening, old friend."

"All these years, I didn't know how to talk to you about my grandson. I was afraid you would try to stop me from contactin' him. We could'a been talkin' all this time, instead of just racin' our boats. I'm sorry, Paul."

"If you had told me you knew about him, I would have had to tell you he died. Neither of us knew there were two boys. And if Anne's friend hadn't found him, we may have never made contact. There is a time for everything."

"Yes, and like my mama used to say, 'If *ifs an' buts* were hickory nuts, we'd all have a merry Christmas.' I guess we both did what we could. I have always thought of you as my son, and I have never blamed you for Sissy's fall or for her leavin' Pearl. She was all a mother could ask for an' then some. But she was strong willed, and she made her own choices—'bout lovin' you, 'bout givin' her child away, and maybe 'bout leavin' us."

Marjorie sighs and looks into Paul's eyes. "She's been comin' to me, you know, ever since that terrible day on the boat after I got that letter. She's been talkin' to me."

"What does she say?"

"I can never remember. I can just remember the way she makes me feel, all comforted and warm. Tell His Honor for me that I'm not mad at Him anymore."

"I will. But you might tell Him yourself."

"Sure, next time I see Him."

Paul looks away, unable to accept the leaving that she now embraces.

"Luke is like her, isn't he?" he asks.

"Yep. He looks like you, but there's a bunch of our pretty girl in him. Now go on. I'm fallin' asleep while I'm talkin' to you."

Paul kisses her hand and then her forehead. "You're warm."

"Too many covers. Take off that extra blanket, would you?"

"Buenos noche, mi madre. Que Dios te bendiga."

"I know what that means," she says with her eyes already closed. "Celita says that to me every time she leaves. God bless you too, son."

Anne arrives as usual—with a tape recorder and her computer. For the last three nights, she has encouraged Marjorie to rest, but Marjorie has had her own agenda. Her alert times have been fewer, but she has made the most of them. During the day, she has wanted only to hear Luke's stories, but in the evenings, she has told her own stories to Anne's tape recorder. Anne transcribed the tapes to her computer while Marjorie slept. The stories are for Luke. They tell all his grandmother knows of their family history: her remembrances of her own childhood in the mountains, what she knows of John's family and childhood, their romance, and the years of disappointments before her Sissy was finally born. She told all of Sissy's stories except for those concerning Paul. They are for him to tell. She also verbally dictated a new will which Kente formalized and notarized.

Anne is late tonight because of backed-up traffic due to a wreck on the highway. On entering the room, she sees that Marjorie is asleep. She automatically goes to the bed and carefully touches her cheek. It's warm. She leans over and gently puts her lips to Marjorie's forehead. It's too warm. She drops her things and rushes into the hall, searching for a nurse, finding the one that is finally on her way to respond to Paul's same concerns.

Marjorie's temperature spikes and emergency procedures are begun. She awakens and speaks incoherently. But even that ends as she slips again into a coma.

Thirty-six hours later, on a cold late February morning, Marjorie Josephine Hester is pronounced dead. Anne leaves the hospital knowing Paul and Luke will support each other. Celita goes home to her family, and other friends go to their individual support persons or systems. Anne falls back on an old friend of hers. She stops by an ABC liquor store on her way to Pearl.

311

Instead of her own home, she drives to the house at the end of River Road. Luke has been staying here, but his car isn't in the driveway, so Anne assumes he's at the church with Paul. She walks in the front door and tries unsuccessfully to avoid memories of her first visit to Marjorie—the no-fear friend with the sassy mouth, skinny legs, and loving heart.

Anne hasn't cried since her trip to the mountains at Thanksgiving. And since she found Marjorie with a rising fever, she has been in a stupor—just trying to help Paul and Luke, trying to postpone her own sadness by staying busy. She can't stop the tears now, but she ignores them as she walks up the stairs to Sissy's room. She came here for a reason. Except for the dust, the room is just as Sissy left it thirty years ago. Marjorie had gone through her drawers, searching for the diary that told of the birth of a child. Otherwise, the room has been untouched.

Her five-year diary ended at Christmas. *It must have been a Christmas gift when she was twelve years old—just entering puberty. Marjorie apparently never considered the existence of a second diary. You don't write down your feelings and activities every night for your entire adolescence and then just stop.* Believing Sissy must have written about her visit to the hospital, and perhaps what she learned there, Anne paces the room, trying to decide where she would she have written—at her desk or in her bed? *And did she know about Luke?*

Anne goes through the desk drawers, but finds only school papers. She looks through the drawer in the table beside Sissy's bed and finds a collection of folded papers. She opens one and realizes it is a note from Paul, probably passed to her in a high school class or in the hall between classes. She doesn't read it or the others. They're not for her eyes. Anne leaves the room for a box of tissues and then returns.

She sits in the desk chair and thinks. *She didn't hide the first diary very well. Maybe she subconsciously wanted Marjorie to find it. But she didn't want her mother to know about Jonathan's death.* Anne mentally puts herself into Sissy's mindset. *The pain was too great for her to speak of, even to Paul. Maybe especially to Paul. If a genetic weakness was passed to their son from her, could she ever risk having another child?* Anne blows her nose and tries to release herself from the agony Sissy must have felt.

She would have to write it down—to sort out her feelings. There has to be another diary. Anne moves to the bed beside the table and lamp, where Sissy might have written. And suddenly, she knows. She reaches down, between the mattress and springs, in a simple gesture that could be done by someone lying in the bed. Her fingers touch something firm, and she pulls out a notebook. It is spiral bound, and the wires are caught on something—another notebook. She lifts the mattress and finds a total of eight notebooks. Not another five-year diary, but eight notebooks.

Anne opens one book and sees through eyes swollen from crying and blurred with new tears that it is indeed Sissy's diary.

Dear Me,

Happy New Year, 1968. Today was a beautiful day; Paul and I raced our sailboats, and—as usual—he let me win. It was such a perfect day, I could almost believe in his dreams.

Anne sees the thinnest volume and thinks it might be the last. She slowly opens it, and gasps at the date.

Dear me,

Happy New Year 1980. I'm at home with Mama on hiatus at the end of a tiring year. I came here straight from Detroit after spending a glorious week with Paul. I should feel sad or guilty, but I just feel grateful for another time together—another stolen time.

Anne releases a deep sigh. *They saw each other after her fall, and more than once. No wonder he has such contentment and control. No wonder she can't be replaced. No wonder there is no date on her grave marker. She has been more spirit than woman for him for so long, he probably doesn't think of her as gone. He probably expects her to appear without warning . . . and maybe she does.* She closes the journal. Like the folded notes, this is for Paul's eyes—not hers, and not even Luke's. They all belong to Paul. She takes the notebooks and paper treasures downstairs, and puts them in a grocery bag. *A humble container for such precious memories. I'll leave them in the car and deliver them to Paul tomorrow.*

She only plans on a couple of shots of vodka to help her relax. She hasn't slept in days, but she can't seem to close her eyes. The familiar warmth of the first drink flows through her body, dulling the various aches and pains. The second drink seems smoother, and she takes a little longer to savor it. The third and fourth drinks she hardly tastes at all. And finally, she sleeps—somewhere on her living room floor.

Hours later, she's dreaming about bells and rings and beeps. *Is it the emergency room?* Paul and Luke are beside her. She's on all fours, trying unsuccessfully to push the right buttons on her message machine to stop the infernal beeping. Paul tries to lift her to the couch, but she slithers through his arms, back to the floor and into a fetal position.

He kneels beside her, slipping a throw pillow under her head. "Not wishing to be born yet, Anne?"

"Noooo. And would someone answer the damn phone?"

"Are you all right, Anne?"

She opens one distrustful eye and says, "Just get me some water, please."

Luke heads for the kitchen. "And start some coffee," Paul adds as he sits on the floor beside her. He has turned down the volume on the answer machine so the beeping is lower but unfortunately still audible. "Close your eyes, but don't go to sleep. I need to talk to you." He strokes her face, partly to comfort her, partly to keep her awake. Rings of mascara are under her eyes from crying, and she smells strongly of alcohol and neglect. He realizes that he has probably never loved her more. "Do you know how old Marjorie was?"

No answer, because Anne doesn't care how old she was.

"She was eighty-eight—older even than I thought."

"That's not possible, and I'm not as drunk as I'd like to be."

"You're drunk enough. But I suspect you finished that bottle a while ago and you're on your way to recovery. She was forty-one when Sissy was born; Sissy was sixteen when Luke was born; Luke is thirty-one now. Do the math. There were miscarriages, stillbirths, and a crib death before Marjorie finally produced a child that would survive. That's why her world was built around her husband and daughter. It's a miracle she lasted this long. I believe she was just waiting for her grandson. I also believe her soul is at rest and that she and John and Sissy and Jonathan are together again. And she's finally holding baby Jonathan and her own lost boys. Anne rises up to her knees and leans against Paul who holds and rocks her.

"The coffee is dripping," Luke says as he offers a glass of water. "Can I please turn off the message machine? It's making me nuts."

"No," Anne says. "Better listen. It might be one of the girls." And as she says the words, Anne's eyes meet Paul's. "Oh God—Summer!"

Luke pushes the message button to hear Joe's voice telling them that Summer's in labor and to come as soon as possible to help with Lindsay. The time of the message is five o'clock p.m.—two hours ago.

"Ok, let's get you in the shower. The coffee will be ready when you get out." Adrenalin works miracles, and Anne moves, with Paul's help, up her stairs and into her bathroom.

Thirty minutes later she enters the kitchen with wet hair, a clean face, clean clothes, and a packed bag. "I'll be fine after some coffee and ibuprofen. Did you call the hospital?"

"Yes, and I talked to Joe. He understands that you'll be delayed. He called as they left the house for the hospital. He said she's just received medication and will probably deliver in an hour or so. He said Lindsay came fast, so they expect this one to be the same."

"Thank you, guys. I'd better get going—or, as Marjorie would say, 'get gone'."

"You make a quick recovery, Anne, but you're in no condition to drive. Would this be a good time for me to meet your mom, Luke?"

Luke grins. "If you're up to it."

"Why don't I drive Anne's car, and follow you to Raleigh? Do you know the way to the Wake Med Birthing Pavilion?"

"You bet. Here's your coffee, Anne, and a thermos for the road."

Unused to so much mothering, Anne takes the mug and blinks back more tears.

Paul grabs a handful of tissues. "Get a pillow. It's a long drive and you could use more sleep."

Chapter 20

The Story of a Day

Anne curses and prays, feeling both angry and helpless. She's angry with herself for escaping reality in a bottle, making her unable to answer her own phone and unable to leave at the earliest moment to be by her daughter's side. She feels helpless because she's trapped in a vehicle Paul insists on driving at exactly the speed limit. When she complains, he reminds her, "We're following Luke. This is the speed he chooses to drive."

"He probably thinks we're old and can't keep up," she murmurs.

"I have ridden with him numerous times this last week. It's how he drives. He's possibly a throwback to my father and uncle. They were both very relaxed about travel—never in a rush."

"Even in emergencies?"

"Anne, this isn't an emergency. Summer will do fine without us."

"I know. I just feel like I've failed her. My presence would give her comfort."

"I know why you're upset, Anne. But you expect too much of yourself. I shouldn't have let you go home alone. I was helping Luke

317

take care of paperwork at the hospital, and I didn't realize you were gone. I thought you might want to be by yourself."

"I should be able to be by myself, Paul. I have to learn to get through difficult times without resorting to booze for comfort and oblivion." She knows it was not only Marjorie's loss, but also the knowledge of Steven's death that drew her to the bottle for the first time in years.

"Once again, I have to remind you, Anne. You are human. Losing Marjorie was not merely a difficult time. She was your best friend, and she was an important part of your connection to Pearl." Paul pauses to smile and wave at an irate driver that passes them with an insistent display of an erect middle finger. "Pearl will never be the same without her. Take comfort in the fact that her spirit had been burdened with sadness and anger . . . until you came along. You brought back the Marjorie I knew when Sissy and I were children."

"I would cry again, but I'm all cried out. When I was thirteen years old, I watched a movie about Davy Crockett. Being a Texan, I loved all the heroes of the Alamo. But I especially loved him, maybe because he chose to be there. Texas wasn't his home. He had lost his family, and I thought he just went to the Alamo because he knew they were hopelessly outnumbered and it was a good place to die. Anyway, I thought he was so brave, and he didn't even cry, at least not in the movie. So I decided I wouldn't cry again. And I didn't, for over a year. I didn't cry again until some boy broke my heart. I've cried enough since I came to Pearl to make up for that lost year— and then some."

"Crying is healthy, Anne. It's a release. And in some ways, Marjorie's death is a release."

"Well, of course it's a release for her."

"And for you," he says as his own eyes fill with unshed tears. "Maybe her leaving will free you to go where your heart is."

"You mean Logan," she responds in a small voice.

"Yes, your mountain man."

"I loved Marjorie, but I love you, too, Paul. And I love Celita and Carlos and Kente, and I think I could even develop a real connection with Ayesha."

"Now there's a positive attitude."

"She came to the hospital one evening while I was sitting with Marjorie. She came on the pretense of talking business—you know, the rentals. But she really wanted to get to know me better. She told me a story about when she was a teenager and she was best friends with Sissy. She said something terrible happened. Sissy and Marjorie were the only people in town who believed and supported her. She said that in her anger at the town, she never thanked Marjorie. She and her mother just left. So she came to the hospital to finally thank her, and to see if I was worth getting to know."

"And what was her decision?"

"She offered to help with the business end of the flea market—no charge."

Paul releases a deep breath. "Ayesha has a long story of her own to tell. We were all schoolmates: Ayesha, Sissy, Billy O'Brian, and some others that are no longer in town. But it's her story to tell."

"Speaking of Billy, I didn't tell you that his wife, Sherry, came to the hospital one evening. She seemed so different. She was smiling. It made her look ten years younger. She said she's living and working in Wilmington now."

"Good! I'm glad she came to see you. She was probably smiling because Billy is no longer her problem."

"What?"

Paul laughs. "I pulled in a favor from a friend in Fayetteville. He runs an auto shop near the military base there. Billy left school before graduating and joined the army. His time in Vietnam was spent repairing jeeps and other military vehicles. He's working for my friend now and goes to AA meetings every day at noon. That's part of his job description—that and staying sober."

"Do you think he'll make it?"

"Stay sober?" Paul shrugs. "Who knows? I beat him up once, when we were kids—for all the wrong reasons. I asked for his forgiveness before he left. He asked for mine. I want to have faith in his desire to change his life. But change is hard."

They ride in silence for a while. Anne clears her throat. "For me, change is impossible. I have no intention of leaving Pearl. I am in love with Logan." *There, I've said it.* "And if he *needed* me to follow him to the moon, I guess I'd go. But he doesn't. If I give up all I care about just to let him have all of his desires, then I will eventually resent him and lose confidence in myself again. I won't do that. We're both retired. We're both financially independent. We'll find a way to be together without one of us sacrificing everything."

"Compromise?"

"I hate that word."

"Mexican stand-off?"

"I hope not."

"I'll be interested to hear what you decide."

"Me too."

"Why don't you sleep? It may be a long night ahead.

Almost to Raleigh, Anne's cell phone rings. She pulls herself out of sleep to answer it. It's Joe.

"Relax, Nana, you have another granddaughter."

"Is Summer okay?"

"She's fine."

"And the baby's all right?"

"Yes, and you won't believe the head of hair on this kid. People won't stop ragging me."

"Why?"

"Because it's black."

"She's black?"

"No, her hair. Did I wake you? Anne, tell me you're not driving."

Anne takes a moment and then she begins to laugh. "We have a dark-haired baby girl. I love it. Ignore the stupid people. You know Robert's hair is dark. And my parents and my brother had dark hair. So a couple of dominant genes got together. I can't wait to see her."

"That's why I called. The babysitter has to leave, so I'm going home to get Lindsay. We'll meet you at the hospital."

"I'll see you there. By the way, what's her name?"

"Josie."

"Oh, that's sweet." Anne hesitates. "Is it short for Josephine?"

"Yes, but we're calling her Josie—Josie Anne."

"Oh my, and I thought I couldn't cry anymore."

"Father Paul told me about Marjorie. I'm sorry. I know she was a close friend."

"Thank you, Joe. We should be there within the hour. Kiss Summer and Josie for me. I wish I could see Lindsay when she first lays eyes on her. Take a picture."

After hanging up, Anne finds some moist wipes in her purse and gently rubs her eyes and face.

"Are they naming her Josephine?" Paul asks, softly.

"Yes. But they're calling her Josie Anne."

"I like that. Anne, do you know Marjorie's middle name?"

"Yes, Josephine. Did you tell them her name?"

"Joe asked when I talked to him while you were in the shower. You are one blessed woman."

"Yes, more than I will ever deserve. Since we'll be there soon, and you will probably leave in Luke's car, I have something for you to take with you. I hope it will lead you to some of the answers you've sought."

Paul says nothing, but Anne can feel the tension rising in his frame as she continues. "Marjorie told you about Sissy's diary that revealed her pregnancy and the birth of a son. The diary was finished that Christmas. I believed there had to be another diary, but I never said anything to her for fear it would contain more information than she wanted to know. I never dreamed that it might tell of the death of her son."

She pauses, but Paul still says nothing. "Anyway, I thought you and Luke might want to know as much as you can about her last winter and spring here. I hope it will give you closure."

"You found it?"

"I found eight notebooks. I noticed there were photographs as well as a narrative. They're in the back seat in a bag with some notes and the first diary. I haven't read any of it," she lies, omitting the fact that the last notebook told of Sissy's encounters with Paul after her fall. "It's your choice: read them, share them with Luke—or don't."

Paul's jaw tightens and his right leg begins to jerk in small contractions. Anne puts her hand on his thigh, not realizing how tightly she holds on to him until he releases his death grip on the steering wheel and covers her hand with his, calming them both.

She pretends to sleep to allow him the privacy of his own thoughts as hers return to Summer.

In the maternity ward, Paul asks the receptionist for Summer's room number. Anne has grown increasingly more strained in the final thirty minutes of driving and now can barely speak. She remembers feeling this way when Robert's parents were driving two-year-old Greer to North Carolina from Ohio, where she had visited them for a week while the move from a rental house to their new home took place. They were late, and each moment of waiting had seemed like an eternity. When they finally arrived, a pregnant Anne ran to her toddler and held her as if both their lives depended on it . . . until Robert pried her away so he could get a hug as well.

"Nana?"

Anne turns to the door of the waiting room where she sees Lindsay, sleepily holding three of her Barbie dolls, all naked and all headless. *Click.*

"Can I hold you?" Lindsay asks.

"I was just going to ask you the same thing."

Lindsay smiles and runs to Anne who scoops up the whole essence of her granddaughter in her arms, and buries her face in the silky strawberry blonde hair. "Where is your new sister?" she asks, laughing.

"We were waiting for you. I need to see her and my Mommy."

Joe walks up and adds his long arms to the embrace. "We knew you'd be here soon, so I grabbed a bite at home and stalled a little before coming back. We've only been waiting a few minutes. I thought you'd like to see Lindsay introduced to Josie with your own eyes."

"Thanks, Joe. You'll get a painting from it."

After introducing Luke, the five of them head for Summer's room. Paul and Luke wait outside while the small family meets its new member.

Summer is holding her swaddled baby. She shifts a little to the side and pats the opened spot for her daughter to fill. Lindsay drops her dolls on the floor and runs for her mother. Joe lifts her onto the bed beside Summer, who kisses her daughter and then shifts the bundle to her other arm—between herself and Lindsay. Joe grabs the digital camera from the nightstand and focuses it. Summer slowly opens the blanket to give Lindsay a better view. And Joe captures the moment, the look of delight as she sees, for the first time, the best friend she will ever have. Anne captures, in her photographic memory, the look of wonder on Lindsay's face as her eyes move from her sister to her mother.

Paul steps inside in time to witness Lindsay's face change from awe to surprise. "But her hair is black. It's not like mine."

Joe sits at the foot of the bed. "You're right. She has dark hair, like Grandpa used to have and like your great Uncle Earl has. Do you know what that means?"

"No."

"That means that Mommy and I will now have a Cinderella girl and a baby Snow White," the big ex-Marine says in his Daddy-to-child voice.

Lindsay's eyes widen. "That's right, Snow White has black hair." She snuggles beside the infant and says into the tiny ear, "You get to be Snow White, Josie."

Anne shrugs off the days of tension and sadness. She takes a cleansing breath and calls to Luke, who meets Summer and his grandmother's namesake. "I wish she could have seen this," he says, and no one speaks. Realizing his mistake, he mutters, "I guess I underestimate her."

"Thank God, she got to meet you, Luke," Summer says, still filled with her own wonder of childbirth and family. She turns to Paul, who is standing beside Anne. "Will you bless Josephine Anne, Father?"

"I would be happy to, and I would be honored to baptize her in Pearl at Saint Angelica's if you would like."

"That would be wonderful. Just give me a little time to recover. Late spring would be nice."

Joe beams. His Protestant wife is finally willing to do something Catholic.

Lindsay looks shyly at the tall priest. "Will you bless my dolls? I lost their heads."

Amidst the laughter, Joe says, "It's alright, Lindsay. Their heads are in my pocket. Just don't put the Ken head on a Barbie body."

Anne's phone begins ringing. She steps into the hall, trying to turn it off. She sees that it's Logan. She answers, giving the good news of Josie and the sad news of Marjorie. She feels and shares his frustration at being two hundred miles away.

"They're grading the roads here in the development tomorrow, and I'm supposed to oversee it. I can get someone to take my place and drive down."

Anne hears his reluctance and says, "It's all right. I'm going to be busy helping with Lindsay. We wouldn't have much time together, and I doubt they'd do the roads right without you."

"I know that sounds obsessive, but it's true. Kiss Summer and Lindsay and the little one for me. I can't wait to hold Josie. And I can't wait to hold you. Every time I think you're coming here, some personal crisis keeps you away. Is this a preview of the future?"

"Well, my daughters tell me there will be no more grandchildren, and I pray to God there will be no more losses of friends—at least not for a long while." And as Anne tells Logan goodnight, she wonders if, in fact, they do let too many things interfere with being together. She could have asked; he could have insisted. It's as if they are square dancing, an ongoing do-si-do, two-stepping around each other, rarely touching. What happened to the sky-dancing?

Luke calls his mother, and he and Paul leave for her apartment.

Anne asks to spend the night with Summer, and Joe gratefully takes Lindsay home for a good night's rest. Summer sleeps. Anne should sleep, but she doesn't. Paul brought her duffle bag and her backpack with her laptop to the room before he left. She opens the computer.

EMAIL TO NOAH:

Lost a friend; gained a granddaughter. Miserably happy. Giving up people is harder than giving up things. I'm at Wake Med's Birthing Pavilion with my Summer and her Josie Anne. I wish my arms could reach around all that I love and keep each of you safe and out of pain's way.—*Always, Anne*

The next morning, Anne freshens up in the bathroom and changes clothes while Summer's doctor visits during his rounds. When she emerges, revitalized, Joe and Lindsay burst into the room with kisses, ham biscuits and, more importantly, coffee.

Food finished, Lindsay gets her first chance to hold Josie. "Hi, sweetheart," she says as her sister is placed in her arms. Joe bursts into laughter.

"You southern women! Three generations in this room, and you all call every child and most of your friends sweetheart. Now tell me the truth. Do you just have trouble remembering names?"

"Actually,' Anne answers, "I did use it to help cover forgotten students' names. Then administration became rigid about sexual harassment, and I had to stop calling them honey or sweetheart. Sad! It turned into, 'hey, you'. I sounded like a damn Yankee. Sorry, you didn't hear that Lindsay."

"I did too, Nana. You said Yankee."

"True, and that's a bad word." Anne jokes.

"Hey, lighten up Nana." Summer laughs. "We have a Yankee Doodle Daddy, don't we Lindy?"

Mimicking her mother, Lindsay whispers loudly to Josie, "We have a Yankee Doodle Daddy, sweetheart."

At that moment, Noah steps into the open doorway. Anne quickly recovers from her reaction to the strained look on his face and smiles her welcome. "Somehow, I'm not surprised."

"You didn't get my email?"

"No," she says as she crosses the room and gives him a friendly hug. "I signed off after I sent out my own, assuming the rest of the world was asleep." She turns to her family. "This is Noah Levinson. Noah, this is my daughter Summer, her husband Joe, and my granddaughter Lindsay, holding her new sister Josie Anne. Noah bought the house you grew up in, Summer."

"Oh, now I understand," Summer says.

"Understand what?" Noah responds.

"Things Mom said when you were in the negotiating process."

"So you agree?" Anne asks.

"Oh yes!"

Confused and flustered by the suggestive comments, Noah asks Anne to speak to him in the hall.

"Elizabeth wants to meet you. Will you come to Duke Hospital with me?"

"I thought she left the hospital. She's in again?"

"We live in a revolving door. Her back pains increased. They're running still more tests."

Anne feels her own strength fading. But she pulls on her reserves and returns to Summer's room. "Could you guys do without me for a while? Noah wants me to talk with his wife at Duke."

Summer winces, knowing this will probably be another emotional ordeal for Anne.

"Sure, Mom. We're fine here. Lindsay brought a movie for entertainment."

"Take your time," Joe adds. "If you're back around one o'clock, you can take Lindsay home for a nap. You could probably use one yourself. I know how that recliner feels."

"Does she know I'm coming?" Anne asks Noah as they walk to the parking lot.

"No. She had a bad night and finally fell asleep this morning. I wasn't sure you would be able to come, so I didn't tell her you're in town."

"I'll be honest, Noah. I'm not comfortable with this. I don't know how to talk to her."

"She isn't hard to talk to. But, in spite of what it might cost, don't lie to her. She'll know. With nothing else to do with her time and mind, she focuses on reading people. Even the doctors have stopped lying or dancing around reality with her."

Anne follows Noah in her car so he won't have to drive back to this hospital. The morning work traffic has thinned but is still intense. She is reminded that this is one of the reasons she left the busy Research Triangle of Raleigh, Durham, and Chapel Hill, in search of a quieter place.

When they arrive, Anne is almost relieved to find Elizabeth still asleep. The frail woman in the bed with perhaps an inch of dark hair and pronounced cheekbones and eye sockets looks nothing like the pictures Noah had emailed of his wife and son. She sees the tubes and the needle bruises on her arms and is shocked by the ravages of a slow dying from disease. *Let it come quickly for me,* she prays. *And if she must die, let it come soon for her. And please, Dear Lord, don't let my words cause her more pain.*

Noah brings a chair to the side of Elizabeth's bed, and Anne reluctantly sits. Noah goes for soft drinks. A smile crosses Elizabeth's lips, but her eyes remain closed.

"That must be you, Anne." A barely audible whisper.

Anne can't speak. Elizabeth's smile slowly grows. She lifts her hand and Anne takes it and holds it in her lap, adjusting her chair to make the connection an easy one for Elizabeth.

"How did you know me?"

"By your perfume. It's Anais Anais."

Knowing instantly what she means, Anne would like to escape this thread but can't. So she admits it. "You must have smelled it on Noah's clothes after we met for lunch before Christmas. You have a great nose."

"If we came back as dogs, I'd be a hound. What would you be?"

A bitch in heat, Anne thinks. "A mutt with no sense of smell and no good tricks, but pretty affectionate."

Elizabeth opens her eyes, gradually adjusting to the light, but not looking at Anne. "I love your sense of humor—and your kindness." Her thoughts are broken by the need of a shallow breath. "You have been very kind to us, especially to Noah. . . . When we ran out of stories, he read me your emails. . . . You two have a real friendship. I'm glad. He needs that."

"So do I." And Anne settles back, no longer afraid of Elizabeth. She tells her of Marjorie's death and Josie's birth. "Since you've heard my stories and my emails, I imagine you know more about me than you ever wanted to know."

"Your stories were like reading a biography . . . of someone I would like to meet but probably never would." She pauses longer between each phrase. "I admit that when you two met for lunch . . . and I wasn't included . . . I did feel a little hurt."

For the first time, she looks at Anne, who looks back while praying. *Tell me what to say.*

A nurse enters and checks Elizabeth's IV drip and her vitals. She refills her water glass and removes the uneaten breakfast. "If you don't take in some nourishment, we're going to have to insert a feeding tube."

"Do I look like a child that responds to threats?" Elizabeth demands in a whisper.

"No, dear. Would you like to try some pudding?"

"Sure." A lack luster response. When the nurse leaves, Elizabeth tries to roll on to her side.

"Do you want a pillow behind your back, or maybe one between your knees? That helps me when my hip is acting up."

"I'll try anything." Elizabeth gasps as a pain shoots through her lower back.

Anne carefully arranges the pillows to relieve strain and sits again beside the bed. "Better?"

"I think so."

Anne realizes that she too is practicing the Lamaze breathing, inhaling and exhaling with Elizabeth. *Too much empathy*, she warns. "Are the books finished?"

"Yes, they're being printed as we speak."

"That's wonderful. I can't wait to read them to my grandchildren."

There is a pause in the small talk. Anne knows that this woman's time is too precious to waste, so she steels herself and begins, "Noah said you wanted to meet me. I have always wanted to meet you and questioned his wisdom in keeping us apart."

"For a while, I was irrationally jealous of every woman . . . that might get a piece of him after I'm gone . . . He was probably afraid I would be jealous of you . . . I was, but I don't feel that way anymore . . . I guess I just feel disappointed."

"Disappointed?"

"Yes, and sad . . . that I won't be the one to grow old with him."

"So you're a quitter?"

"Yeah. I'm smart that way . . . When there's nothing to fight for, I stop fighting . . . The books are finished. Me too."

"What about Noah?"

"Noah's tired of the dead and dying . . . Without this albatross, he can get on with his life."

Anne doesn't care for self-pity, even though she understands that this woman, more than many, has a right to feel sorry for herself. But sorry doesn't help. So Anne tries another tactic.

"I can't stay. I have to get back to Raleigh to take Lindsay home from the hospital for a nap. I have one last story to tell you. Do you want to hear it?"

"Are you going to lecture me?"

"No."

"Will it make me sad?"

"No."

"Will you eat my pudding so they won't insert a feeding tube?"

"I'll think about it."

"Okay."

"This might be called *The Story of a Day*. Last Thanksgiving, I went to Hickory to visit family. While I was there, I drove up the mountain to see Logan and the cabin he's been building. It was a frustrating visit, full of desire and need trapped together on opposite sides of a hand hewn wall."

"You should be a writer."

"You should be quiet."

Noah slips into the room and hands Anne a Diet Coke, then sits in a chair by the window. The two women ignore him. Elizabeth does not take her eyes off Anne.

"If my grandson had not been with me, I might have made the mistake of sleeping with him."

"Why a mistake?"

"Because he wants to take care of me."

"I understand."

Noah shakes his head, not understanding.

"The following day I drove to Durham to visit Summer."

"I thought this was called *The Story of A Day*," Elizabeth says with fake sarcasm. "You're on the third day."

"The first two were prologue. This is the story. I had emailed Noah that I would be in town, and he suggested lunch. He wanted to tell me something." Anne isn't sure that Noah read all of the emails to Elizabeth, especially concerning this visit, but she continues as if Elizabeth knows nothing.

"We met at my favorite Thai restaurant. I almost didn't recognize him with his short hair and runner's physique. You have a good-looking husband. Anyway, he caught me up on your health, your books, and my blue heron. I accept that men are fickle, but the blue heron knows he belongs to me. You're just borrowing him."

Anne ignores Elizabeth's sly smile. *Don't get ahead of me.* "After lunch, he dropped the bomb. He told me about the existence of an accidental life insurance policy in my name. Steven was the owner and the benefactor, and had doubled the value of the policy. I had continued to feel threatened by him in a subliminal way, even though our divorce had been final for years. I have never felt quite so alone and vulnerable as I did when Noah told me that Steven was apparently still planning his fortune through my death. I didn't know then that Steven had been dead for months and the increased policy was on his life, not mine."

"When we left the restaurant, I was in a daze. I almost walked in front of a speeding car. Noah pulled me out of harm's way, and I held on to him for dear life. I couldn't let him go. All the frustrations and fears I had carried with me for the last years seemed to gel—right there. And I am telling you the truth when I say this. If he had asked me to go with him at that moment, to anywhere, I would have gone."

Noah sits in his chair, looking out the window—not breathing.

"But he didn't ask. He held me, and he made me feel safe, and then he took me for a long walk. That's why he was late getting home. That's why he smelled of my perfume. You may think he could step into a new life without you, Elizabeth. But he belongs to you; he will always belong to you. I just borrowed him for a day."

A tear slides down Elizabeth's cheek. "Thank you, Anne. Don't tell me anymore. . . . That's exactly enough. And by the way . . . how is your textbook doing?"

Anne gasps. "How long have you known?"

"Almost from the beginning. I hope Noah explained . . . why we had to drop the opportunity to work with you."

331

"He did. And then he gave me another opportunity. I hope my stories helped you even half as much as they did me. Thank you for telling me that you know. I hate secrets, and now they are all revealed." Anne rises and leans over to kiss Elizabeth's forehead. "I have to get back to Raleigh and help my son-in-law. Will you sign your books for me?"

"I am beyond pretense, Anne . . . If I can't, Noah will, and his words will be mine . . . I thought you might take care of him after I'm gone . . . but I think you and Logan will finish your dance and then make a life together . . . I am happy for you. Be happy for yourself."

In the hallway, Anne leans against the wall. Noah joins her.

"Thank you," he sighs, emotionally exhausted. "I'm as surprised as you that she guessed who you are."

"She knows there's more to the story of a day."

"What you said was true. And it's all she wants to know."

"Correction. That's all she wants to hear."

Anne stands up, away from the supporting wall. Noah still leans, his eyes closed, his face strained.

"I have to go. Relax, Noah. For as long as I have known you, you have been a good husband. You have also been a good friend to me." He opens his eyes and looks into hers. "And if you had to choose between the two, you would choose Elizabeth. Hell! I would choose Elizabeth! She's wonderful! Don't waste your energy or hers by kicking yourself or by confessing to something that isn't important in the end."

"I wasn't thinking about myself, Anne. Did you see a boy in the room?"

"A boy?" Anne asks, willing the image away—not wanting to admit even to herself, that she saw the smiling child, waiting.

"Never mind, just my imagination." He straightens and watches Anne leave.

In her room, Elizabeth looks with wonder and welcome at her son. And another tear rolls down her cheek as she watches Joshua fade.

Anne enters Summer's room to find Logan sitting in the chair she slept on the night before. He's holding little Josie and speaking in baby-babble. Once again, her burdens melt and slide without resistance to the floor. She steps over them, and crosses the room to kneel beside Logan for a kiss.

Chapter 21

Another May

THE SEARCH FOR OSAMA Bin Laden continues; the war in Iraq continues; the president's rejection of stem-cell research continues; the sexual abuse trial of the world famous entertainer continues; and Logan and Anne's effort to find a way to be together while maintaining their individual dreams continues. Anne's favorite play on Broadway is *Doubt*, but that is not what she feels. Logan's favorite country song is "My Give-a-Damn's Busted", but it's not how either of them feels. They find themselves in an enviable frustration.

"I know that spending six months in the mountains and six months at the coast seems like a painless choice, but it isn't," Anne argues. "You won't want to be away from your plants for that long. And as president of your homeowner's association, you'll constantly be called on for one emergency or another."

"I'm sure we'll both have to make compromises, Anne. But I won't be president forever, and my plants are wildflowers. After they're established, they mostly take care of themselves."

"I hate the whole idea of compromise, Logan. It's a giving up—on both sides. And knowing me, I'll be the one giving up most of the time. I have a life and friends here that I don't want to abandon."

"I thought compromise is what the theatre is all about."

"Collaboration, Logan, not compromise. There's a humongous difference."

"Semantics. There's no difference."

They're sitting on Anne's balcony, watching the sunrise, much as Anne did on her deck in Durham, a year ago. This time, she is not troubled by the nightmares of her past. This time, instead of communicating with the blue heron, she is watching pelicans in the sky, egrets in the grasses, and fishermen in their boats, all with a common purpose. If she were alone, it would be peaceful. Instead, the air is charged with Logan's inability to settle for the moment, his need for a plan, a decision. Most of all, she feels his need for her to agree to follow his lead—wherever it takes them. Her greatest concern is she might do that. For an insane moment, she thinks that if she stood on the balcony rail and flapped her arms, she could catch a wind current and fly with the birds. She and Marjorie and Sissy, and then she stops—suddenly seeing in her mind's eye what she has avoided knowing. She sets the image aside as she takes Logan's hand.

"Collaboration, my love, is the opposite of compromise. Compromise is taking two things that may be whole and good, and slicing away a part of each in order to make the remaining two parts fit into one space. Imagine taking two landscapes, cutting them down the middle, and then joining two different halves together. Or imagine taking the body of a sparrow and attaching it to the legs of a crane. He would not be able to fly or to forage. A freak of nature, he would have to evolve into something entirely different or he would cease to exist. I like who I am. I don't want to become the other half of you, each half struggling for dominance until one ceases to exist."

"And collaboration?" Logan smiles at her analogies, knowing he is not at risk of losing her, feeling he is more at risk of losing himself. And in that moment, he glimpses her concerns.

"Collaboration is when two or more people share their knowledge, experience, and creativity to solve a problem or develop a concept. From this sharing and exploring, something entirely new emerges—something that neither of them could have come up with on their own."

"You mean like the whole is greater than the sum of its parts?"

"Exactly. And it doesn't matter who initiates the solution or concept. Ownership or control is not important."

Logan brings her hand to his lips and kisses the inside of her wrist. "Stick your foot up here, and I'll kiss it, too."

Anne playfully hits his arm, moaning her disapproval of his unfair tactics.

"All right," he says. "You want significant time here; I want the same at the cabin. I also want you in my arms at night, and I want you happy."

"How about this, Logan? Six months here that includes the winter; and six months at the cabin that includes the summer. But one week of each month will be spent at the other place. I'm sure your children and mine will want to visit us here in the summer, and we might want to spend Thanksgiving or Christmas at the cabin. Some of the kids would want to visit us there in the winter and go skiing."

"I think I'm the one being compromised—half recluse, half social butterfly. I don't know, Anne. Twelve trips a year, never in one place more than three weeks. What about other travel? I've always wanted to go out west and explore the Anasazi Indian ruins. I have a sister in Alaska. Wouldn't you like to go visit her? We'll also want to visit your brother in Michigan."

I haven't told Earl yet that I live next to water. But Anne smiles as she feels herself letting go—letting go of the death-grip she has on Pearl, letting go of the death-grip she has on independence and control. "We're doing it, Logan. We're collaborating. We're listening to each other and opening ourselves to new possibilities. We don't need to have a plan carved in stone. We'll take baby steps and see where they lead us. I will spend this summer with you, but I'll need to come back here now and then. You can come with me or not. You're used to solitude." *And I already need time alone; I'm already feeling suffocated.*

Logan pulls her into his lap and kisses her hard and long. "Screw solitude!"

Okay, I'm going to have to introduce 'time alone'.

Tio, sleeping on the front porch below the balcony, barks at the approach of a moving van, disturbing the quiet and frightening the wading and flying birds. The van turns on the road to the church and stops at Anne's house. She rises from Logan's lap and leans on the balcony rail.

The driver's door opens and Noah steps out. "Áhoy to the house," he calls.

"Hooray! You made it!" Anne runs to the stairs, sprinting down them to greet her friend, dismissing thoughts of compromise and restructuring her life to mesh with Logan's.

After breakfast they linger around the table, drinking coffee and catching up on each other's lives.

"I wish I could have been there when you talked with Steven's wife," Noah says to Logan. "Anne wouldn't write about it on email, but I think there's more to that story."

"I don't talk about it, period," her eyes flash a warning.

"I just need to know one thing, Logan. Who was the beneficiary on the life insurance policy Stephen had on Anne?"

"I don't know if Anne has looked at it."

"I have," she whispers. "I'm not hiding my head in the sand, but I really don't want to talk about this, guys. Let's talk about something happier, like Tio." She pets the adoring dog leaning against her knee. "Juan, asked me to take care of him because his family had to move. But more importantly, how is Elizabeth? And where is she?"

"She's in Chicago, getting ready for her first book signing. I'm heading there tomorrow. She's still trying to figure out how to live her life as a survivor. She wakes up every morning trying to readjust to life instead of death."

"Have the doctors declared her cured?"

"No. She's in remission. We don't think about the future. We're just making the most of the present."

"A good lesson to us all. Is her hair growing back?"

"It's finally long enough to style. Ian gave her the first post-cancer haircut. I may have to add a room to our house in Chicago for him."

Logan watches the two of them, unthreatened and content. Anne smiles at him. "What about advance sales on Elizabeth's books?"

"Going very well, considering they will appeal to a limited audience. Her profits will be donated to cancer-related charities. Her assistant and close friend from the office is staying at the house with her, screening phone calls. She still isn't strong enough to absorb all the pain that cancer victims and parents of sick children try to dump on her. She wants to help, but they use up her energy, and often leave her depressed. It's only going to get worse after the books are on the shelves. So, we're going on an extended vacation this summer—with no forwarding address. By the way, she told me to thank you for the Queen Bess plaque. It's already beside our front door. She sent a package to you. She said that you aren't to open it until after I leave. Everything else we borrowed from you is in the truck. Where do you want it?"

"I just want a few personal things, like Lindsay's journal and my wooden box, and of course the hobnail vase—the things that tell my stories. The furniture and other décor will be used in the new triplexes below the church. Did you notice them?"

"How could I miss them? It looks like an upscale Spanish village. When will they be finished?"

"One already is. The others should be completed by fall."

Noah sips his coffee. "And how are Paul and Luke doing?"

"Well, Paul introduced his son in a Sunday morning mass. The old folks weren't surprised, and the young folks were delighted. It was those in-between the young and old who complained."

"What will he do?"

"Give them time to get over it. He's not leaving, and he won't send Luke away."

"What will Luke do here?" Logan asks.

"The first thing he's doing is turning Marjorie's home into a board-ing house for Mexican men without their families—those that have to go back and forth to Mexico, renewing their green cards. Now that we have more work in Pearl, we're getting more immigrants".

Noah laughs. "And how do his neighbors feel about that?"

"Like his father, Luke's giving them time to get over it. He's also teaching English as a Second Language, ESL. That's what he did in the Peace Corp. He's learning their culture while they're learning ours. There's nothing for his neighbors to complain about."

"What happened to his job in Raleigh? And didn't he have a girl-friend there?"

"He quit his job, and his girlfriend quit him. Now Celita follows him around like a puppy."

"And who is Celita?" Noah asks.

"I'm not sure. She used to be the slightly chubby and cheerful manager of our art co-op. Now she's the slightly thin, wistful man-ager of the Luke fan club. I hardly recognize her. With Paul's good looks and Sissy's blue eyes, he has turned all the female heads in Pearl."

"Except yours," Noah grins as Anne takes the dishes from the ta-ble and returns with the coffee pot.

Logan pulls her into his lap. "Nope," he says, "this one's mine. And whether she knows it or not, she's mine forever."

Anne sets the coffee pot on a trivet and settles back against Logan. While the two men talk, she luxuriates in the warmth of love and friendship. And she knows it is true. She and Logan will stick. It's not about hormones or a fluttering heart—although she's happy to note that they both still make their presence felt. Deep in the core of her being, she knows that Logan will be the last man in her life. She isn't ready for marriage until she meets his children and until they iron out the logistics of their lives together, but she knows it will happen. Paul will continue to be an integral part of her life; Noah will continue to be her friend, if only through email—each being exit time for the other. Paul may never approve or understand about exit time, but Logan does because it doesn't threaten him. Logan knows that he is her old and new and best adventure.

The doorbell rings, and Paul calls in through the open door, "Anyone for a sail?"

Logan is on the *Espirita* with Paul. Anne thought he would feel safer on his first sail with a more experienced sailor. She and Noah are on the *Peli*, a gift to her from Marjorie.

The breeze is mild and the two boats move slowly and smoothly along, the sailors enjoying the cool spring morning, the blue-gray sky, and the friendly presence of pelicans flying close to the water's surface, catching an updraft and watching for food. In the distance, they see a fishing boat surrounded by seagulls.

"Do you see why I love it here?" Anne asks.

"Of course, but for some strange reason, in spite of how relaxing and beautiful this all is, I can't wait to get back to my work and . . ."

"And Elizabeth," Anne completes his thought.

He smiles. But they both know what he wants to talk about—the afternoon six months before when he pulled Anne from the path of the speeding car, and how he could not let go of her.

"If I fell into the water right now and could get to a buoy, I would cling to it in much the same way I clung to you last November," he says. And they each remember what followed.

On that brisk fall day, Noah did not ask Anne to go with him; she asked him to go with her. And, for a time, they both abandoned their realities. They walked to and through the UNC campus, Noah's hands stuffed deep in his pockets, his pace fast, his body stiff. Across the street, Anne spied an old refurbished hotel. She looked away as she asked if he wanted to get a room. Her unwillingness to make eye contact, made his lie easier. "No!" he whispered.

He stopped at a park bench where he pulled her onto his lap and buried his face in her breast, screaming, then cursing, then crying, her body muffling his sounds of anguish and despair. She stroked his head and murmured soft calming words as she felt his emotions release and finally ebb.

When his grip relaxed, she slid off his lap and sat beside him, reaching under the bench to retrieve the bright yellow-green tennis ball she had spied through the open slats of the seat. She began tossing the ball in the air and catching it—short tosses, as she edged away from him—giving him space. Emotionally exhausted, he watched her for a minute and then reached over to intercept her toss. But she grabbed it out of the air before he could. He looked at her in surprise.

She jumped up and dropped her purse on the bench, continuing to toss the ball to herself, higher each time, daring him to capture it. He rose, removed his coat, and took the challenge. She ran; he chased. When he was about to catch her, she stopped and threw the ball high into the air. He paused to catch it, and she ran to the sidewalk where they had passed an abandoned hopscotch game. He watched her hop its length, like the girl she must have been.

"Your turn, girlfriend," Anne teased.

He threw the ball to her, and began hopping. She tossed it back, making him focus on his feet and hands at once. His laughter began as a suppressed chuckle and built. By the end of the hopscotch game, they were both laughing hysterically. Anne was throwing the ball, not to him—*at* him. It was all he could do to catch it and keep his balance.

And then it started. Noah took the lead. He began running—flapping his arms, jumping over low obstacles, hiding behind a tree only to jump out and race away just as she reached him, all the while, tossing the ball between them. He led her back to the bench where they rested, occasionally laughing but not talking, each alone in memories and wishes.

On their way back, they passed the hotel again, and this time he asked if she wanted to get a room. Again looking away, not making eye contact, which would expose her truth, she said, "No! By the way, you make a good Pied Piper."

And now, six months later, he asks what he has wondered about since that day. "Why did you go with me? You spent the entire lunch telling me how you wouldn't use sex as a balm for a needy man again."

"I'm the one who suggested it, remember? And it wasn't sex after all."

"I would argue with that. I've never felt so naked and so deeply touched and so aroused and satisfied. I think Elizabeth would have felt more betrayed by our play—that incredible abandon, that shedding of tension and emotion—than if we'd had ordinary sex. But why did you ask me to go with you?"

"Because you wouldn't ask, and you wouldn't let go of me, and I was afraid a car would hit us, standing there in the middle of the parking lot." They both chuckle at the memory and the thought. "But maybe that was all just an excuse," she added. "I was vulnerable, too; I wanted to be held."

"Why didn't you turn to Logan?"

"He wanted forever, and I wasn't ready for that. I knew ours would just be *the story of a day*, and you would go back to Elizabeth."

"Why didn't we get a room?"

"Because, in the end, that's not what we wanted."

He teases. "You could have fooled me. I've been kicking myself ever since."

"You'd be kicking yourself harder if we'd gotten a room."

The sail waffles, and Anne adjusts their position. The wind is picking up. Paul signals for a race, and Logan has his first experience with life on the slant. Noah, like Joe, is a ringer, an experienced sailor. But he keeps this knowledge to himself.

Anne calls out to Paul that if he lets her win, she'll never speak to him again. As the *Espirita* passes the *Peli*, Anne sees Logan leaning out over the water, a look of fear, discovery, and exhilaration on his upturned face. Paul pushes at glasses that aren't there, and she laughs aloud. *Finally, everyone and everything is in its time and place.*

Paul and Logan finish first, and Noah supports Anne in accusing them of cheating. But Anne is smiling inside, knowing that—just this once—Paul's win was her choice, and only one of many good choices to come.

EMAIL TO NOAH:

I know that a phase of our lives has ended, but our friendship will continue. Keep that Chicago CEO persona in check. Do the work, but don't wear the hat. It no longer suits you, sweetheart, girlfriend, whatever.—*Always, always, Anne*

Epilogue

ANNE LEANS BACK ON HER willow chaise, now relocated to the back porch of Logan's cabin. Her computer in her lap and Tio curled up at her feet, she begins her Father's Day notes to all the men who would welcome her remembrance.

She looks up and sighs at the magical beauty of the trees surrounded by mist, with only the rhododendrons and mountain laurels close enough to gain focus. *Click. If I completed one painting a week, how many years would it take to finish the thousand images I can already envision? I wonder if time will allow.*

Anne loves getting up before Logan and spending the precious alone-time in cyber conversations with family and friends. She misses the blue heron in Durham and the white egrets and brown pelicans of Pearl. But she's getting to know the chattering chipmunks and Logan's snake, and has matched whistles with the summer birds. There are also bears and coyotes and surprisingly few deer—maybe because of the bears and coyotes. She sets the computer aside and crosses her legs, leaning forward to peer into the mist. Strangely, in spite of the constant movement of the creek below, she feels crowded by the trees and the enveloping thickets of rhododendron, as if she were in a cocoon. *Shake it off, Anne. You'll adapt.* She looks at the multitudes of flower buds, swelling and beginning to show color, some already blooming. It's a banner year for rhododendron, even in this heavily shaded valley on the mountain. It has been a banner year for all those she holds dear—even for Marjorie who found her grandson and is finally with her beloved daughter.

How did we get here? How did so much happen in one year—one cycle around the sun? I buried Pollyanna before I left Pearl, releasing her from the Peli *as I sailed solo behind the* Espirita *while Paul and Luke scattered Marjorie's ashes. Pollyanna deserves a rest. She's been kicked around enough. My new reality-based thinking gets some nice surprises and fewer bruises. I'm no longer sure how I feel about romantic love and all those take-your-breath-away expectations. They're under the sea with Polly. I'm looking forward to finding the truth of us, of Logan and me—with no expectations, just joy at each new revelation.*

Knowing her brother to be an early riser, Anne picks up the extra phone she carried to the porch and dials his number. After wishing him a happy Father's Day, she hesitates and then tells him about the deep water bay in front of her home.

Earl laughs. "Did you really think I didn't know that you're tempting fate beside water you could drown in?"

"I swim better than I did as a girl and I now care about staying alive for the sake of others. I even wear a life jacket when I'm sailing."

"I know. My nieces told me. And I also know you're a smart capable woman, little sister. I need to come and see you. Is the fishing good?"

"You'll love it. And I have a friend who would gladly show you all the good places to catch flounder, speckled trout, rock fish, you name it. He's a fisherman priest."

Anne sighs in relief and happiness after she says goodbye. She has saved the last Father's Day message for Noah. She opens her computer again. But before she begins her missive to him, she pulls a letter from her pocket. It was included in the books Elizabeth had sent to Anne with Noah. She unfolds it and reads.

Dear Anne,

I instructed Noah to have you open the package after he left because this is a conversation just between us. I know how you feel about secrets and lies. None of us have lied to one another; we just haven't revealed all we know. For example, I realized almost from the beginning that your stories were not by a writer-in-the-raw, but by an accomplished writer whose style I recognized, whose book on scene design I had once hoped to publish. I didn't tell Noah that I guessed his subterfuge because I sensed this complicated gift the two of you had wrought for me would only work if I played your game.

You were each at a vulnerable place in your lives when this began. You could easily have taken him from me. Your stories made me fight for Noah's love; they stimulated the idea for Joshua's books and made me fight for the time I needed to complete them; and ultimately, they made me fight for my own life. It was a game we all played, and we all won.

I don't know what our future holds regarding my cancer's remission, but we are choosing to live and love in the present, enjoying every day, every hour, every moment.

Yours,

Elizabeth

Anne folds the letter and puts it back in her pocket. *Time, my friend, it always comes back to Time.*

EMAIL TO NOAH:

One last story. When you visited me in Pearl, you asked a question I never answered. Steven was, of course, the beneficiary of the life insurance policy on me. As you know, his wife cancelled it. Why did she then take out a policy on Steven? My best guess is that she saw his hope for a financial reward through my death as a threat—not only to me, but to herself as well. She probably saw herself as his next victim. Marjorie would say, "Call the law!" I don't think I would. Even if she's guilty (and she may not be), I don't think she's likely to strike again.

In the end, she was smarter than him. The beneficiary of the policy on Steven was not his wife. That would have been a red flag of guilt. The money is to be used as a memorial, to promote the music Steven wrote, the music that had never received the attention it deserved. His one great gift will finally be heard, and will probably eventually make a lot of money. Who will get that money? His surviving spouse, of course. It's just a theory. Call the law if you want.

I suppose what goes around, goes around. Maybe I'll visit a Buddhist monastery. Maybe I'll stop painting triangles and try circles. I feel freed.

Speaking of the law and freedom, Billy O'Brian is in jail. He couldn't give up the booze and the brawling. Paul plans to bring him back to Pearl when he's released, and has already started an AA program. Billy will have to sit with Mexicans, blacks, and other rednecks, and maybe me. Sherry wants nothing to do with him, but Paul's determined to help Billy. He says they have a history, and he owes him.

I read and re-read Elizabeth's books. I'm glad she wanted me to open them in private. Her kind acknowledgement brought me to tears. What a wonderful gift.

Happy Father's Day, Noah.—*Always, Anne*

She closes her computer again, looks at Tio and says, "Screw it, Tio. I can't be here today. Let's go to Pearl. He jumps off the chaise and turns in circles before bounding off the porch, running for her Honda.

"On the Road Again". . . She whistles as she drives the familiar road from Greer's home, where she had breakfast, to Summer's home, where she had lunch, and now on to Pearl. Before leaving, she woke Logan, and told him she had to leave for a week. He seemed to understand. Now she reaches across to the seat beside her and finds a small digital recorder. She clicks it on and then sets it down again.

How shall I begin? Not with Dear Diary or Dear Me. One is too boring; the other belongs to Sissy. Ah! I know who I'm addressing. She smiles as she begins her oral journal.

"Dear Time,

I can see you in your long gray cloak, waiting. I have come to think of you in a kind way. We humans ignore, waste, borrow, buy, and spend you as if you would be ours forever. I want to use the rest of what I have of you with joy and thoughtfulness.

I wrote about my past for Noah and Elizabeth, and ultimately for myself. But from now on, I want to write about the present. Before that however, I need to tell the stories of Marjorie, Paul, and Pearl.

When I returned to Pearl from Raleigh after Josie was born, Paul held a memorial service for Marjorie. His eyes kept looking at the back, at the doors, as if he was expecting someone else to arrive. I didn't understand until late that night.

Unable to sleep, I was sitting on my balcony. The moon was full and bright, eerily lighting the bank and the marina in front of my home and the small cemetery to the left. Beyond it, Paul's home and his open kitchen window drew my attention. He entered the room, his hair still wet from the shower, wearing a white t-shirt and soccer shorts. He sat at his old oak table where the notebooks I had given him were scattered. He drew them to him, touching each one lovingly. He poured a glass of wine and, without tasting it, lifted his hands to his face and leaned forward, exhaustion and grief shaping his form.

I don't know if he cried, but my own tears flowed freely as I felt his emotions enter and overwhelm me. I leaned back in my chair and closed my eyes to create a weak shield. When I looked again, he was arranging the journals in an order. He selected the top journal in his stack and began reading.

I felt like a voyeur, and so rose to go inside. But before I turned away, something drew my eyes to the cemetery. A woman stood there, also watching him. After a moment, she sat on the nearest gravestone as if preparing for a long wait. At first, I wondered who she might be, but then I remembered the child in the shadows of Elizabeth's room—and I knew the watcher. I whispered her name,

348

and she looked up at me with clear blue eyes.

In that moment, I understood my feelings for Paul had stood in the way of choosing Logan. When I saw Sissy there, I knew I did not want what was left of Paul's worn and shadowed heart. I wanted the whole heart Logan offered. I wanted to make a life with him that was not about a house or a town. I wanted to give all the love I have to him without measuring the difference.

So, Dear Time, here I am on my way back to Pearl. It has been a year since I first travelled this road in search of my future. I have learned much in those brief months. The most important thing is that being alone is a state of mind. You can live alone and not *be* alone.

I spent several weeks with Logan at his cabin and then felt the need to escape the rhododendrons' twisting grasp. It's Father's Day. His children are coming, and now I am the one who isn't ready to meet them. It's too important a day. All of their family memories and loyalties are tied to this day. I will meet them on an ordinary visit when I feel less an intruder. That day will come soon.

Thankfully, Logan has a graceful acceptance of the other people in my life—even Paul, who is my primary reason for driving to Pearl. Although he has the memory of past love to sustain him, I know Paul aches for companionship, and I can give him that. Luke still has his adopted parents to care for and a career to pursue. Although their relationship is real and strong, it is limited by a young man's need for adventure. He plans to give a year to Pearl and then return to the Peace Corp—unless Celita convinces him to stay.

I suppose, in spite of my long concern about the men in my life, I haven't really had to choose between them."

She clicks the recorder off as she drives into town and is pleased to see how much work has been done on the Pearl Flea Market, scheduled to open on the July 4th weekend.

It's evening now, and Anne watches the sunset from her balcony. A breeze lifts her hair and brings the scents of the flowers now thriving on the terraced bank. Tio lies on the floor, his head at her feet.

Paul didn't look into her eyes earlier when he told her that Sissy's journals made him believe her fall during their senior trip was no more than a freak accident of careless youth. Anne remembers her own careless youth, her disregard for life—until she became a mother. How that changed her. The thought leads her to something about Sissy that she can't quite visualize, something she had almost seen while arguing with Logan here on this balcony—when she had felt the desire to fly—to fly away from his wants and determination.

Sissy couldn't have known about Luke or she would not have been leaning out from that precipice. She would have protected herself for the day he would find and need her. Instead, what she knew was that her baby Jonathan was gone and she couldn't risk the possibility that she was like her mother and would have one doomed son after another—because of her inherited genes. *She perhaps did not plan her fall, but I can imagine myself in Sissy's place.*

I can imagine not caring whether I lived or died. I can imagine, in the midst of such depression, thinking Paul might be better off without me. I can imagine leaning out to get a great shot of this surreal moment. I can hear a sound, maybe the snapping of a twig that breaks my concentration. I'm losing my balance. The choice is there, sitting behind my eyes. Paul's hand is reaching for me. I can try to help myself or simply let it all go and join my lost baby. I choose, then turn my head toward him—for one last look at love.

Anne covers her face with her hands, trying to block the image of tangled tree branches and the sound and pain of crashing through them. Somehow she knows it was a choice, a choice that reshaped their lives, changed their destinies. She will never share these thoughts with Paul. Perhaps he couldn't look at her because he already knows.

In this moment, she accepts, profoundly, that everything is fragile; everything is fleeting; everything is borrowed—the passions, the loves, the joys, even the sadness, certainly possessions, and even more certainly—time. They are all temporarily held gifts—gifts that one should not clutch, but hold with open hands. Even her body is a temporary thing. Nothing is permanent and nothing is static. *Is life indeed a wheel, and do we recycle not only aluminum cans and plastic, but also ourselves—over and over? Or do we instead move forward in a straight line, eventually changing lanes to a parallel universe of the spirit?*

A smile crosses her face as she closes her eyes again and tries to momentarily erase logic and knowledge, making room for anticipation of that which is beyond time and comprehension.

Tio brushes against Anne's leg, and whines for her attention. She absentmindedly rubs his ear. He gently nips a finger. She looks down at his upturned eyes. "Tio, who were you in your last life?" She smiles as he licks her hand and then rests his head in her palm, gazing intently into her eyes. She pats her lap, and Tio jumps into it, licking her face and barking with pleasure and adoration, turning her smile into helpless laughter which stops as abruptly as it began.

Oh God! I told Logan I would give my answer to his proposal after I met his children. Then I left the cabin today before they arrived. Oh, sweetheart, what must you think?

Her cell phone rings, and she picks it up, checking the caller ID. It's Logan. "Yes!" she says. "Yes, yes, yes!!!"

END

About the Book

Borrowed Things was conceived in a tent where my husband and I lived while we built our log home in the Blue Ridge Mountains of North Carolina.

Having lived through divorce and remarriage in the midst of dramatic social change, I wanted to develop a story that honestly addresses issues about relationships and the struggle to bridge the gap between a conservative upbringing and an evolving, sometimes permissive, society. I am drawn to stories about smart courageous women who are able to acknowledge their fears and weaknesses but still take the risks necessary to overcome them and build a life unfettered by past mistakes. And that, with a touch of suspense and irony thrown in, became the meat of my novel. It is a mix of daydreams and true stories based on imagined and true characters.

Many people who read this book asked for Father Paul's and Sissy's story. As a result, I am currently writing *By Way of Water*. The story begins in the turbulent 60's, when Sissy is twelve and Paul, recently smuggled into America following the political assassinations of his parents in Mexico, is thirteen. Look for it in 2014.

ABOUT THE AUTHOR

Doris Schneider is a writer, artist, and former professor of theatre at North Carolina Central University. While directing a play in Singapore, extra time in a lush hotel room prompted her to continue writing a story she had begun years before in a not-so-lush tent in the Blue Ridge Mountains. The result is *Borrowed Things*.

CONNECT WITH ME ONLINE:

Follow Doris Schneider on her blog, *Rock My Words* at
http://dorisschneider252.com
Facebook: https://www.facebook.com/dorisschneiderbooks

Made in the USA
Charleston, SC
18 January 2015